Surrender My Heart

"Don't you remember me, Mary?" His tone was as throaty as a lover's and he smelled of fresh meadow. "What can I do to make you recall that wondrous night?"

His face was only inches from hers. She could feel his warm breath on her face and stared at him in speechless awe. He drew closer, his lips nearly touching hers, then straightened with regretful slowness. His hands drew away from her, reaching for the buttons that held his trousers in place. With aching slowness his fingers loosened one button, then another.

Megan's eyes bugged. "Wha-what are you doing?" she stammered.

His gaze was as hot as boiled molasses with the thick fringes of his lashes half-mast over his deadly eyes. "I know you like your men to undress in front of you."

"I-I don't know what you're talking about."

"No? You don't remember me?" He looked devastated, but smiled finally. "You will, love. You will."

Other **AVON ROMANCES**

SURRENDER MY HEART

LOIS GREIMAN

AVON BOOKS ◆ NEW YORK

To my husband, Scott,
who has paid the bills,
nurtured my dreams, and captured my heart—
with all my love forever.

SURRENDER MY HEART is an original publication of Avon Books.
This work has never before appeared in book form. This work is a
novel. Any similarity to actual persons or events is purely coinciden-
tal.

AVON BOOKS
A division of
The Hearst Corporation
1350 Avenue of the Americas
New York, New York 10019

Copyright © 1993 by Lois Greiman
Published by arrangement with the author
Library of Congress Catalog Card Number: 92-96997
ISBN: 0-380-77181-0

First Avon Books Printing: March 1993

AVON TRADEMARK REG. U.S. PAT. OFF. AND IN OTHER COUNTRIES, MARCA
REGISTRADA, HECHO EN U.S.A.

Printed in the U.S.A.

RA   10 9 8 7 6 5 4 3 2 1

Chapter 1

Charleston, South Carolina 1850

Megan O'Rourke paced the short length of her rented room, treading the same worn course she'd followed for the past several hours. If Michael was so set on using her as the lead idiot in his confounded schemes, he might, at least, be quick about it.

She paced again, her strides short and irritable. Mother Mary, he was as slow as a three-legged mule with a bellyache.

Voices sounded from the hallway. Megan's breath caught in her throat. Who was it? Hurrying silently to the door, she pressed her ear to the marred portal. The lone, bedside candle flickered unsteadily, casting wavering shadows across the room's sparse furnishings. From the hall raucous voices swelled to a crescendo, then faded.

Drawing a heavy breath, Megan let her shoulders round with fatigue. She was sick of these damnable swindles, sick of the fear, the interminable wait, and her brother. She was God-awful, sure as death, sick of her brother. She should never have begun traveling with him, but to a frightened, knobby-kneed orphan, his devilish plans had seemed preferable to starvation. Now, however, she wasn't so sure, although the memory of abject loneliness still haunted her.

He was her brother, her only kin and he'd cared for her when there was no one else. She'd not forget that despite his shortcomings—but she was weary.

Glancing fleetingly across the room, Megan eyed the humble bed longingly. It was late. Perhaps it would do no harm to rest for a moment. After all, she'd already shown herself to the prospective pigeon. All she need do now was wait for their arrival, watch her Romeo fall into an insensible stupor, and help Michael tuck him neatly into bed.

In the morning, the sleepy fellow would awake to a slight headache, a vague memory of her face looming over him and empty pockets. But she'd been told by Michael who'd been told by a friend of a friend of another scoundrel that at least one of their victims thought his lurid memories of the night well worth the loss of funds. It made one wonder just what was in Michael's sleeping powder.

Pacing the bare floor, Megan scowled wearily at the sagging straw tick and tried to squelch her feelings of guilt. Any man who could be persuaded to buy a daft woman's favors was not worth her pity, she assured herself. And besides, the men were never hurt. Just robbed— and somewhat humiliated perhaps. Still, the swindle as a whole was far preferable to most of Michael's grand schemes, which generally put life and limb in dire danger and left Megan to pull them from the jaws of destruction at the last moment.

This was a simple swindle—nearly foolproof, Megan reminded herself. Lowdown, rotten, and immoral—but nearly foolproof. And that was as good as she could expect from her only brother.

She stared covetously at the down-filled pillows. Perhaps it would be good to rest, she deduced, for she never knew when she might need all her strength, and surely a few minutes of rest would ruin no monumental plans. She hesitated, weakened, then sank slowly to the edge of the bed.

Smoothing her palm across the lumpy surface, Megan tested the softness of the thing. Wonderful. She sighed. Heavenly. Biting her lip, she studied the door with a scowl, then with sudden decisiveness she kicked off her worn slippers, exposing her bare feet beneath. She should have purchased stockings, but she'd hated to part with the coin. Lying back against the pillows, she smiled. She'd rest only a few minutes. Just a few.

Below her in the smoke-filled saloon, Michael flashed his congenial grin across the table at his companion. The bulky, side-whiskered fellow had seemed to be the perfect pigeon but had, by now, consumed extraordinary amounts of liquor without reaching the necessary level of intoxication. Glancing about, Michael noted the quiet of the place. Only a few dedicated drinkers remained. Three hearty companions leaned their weight against the bar, while one large, dark-haired fellow sat alone, seeming deep in thought.

"Well, Mr. Gregory, you ready for a night of carnal pleasure?" questioned Michael, grinning lopsidedly and employing his best southern accent.

Gregory, who was far past sobriety, returned the leer with a chuckle. "I was born ready, boy. And I'm primed for action."

Michael threw back his head and guffawed, slapping his sagging companion on the back and watching as his loose-muscled body lurched with the stroke of his hand.

"That's what I like to hear, Gregory," he admitted, then leaned closer with a whisper. "Suzanne likes her men primed."

"Hell, I been rearing t' go fer over an hour," complained the heavy man.

"Yes well, she likes to get herself . . ." Michael paused, grinning again and allowing Gregory's imagination some time to heat up. "She likes to get herself good and ready." He raised his brows. "She lives for this you know. She needs a man." Michael nodded sagely.

"Yeah?" Gregory all but drooled. "And her so young and fresh, too."

"Shhh," admonished Michael, letting his eyes skim the room as if fearing they'd be mobbed. "We don't want to cause no ruckus," he whispered, "but I have to admit, she's a pretty thing."

"Pretty ain't the word," whispered the other in return. "Mouthwaterin' would be more likely. But tell me, why don't you set the girl up in a proper house somewhere? Make a real business out of it?"

"Well," Michael began, leaning back in his chair, "the way I see it it wouldn't be fair."

"Fair?"

"Sure. A woman like this comes along only once in a lifetime. It wouldn't be fair t' keep her for a select few. So we keep movin' around."

Gregory nodded loosely, narrowing his eyes and seeming to understand the entire theory before another question sparked in his slowing brain. "Tell me though, how can you bear to share her? Her being what she is?"

"Well . . ." Michael bent forward, his red hair glowing in the lamplight as a modest blush stole across his freckled features. "I won't lie to y', Gregory. I ain't enough man fer a woman like her. Not half enough. But you . . ." He paused, clapping the other on the back again. "You're the type she was made for."

Gregory accepted this in silence for a moment before he said, "Are you sure she's quite right in the head? I mean—not that I ain't memorable, but she didn't say nothing when she come down."

"I tell you Gregory, she ain't a big talker," confided Michael, not admitting that she refused to simper and was notably lousy at acting daft. And southern men, in his own opinion, liked women they could easily outthink— women not like his sister Megan. "Some say she's daft," Michael lied with well-practiced ease. "But if you ask me, a woman's got no need for brains. Not if she looks and acts like Suzanne anyhow."

"Amen," breathed the man. "Amen to that." He took another gulp of his beer. "My wife— real smart woman. Orders me about most the day. But she don't want to . . ." He waved a beefy hand about vaguely. "Well, she don't want to do *nothin'* more than once a month hardly."

"No! And with a stallion like you in her stable," said Michael in disbelief, leaning aside slightly to avoid the man's fermented breath. "Don't hardly seem possible."

"No, it don't," agreed the other, gloomily scratching his drooping belly.

"Well, never mind that. I'm bettin' Suzanne's bout ready if you are."

Gregory licked his lips. "If I was any readier, I'd bust."

Michael laughed, sliding his chair back and rising to his feet. "Good man, but hold your pants on. I'll get us one more drink."

"I don't need no—"

"A toast to your good fortune," explained Michael, patting the man on the arm with a grin. "Only be a minute." With that Michael marched quickly off to the worn length of the mahogany bar where he casually dropped a fractional gram of drowsy powder into Gregory's brew. Swirling the stuff about, he smiled at his own cleverness and sent up silent thanksgiving for men of Mr. Sidewhiskers' ilk.

"Here you are then," beamed Michael, handing the final drink to the bleary-eyed planter. "To Suzanne."

"Suzanne," intoned the other with a sloshy grin before hefting his mug and gulping the beer.

"To women with sense enough to be silent," prompted Michael, taking another swig of his own brew.

"Here, here." Sidewhiskers burped enthusiastically. His words were already slurred almost beyond comprehension while his thick neck was barely able to support his oversized head.

"Good," said Michael with his most benevolent smile. Once again his magic powder was combining beautifully with the liquor in the man's system. "I'll want a full report in the morning—if you're done by then."

"Y' mean," grunted the man, his eyes wide, his head bobbing slightly. "Even in the morning?"

"And all day," assured Michael, quieting his faded sense of guilt for lying so shamelessly about his little sister.

" 'Nough talk"—the man belched—"show me to her."

"Thata boy. Wonderful. Well, I guess we're ready then." It was a very delicate matter, choosing just the right moment to begin the sojourn upstairs. The prospective suitor had to remain mobile while being inebriated enough to assure his collapse upon the journey's end.

"Up we go," Michael urged. Taking the heavy man's arm in a firm grasp, he endeavored to raise the hulk to his feet, but the southerner's balding head was now drooping sideways while his beefy legs did nothing to assist Michael's efforts.

"Finally agreed on a price?"

The question came from behind them. Michael jerked about, half-dragging his victim from his chair as he strained to see the intruder in the dimness.

It was the dark-haired man. His chair now stood empty as he leaned his solid weight against the nearby wall. He was built like a thoroughbred, tall and well-proportioned, with hawkish, inscrutable eyes that seemed to pierce the haze without undue difficulty.

Hell's bells, Michael groaned in silence. What made him pop up now? The imposing fellow had obviously imbibed a bit of liquor. Yet there remained an unwelcome sober intelligence on his sharply chiseled features. Michael scrambled for words.

"I'm sorry, sir, but this conversation is exclusively between Mr. Sidew ... I mean, Mr. Gregory and myself." It was the best he could think up on a moment's notice. But glancing down at the mentioned fellow, he realized with a scowl that his companion was far beyond coherent support.

"Gregory here seemed quite taken by the girl. I'm sorry I didn't see her myself. What's a fresh, young girl worth in ready cash these days?" asked the interfering gentleman nonchalantly, showing no expression on his impenetrable features.

"What?" gasped Michael, seeming shocked by the stranger's blatant assessment of the situation. "You misunderstand, sir," he argued, doing his best to sound indignant while fighting to keep Gregory from plopping face first onto the hardwood. "Mr. Gregory here has asked—ahhh to *court* little Suzanne."

"Really?" the stranger drawled. "And how

would *Mrs.* Gregory feel about such a proposition?"

"Mrs—ahhh—Mrs. Gregory?" Michael gulped. He'd been grooming Gregory for a good two hours. It was too late to change pigeons now and even if he were so inclined, this big stud was not the kind he would care to pit himself up against. He preferred his gulls to be slow, both in gait and wit. This man looked to be neither. "I was unaware there was a Mrs. Gregory," Michael lied speedily, hoping the other had heard only a small portion of his condemning conversation.

"Disappointed?" asked the stranger.

"Well, certainly. It's so difficult to find a proper match these days, what with all the scoundrels about." Michael was sweating profusely and praying he wasn't digging himself a deeper grave.

"Are you some kin to the girl, then?"

Oh Lord, how was he to answer that? How much had the stranger heard? How much did he suspect? "Why—ah—yes. I'm um—her . . ." Michael paused, trying to read the man's expression, but it was no use. "Her brother."

"The devil you say!" Suddenly the man had jerked away from the wall, all sign of nonchalance gone as his fists clenched and muscles tightened. "What kind of man would sell his own sister!"

"Selling her!" squawked Michael, bolting back a step and letting Gregory's head bump unconsciously to the table.

Justin Stearns remained motionless. Anger welled within him. Had the south sunk so low as this—going beyond the degradation of slavery to allow a man to sell his own sister for a few dollars a night? Lord help them all. He clenched his fists and rethought his options. He'd heard enough of the conversation to know the little red-headed weasel wasn't worthy of alligator bait. The solution seemed simple. He'd merely threaten the rapscallion with a visit from the sheriff if he refused to let the girl go. Justin himself would pay the girl's fare to find a better way of life.

But the weasel *must* be the girl's brother, for who would admit to prostituting his own sister if it weren't true?

Justin glowered. Kinship created all kinds of problems, for a brother had a legal right to do most anything he willed with his sister. It was a kind of ownership by blood.

"I'll buy her from you." Justin's low words were as hard as granite.

"What?" Michael drew himself up behind Gregory's table, trying to find some expression of indignation and hoping he'd live through the night. "I can't sell my own sister."

"Seven hundred dollars to get her out of your grimy hands!"

"What?" repeated Michael squeakily.

"Seven hundred. And you'll not show your face in these parts again."

"See here. She's my sis—"

"Not anymore!" growled Justin, pulling bills from a thick roll and slapping them against the smaller man's chest. "Now she's mine. Get out and don't come back cause if I ever see your face again you'll wish I'd killed you the first time. You hear?"

"Seven—" Michael backed away, trying not to grin. "Seven hundred!"

"It's not too late to kill you now," warned Justin darkly.

No. Indeed it wasn't, Michael thought. And why die when he could have the seven hundred and Megan too. After all, the girl was sharp as a whip and twice as dangerous when riled. And she was likely to be riled. "Take care of her," he said merrily.

"Get out of my sight!"

Michael smiled happily. "All right then." If he wasn't mistaken, Mr. Congeniality here meant to do the honorable thing—had actually paid seven hundred dollars to see that the poor girl was no longer mistreated.

It would be a particular pleasure to witness the meeting between the gentleman and Megan. But, he reasoned, one couldn't have everything and now that he had a choice—he'd take the money. Lifting his hat from a nearby hook, Michael tipped it onto his head and left.

Justin watched the door close behind him, then turned to walk slowly to the bottom of the uncarpeted stairs. His movements were fluid despite the whiskey he'd consumed. Stopping short of the lowest step, he glanced upwards for a moment, pausing with a hand on the rail. Placing one booted foot on the bottom step, he frowned, then pivoted, returning to his seat to consider the situation.

Seating himself, he glared at the half-empty glass before him. What had he done? He hadn't come to town to buy himself a half-witted white girl. He'd come to town for another purpose entirely.

Justin took a sip of whiskey, not quite able to dim the thrill of his success.

He had bought Manchester's stallion. True, he'd had to send Zeke to actually make the purchase. True, they'd lied like fiends to convince Manchester to sell him the animal. And true, the man was going to be madder than a hornet when he found out the truth, but Justin owed him a trick or two. Horace Manchester had been a rival ever since he took Emmylou to the barbecue.

Justin chuckled quietly. The entire episode had gone like clockwork. Zeke had used his little known Christian name, Benjamin Ezekial Willard. He'd dressed like the successful plantation owner he was not, proclaimed he'd heard of Manchester's outstanding walker stallion, and insisted he needed to buy the horse and was ready with cash. It had taken less haggling than Justin had anticipated. Manchester had even escorted the horse to Charleston himself, after which Zeke had returned to Justin at the inn and formally made Justin the rightful owner.

It'd been quite a day. The stallion was safely in the livery stable, Zeke had returned home to his family, and Justin's herd of horses looked a damned sight better. He took another drink and smiled outright.

Zeke had played the hand perfectly—even agreeing to breakfast with Manchester in the morning. Of course Manchester was in Charleston for his Saturday night poker. Perhaps it was even the man's impatience to get to that game that had prompted him to sell Sure Gold. Or perhaps it was simply because he no longer needed the stallion, for surely he had a pasture full of the horse's get by now.

Whatever the reason, the stallion was now Justin's and tomorrow morning he could leave this sorry inn, which he had chosen for the express purpose of avoiding Manchester. He would meet Horace at a posh eating establishment and gloat, bill of sale in hand. Life was good. But. . . .

Justin's smile faded. What about the girl he'd just purchased? Justin glanced toward the intended suitor who dozed peacefully, his fat cheek squished against the tabletop as he snored an annoying tune. Lord help them all when people could be bought and sold like so many cattle. The poor girl was probably no more than a child, abused and neglected by her brother. But he'd set the matter right. He'd send her wherever she wished to go. He hoped she had enough wits to tell him her name and the address of some friend or relative who might care for her.

Justin scowled at this new thought. He hadn't considered that she might not even be coherent. The brother had not said just how daft she was. But it was too late to change his course now. Luck had been with him when Manchester accepted Zeke's offer for the stallion. It was only right that he be willing to help another with the money saved. And help her he would.

Bolstered with the sure knowledge that right was on his side, Justin rose from his chair and mounted the worn steps in search of the poor child he'd just rescued.

Chapter 2

$\sim$ ⟨⟨ $\sim$

Shifting his weight and knocking a bit louder,
Justin considered how best to inform the girl
she had just been sold by her brother. Even having grown up around the use of slave labor,
Justin had rarely encountered such a cold-
hearted act. But what else could he expect from
a system that for centuries had enslaved its fellow humans? The only difference here was the
color of the poor girl's skin.

Frowning at the unopened door, Justin wondered if the girl was asleep. It was, after all,
very late. Easing the door open, Justin peered
into the dim interior.

A single, stubby candle stood upon the bedside commode. Its flame wavered, spreading a
fitful tide of shadows and light across the back
of a peacefully slumbering figure. There she
was. She lay on her side, oblivious to the foul
goings-on of her kin, curled away from him like
a small, helpless kitten with no defense save her
own innocence.

Justin's jaw hardened. He hated the injustice
of the thing. Judging by her size she was no
more than a child, far too young to hear the

15

news he was about to deliver. And yet he couldn't wait; the words needed saying. With tension stiffening his gait, he strode across the bare floor to the bedside.

"Suzanne . . ." he began in a gentle whisper, but as he touched the girl's arm his gaze fell past her shoulder to the swelling softness of her breasts, half-freed from the emerald velvet of her gown. Suzanne! Justin's breath caught abruptly in his throat. Good Lord, for a child she certainly had large. . . . She certainly was mature. Could this be the poor waif he had imagined so clearly only moments before?

Releasing his trapped breath with a conscious effort, Justin forced his gaze from the girl's luscious bosom to her delicate face. With slow thoroughness he studied each feature—the slightly parted lips, the satiny skin.

Seating himself beside the neat little form, Justin leaned sideways to better view her.

Upon the aged pillowcasing, the girl's hair flowed like rivers of flaming honey, framing the small, angelic face that defined perfection. Dark forests of lashes lay against the slight flush of her silken cheeks, and between the drowsy lids and petal soft mouth resided a slightly upturned nose. There was something about her nose, some pixielike quality that made Justin smile, despite the awful circumstances.

Drawing his gaze from her stunning face, he allowed it to fall on her half-exposed bosom. The two tantalizing mounds were pressed gently together, as soft, firm, and round as twin melons. Framed by a heart-shaped bodice of lace, they rose and fell slightly with each breath she took.

Justin let his gaze drop lower, noting the steep decline from her ribs to her waist.

She was perfect, he thought, slowing his breath with an effort. But then he scowled. She was perfect physically but what of mentally? Blast it all! It wasn't fair that such a wondrous creature was deranged and sullied.

She was a lovely, defenseless creature at heart. Anyone with eyes could see that.

With slow tenderness, Justin reached out, lightly touching the feathered glory of her flaming hair. It was as soft as thistledown, as bright as firelight. What kind of animal could possibly desert such an innocent angel? Surely the brother was the one deranged. Who knew what kind of horrendous treatment she had endured at his hands?

But perhaps Justin could make things right. Perhaps it he took her home with him, he might show her enough kindness to heal her.

With this new thought, Justin was filled with titillating anticipation. Leaning closer, he smoothed back a strand of the girl's auburn-gold hair. He'd give her the news gently for it was clear she was a delicate creature, all soft curves and gentle, drowsy sighs.

"Suzanne." He called her name softly, doing nothing to frighten her. "Suzanne." This time the single word was slightly louder but no more forceful. She certainly slept with the innocence of a child.

"Suzanne," he repeated, raising his voice and leaning closer.

Megan stretched, pushing her arched feet from beneath the warmth of her hem and drawing a deep, contented breath. Her dreams had carried her far afield, causing her to lose all recollection of the here and now. She opened her eyes sleepily.

"Who—" She gasped, pressing herself back into the tick. "Who are you?" Had her dreams materialized into flesh and blood?

Justin drew his thoughts together abruptly. Now was not the time to besmirch her brother's name. Now was the time to win her trust.

"I've come to take care of you, Little One," he said quietly.

Megan's mouth fell slightly ajar. Take care of her?

Justin watched her. Her eyes were the color of emeralds. Wide and deep and utterly entrancing. Suddenly he could think of not a single thing to say and the only thing that seemed worth doing was. . . .

His lips touched hers without a second's thought. They were soft lips, sweet and yielding, drawing him out of himself. She smelled of lavender. Her full breasts pressed up against his chest, sparking flames from her warm body into his.

She hadn't awakened after all, Megan deduced foggily. Her dreams had just heated to a new and wondrous degree. And surely one could not be condemned for one's dreams so she might as well enjoy them.

She opened her mouth to her dream lover, feeling the entrance of his tongue, thrilling at the sensation of his hard chest against hers. He was strong and tender and had come to care for her. He was not like the men Michael found, not the pawing, sweating lechers who soon fell in a sloppy heap at her feet but a gentle, hotblooded lover.

She tentatively touched her tongue to his, feeling a jolt of ecstatic excitement and arching up to meet him.

Justin felt her stir beneath him. She was just a girl, he reminded himself, but never had he felt such arousal, such a need to touch and be touched.

"Suzanne," he murmured. "Suzanne."

Megan froze. Suzanne?

Feverishly she pressed against his chest, pushing him away. Their eyes met again. She shook her head once, clearing her mind.

"Who are you?" she whispered in confusion.

Justin scrambled for his senses. He shouldn't have kissed her. He needed to show her a new kind of man.

"I'm a friend of your brother, Suzanne. There's no need to fear."

Megan's eyes narrowed as memories rushed painfully back to her sleepy mind. A friend of her brother? A friend of. . . . She shook her head again, slowly now. Michael's friends generally drooled and rarely had all their teeth while this man had. . . .

She let herself absorb every stunning detail of his face. This man had everything, she thought dreamily, then snapped her brain into reality and reason. He was no friend of her brother.

"I've come to take you home." His words were a whisper of seductiveness.

Megan mouthed a reply, but the alarm bells drowned her answer, convincing her of her dangerous vulnerability. With one desperate effort she shoved him back and lunged from the bed, fleeing the short distance to the wall. "Get out of my room," she rasped. He may be beautiful. He may be desirable. Holy Patrick, he may be Adonis himself come down to tempt her. But he was *not* the man Michael had intended her to meet, and therefore he was dangerous.

"Listen to me, sweetness," Justin crooned, doing his best to keep from frightening her. She looked terrified, her eyes as wide and bright as a fawn's. "I won't harm you." With slow, deliberate movements he rose from the bed, watching her as he did so. "I can't imagine anyone wishing to harm something as lovely as you."

"Don't come any closer or you'll suffer the consequences," Megan warned abruptly.

Justin froze in place, mulling over her threat. Suffer the consequences? Her words were smooth and succinct although they were tinged with a northern accent—an accent her *brother* had not had. So perhaps they were not kin. And perhaps her thinking apparatus was a bit healthier than Justin had expected.

"Relax, Little One," he soothed, nearly trembling with the possibility that her mind might be as perfectly formed as her body. Without conscious thought he noted the accelerated rise and fall of her breasts, the wild, scattered mass of her hair. "There's no need to rush things. We'll spend the night here if you like." Even across the dim room Justin could sense the girl's increased wariness.

It was the statement that they would spend the night, apparently together, that decided Megan's next move.

"Stay where you are," she ordered. From her pocket appeared a small, weighty weapon. "Stay where you are."

Justin frowned, cautiously eyeing the deadly cylinder pointed directly at his heart. So she *was* deranged! "I won't hurt you," he assured her again as his gaze shifted from the weapon to her sparking green eyes. "I know you don't understand me, Suzanne. But truly, you're completely safe with me."

Perfect white teeth gleamed from the girl's angelic face. She seemed to find something amusing about a man who would assure her safety while she threatened his with the open end of a firearm. Her fine-boned hand remained unmoved, causing Justin to frown as he realized his predicament. The brother had said nothing to suggest a violent nature.

"If you'd drop the pistol, sweetness, we could sit and talk things through."

"I'm hardly likely to succumb to that old ploy," Megan said, realizing the bed was the only available seat.

Justin frowned again. She was suspicious far beyond her tender years and for a half-wit appeared to be surprisingly quick. Perhaps she had moments of lucidness, he decided, nodding mentally at his own clear thinking.

"I'm sorry if you've been taken advantage of in the past, Suzanne," he reassured her gently, believing he understood her distrust. "But honestly, I won't hurt you."

He watched her smile again. The expression was chilled and knowing. "I know you won't hurt me, mister, not so long as I hold the gun, at any rate."

Justin absorbed her words, then tried again, keeping his tone smooth and patient. "Listen, Suzanne, why don't you put the pistol down so we can talk?"

"Why don't you keep still and let me think?" Megan countered irritably, pacing the narrow confines of the room, and focusing the small pistol on her visitor as she did so.

Justin remained still, watching her fretful movements. She was little more than a child, misused and neglected, he reminded himself with some difficulty. "I know you're frightened, but . . ."

"Take off your britches," she interrupted suddenly.

For a moment Justin was stunned to silence. His britches? "I beg your pardon."

"Take off your britches," she repeated, nervously waving her pistol at him.

Wait a moment now. Just wait. Was it his imagination or was she requesting that he disrobe? Justin's whiskey-befuddled mind scurried to unravel the mystery of such an evening. It had begun so peacefully, after all, with just a drink or two to celebrate the purchase of his stallion. How was it now that he found himself threatened by a ravishing beauty who demanded that he undress? Her brother had indicated she needed a man but really. . . . Certainly a deadly weapon was unnecessary.

"Relax sweetness," he said again, handling

her much as he would a skittish filly. "I won't hurt you. Lower the pistol."

Megan's hand remained unmoved. "I don't think you'd truly care to have me aim at lower regions, would you?" she asked. Her small chin dropped fractionally, her enormous eyes studying him in the near darkness.

Justin scowled, trying valiantly to believe his original assessment had been right. Surely the girl was mistreated and needed saving.

"Unbutton them," she ordered nervously, her lace-encircled wrist jerking slightly as she indicated his trousers.

Undress? His brows rose skeptically. For a damsel in distress she had mighty strange requests. "I don't mean to find fault, sweetness, but I don't believe this is quite the proper way for a lady to conduct herself."

"Huh!" Megan spat an expletive. "Look who's telling me the proper way to live my life!"

Justin frowned. "I've meant you no harm, Suzanne. In fact ..."

"Don't you dare tell me your honorable intentions, not after buying me for your own depraved purposes."

She knew!

Justin stared at her in mute disbelief but the truth was obvious now. She knew her brother had sold her and therefore she was a....

Anger sparked within Justin's soul. "You're not only a whore," he determined stonily. "You're a thief as well."

Megan felt the quiver of fear creep up her spine and stiffen her arms. "T——take off your britches," she sputtered.

"And what if I refuse?" He canted his head slightly, causing the candlelight to make dusky kaleidoscopes of his eyes. "What then, love?" he asked, casually crossing his arms over the tight muscles of his chest.

"Then I'll shoot you." Megan's voice sounded shockingly steady, at least to her own disbelieving ears, but her visitor seemed unimpressed and watched her silently, like a large cat might survey his lunch.

"Wouldn't my dead body be a nuisance?" he asked thoughtfully. "All that blood." He shook his head with a distasteful expression, as if he could imagine the scene. "Very messy. And how would you explain it to the authorities?"

Heavenly saints, he was arrogant! It would serve him right and proper if she did shoot him. But what *would* she do with the body? It was so large, and. . . .

"A lady's got a right to protect herself from the drunken vermin who come slinking into her room at night," she said, fighting to clear her head.

"That's true." Justin nodded solemnly. "A lady does, but there's no lady here, my love, just you and me."

"You're a snake!" How dare he slander her when he was the one who had forced himself into her room. Well, perhaps 'forced' was not quite the proper word.

"Snake, am I?" Justin laughed, showing a generous portion of white, even teeth as he watched her.

"What kind of man would buy a woman's favors from her own brother?"

"Well now," he answered slowly, "that depends on the quality of the woman in question, I suppose." Leisurely his eyes roamed from her face, traveling with slow, skin-tingling heat down the length of her body, then upwards to finally settle on the fullness of her breasts. "For a woman like yourself, I imagine any man could be convinced to buy."

Megan could feel the flame of embarrassment lick her face.

"Give me your britches." Her voice quivered, whether from anger or fear even she was uncertain.

In the dimness he studied her until she felt the fire of his scrutiny sear through to her backbone. She felt as if he was looking into her very soul, but refused to lower her gaze. "Give them here," she demanded shakily, but he only smiled again and in that moment Megan was absolutely certain she faced the son of Satan. Battling an impulse to cross herself, she warned, "I'm counting to five, then I shoot." How it was that her voice still functioned, she had no idea. "One." Oh God! Dear God, please make him give up his pants. "Two." He wasn't going to do it. She could feel sweat prickle her palms and longed to run screaming from the room. "Three." Silence stretched for a timeless eternity between each number she spoke. Her body felt like petrified lava while his appeared as calm and relaxed as if he did this sort of thing each day before breakfast. "Four."

Justin's nod was almost imperceptible, but his hands finally dropped to the buttons of his trousers. "All right, sweetness, if you insist." He smiled as he said it. "You know, your brother said you were desperate for a man, but I can assure you, there are more pleasant ways to go about it."

The muzzle of her weapon waved slightly and she grasped it with both hands now, praying he had not witnessed her weakness. "Keep your mouth shut."

"As you wish, my love," Justin said evenly, "but what I had in mind is much more enjoyable with our mouths open, as I'm sure you know."

"Keep still," she panted. "Unbutton your pants and get on the bed."

"Yes, ma'am." The anger was gone from his face now, replaced by . . .

Holy Patrick, she thought in horror. He was laughing at her. "Hurry up," she squeaked, then winced at the tone. Please, oh please hurry, she wanted to plead but he did not. Instead his hands moved with exaggerated slowness on the buttons that bound his trousers. Against her will her gaze was drawn there.

Beneath the fine fabric of his pants a broad, heavy bulge pressed against the white cloth of his undergarment. Megan's eyes widened to enormous widths, then snapped back to her prisoner's face, her own burning like fire. Hail Mary full of grace, she began in a panic. "Hurry up," she ordered again, made frantic by the sight of his overwhelming masculinity.

"Your impatience is very flattering. But why not enjoy the show?" Justin quipped.

Enjoy the. . . . Hail Mary full of. . . .

"What do I do with my boots?"

"Wh——what?" It couldn't possibly be that he was talking about his boots at a time like this. She was sure of it.

"My boots," he explained. "I can't get my britches off until I take off my boots." He canted his head at her, scowling a little. "Would you mind helping?"

"I—you—I most certainly will not," she sputtered.

"Are you sure? It might be fun. I could sit on the bed there and you could . . ."

"I will not," she gasped.

"Well." He sighed. "As you wish. But would you mind if I sit down?"

"No. I mean yes. You can't sit down. You can do it standing up."

There was silence for a moment, then, "Do you think so?" he asked. "Your faith in me makes me very proud, Little One."

Was there a double meaning in that? she wondered. She hated double meanings.

"Just—just get it done," she sputtered. Sweat now trickled down her back and her hands ached, proof of her petrified grip on the pistol.

It took an eternity for him to pry the boots from his feet. But the worst was yet to come, for his trousers were loath to leave his form and needed to be practically peeled from his body.

Megan licked her suddenly dry lips as his steady hands pushed the trousers from his lean hips. Her face steamed as her uncontrolled gaze remained riveted on him. Was he deformed or was all his 'bulk' normal? Eternity passed as, inch by inch, his trousers lowered, pressed down his corded, endless legs and finally falling in a heap at his feet.

"Now get on the bed," she ordered. She was having difficulty forcing enough air into her lungs.

Kicking aside the discarded garment, Justin grinned before leisurely complying. Resting languidly on his back, he laced work-hardened fingers behind his head and graced her with the full force of his dazzling smile. "What now, sweetness?" he asked, not showing an iota of decent embarrassment for his near-nudity.

What now indeed, Megan questioned silently. Merciful Mary, he had a body like a marble god! "Now you stay precisely where you are," she improvised, whipping her imagination into submission. "Cuz, cuz," she explained, shakily retrieving his trousers from the floor and edging around the bed toward the door. "If you come into the hall before I count to fifty, I swear, you'll regret meeting me."

"Surely you jest," Justin commented, his voice filled with an emotion she failed to interpret. "How could any man regret meeting you? And I doubt you can really count to fifty. I noticed you had difficulty just counting to five."

Megan could only assume he meant to insult her but found she was far past caring. "You'll regret it," she repeated, fumbling around his britches for the door latch. Her hands trembled. She was nearly free and turned now, but his voice stopped her.

"Suzanne. Have you ever heard of justice? No? I thought not, but I believe in justice and I feel it's only fair to warn you that justice will be served. So I'm giving you one chance and one chance only." He sat up, resting his hands on the bed and holding her gaze with his own. "If you give me the gun now and return my possessions, I'll not press charges." He paused, studying her in the silence. "But if you don't, I swear I'll find you and when I do . . . justice is not always a pretty thing, my love."

Hail Mary. . . . Hail Mary. . . . Hail Mary. . . . Good Lord, she couldn't remember the prayer and here she was, face to face with the devil himself.

Trembling like a wind-blown leaf, Megan jerked the door wide. "You won't find me!" she said, stumbling on his pants and hurrying to right herself and her aim. "You'll never find me."

His laughter filled the room with eerie reverberations. Megan felt the chill of his humor like the howl of a ghost and crossed herself hurriedly, still gripping his trousers like a souvenier of war.

"Don't fool yourself, little girl," Justin growled, dropping his laughter. "I'll find you and when I do your questionable soul will be left without a body to encase it." He laughed again, savoring her terrified expression and stopping her exit with another warning.

"Beware of strangers. I'd hate for another to enjoy my revenge before I get the pleasure."

Eyes locked, green on brown, causing Megan's small neck hairs to creep upward as the threat came home to her. If it weren't for her pistol, she thought, he'd kill her, without regret or the slightest bit of trouble. Breaking free of his spell, she jerked the door open wide and escaped into the darkness of the hall where she gasped for breath.

She was free. She was alive. Trembling relief shook her, but she calmed herself as best she could. She should wait there and make sure he stayed put, she thought, but what if he didn't? What if he came charging through that door after her?

With one wild glance down the hall she fled, her bare feet noiseless against the wooden floor.

Chapter 3

M ichael was the picture of contentment, seated before a cheery flame as if he had not a care in the world.

"Didn't have no trouble finding me, huh?" he asked, rising leisurely to stretch the kinks from his back.

"No." Megan remained astride for a moment, still holding her stolen treasure, as she watched him from her mount's back.

"What's that you got in your hand?" he asked.

Kicking her feet from the stirrups, Megan slid to the ground before rounding the fire to face him. "His britches," she stated flatly, lifting the stolen garment high as proof of her statement.

Michael stared in disbelief, seeming stunned by her possession. "Whatever for?"

"What for?" She smiled. "You want to know what for?"

He nodded but in that moment she dropped the trousers to slam her small fist into his abdomen. Air whooshed from Michael's lungs, hissing with its exit.

"Hell's bells, Meg," he scolded from his doubled up position, glancing upwards at a crooked angle. "What'd y' do that for?"

"What'd I do that for?" Megan mimicked in a shrill tone, her arms akimbo. "I'll tell you why. I'll tell you!" Her words were a shriek of inarticulate anger. "I did that cuz you sent some big, ornery bull moose into my room without so much as a warning, that's why. And you never considered he might kill me, did you? Did you? I could be dead!" she raved. "Or worse."

Straightening gingerly Michael ventured, "Worse than dead, Megan?" There was laughter in his tone as if he were attempting to imagine how one could be worse off than dead.

"It's not funny, you low-bellied wart hog," she fumed, taking a threatening step closer. "You sit here nice and safe by the fire while I nearly get myself . . ." Her breathing was erratic, her memories terrifying. "Killed!"

"Now listen, Meg," Michael soothed, backing away cautiously. "I didn't want to send him up. But he overheard more than he shoulda heard and started causin' a ruckus. And Mr. Sidewhiskers had fallen asleep and that big stud wasn't gonna take no fer an answer. Not after hearin' Sidewhiskers spoutin' how pretty you was. And you was specially pretty tonight, Meg. Did I tell you that?" he asked with all the charm he could muster.

Having backed him against a tree, Megan paused for a moment. He was her only brother, she reminded herself. Blood kin. All she had left.

"Honest Injun, Meg. I did my best to get him outta there, but he wasn't havin' none of it. Be-

sides," Michael added quickly, "I knew you
could outwit him. Never doubted it fer a minute. I sure wouldn't have let him go up if I
hadn't a know'd you could handle him."

"And no thanks to you," Megan said, steaming mad. "You should be slow-roasted over that
fire instead of sitting there so cozy."

"What do y' mean? I'm here, ain't I? Just
where we said we'd meet? And we got double
the money," he lied, seeing no reason to tell her
the extraordinary sum he had received.

"You . . ." She glared at him, her mind scrambling as she tried to understand him. "It's not
even the money, is it Michael? It's just the thrill,
isn't it? It's like one big game of chance."

"What're you sayin'? Course it's the money.
We need it to buy them farm—"

"Don't bother sayin' it," she warned. "It's all
just a game to you. Only you're not risking
money. You're risking my neck."

"Nah, Meg. You take it so serious."

"It *is* serious!" she stormed. "It's my life."

"Where's your sense of fun?"

"Sense of . . . You're just like Uncle Chester,
aren't you? Ma knew. She knew ever since that
time you put the snake in her copper kettle. She
knew when you hung yourself up by your toes
in the outhouse just to hear her scream. And
when you wagered Billy Swaggert a peppermint
stick that I could best Suzie in a footrace, and I
won and you got the peppermint—then she
knew for sure. She said there was one in every
generation."

"One what?" asked Michael dubiously, planting his own hands on his hips and staring at her.

One no-good, she thought. One man who would never do an honest day's work in his life. One man who would never walk the straight and narrow. "One man like you," Megan said. "But she loved you anyhow."

They were silent for a moment before he said, "That's me." He grinned, his freckled countenance splitting into an irresistible expression. "Y' can't hardly help but love me."

"You're a toad," she said wearily, knowing he was right and knowing she was a fool. "A toad," she repeated and stomped stiffly off to her mare.

The gray nuzzled Megan, her solid presence soothing the girl. "Rain," Megan crooned, addressing the mare as she stroked the delicate equine face. "I almost got myself killed back there." Without the slightest effort she could remember the man's eyes, narrowed with hate and cold as a north wind. He could have killed her. And what had her ninny-hammer brother done to prevent it?

"Ah, Meg." Ninny-hammer approached, carrying the purloined trousers. "Why *did* you take the fella's pants?"

Mother Mary! Why did she put up with him? Why? Loneliness? Fear? Loyalty? The usual answers no longer seemed sufficient, for the terror of being alone was far less threatening than the terror of the man at the inn.

"And how did you expect me to get out of there without him following me?" she asked, snapping open the carpet bag that contained her extra clothing. "Sweet talk? I'm sorry sah," she began in a sugary southern soprano. "I know we duped y'all, but little ol' me has gotta go now, so would you mind stayin' put for a spell so I can leave town with your money?"

"Meg." Michael laughed appreciatively. "That's real good. Your drawl's comin' along real good. Couple more months down here and you'll be able to do some talkin' next time we meet your men friends."

Men friends! It was like Michael to put such a harmless term to the devil himself. "I'm going to tell you something, Michael Shane O'Rourke," she began. "I won't be pulling any more swindles. Do you hear me? Not if I have to *walk* all the way to Indiana and strap the plow to my own shoulders."

"Now, Meg. You're just wore out. You know this is the best scheme we ever hit on."

"Best? Best for what? For getting me killed?"

"You're talkin' outta your head. Them southern boys ain't gonna hurt y'. What do y' think that big stud back there is gonna do? Challenge y' to a duel? And with no britches?" he asked, hefting the stolen garment.

There was silence for a moment then, "He was real mad, Mike," she said, her anger weakening. She was tired, too tired to hide the fear in her eyes.

"He was just a man," Michael said, his tone dismissive. "Just like all the rest. You know them southern gents; they wouldn't hurt no lady if their cotton depended on it."

"Not a lady," Megan murmured, remembering the man's words. "But me, he'd hurt me."

Tilting his head sideways, Michael scowled, hearing the fear in her tone. It wasn't like little Megan to get so jittery. Even when Pa's old mule had gotten a wild hair and gone bucking circles around the corn field with her hanging on his back by the harness leather—even then she'd kept her head. "What?" he asked, trying to figure the change in her.

"He was different, Mike," she said, not able to stop the quiver that shook her. "You should have seen his eyes. He looked at me like he didn't care if I shot him or not."

"Now Meg, really ..."

"I'm not fooling, Mike. He was burning mad."

"Well, a little tiffed maybe, but he weren't—"

"A little tiffed?" Megan asked slowly. "A little tiffed, Mike? We stole his money, his britches, and his pride, and you think he's going to be a little tiffed?"

"Well, what do you think he's—"

"I'll tell you what I think," Megan answered, her tone measured. "I think he's going to give us what we right and well deserve. I think he's the devil himself, sent to make us pay for our sins. I think he's going to track us down and feed us to the ..."

A noise sounded from the nearby brush. Megan froze in her tracks, her heart as heavy as lead within her chest. Sweet Jesus, she prayed, don't let it be him!

The bushes rustled. A deer stepped out, antlers raised, nostrils distended. And then he was gone, back into the woods behind him.

Megan lowered herself weakly onto the log beside her. Every limb trembled as her blood pounded along its burning course. "I'm not doing any more swindles, Mike," she said, her voice barely audible.

"Now Meg . . ."

"No." Her brows lowered above her narrowed eyes. "I'm not."

No more swindles? Michael stared at her in mute disbelief. What would he do for sport? Things were just beginning to go so well. For three years he'd cared for his skinny little sister. Perhaps he hadn't kept her in quite the style some might have thought proper, but he'd kept her alive. And then it had happened—she'd blossomed like a rose. Almost overnight. She'd bloomed into a flower too delectable for men to resist. And suddenly the pickings were juicier, the purses fatter.

He glanced at her again, studying her in the firelight. In the past months she'd developed into a woman, a woman with their father's quick temper and fine looks. And yet she failed to realize the change, still seeing herself as the knobby-kneed orphan he'd dragged from their mother's grave beside that run-down corn field.

"Get some sleep, Meg. We'll talk about it in the mornin'."

Her face lifted from the fire, as somber and still as the night itself. "No more swindles, Michael."

Damn. "I know you're tired, but we need money. We can't hardly work the farm without some cash, can we?"

"I'll find a way."

"Don't be a goose, Meg. Listen, I set up a little scheme a couple months back. Just a simple thing, but real sweet. And I can collect any time now. Tomorrow if you like. It'll just take a half a day and it'll bring in a bundle."

"No."

"It's my best plan yet. There was this pretty girl in Charleston. Looked somethin' like you. Hair just your color. Ain't that somethin'. Well, she and I took a shine to each another right off and she knew of this rich planter fella see. So I thought—"

"No!" Megan's voice exploded into the night, trembling with emotion. "I said no, Michael. Don't you understand? I'm sick of it. Sick and tired and scared."

Silence echoed in the forest and Michael turned abruptly away, grinding his teeth and dipping his hand into the pocket of the stolen trousers. It was the owner of those trousers who had caused the trouble. The revelation hit him suddenly. She had turned away from her own brother because of him.

There were only a few small bills remaining in the man's pockets. Michael shuffled through them before noting a folded square of crisp paper. Without thought he opened the thing, then read it silently.

It was a bill of sale for a plantation walker stallion named Sure Gold, a horse whose full description and price followed.

Five thousand dollars! Michael's jaw dropped as his gaze skimmed up the page. The animal had been sold to a Benjamin Ezekial Willard for five thousand dollars.

So the big intruder at the inn was named Benjamin Willard and had not only lost Megan but had also lost his bill of sale for his ridiculously expensive stallion.

And what did that mean for Michael O'Rourke?

It would be interesting to see such a stallion, he thought, to determine whether this Benjamin was any judge of horseflesh, and perhaps, just perhaps. . . .

Michael smiled into the darkness. Perhaps he'd inherit himself a horse. Or maybe he'd give the animal to Megan. She had an eye for a good horse and who'd stop him? After all, he held the bill of sale. Who was to say the stallion wasn't his?

Horace Manchester trod along the hard-packed street. It was dark except for the islands of yellow illumination that glowed from the gas street lights.

His winnings had been substantial at the gaming tables. His mood should be good but. . . .

He sighed, tipping back his hat and mentally chuckling at his own melancholy. Call him a sentimental fool, but he'd miss the old horse. He sighed again. It wasn't as if he needed the stallion. In fact, for the animal's own good it was time for him to move on to new pastures and new mares, for to tell the truth most of Manchester's mares were Sure Gold's own get and therefore undesirable to mate him to.

Still, he'd miss the old boy—and so he took this late night walk alone—this one last chance to say farewell without an audience. He knew where the horse was kept for he'd stabled him himself since Willard was from Savannah and didn't know of a reputable livery in Charleston.

The barn was nearly dark when Horace entered it. Only one light shone from within. A towheaded stable boy of thirteen years slept on a pile of straw by the door and Horace smiled, thinking there was no reason to wake him.

Inside a horse nickered and equine smells assailed him, and then it struck him. . . . Who would leave an unguarded light burning in a barn? He scowled, suddenly less tolerant of the boy in the straw; a scraping of boots alerted him to another's presence.

Walking down the broad aisle, Horace noticed the light hanging on a peg about midway down. A stall door opened. Sure Gold stepped out.

"Hello," he called, unable to see the horse's handler.

Behind the horse's muscular shoulder Michael O'Rourke froze. Damn!

"Ah—Hello." Michael smiled, stopping the stallion to step into view.

"Going for a ride?" Manchester asked.

Michael's mind raced. It had been so simple thus far. He'd found the stallion without a hitch. The boy had been blessedly asleep. He'd been almost free and clear. But perhaps this gentlemanly intruder meant no harm. Then again, maybe he knew Benjamin or Horace Manchester or simply knew of the stallion. It was time for caution.

"No. Oh no. I work for Mr. Willard," Michael lied smoothly. "He asked me to fetch the horse."

"I see." Manchester nodded, wordlessly assessing the lad. It was well past midnight yet long before dawn. He could think of no reason to move the horse now and he knew of no employee Benjamin had brought along.

"You're heading back to Georgetown then?"

"Yes. Georgetown." Michael smiled. "You own the livery? I was told to show the animal's bill of sale to the boy at the door but ..." He chuckled. The stallion pawed and reached his white-blazed nose toward the other man. "The boy needs his sleep."

"Yes." Manchester tensed and chanced a glimpse in the stable boy's direction. What was the game here? "Daniel's a good lad, but he gets weary—works at the mill when he doesn't work for me, you know. Could I see that bill of sale?"

"Certainly." Michael reached in the pocket of his breeches. Everything was going fine. The man didn't suspect a thing.

The paper crackled in Manchester's hand. He smoothed it open, revealing his own spidery script on the wrinkled page and pretending to read the horse's description. "It looks like everything's in order. But I'd like to know one thing." He handed the paper toward Michael who reached to receive it but suddenly his wrist was locked in the other's steely grip. "Where'd you get the bill of sale?" he growled.

"From Mr. Willard."

"The hell you did. Willard's from Savannah, not Georgetown."

Michael went limp. "I'm sorry," he whimpered. "It's all my fault. I just ..." Without warning he twisted his arm upward, breaking Manchester's grip as he dropped the stallion's rope and bolted for the door.

"Hey!" Horace shouted. "Hey! He's getting away. Thief! Stop that thief!"

But Michael was already lost in the darkness outside the barn and Sure Gold was rearing, frightened by the commotion and threatening to follow the thief's exit.

"Dammit!" yelled Manchester, lunging for and catching the stallion's rope. "Dammit boy! Wake up!"

A bleary-eyed lad stumbled in, his hair generously sprinkled with straw.

"What—"

"A thief. Here. Take this horse. Do you have a weapon?"

"Huh?"

"A weapon? A gun. Oh damn it all. Put the horse up and yell your fool head off if anyone steps through that door. You hear?"

"You going after the thief?" the boy asked, his eyes finally widening.

"I'm going for the horse's owner," said Manchester, shoving the receipt in his pocket. "Where's he staying?"

"Ahhh—" The boy's mental wheels creaked and Manchester scowled impatiently. "Ahh—the Red Dog Inn," he finally blurted. "The Dog. Just down the street."

Manchester found the inn easily and grimaced at the shabby exterior. Willard must have been too concerned about Sure Gold's well-being to rent a better room farther from the livery.

Stepping into the inn's nearly empty saloon, Manchester noted the setting. Two men stood talking, one very tall, his hair dark, his back toward the door. The other was an elderly, weary-looking sheriff with a badge slightly askew on his plaid vest. An inn employee was halfheartedly cleaning the place, and draped across a nearby table was a balding, sidewhiskered man who snored and wheezed in his sleep.

"Sheriff?" interrupted Manchester, thinking himself lucky to find a lawman so close to hand.

The tall man turned.

"Stearns!" Manchester said in utter surprise.

"Manchester." Justin narrowed his eyes. It had been a hell of a night. He wasn't ready for this encounter just yet. "Not right now, Horace. I've got a situation of some importance to discuss with the sheriff."

"The hell you do. I need his attention. There's been trouble at the livery."

"What livery?" Justin snapped, all attention riveted on his rival. "Is Sure Gold safe?"

"How did you know Gold was here?" demanded Manchester, immediately suspicious.

"Is my horse all right?" stormed Justin.

"*Your* horse!" Manchester snarled. "The hell he is!"

"Ezekial purchased him for me for a fair price," Justin bristled, "knowing you'd not sell the animal to me."

"You'll have the stallion when I die of hoof rot," promised Manchester hoarsely, grasping the truth with quick intellect.

"I already—"

"Hey!" shouted the sheriff abruptly. "What's this all about?"

"I bought the horse for a goodly sum," growled Justin.

"And what have you to say, mister?" asked the sheriff gruffly.

Manchester was silent. The bill of sale was safely tucked into his own pocket now. How the scoundrel in the barn had laid hands on the thing he had no idea but the fact was Stearns had no proof of purchase.

Now was the time to make old Justin pay for snatching little Emmylou Bartell from out of his grip.

"The horse is mine, sheriff," Horace said calmly. "This man stole him."

Chapter 4

B last it to cinders! She was gone!

Wearily Justin lowered himself to his rented bath. Suzanne, or whatever her true name was, was gone. She'd disappeared while he paced the confines of a jail cell like some half-crazed jungle cat.

He'd been imprisoned! Justin Stearns in jail! God Almighty!

It was bad enough she had deceived, robbed, and humiliated him. But to take his bill of sale, then. . . .

Then what? How had Manchester known of Justin's lost receipt?

Perhaps he had known all along that Zeke worked for Justin. Perhaps Manchester had been aware of Justin's trickery all along and had hired the two scoundrels to get the bill of sale back. Or perhaps it had simply been fate that had brought the girl into his path. Or perhaps. . . .

Blast it all! Cooling water splashed over the tub's rim as Justin yanked himself to an upright position. He didn't have the answers, but he knew one thing for certain, she was a demon, a little angel-faced witch who deserved the worst he could concoct for her. But how would he find her?

The sheriff had refused to look for her, preferring to believe Manchester's cockeyed tale.

Justin steamed in silence. The rotten, tricky bastard had had him jailed while he took the stallion back home, and now Justin was left with considerably less money, no stallion, and one less pair of riding breeches.

Damn!

He should have gone straight home with Sure Gold instead of waiting to gloat to Manchester. But how was he to know? How could he have guessed the wave of events he would set in motion? How could he have predicted Suzanne? How could any man. . . .

Drawing a deep breath, Justin loosened his grip with a conscious effort, easing himself back against the smooth metal. He'd find her. If it took a thousand lifetimes, he'd find her and when he did he'd strip every inch of hide from her luscious body and tack it to his bedroom wall for decoration. But until then he could only hope he'd scared her with his threats.

Good Lord! His father would never forgive him for being imprisoned. No Stearns had ever been imprisoned. Not until a week ago when he'd met a half-sized sea nymph with the body of a heathen goddess and the cunning of a red vixen. How could he have been so idiotic as to hand over his bill of sale to her? How?

The memory of his foolishness tormented him. But even more painful were the memories of her. Every night she haunted his dreams. Every night she floated through his mind like an unholy, haunting spirit. Without the slightest effort he could recall every detail of her—her hair, her form, the wonderful innocence of her face. Her kiss . . . sweet, yielding. . . .

Slamming his fist against the rim, Justin ground his teeth in vexation. It wasn't her innocent beauty that made him search for her, after all. Hardly that! In fact, it was the opposite. It was her deceit, her cunning, her callous use of his sense of justice that galled him.

She'd won the first battle, but there would be another. Abruptly pushing himself to his feet, Justin reached for a towel. There was little he could do now but return home to Free Winds as he had promised his father. Contacting Manchester would wait. Horace could be a rare pain in the hindquarters, but despite their longstanding rivalry he was bound to return Sure Gold to Justin—eventually. But more importantly, Justin would find the girl. And when he did. . . .

Megan stared absently from the small square of the multi-paned window. It was late, long past dark, and Michael should have returned home by now. They shouldn't have stayed in Charleston. They should have moved on. She'd begged Michael to do so, but he'd insisted they stay, saying he was ready to make a fresh start—that he was ready to settle down.

She almost believed him. She wanted to. But why here? What if they met up with the devil from the inn again?

Megan fussed with the curtain and scowled.

Michael had assured her the man was not from these parts and had left town the very next morning.

"Pretty lady like you shouldn't think so hard."

Megan jumped at the drawled words. In her reverie she'd completely forgotten the presence of her guest.

Robert Tolbert was an acquaintance of Michael's, a dapper, southern gent who had not missed visiting the O'Rourke's rented cottage for a single day since his introduction to Megan. And yet she wasn't certain why he was there. Was Michael grooming him to be his next pigeon and encouraging him to come around, or was the young man interested in her on his own?

He seemed a decent enough man, Megan thought, though a bit irritating in manner.

"I'm sorry," she said with a scowl for her own lacking manners. "I'm afraid I'm not very good company. I just—I was wondering what was keeping Michael so long."

"Don't you trust me?" Robert asked, watching her with sleepy, heavy-lidded eyes.

He wasn't an unattractive man, Megan thought. But he wasn't built like a finely bred stallion. He wasn't tall and muscular with eyes that seared through her flesh and probed her soul. He wasn't like the man at the . . .

"It's not that I don't trust you," she lied, for in truth she didn't trust any man, especially the kind like the man at the inn. She'd tried to forget him. God knew she had tried. But perhaps it was her curse. Perhaps she was more like

Michael than she knew and was simply attracted to the wrong kind of people, people who would hurt her, people like the devil at the inn who had burned her lips with that one kiss, then promised to see her hang. "It's just . . ." she mumbled, trying to straighten her thought. "Michael should have been home by now."

"I think he'll be busy for a good spell yet," Robert said, his mouth lifting into a confident grin. "Leastways till his luck runs out."

"Luck?" she asked cautiously. "He said he was looking for a job."

"Then I'm certain he is," Tolbert replied. "No man could lie to you, Buttercup."

She didn't like it when he called her Buttercup—but the man at the inn had called her far worse. "He should be home by now," she repeated, turning again to the window.

"If I was out late, would you carry on so about me, Miss Welsh?"

He was watching her again. She could feel his gaze, heavy and binding.

"He's my brother," she said, trying hard to stifle the regret in her voice. "That's why I worry."

"Well, I wouldn't," Robert said. "He's a very industrious young man."

Megan frowned. This Robert-person was either terribly naive or searching very hard for the good in everyone. Either way, perhaps he was the kind of man she needed. Certainly the man at the inn was not her type and the fact that she remembered his kiss each night in her dreams was no reason to think otherwise.

The fact was, she'd never been kissed by a man before. Probably every man's kiss would feel just the same. Probably if she kissed Robert she would dream of *him* each night. And what better time to find out than now?

"You think Michael's all right then?" she asked, lowering her lashes and trying to recall how girls were supposed to flirt.

"I'm certain he is."

"That's very nice of you to say," she simpered, and wondering if her remaining scraps of morality had finally left her, she lifted her hand delicately to her throat. "I worry so for him. He's my only remaining kin, you know."

"But you mustn't worry," Robert said, rising from the settee. "It pains me so."

"Does it?" He was directly in front of her now and she lifted her lashes to look up at him. Perhaps he could really care for her as a man should care for a woman, as her father had loved her mother.

"I think of you night and day, Buttercup," he said, gripping her arms. "All the time," he gasped and suddenly he was kissing her.

She remained motionless for just a moment, waiting for the flash of desire, the warm surge of feeling, but there was none. His lips were wet and loose, his hands groping, and she struggled to get free.

"No," she said, trying to jerk free, but he refused to release her.

"My daddy is rich, Buttercup. I could care for you."

She stilled for an instant.

"I could keep you in a fine house and come to you at night. I could—"

"Keep me?" Her tone was stunned. He didn't

care about her. He was no different than all the pawing lechers of her past. "Let go of me." She jerked her arms again. "I don't want that."

"Don't play coy, Buttercup. I know your kind. I know what you like," he said, and suddenly his arms were around her, squeezing into her as he splashed wet kisses across her face.

"No," she gasped, turning her face away as she pushed against him with all her might.

The sound of tearing fabric stopped the struggle. For an instant both combatants stared at the small rend in her gown and the ivory flesh of her shoulder.

"You tore my dress," Megan said, momentarily stunned. She'd paid good money for that dress, money that could have been spent on more practical things.

"I'll buy you a hundred more," Robert panted, his eyes not leaving her exposed shoulder. "I'm rich beyond your wildest dreams. I'll. . . ."

"You tore my dress," she repeated, scowling at him.

"I'm going to make you mine," he rasped feverishly. "I know what you want." With a yank he pulled her atop him. His hands were everywhere, mauling her.

She couldn't breath. Fear choked her. "No. Please." She pushed against him, desperate for breath, for space. Cramming her elbows against his chest, she wedged some distance between them, then with a lurch jerked free.

His hands fumbled, grasping, catching her ruffled wristband. The sound of ripping fabric filled the room as the sleeve tore clean away from the bodice. Robert gaped dumbly at the limp cloth in his hand while Megan looked from her bare arm to her uninvited guest.

"You tore my dress," she said again, the pitch of her voice rising with vexation.

Robert remained mute for an instant, then tossed the sleeve dramatically aside and declared, "It's nothing. Only an unnecessary barrier between your flesh and mine."

Well, that was it then, Megan deduced. He'd lost his mind. Her eyes narrowed as she watched him, carefully, as one might watch a poisonous lizard. He was about to attack. She could see it in his eyes and gathered herself for the impact, tightening her fists and planting her slippered feet firmly on the floor.

His charge was swift, if a bit predictable, and as her sharp knuckles contacted his nose, the sound of crunching cartilage filled the room.

"Oh God!" he gasped, falling back against the settee, his fingers splayed across his broken face. "Oh God."

"What's goin' on?"

"Michael!" Megan spun on her brother, her fists clenched and ready. "Where've you been?"

"I've been—looking for a job—of course."

"No, you haven't," she countered, advancing on him. "I want the truth."

"Ohhh . . ." Tolbert moaned.

"What's he been tellin' you?" Michael queried, indicating the downed fellow.

"He hasn't been telling me anything. But you're going to. What have you been doing all this time?"

"She broke my nose," Tolbert wailed, his complaints finally breaking through their argument, causing Megan to pivot angrily toward him.

"And what did you expect?" she asked, arms akimbo. "You think just because you're rich you can treat people any way you please? You think cuz your pa's got a lot of money you can handle me like I'm some—some overripe melon? Well, you can't!" she stormed, taking a step toward him.

"Keep her away," Tolbert squealed, scrambling backwards over the arm of the settee.

"See what y' done?" Michael complained. "Y' scared him—and him the heir of Tolbert acres too."

"I don't want to hear about it, Michael."

"Ain't it just like you? Here I go outta my way t' meet y' up with some nice fella and what do y' do? Y' bust him in the nose," Michael said, raising his hand toward the injured gentleman. But before his arm fell back, Robert had raced past them, fleeing the house as if hornets bedeviled his backside.

"Hell's bells, Meg, I just can't understand you."

She studied him in silence, her thoughts boiling within her. The strange truth was he truly didn't understand her, she thought. He honestly saw no harm in the swindles, no loneliness in the endless travels. He was an entirely different animal than she, exhilarated by the thrills and dangers of their nefarious lifestyle. While she. . . .

"I'm going home, Michael," she declared solemnly. "Tomorrow."

His jaw dropped open as he groped for

words. Never had she threatened to leave him. Never. "What for?" he asked incredulously. "T' farm that worthless hunk of hillside? T' be some martyr? Buried beside Ma and Pa. It killed them, y' know. And it sure as hoot woulda killed you too if I hadn't come home when I did."

"And why did you come home, Michael? Why after all those years? After you told Pa you wouldn't?"

"Maybe I missed Ma," he said quietly. "And maybe I missed you, too, Meg."

She didn't doubt his word. He had a need for excitement, for danger, for travel, but she didn't doubt he cared for her, and in truth that was why she'd stayed with him for so long. Because he was the only person on earth who cared— even a smidgen.

"I need an honest living," she said gently. "A home."

"And what do y' call this?" he asked, raising his hand to indicate the humble cottage they rented. "Ain't it grand enough for y'?"

Megan was quiet for a moment, absorbing the stifling tension of their dispute. "This would be heaven," she whispered finally, "if it was mine. But it's not. It's not mine. Not home. Don't you see? I need to go home, to wake up with the sunrise and put my hand to work I take pride in." She curled her empty fist as if holding something precious. The silence was painful. Her hand uncurled. She wished he understood. He was her brother—her only kin. "I need to go home, Michael. I need to."

The silence was as thick as night but went unbroken for mere moments. "Go on then. Go on home," he ordered. "But I'm not goin'. I got outta there when I was no taller than a hound and I ain't never goin' back t' break my back on that farm."

"I'm not going to farm." Megan blinked, biting her lip, hating her weakness. Her words were little more than a whisper to her own ears. "I'm going to raise horses."

"Raise horses?" Michael guffawed finally, his expression incredulous. "Raise horses?"

"I've been thinking on it a long time, Michael. I know horses. I'm good with them. I am," she defended, though he didn't argue. "Pa always said I was. And I picked Rain. I can find others as good in time. My share of the money'll last me a while if I'm careful, and you know how I can stretch a coin. I'll build my herd slow and careful."

She bit her lip again, scowling at her brother, suddenly nervous now that her plans were laid bare to scrutiny. "What—what do you think?" she asked softly, but he was speechless, dumbfounded.

"You're—not jokin'," he said finally.

"No." Her answer lay deadly still in the tension. "I'm not. I'll need my share of the money. Tonight."

Silence filled the house, blanketing the area like a fog. Michael's eyes were as round as dinner plates. He opened his mouth once, failed to speak, then tried again.

"Listen Meg." His voice cracked as he said her name. "'Bout the money . . ."

Silence again. Deep and eerie. Megan watched him.

"What about the money?"

He couldn't seem to answer but stood like a beached catfish, gasping hopelessly for air.

"Tell me you didn't gamble away my money." She said the words slowly. "Tell me you didn't. You're a poor excuse for a brother, Michael, but I know. I *know* you wouldn't lose my money, not after telling me you'd guard it with your life, not after swearing you'd save it for me, so I could go home. Tell me." She took a step toward him, the entirety of her attention focused on his suddenly sweating face. "Tell me."

"I got it!" Michael shrieked, backing away from her. "I got the money sure enough. I just—I just don't got it on me."

"Where is it?"

"I . . ." His voice creaked with the single word. I loaned it to a fella." The words tumbled out. "But not just any ol' fella. This one was rich. Filthy rich." He paused for her question but when she said nothing he hurried on. "Gambling. He was gambling see, and he was outta cash and needed a stake. So I loaned him some."

"How much?"

"Well, I . . ."

"How much?"

"All of it."

"All of it!" she screamed. She was going to kill him. God forgive her. She had to do it.

"Now listen, Meg." He backed away again, praying for divine intervention. "It ain't so bad as it sounds. He's good for it. Promise. Got hisself one of them big plantations. We just gotta pick up the money, that's all."

She continued her advance.

"With interest," he sputtered quickly. "He promised t' pay interest. We can collect it tomorrow, then head north. I'll go with you. Help pick out them horses." She had stopped. Sweat beaded his brow. "I'll go all the way home with y'. It's the least I can do. I'll fix them old fences. We'll work together. It'll be great, Meg."

"He'll pay interest?" she asked. Her attention had focused on that one detail. "Tomorrow?"

"Yup. Sure. You bet he will and gladly too. The way I got him outta a bind. He was real grateful. And he won the hand too."

"Why didn't he pay you back immediately?"

"I had to get right home. It was almost dark and I didn't want y' worryin' bout me. But I heard later that he'd won real big."

She stared at him. Holy saints, he was a liar. It was a wonder he hadn't been struck dead long before. But where was the lie exactly? It was difficult to know. There was almost always a shred of truth in his tales. A minute shred, true, but a shred nonetheless.

"All right." She was so tired. Too tired to attempt to extract the truth from the lies. "And you'll help me with the fences?"

"I sure will, Meg. I'll plant them rotten posts myself."

His tone sounded utterly honest now and Megan shook her head, closing her eyes for an instant as she did so. "All right," she repeated wearily. "We'll go tomorrow then."

"Thatta girl, Meg. Thatta girl. I knew you'd forgive me."

She stared at him mutely, her expression suggesting no forgiveness whatsoever.

"He's good for it," Michael promised again, seeing her doubt. "He is. Hell's bells, Meg, them Stearns's is richer than the devil hisself."

Chapter 5

"If God had wanted us to ride in carriages he'd have given us wheels instead of legs," Megan complained, scowling at the high-stepping chestnuts that pulled their borrowed conveyance. "I don't know why you wanted to take this contraption."

"I told y'," Michael explained again. "Old Matt owed me a favor. Lent me this here rig. I was just thinkin' of you. Can't hardly ride yer mare all the way to Indiana without givin' her a little rest and some barley, can y'?"

Megan shrugged noncommittally and Michael smiled. She was pretty as a picture, dressed in the rose-hued gown he had purchased for her just the day before. He'd been obliged to say he'd bought the thing months ago. Lord only knew what she'd do if she learned the truth. He shrugged mentally, remembering her temper. She used to be such a sweet kid, like their ma, small, plain—compliant. Maybe it was her death that had changed Megan. Maybe it had been her calming influence that had made his sister so sweet tempered as a child.

Those were the days, when she was just a

gaptoothed kid. When she thought he could do no wrong. When he'd still helped his Pa on the farm. She'd adored him then. He remembered her eyes, huge as a fawn's—and as trusting—watching him like he was St. Patrick himself.

But he'd had a chance to travel to town with their neighbors and he'd known right off that he belonged there amidst the bustle and crowds.

At twelve he and Pa had had a quarrel and Michael had walked out for good, planning never to return. But seven years later he had.

The old farm had been a shocking sight. Pa had died two years before and Ma a year and a half after him. Megan had tried to farm alone. She was skin and bone, wearing rags and working herself toward her own grave. Still she'd wanted to stay, had said it was their land—all they had.

Michael sighed mentally and studied her profile. She was a beauty now and her eyes were the same. It was her way of thinking that had changed. She didn't trust him no more, and gambling away their money hadn't helped. But he'd get it back. He had it all figured out. Sure, she'd be mad for a spell, but she'd see the humor in it after a bit. That good old Irish sense of fun must be hidden in her somewhere. And then, once their funds were replenished she could go home if she wished.

"We're almost there, Meg," Michael explained, seeing the double row of oaks that had been clearly described to him. "Now you just let me do the talkin'."

"Why?"

Hell's bells, she was ornery. Now he missed

the little critter she had once been. But Megan was what she was, all woman now, and well able to tempt any man out of his life's savings. The gown's top part fit right-snug, he noted, causing her to appear even more gifted than she was, while the skirt started high up, just under her bosom.

"Cuz I told Sonny we was from Georgia," Michael explained curtly. "He's expectin' a southern drawl."

"I can drawl," she said flatly.

"Well don't. Just keep yer mouth shut and let me do the talkin'."

"Certainly," she said primly. "And you'll take care of everything, right, Michael?"

"That's right."

"Like you took care of things when we were in Tennessee. When you told me to sit on the street and pretend I couldn't walk and that fellow came along and said I was his long lost Lizzy Ann and started dragging me away. Like that time?"

"Well, no, I—"

"You what? You forgot I was stricken by a paralyzing malady and had stopped in at the saloon for a drink? Forgot to consider that there are people out there even sicker in the head than you who might think I'd make interesting sport?"

"No, I—"

"No, *I*," she interrupted brusquely. "*I* was the one who had to miraculously become cured and hide under that wagon for six hours until the commotion died down. *Me*, Michael, not you, so I'll tell you something—I won't be going in that house unless you let me know what you've got planned."

Michael scowled. She was so suspicious these days. He couldn't understand why.

"It's just like I said, I loaned a fella some money and we're going to collect," he insisted.

She smiled, an expression that made the small hairs on Michael's neck creep upward. "Don't tell me your cock-and-bull story, Michael, or I swear I'll walk in that house and tell them the truth—all about you."

"I'm telling you straight. I—"

"I swear I'll do it, Michael. Don't doubt me."

He stared at her. "What's become of your family loyalty? Your—"

"Tell me."

"All right. All right." Michael scrambled mentally. "It's like this. I had a real sweet scheme planned—like I told y' a few weeks back. I had met this gal name of Ruby in Charleston and she knew of this fella—Sonny Stearns—said he was a rich man's son who was known to get in a bit of trouble now and again—a good lookin' lad that she'd had her eye on fer a spell. So I.... Well, I ..."

Michael dropped his eyes and willed a blush. "I know it was wrong, Meg, but I told her t' take the fella t' her bed after he got hisself good and drunk. Y' see, then I thought we could show up three months later, which is just about now, and pretend he'd bedded *you* and that you was, in the family way, and he'd have t' pay up."

Megan stared at him.

"But then," Michael hurried on, "then a couple weeks ago, when we had that trouble at the inn. Y' know when that big dark fella scared y' so bad, and I knew you was wantin' t' quit the schemin'? So I decided you was right and I decided to go straight. And then—ah—just by coincidence I saw this Sonny fella gamblin' again and he was short of money and I thought, what better way t' redeem myself than t' loan him some. I mean, after the awful thing I'd been plannin' t' do."

Michael took a deep breath, slowed the team, and lied some more. "So I ups and loaned him my, *our*, money, thinkin' he'd pay us back soon as he could. But he refused. Refused!"

He chanced a glance in Megan's direction. "Do y' believe it? Says he didn't owe me a thing." Michael ran a hand through his red curls and shook his head. "What could I do? I couldn't hardly bear t' tell you I'd lost the money so I decided t' go ahead with the original swindle."

Megan still remained mute, staring at him.

"It's the Lord's truth, Megan. I swear it—"

"No." She lifted a hand wearily. "Don't swear to it, Michael." Turning her gaze toward the road, she noticed the stately, well-tended lane they'd just turned down. Slaves toiled in a nearby field.

At times she felt as if she herself was in bondage. She watched them in silence.

Michael was probably lying through his teeth, she thought grimly. But perhaps not and she was certain of one thing. Her money was gone. And with no money she couldn't go home; she couldn't have an honest life.

"He owes you the money?" she asked quietly, knowing better than to believe but trying to nevertheless.

"He sure does, Meg. All that money. And they can afford it, too. Look around. Slave labor! Cruel! They deserve t' lose a little if y' ask—"

"God forgive me." Her words were soft. "I'll do it."

"Y' will?"

She turned to him soberly. "But this is the last one, Michael. The last. Never again."

"Sure. Yep. Great," Michael chimed. They were past the slaves yet well out of sight of anyone at the big house. "This is gonna be simple. We'll walk in there. I'll tell 'em you're with child—that it was their son that done it. You just look pretty like you always do. And keep still until you see the lad. He's a strappin', fairhaired boy. I'll give you the sign." Michael rubbed his nose. "Then you say, good and loud, say 'Sonny', like you been missin' him. Understand?"

Megan nodded, praying silently for her immortal soul.

"Great! This'll be grand. You won't regret it, Meg. I promise."

"Might there be a Mr. or Mrs. Stearns about?" Michael held tightly to Megan's elbow as they stood stiff and proper upon the endless, white veranda of Manor Royal.

"Yassah." The doorman was black as ebony, somber as a storm cloud. "Who do I say be callin'?"

"Mr. Royce Edwards and my sister, Mary."

The doorman turned his back, regal as a crowned prince. Seconds ticked by with heart-thumping slowness. Hell's bells, the house was big as their entire farm back home. Michael smiled.

The humorless doorman returned. "Follow me."

The entry of the house was gargantuan, spreading out in immaculate splendor to join the grand, sweeping stairway that curved upwards to the top floor. The morning room where they were shown was large and airy, centered on broad, sparkling glass doors that overlooked a duck pond set amidst an emerald lawn. One door stood open, letting in the sweet scent of the Carolina morning. Michael nudged Megan into a chair not far from that opened portal.

"Mister Edwards?" questioned a gray-haired man, entering from the hallway.

Michael steadied his nerves. "Yes sir. I'm Royce Edwards, and you must be Thomas Stearns. I've heard nothing but good about you, sir." Michael extended his hand, crossing the floor to grasp the big man's palm in his own. "It's good to meet you."

A woman entered and Michael turned to share his effervescent smile with her. "Mrs. Stearns," he drawled.

Agatha Stearns was slim and delicate, surrounded by a gentle self-assurance.

"I'm Royce Edwards and this is my sister, Mary." Michael waved a quick hand in her direction. "Perhaps I should have contacted you before barging in like this, but, well, I simply wasn't sure how to preempt our meeting." He frowned slightly, then turned to stride pensively toward the window. "I'm afraid what I have to say is not—well, it's not of a pleasant nature, I'm afraid."

Silence filled the house and Michael shivered slightly, feeling exhilarated like never before.

"Speak your piece, Mr. Edwards," prompted the elder man. His voice was deep and steady, rumbling through Michael's mind for an instant. Was there something familiar about it? No. It was just the southern accent—hard to distinguish from all the others he'd heard in this part of the country.

"Yes, of course," agreed Michael hurriedly. This was no time to delay. He glanced once at Megan, who sat silent and still.

"My story begins about three months ago when I was on a business trip in Charleston. As usual my sister was with me. We always travel together, you see, since the death of our parents." Pacing across the room, Michael joined his hands behind his back, looking saddened by his own words, but continuing on with obvious difficulty. "As it happened on this particular occasion, business went well. I finished up early and thought I might enjoy a quick drink before returning to check on Mary's well-being.

"I fear I can't leave her for long." He paused again to shake his head with slow regret. "You see, since our parents' deaths she's been—well, she's simply not quite right. You know." He lifted a hand toward his own temple. "In the head." He didn't look at her when he said the words. She had a tendency to dislike hearing of her lunacy. But she'd taken the news of the im-

pending birth much better than he had hoped
and she made a cute little mama, too. "The doc-
tors are baffled. There seems to be no cause for
her malady and yet, she's spoken not a word
since their passing."

"How awful." The sentiment was the silver-
haired Mrs. Stearns', who stared past Michael to
rest her sympathetic gaze on the poor girl's
lovely face.

"Go on," prompted her spouse, his expression
unchanged.

He was a tough old badger, Michael thought,
not to be taken lightly.

"As I was saying, business went well, allowing me to stop at a small saloon where I . . . Oh
God." Michael lifted his hand abruptly, covering
his face for an instant. "It's so hard. I'm
ashamed to tell you good folks the rest. But the
truth is always the wisest course." He sighed,
dropping his hand and his eyes. "I got involved
in a game of chance that night. The hour became late and I assumed my sister was asleep,
but when I went to check on her, she . . ."

Michael closed his eyes in abject misery. "It
seems," he began again, opening his eyes finally
to stare mournfully at the couple before him. "It
seems that while I was about, my sister met
your son. I'm sorry," he moaned, wringing his
hands as if in agony. "What I wouldn't give to
spare you folks the truth, but it happened." This
was it, the cutting stroke. "It's not her fault.
She's unable to understand the moral aspects of
such an act outside of marriage. Of course," he
added quickly, "I'm not blaming your son either."

Michael blushed artfully. Any moment now they should realize his implications. Any moment. . . .

Agatha's gasp filled the room. Her hand fluttered upward, covering her mouth. "No."

Success! He could hear it in the sorrowful tone of the mother's despair. Her love for her son would save the day. They'd gladly pay any amount to clear his name. Life was good.

"What are you saying?" Tom demanded, his tone hoarse and gravelly. Agatha may have been shaken, but her husband was not and glared at Michael with scalding heat. "Do you mean to tell us our son spent the night with your sister?"

His eyes—there was something about them. "Yes." Michael spoke the untruth in a soft, convincing tone, his expression pained and utterly broken. "I'm afraid that's the way of it."

Silence ruled the house. A pin could have been heard falling from thirty yards.

"I'm not expecting anything from you folks, of course." He sighed. "I simply thought the father, and his parents, should know of the impending birth."

"A baby?" It was Agatha who posed the painful question, her voice as soft as sorrow could make it.

"I fear so," came Michael's tortured response. "There will be a child. Your son's child. But," he hurried on, "I don't expect any kind of compensation. I was simply concerned about what the people in your community might think if they got wind of your son's . . . lack of . . . responsibility. And, too," he added, "the child may be like its mother." He touched his head, indicating her mental instability. "It would be a shame if folks thought your blood was somehow tainted, when in fact it's no fault of yours at all.

"No." He lifted his chin proudly. "We'll be moving on—just as soon as we can afford to do—"

"God damn it!" Tom exploded suddenly.

Michael jumped, his jaw dropping slightly and his breath catching in his throat. "I, I beg your pardon."

"Which boy is it?"

"Huh?" Michael asked inarticulately.

"It must be Sonny. Was it Sonny? Or was it Justin?"

"I—think . . ." Michael glanced frantically toward Megan whose eyes were as wide as an emerald sea. "I—Mary can't talk so—"

"So how'd you know it was a Stearns?" Tom's square jaw was thrust out, his expression wary.

"Well . . ." Michael fought for control. "She writes quite legibly and—"

"Writes?" Stearns growled, his tone sounding disbelieving. "She writes but doesn't talk?"

"Ahh—yes sir."

"Then what'd she write, boy? Spit it out."

"Sonny. Sonny Stearns."

"I've never heard of such a ridiculous—" he began, then shouted, "Peter!" His voice bellowed through the house, reverberating the very walls with its volume. As if by magic a dark face appeared in the doorway, his eyes round and cautious.

"Yassah."

"Tell Nat to bring my sons," he growled. "And hurry."

"Thank you." Michael accepted a lemonade from the neatly dressed slave, then chanced a look at Megan and wished he hadn't. She didn't look happy and he wasn't sure why. After all, things were going well. True, he'd been a bit worried himself for a spell, but surely if the Stearns doubted his word, they'd have already been thrown out on their ears. The simple fact that they were still in the house meant they would be successful. It must also mean that the Stearns boys had gotten in enough trouble in the past to make this new scandal believable.

God he was clever. He smiled. "Take some ade Mary, dear," he urged as the serving girl offered a glass to the frozen little mother-to-be. But when his sister made no response, he cleared his throat and announced to the room at large, "How silly of me to forget. Mary can't keep a single thing in her stomach these days. Her condition, you know."

At his words Agatha looked increasingly nervous, while her spouse glowered even more fiercely toward the door, as if his glare alone would bring his two sons marching through that entrance. The tension in the room was as thick as bread pudding, but Michael smiled. They were almost through it, after all. The worst was over. Venturing one more glance toward Megan, Michael smiled with all the brotherly warmth he could muster. She'd thank him when this was all over. Oh, she might not admit the cleverness of his ploy, but she wouldn't be able to deny it in her own heart.

A dog barked, then another. Megan's hands gripped the arms of her chair with ferocious anxiety, her face going pale, and Michael smiled again. "There's no need to be nervous, Mary. We've done the right thing. Honesty is always the best course."

"Sonny!" Thomas Stearns propelled himself to his feet, facing the young man who entered by the door he had watched with such concentrated attention. "What the devil is all this about now?" he asked, glaring into his son's face and demanding an answer to his unexplained question.

Sonny stood for a moment, his so-blue eyes taking in the scene before him with quiet intelligence. "What's what all about?" he asked finally, seeming nonplussed by his sire's obvious agitation.

"This!" stormed Tom, throwing a wave toward the two who had so abruptly invaded his peace. "This . . ."

"Perhaps I can be of some help in explaining things," offered Michael graciously. Calmly setting his ade aside, he rose to his feet, tugged his vest into alignment, and strode toward father and son. "I'm Royce Edwards," he began, offering Sonny his hand. "We haven't met, but this," he explained, waving a hand gently toward Megan, "is my sister." He paused for a moment, watching as Sonny's eyes widened at the sight of the girl. At first there was only the usual reaction of a young man noticing a beautiful woman. It took only a moment, however, for another expression to cross his face. Was it recognition, uncertainty?

"We were in Charleston about three months ago. February the third was the exact date we arrived," explained Michael. "We stayed at the Grand Oak." He paused again, allowing the young man enough time to garner the information. "It was a Friday night. I—" He glanced at his sister, looking uncertain now, as if his emotional distance could no longer be maintained. "I—or perhaps I should say, my sister—believes you met her that night."

Sonny was indeed a good-looking lad, Michael thought, even better than he remembered, with his lengthy grace and tousled blond hair. It was no wonder Ruby had been so eager to take the man to bed. Ah, Ruby, he remembered, with the gleaming red hair and curvaceous body. She'd had the wonderful morals of a stray cat and an insatiable lust to match. She'd been the perfect woman to entertain Sonny Stearns those three months earlier. Michael laughed inside, somewhere near where his soul should have been, then reprimanded himself. After all, Sonny seemed to be a likable fellow. It was almost a shame to accuse him of such a dastardly deed. But then. . . .

"Did you bed the girl or not?" roared Tom suddenly, all patience gone.

"What?" Sonny choked, his jaw dropping at the accusation.

"I said," repeated the father, leaning toward his youngest son, "did you bed the girl or not?"

"No," Sonny exclaimed, then stiffened, dropping his jaw to an even lower position. "Well, I, I'm not sure. I . . ."

It was coming: the culmination of months of work, the final stroke of genius, the greatest of Michael O'Rourke's victories.

A gasp split the room, the terrified sound of it freezing all inhabitants to immobility, except Michael, who turned toward his sister with an irritated scowl. How dare she interrupt his finest hour?

"Justin!" Tom exploded. "It's about time you showed up."

In the glass doorway a man stood, facing Megan from not three feet away. His hair was dark, his body long and muscular. There was something familiar about him. Michael's mind scurried for information. There was something about him. . . .

"I'm sorry I'm late." Justin slowly turned toward his father, finally granting Michael a full view of his unforgettable features.

"No!" Michael rasped hoarsely. His mouth opened, closed, then opened again. "I mean no!" he amended, willing his voice to sound calmer. Which it didn't. "I mean—my sister is very upset." Screwing his head away from Justin's hawkish eyes, Michael fled past the man to Megan's side. Taking her arm in a frantic grip, he jerked her to her feet.

"Come now, Mary," he mumbled in a voice far different from his usual tone. "I am *dearly* sorry to have put you through this, but we'll go straight home now. Straight home!" he promised, trying to pry Megan's feet from the spot where they remained nailed to the floor. "Don't you understand me? We have to leave these good people. We came to the *wrong place*," he ground out, pulling at her with all his trembling strength. "You were mistaken. We've never met these good folk before. *They don't know us!*" he said, emphasizing each word as if their very lives depended on them. "They don't know us. *Yet*." With the word *yet*, he yanked at her arm, but Megan didn't budge.

Her eyes were glued to the man in the doorway. He had come! Somehow he had ascended from the depths of her nightmares to step into the reality of her life. She could feel Michael pulling at her. Vaguely she heard the terror in his tone. He was trying to pull her to safety. She knew that much. But it was no use for in the depths of the man's murky gaze there had been a recognition so clear as to leave not the faintest hope of continued survival.

"Don't worry, Mother," Justin said calmly. "Sonny and I are innocent this time. You see, I've met these two before. A few weeks back in Charleston." His gaze struck Megan like a bolt of lightning. "The boy's a charlatan," he said simply. "And the girl." He paused and smiled, chilling Megan's heart to stillness. "The girl's mine. Bought and paid for."

Chapter 6

Megan's world spun inward, spiraling downward in slow, erratic circles. No, her mind screamed but her lips remained motionless, slightly parted as if she panted for air. No.

His face was as perfect and dark as she remembered.

"Her name was Suzanne then," he said quietly. "And I've looked everywhere for her."

He stepped toward her. She watched him as a hare does a wolf. Was he going to kill her here and now? Mother Mary full of grace, her mind moaned, and then she fell, melting toward the floor in her most beautifully executed swoon, with one hand still caught in her brother's petrified grip.

"Mary?" Michael questioned, staring dumbfounded at Megan's limp form. For a moment he had forgotten his sister's tender condition, but his oversight lasted only a second. "Mary!" he called with sudden drama as he realized her ploy. "Mary." With a flourish he knelt beside her, his freckled face contorted with pain. Patting her hand, he glanced up at the Stearns, who stood watching with open-mouthed dismay. Apparently it wasn't every day that young mothers-to-be collapsed upon their morning room floor.

"Look what you've done," Michael railed, struck by sudden inspiration as he stared up at Justin. "Your wild accusations have shocked her into a stupor. How dare you say—"

"One more word from you and I'll fetch the sheriff here and now," Justin informed him quietly.

Michael's mouth snapped closed. Justin strode closer, then bent lithely to scoop Megan into his arms.

"I'm taking 'Mary' upstairs to rest."

With long, easy strides he headed for the stairs. Four pairs of shocked eyes followed.

"What's all this about?" questioned Thomas gruffly.

"It's just as I said," Justin replied, pausing in the doorway. "The man's a four-flusher— dishonest to the core." He allowed his scathing gaze to burn Michael for a moment. "Don't blink or he'll steal the gold right out of your teeth," he added, and then he was through the door, out of hearing of the others and striding up the stairs.

Her world had ended. Megan opened her eyes slowly, completely forgetting her ploy as she stared into the mahogany depths of her captor's eyes.

"Let me go," she whispered hopelessly, the words creeping from the bottom of her soul.

"You're awake." No expression showed on Justin's granite features. "Good." He was climbing the steps as easily as if she were no more trouble than a soiled coverlet. "I hope next time you swoon you'll have the good sense to choose a softer landing."

"Let me go," she whispered again, knowing it was useless.

"After our one, unforgettable night together?" asked Justin. "After all the days I've dreamed about having you back?"

"What are you talking about?" They'd reached the top of the stairs and turned to travel swiftly into a bedroom. Her tone was no more than a breathy murmur, but as her words registered in her own brain she grasped onto the idea as her last chance for life. "What are you saying? I've never seen you before in my life."

He stared at her, wordless, expressionless, then bent to carefully place her on the broad expanse of a canopied bed. "Don't you remember me, Mary?" His tone was as throaty as a lover's and he smelled of fresh meadow. "What can I do to make you recall that wondrous night?"

His face was only inches from hers. His arms cradled her, refusing to withdraw. She could feel his warm breath on her face and stared at him in speechless awe.

"I know what'll jar your memory," he whispered finally. He drew fractionally closer, his lips nearly touching hers, then straightened with regretful slowness. His hands drew away from her, reaching for the buttons that held his trousers in place. "Surely you'll remember this." With aching slowness his fingers loosened one button, then another.

Megan's eyes bugged. He was undressing.

Right there in front of God and everyone.
"Wha——what are you doing?" she stammered.

"I'm disrobing! I'm sure you'll appreciate it. I
know that's the way you like me best." His gaze
was as hot as boiled molasses with the thick
fringes of his lashes half-mast over his deadly
eyes. "Naked!"

"No," she whispered, launching herself from
the bed, but he was after her, grabbing her by
one wrist to pull her into his arms.

"Why not?" he crooned, but his teeth were
gritted. "I know how you like your men to undress in front of you."

"I—I don't know what you're talking about."

"No? You don't remember me?" He looked
devastated, but smiled finally. "You will, love.
You will," he said with steady confidence. "And
when you do, the memory will burn within you
as it does in me."

"Let me go," she gasped, stiffled by his close-
ness. "You're mad."

He smiled again, but the expression was
frightening, immobilizing her struggles. "I may
be, love. I may be." His eyes held her for a moment longer before he released her.

She stepped back, eyeing him in horror, but
he seemed to fail to notice her expression.

"Missy!" he boomed, causing Megan to jump
in fear. Footsteps sounded in the hall. A slave
girl appeared, her fresh, lovely face tense, her
eyes wide and startled.

"Yassa, Massa Justin?"

"Don't call me master," he reminded her
gently.

"Yassa Ma . . . Justin." She nodded solemnly.

His face softened and he grinned. "The *lady's* not feeling well, Missy. Don't leave her side until Tia comes to relieve you. All right?"

"Yassa."

"Thank you." He nodded brusquely. "You rest for a spell, *Mary*. I won't be gone long. I promise you that."

Megan watched him leave, wondering frantically if his words were meant to comfort her.

She had always known she'd eventually pay for her crimes. But not like this, locked away in some fairy-tale mansion by a raving lunatic.

Silence held the room. Megan stared at Missy, who stared back. They shuffled their feet, shifted their gazes, and eyed the door with yearning.

She had to get away before he came back, Megan reasoned, trying to contain her panic. She had to leave—before it was too late.

"You're still here," Justin said, eyeing Michael as he reentered the morning room.

"See—see here," Michael said, puffing his chest in indignant anger. "The girl's my poor, daft sister. You've made serious accusations against us."

Justin crossed his arms over his chest and smiled. "And you've made a serious mistake, haven't you boy? I heard your ridiculous tale and know you planned to cheat this family out of a fortune."

"Hardly that. I—"

"You!" Justin raged, stepping nearer. Michael backed away, but Justin followed, grasping him by vest and shirt front. "You are a low-bellied snake." He shook the smaller man as if he were just that. "And if you wish to see the daylight tomorrow, you'll leave now while my good humor holds."

"But, my sister—" Michael squeaked.

"Is mine," Justin said wickedly. "Paid for with cold cash, remember?"

"You bought the girl?" Sonny piped up from behind. "You must be joking, Justin."

"I assure you I'm not in the mood for jests, Sonny."

"But—" Agatha said, scowling at her son's back. "The girl's not a Negro, Justin. What are you thinking?"

"Her brother here sold her to me," Justin said. "I can only assume that means she's got Negro blood."

"But she's—" Michael began again.

"Mine!" Justin repeated, grinding the word into his face. "She's mine and you'd be wise to not forget it. I warned you before about showing your face. I'm warning you again." Half-dragging the man toward the door, Justin propelled him down the hall and out the front entrance.

Michael stumbled onto the veranda.

"Consider yourself lucky," Justin said, his chest heaving. "Come again and your luck will fall short."

Michael delayed only a moment before scurrying down the stairs to the buggy. Best to leave alive, he deduced wisely. There was nothing else to be done right now. Megan would have to hold her own until he could figure a way to get her back. Climbing up behind the rented team,

Michael lifted the lines and hurried from the yard.

The morning room was still littered with his family's stunned, motionless bodies when Justin returned.

"What the hell is this all about?" his father demanded.

"I know little more than you do," Justin said blandly. "I met the two of them in Charleston. The little red-topped rat was selling the girl. I bought her."

Silence as heavy as lead.

"Bought her?" asked his mother, her hands clutching each other. "But how could you ... I mean, she's his sister."

Justin shrugged. In truth he had no idea what to do now and only wanted time to think. "It's altogether possible they're not related by blood at all."

"Still," Agatha said, looking not the least relieved, "the girl's so—fair. She can't be ..." Her voice trailed off.

"Black?" Justin asked quietly. "You know as well as I do, Mother, that if she's even one-sixteenth Negroid she can be bought and sold."

Thomas scowled darkly and Sonny shuffled his feet. Apparently they were uncomfortable with purchasing someone whose skin was paler than their own.

"It's your rules," Justin reminded casually, "not mine."

"Damn it, boy!" Thomas stormed. "The girl looks white to me. What are you thinking, enslaving the girl? And her expecting a child."

"There's no reason to believe she's with

child," Justin reminded them. "More likely the brother told her to pretend."

"But she wouldn't—" began Agatha, sounding scandalized.

Like hell, thought Justin, but he was not ready to nail the girl to the same cross as her brother until he learned more of the facts. "She's daft, remember?" he said, trying not to grin at the prospect of using her own ploy against her. "Perhaps she doesn't realize the seriousness of her actions."

"But—"

Justin raised a hand. His mind buzzed with questions. Where had she come from? What had brought her there? Good fortune! Nothing else. Just his own God-given luck. She'd come! Glory be! His mind screamed with glee, but he held his face expressionless as he watched his father.

"I need some time to myself. I'm going for a ride." He turned to leave, but the sight of his mother's anguished face stopped him. If there was a person in his family who shared his views on slavery, it was she, he knew, and he'd had no right to hurt her with his words. "Don't worry, Mother." He wished he could tell her the facts, could ease the pain he read in her eyes, but what could he say? He understood the circumstances only slightly better than she. "Everything will come out right. You'll see. Send Tia to relieve Missy, please. I don't want Mary left alone. There's no telling what she might do."

Agatha's face, which had already been pale with worry, blanched to chalk white.

"I mean," Justin amended quickly, realizing she thought his little white slave might throw herself from the window. "She may faint again or need something." It hardly seemed the time to admit the angel-faced madonna might very well steal the very clothes from their bodies before vanishing up the chimney in a cloud of smoke.

Once outside, Justin drew a heavy breath.

He needed a ride, fresh air, time. . . . God, he needed time. Striding to the stable, he found his gelding still saddled and waiting, but paused to glance back in the direction he'd just come. He couldn't risk leaving, he realized suddenly. Tia was big as a barn and meaner than last year's toothache. But Suzanne, or Mary, or whatever she chose to call herself today, might just wrestle the big buffalo into submission before organizing a slave revolt. Who knew what she was capable of doing? Blast it all! Who even knew who she was?

Perhaps he should have told his family the truth about her part in her brother's loathsome plots, but Justin wanted to mete out her punishment in his own sweet time without the aid or hindrance of his family. They needn't know what his plans were for her. After all . . . he owned her.

Justin smiled, stalking around the barn, and ducking between the rails of the fence. He'd walk a ways, he decided, but would watch the house. It wouldn't hurt to keep an eye on Mary's window. Just in case. He smiled again.

She'd come! It was the only coherent thought in his mind. God, fate, or the devil himself had made her appear in his parents' morning room like an unfolding bird of paradise.

He'd been shocked to immobility when he'd heard the brother's voice through the open glass doors. He'd recognized the voice immediately and had waited, listening to the scheming little weasel dig his own grave.

Perhaps he should have held the man for the sheriff, but in truth Justin didn't care about her brother. He was just a slippery reptile out for a quick coin. While she. . . .

Justin's nostrils flared. She was a scheming little temptress who used her God-given beauty to seduce and manipulate. But she'd be the one manipulated now for she'd messed with the wrong man. She had come, had walked in like a lamb to slaughter. Justice lived. And justice would be served. It was impossible to guess what her plans had been but one thing was certain; he had not been included in them. Her stark expression of terror had made that much perfectly clear. Whatever she had come to do, it had not been to meet him.

Justin nearly rubbed his hands with glee. She'd been terrified. Her flawless little face had revealed her trembling emotions. The memory remained in his mind like a haunting melody. The mere sight of him had rendered her speechless. Just imagine what the thought of being his slave would do to her!

He chuckled to himself. She must be terrified this very moment—quaking at the idea of being under his thumb.

And she thought he was crazy. Justin chuckled again. The little cat-eyed temptress thought him mad, just as he had believed her to be on their first meeting. Life was good, and it would only get better after the little vixen had had some time to anticipate what bondage to a madman would mean. Let her believe he was insane. Let her stew in that misbegotten idea for a spell. Justin laughed aloud now.

He was going to enjoy this to the fullest. Oh, he wouldn't hurt her, and eventually he'd have to set her free, of course. But first she'd tell him how she'd hooked up with Manchester and then she'd be the one to convince Horace to return the precious stallion to his rightful owner.

Revenge was sweet.

Give him twenty-four hours with her and she'd be begging to tell the truth. Give him forty-eight hours and she'd be a sniveling lump of penitent jelly. Hell, give him a week and she'd be kissing his. . . .

Life was good. It was grand, wonderful, a veritable. . . . Justin's celebration ground to a halt as his jaw fell lax.

Merciful heavens, what was that? It was—it was. . . . Blast it to cinders. It was Mary!

Chapter 7

S he clung to the sill of the second story window, her feet bare, her toes scrambling for a hold amongst the climbing vines.

Justin's breath caught in his throat as she slipped an inch. God help them all; she was actually going to attempt to climb down the tangled vines. For an instant longer Justin stood watching in mind-boggled amazement.

She slipped again. A tendril of ivy tore away from the aged brick. Her legs, bared to the knee with her mauve skirt hiked up between them, pistoned wildly, searching for a firmer grip.

She was going to kill herself. The thought suddenly implanted itself into Justin's brain. Blast it all, she was going to kill herself. He was running before he knew it, sprinting through the trees toward the small, fiery-haired creature who clung to the wall.

How dare she take such a risk with her neck? It was his neck, too, after all, bought and paid for, and he'd be damned if he was about to let her die prematurely. When she died, he fully planned to do the deed himself.

He was at the edge of the trees now, less than

two hundred yards from the house but hidden
by the foliage. Justin paused, glancing through
the leaves toward the wall. She was still there,
laboriously lowering herself by quick but careful inches.

She was going to make it. The little urchin
had actually scaled the side of Manor Royal like
some outlandish monkey. Justin shook his head
in amazement, drawing a relieved breath. She'd
scared the wits out of him, but two could play
her game. A crafty grin lifted the corners of his
mouth and he chuckled quietly. The girl deserved to be taught a lesson.

Megan's entire body trembled with fatigue,
but she'd made it. There was no one in sight.
All she needed now was a horse and she'd be
free. With one frenzied glance over her shoulder,
Megan sent up a silent prayer and ducked
around the corner.

"Mary." Justin caught her against his body
with amorous glee, muffling her screams against
his chest.

It couldn't be him! It couldn't be!

"Mary," he crooned again. "You couldn't bear
the separation either, could you, love. I've been
waiting forever, wondering when you'd come."

He smothered her to him, pressing the breath
from her body. "Every minute without you is
like a lifetime, every second an eternity in hell.
Mary. Let me look at you."

He snapped her out to arms' length. "Oh my
love, you're more beautiful than ever. I was. . . .
I was. . . ." Again he snatched her to his body,

crushing her soft curves against his hard chest. "I'm so sorry I killed you, Beatrice," he moaned suddenly, his wild thoughts careening him into uncharted territory. Heaving sobs wracked his body, bumping his large frame against hers. "I didn't mean to kill you. You're the love of my life." Again he pushed her from him to stare into the depths of her dilated eyes. "You must believe me. I didn't mean to kill you. I just . . ." He drew in a deep, shuddering breath. "I was just overcome with passion. Our love play . . . your flesh, naked against mine. And you crying out in rapture, in pain. Oh Lord, Bea. The thought of it drives me nearly mad. I could take you this very minute. Right now. Here!"

His hands grasped the neckline of her gown and suddenly Megan realized his intent. He was going to rip the garment from her body. "No!" Her plea was barely more than a squeak.

"No?" He stopped suddenly, looking puzzled. "No?" There was an insane light in his eyes, as frightful as a banshee's howl. She cowered against the wall, certain she was about to die, but Justin calmed abruptly. "You're right." He closed his eyes, shaking his head slowly. "Of course. You're always right, my love. We must wait—until tonight. We mustn't let them know." He nodded toward the house, but kept his eyes on hers. "We'll wait," he decreed. "But I can't go without a kiss. I'll die without it."

She gaped at him, speechless.

"You're not still angry that I killed you, are you, Bea? Tell me you're not."

She dared not breath, but stared at him in horrified disbelief. He was as crazy as a hoot owl and she was trapped.

"Tell me." He shook her suddenly, seeming overwhelmed by the thought that she might resent such an inconsequential thing as murder. "Tell me you're not angry."

"N——n——no," she stuttered, her lips too stiff to form anything more coherent.

"Thank you. Thank you. I won't do it again, Bea. I promise. Next time I pleasure you I won't use the knife," he whispered. "I'll use the club— just the way you like it."

Mother Mary full of grace . . .

Her prayer was pathetic, her mind too weak to focus on anything but Justin's face, dark, intense, and utterly mad.

"It'll be better than ever, love. But we must wait. You were right. Just one kiss. Just one and then you must go."

She had no idea what he spoke of for her mind had ceased to function, but he shook her again.

"Give me a kiss, Beatrice, or I won't bear the wait. I'll have to take you—" His voice deepened with intensity. "Here and now."

For a moment she honestly thought she might faint, but what would it help? With every limb atremble she rose on her bare toes. Her lips were cold as ice against his warm cheek.

"Beatrice." He chuckled as she drew away. "You're such a tease sometimes."

Suddenly he pulled her into his embrace. Bending her stiff body slightly, he leaned her over his arm and placed his lips to hers.

The heat of his kiss was shocking. It hit

Megan's numbed system like a volcanic blast. His mouth moved against hers. His tongue caressed her. Pure chaos exploded within her. She was pressed so tightly against him that she could feel every muscle, every hard, flexing irregularity of his form. And suddenly she was hot, burning hot.

"There." He straightened suddenly, pulling her along with him. She felt like a rag doll in his arms as she stared at him, lips parted slightly. "I can wait now." He smiled, the grin of Satan's son. "Until tonight."

Taking her arm in a firm grasp, he turned her about and guided her around the corner toward Royal's pillared veranda.

Just inside the huge double doors, Agatha stood arranging flowers on a small walnut table. She turned from her task just as they entered. Her jaw dropped and her eyes widened in wordless wonder. She attempted a few words, but nothing came.

"We went for a walk," Justin said, as if that explained the tattered lengths of dismembered vines that clung to Megan's hair. "She needed some air," he added, pulling his stiff, little thrall toward the stairs.

Three house slaves ceased their duties to watch the pair ascend and then a door opened above and Sonny stepped out. His square jaw dropped to an angle similar to his mother's. He noted Megan's littered hair, her bare legs, her scraped knees, then, lacking the discipline of silent acceptance, he lifted an uncertain hand to indicate the room she had occupied. "Wasn't she . . ."

"Went for a walk," Justin explained curtly, pulling her around the corner to her room. The door was still closed, apparently to prevent her escape, and he pressed her back against the wall, gazing into her terrified eyes. "Beatrice," he whispered, then kissed her again. This time the caress was as soft as a butterfly's breath. "I'll be back tonight. I promise." He stood for a moment, watching her, but suddenly his expression changed to one of stunned bewilderment. "Mary?" He spoke the name questioningly. "When did you arrive?"

Megan stared dumbly at the picnic basket. It was proof of Justin's insanity—proof of her own insanity for ever considering her brother's plans. Her eyes itched. Her head hurt. Every muscle in her body ached. She hadn't slept a wink for over thirty hours. All night she had lain in petrified terror, listening to every squeak, every scrape against the window. But he hadn't come. She closed her eyes for an instant. She'd been thankful for that small reprieve but morning had brought new horrors: A picnic—away from the relative safety of Manor Royal, away from the people who apparently kept Justin from becoming blatantly dangerous.

"Are you ready, my love?"

Megan jumped at the sound of his voice. Ready? Ready to die? Ready to be raped and mutilated? Ready for sexual torture? No. She didn't think so.

"We may be gone for quite some time, Mother." He turned toward the elder woman, his face as clear and intelligent as any Megan could recall. Who could have guessed he was mad? "But we'll be back for dinner. I don't want to overtax my little Mary."

Taking the basket in one hand and her elbow in the other, Justin steered her toward the door. A lightweight carriage waited a short distance from the broad veranda. A team of glistening black horses tossed their heads and chewed their bits, eager to be off.

It was a perfect morning, the sky as blue as a robin's egg, the air as fresh as wintergreen. A bad morning to die, Megan thought.

Justin handed her up to the leather upholstery of the carriage seat. She pulled her rose-hued skirt about her and pressed herself against the vehicle's padded arm, as far from the driver's seat as possible. He rose beside her, not seeming to notice her distance. Lifting the lines, he set the team in motion.

The road rolled beneath them, bordered by dark-earthed fields where slaves, armed with rakes and hoes, readied the soil for planting. Justin was silent, eerily so. Megan watched him from the corner of her eye. One would think, after his ramblings of yesterday, that she would be grateful for his silence, but the quiet was almost more frightening than his delusions. Who—or what—did he think she was today? Perhaps he believed she was an inanimate object, a door handle, a flyswatter. Oh Lord, what if he thought she was something undesirable? Perhaps a rodent, or. . . .

Mother Mary! She couldn't bear the silence. It was too much.

"Is—is this your father's property?" she asked abruptly.

"Yes." His answer was curt, devoid of expression.

"And—and the horses—they're very handsome. Are they his?" Lord, what a stupid question. Who else would own them?

"Yes." Silence stretched behind his answer, like the empty road they traveled, but before Megan could think of some other, clever query, he added, "Nat trained them."

Megan watched him. He seemed different today, although he looked the same—crisp, commanding, larger than life itself. "Nat? Is he a—a friend of yours?" It was so difficult to know what to ask a madman.

"Nat?" Justin turned to her for the first time. In the early sunlight his hair appeared to be flecked with reddish highlights. "Nat's a slave. One of my father's two hundred or so," he said, then turned solemnly back to the road.

What did his tone imply? And his expression, almost of disapproval. His body seemed stiff. She could see the corded strength of his arms where his white sleeves were rolled away from his wrists.

"He's got the lightest hands I've ever seen." Justin scowled at the glistening blacks. "Sensitive as a . . ." He paused, lifting one large palm from the lines. It was crisscrossed with callouses, the hand of a working man. "Soft as a woman's." He turned toward her again.

Megan flinched under his gaze and turned quickly away, hiding her face beneath the brim of her straw bonnet.

"Here we are."

They stopped by a small copse of trees where the grass grew in perfect emerald luxury beside a small stream.

Megan's throat constricted. What if she refused to get down? What if she grabbed the lines and galloped off with the team? What if she. . . .

"Come on down, love."

He stood waiting for her. How long he'd been there she wasn't sure, but his hands felt steady and strong as he lifted her. He held her longer than necessary. There was a magnetism about him, a frightening, irresistible pull that left Megan petrified in his grip. His hands were on her waist. Warmth seeped from his fingertips, spreading throughout her body.

"I'll get our things," he said finally, and drew away jerkily, like a puppet in unskilled hands.

Retrieving a blanket from the carriage, he smoothed it beneath the spreading branches of an elm, where the shade dappled the grass like a mosaic.

"Sit down, Mary. Don't be shy."

Hesitantly, Megan lowered herself to a corner of the patchwork quilt. It was very quiet. There was no one near—no one within sight.

"We've got a veritable feast here." He took the picnic basket from the carriage, then strode with slow, liquid steps toward her. "But I'm not hungry just now. Do you mind if we wait to eat?"

Megan meant to speak, but no words came. She shook her head dumbly, not daring to take her eyes from him. Holy Patrick, he was big, she thought as he lowered himself and the basket to the quilt. Surely he outweighed her by double.

And the mass of his body. . . . It wasn't fat, but lay in long, graceful mounds beneath his clothing, as if each muscle waited impatiently to be set to motion. She gulped convulsively.

"This—this Nat fellow," she blurted suddenly, having no idea what she was about to say. "Has he been with your father long?"

"Not so long. Four or five years." Justin reclined onto an elbow, facing her across the multicolored blanket. "It doesn't seem long to me, but maybe if I were a slave I'd feel differently."

His eyes were flecked with golden highlights. They were the most incredible eyes. The eyes of a genius—or a madman.

"What do you think?"

The question caught her off guard and she blinked twice, staring at him.

"What do you think?" he repeated. "Do you think time is a standard unit or does it vary, depending on your perspective?"

"I . . ." She was no scholar. She'd readily admit it. "I don't know."

"And what about slavery?" His voice had a rich, melodious rhythm, like a snake charmer, coaxing the serpent from the basket. "Do you think it's right to enslave our fellow man?"

She stared at him mutely. But he remained silent, awaiting an answer. Was *she* his slave? Was he toying with her? "My parents believed slavery was an evil thing," she said finally. "We were taught to believe the same."

"Ahhh." Justin nodded. "And how do your parents feel about your present line of business?"

Megan drew her arms tightly against her body as if she might shield herself from him. "My ..." She gulped. "My parents are dead."

Justin scowled. Who could guess if she was lying? "I'm sorry. How long ago?"

She raised her eyes. "Several years."

Justin's scowl deepened. She was probably lying through her teeth, he reminded himself, but still, the thought of a girl without a mother ripped at his heart. "So you were left in your brother's care?"

She knew better than to answer. He was probably trying to trick her. But trick her into what? At any time he had the right to march her to the sheriff and accuse her of theft—or worse.

"My brother never cared for farming," she said softly. "He'd left long ago."

"So you were left to farm alone?" He wanted to ask how she'd survived on her own, but the question seemed too blunt and perhaps too cruel.

"I'm Irish." She shrugged. There was just the slightest expression of pride as she lifted her small, neatly rounded chin. "Farming is in my blood."

"But not in your brother's."

She shrugged again, thinking she'd said too much and refusing to answer.

Quiet stretched around them. A hawk soared from a distant treetop, soundlessly, on glorious wings.

"What do I call you, Little One?" His question was soft as his eyes remained fixed on her face.

His shirt was open at the neck, exposing a

disturbing amount of smooth, sun-darkened flesh, and when her gaze drifted from his face, it was inclined to fall on that spot.

"Mary." She said the name abruptly, although there had been a delay before the answer.

"Why?"

"I-I beg your pardon?" she stammered.

"Why should I call you Mary? It's not the name your brother used."

He'd talked with Michael? Megan panicked at the thought. What had Michael told him? It was impossible to tell. What was she supposed to say? What if she was caught in a lie? It seemed a foolish thing to lie to a madman—especially when alone with him.

"Mary's my middle name," she corrected quickly.

"Reminiscent of the Virgin Mary?" he asked.

She searched for signs of sarcasm, but his expression was perfectly smooth.

"After—after my mother," she said nervously.

"And your Christian name?" he asked, his gaze sharp enough to cut her to kindling.

"Megan. It's Megan," she blurted. She didn't even care if she was a fool. She couldn't lie, not when he watched her with those ungodly eyes.

"Megan." He said the name almost reverently. "A good Irish name." He stared at her in silence for a moment. "You have a wonderful face, little Megan. Full of character. Has anyone ever told you that?"

"N——no." She felt as if she was slipping into a land of fantasy, where nothing was as it seemed.

"And your hands." He reached out to smooth

one finger gently along a faint vein that ran from her knuckle to her wrist. "You've got such delicate hands." He lifted one, overturning it to study its palm and add with a smile, "For a farmer."

She watched the movement of his fingers and shivered at the touch.

"Are you cold?" He lifted his eyes abruptly from her hand to her face.

"No."

"Oh." He smiled again. "Then I'll assume you enjoy my touch," he said, still holding her hand.

There was nothing she could do but stare. She felt like a ninny-hammer, dumb and helpless, mesmerized by the beautiful masculinity before her.

"How did it happen that you reconnected with your brother if he was gone for all those years?" Justin asked gently.

She bit her lip. Was he mad? Or was he so much her intellectual superior that she couldn't so much as guess the direction of his thoughts? "He came back. After our parents died. He said I couldn't farm alone. He said I'd die trying."

She tugged her hand from his and Justin let it go, watching her face. It was full of mystery, of unspoken knowledge.

"And would you have?" he asked quietly. "Would you have died?"

Megan's breath caught in her throat. What did he care? Who was this man? "Perhaps . . ." she whispered, remembering the shame of her past years. "Perhaps it would have been better than what I've done since."

Justin was caught in her eyes, in her soul. He could feel himself slipping under her spell, bound in the undertow of her emotion.

He shook himself mentally. What was he thinking? The girl was a charlatan. She'd stolen his money, pants, and had caused the loss of his stallion, for God's sake! She was not some little orphan girl for whom he should feel pity. He straightened, trying to do the same with his thoughts. He was supposed to be manipulative, cunning. . . .

"And where was this farm?" he asked.

Megan drew a deep breath. His tone was soft. His eyes were as gentle and warm as an angel's. He could likely enough charm the hide off a horse at fifty feet.

"Up north." Her answer was cautious. She had to preserve something, at least make some attempt to save herself. But she couldn't look him in the eye. Even an evasion of the truth made her lower her face, hiding her fear behind the brim of the pink-ribboned bonnet.

She could feel his gaze on her. Her skin felt warmed by it.

"Up north," he said easily. "And how do you like our southern states?"

It seemed such an urbane question. What in heaven's name was he driving at, or was his mind so scattered he was wont to ramble on without any precise direction? "It's warm," she said, frantically searching for an answer that wasn't likely to cause her immediate death. "And the flowers," she added, lifting her face to gaze out across a flower-bedecked meadow. "I'll miss the flowers when I return home."

She realized her mistake as soon as her words were out and raised wide, frightened eyes to his. But he seemed unconcerned by her answer, only questioning it softly.

"And are you planning to return home soon, little Megan?"

"I—we . . ." Panic gripped her. What was she to say? "I don't know."

He was quiet. The raucous caw of a raven broke the silence. Her nerves stretched like overtight bow strings as he watched her.

"Well. . . ." He drew himself slowly to a sitting position, his eyes never leaving her face. "I'm hungrier than I thought, I guess." Reaching for the basket, he added, "We might as well have our lunch. If I know Kendra, she's packed a feast worthy of a king. And I figure, life's too short to delay its small pleasures, don't you think?"

Megan swallowed convulsively, hoping she wasn't expected to answer for she was entirely uncertain to what he referred.

"Ahhh—look at this. Chicken. You've never tasted chicken until you've tasted Kendra's. And peach cobbler." Justin pulled out one item after another, as excited as a child. "Mrs. Miller's not a bad cook, but she can't match Kendra. Here." He spread a loose weave napkin before Megan. "Don't be shy. Dig in."

Megan watched him. Without a doubt he was the most masculine man she had ever met. How was it now that he could appear so absolutely boyish, so utterly disarming that she could almost believe she were here for no other purpose than to share his picnic?

"Mrs. Miller?" she asked unthinkingly.

"Miller? Oh, yes. She cooks for us. Here. Have some chicken. It's delicious."

Megan stared at the golden breast of chicken on her napkin. It looked delectable. There had been three meals since her arrival at Manor Royal. She had shared in none of them. In fact her stomach had turned over at the mere thought of food. Strange now, that she should feel such sudden hunger. Lifting the breast to her mouth, she took a tentative bite of the succulent meat. It was ambrosia. She was starved.

"Good, isn't it?" he asked, his white teeth visible between his slightly curved lips.

"Um," was all she managed as she tore eagerly into the meat.

He sat with one elbow resting on a bent knee, watching her. His long, well-muscled body looked relaxed and somehow elegant, even in his casual attire. "Can I ask you something, Megan?"

She nodded, reaching for a roll.

"I understand why you might have taken my breeches. I mean, I see now that you had to escape without my following you. But why did you want Manchester to steal my stallion?"

How the breast of chicken landed in her windpipe, Megan was never sure, but she choked spasmodically, heaving and sputtering until she finally emerged from the fit looking wild-eyed and red-faced.

"Are you all right?" Justin banged her back for the third time, seeming painfully concerned for her well-being. "You have to eat more carefully, love. I didn't mean to upset you. I was just wondering—what was in it for you?"

She sat like a petrified tree. What in the name of Mary was he talking about?

"Why did you do it?" he repeated gently.

She was silent for a long while, trying to decipher his thoughts, trying to make sense of his ramblings. But there was no sense. "What?" she whispered finally.

"Why did you want him to take my horse?"

"What horse?" Her voice wasn't strong enough to ruffle a dandelion's seeds.

"The horse I bought from Horace Manchester." He sounded utterly patient and watched her as if he was merely inquiring for curiosity's sake.

"Who?" she murmured.

For a fraction of a second she thought she saw anger on his face, but it was gone too quickly to be sure.

"You're right." He looked at her suddenly as if he marveled at her. "You're right again. Never admit it. Never." He grabbed her shoulders suddenly, gripping them in the strength of his calloused hands. "What was I thinking? Never let them know what you did, Bea. They'll take you from me. They'll take you." He crushed her to him, pressing the remains of her lunch between them. "I couldn't bear it if they took you." He snarled suddenly, jerking his head to the side to glare into the nearby trees. "They'll never have you. Tell me they won't."

Her eyes were glazed. Her stomach sat just below her Adam's apple.

"Tell me they won't," he repeated, shaking her slightly.

"No," she squeaked. "They won't."

Justin nodded, seeming satisfied with her response. "I love you so much." He stared into her eyes from such close proximity that she could feel the warmth of his breath. "Tell me you love me."

She tried to do as requested. She was all for saving her hide in any manner possible, but the words wouldn't be forced past her frozen lips.

"Don't you love me?" His expression was stunned. "Don't you, Beatrice?"

She would have spoken if it were physically possible.

"It's because I killed you, isn't it?" he queried matter-of-factly, seeming to notice nothing strange in his question. "You don't have to tell me. I know you hold that against me. I can't bear it." Suddenly he was on his feet, dragging her up beside him. "I can't bear it. I'm going to drown myself. But I can't go alone. I can't be without my Beatrice. You'll drown with me. We'll go together. Unless . . ." He ceased his movement. She was draped beside his large form like a wooden doll, her face frozen in a horrified expression of shock. "Unless you tell me you love me."

She nodded dumbly, her neck barely mobile.

"You do?" He pulled her to him, flattening her small form against his. "Honestly?" His face was alight. "Say it. Say it, Bea."

"I love you," she managed.

"Ohhh!" Her bones creaked with his embrace. "Say it again."

"I love you." She could barely squeeze enough breath into her lungs to vocalize the words.

"Again. Say it again."

"I love you." She almost managed now to put some semblance of emotion into the words and felt some pride in that accomplishment, but his next words stopped her cold.

"Show me." She was pushed away from him again. "Show me how much. Dance for me." The light in his eyes could have scared a witch from her caldron. "You be the harem girl. I'll be the sheik."

Her knees were going to buckle. She could feel them giving way.

"Take off your clothes. Dance for me. No one does it like you, Bea." He was reaching for her buttons.

"I'm not Beatrice," she whimpered, as terrified of the truth as she was of his delusions.

"What?" His fingers stopped their movement. "Not Bea?" he growled, his hands now curling about her shoulders. "Then who are you?"

"M——Megan."

"Megan? Megan who?"

"M——Megan O'Rourke."

"Oh." He took a deep breath, blinking as he did so. "Megan. Of course." He looked her up and down, then lifted his hand to gently brush away the crumbs he had crushed into her gown. Pieces of chicken and roll clung to her bodice and his knuckles casually floated over her breasts, absently cleaning away the food particles. "I didn't mean to disturb your meal, Megan. Please. Sit down. Eat."

Megan's stiff neck turned woodenly. Her unblinking eyes rested on the food. Her stomach turned. Somehow she had lost her appetite.

Chapter 8

In the darkness Justin's stockinged feet had contacted something hard and solid. He cursed silently, bravely refraining from grabbing his injured toes and dancing wildly about the room.

He'd had a devil of a time getting through the window. And *he'd* used a ladder. How the little monkey girl had ever scaled the walls of Royal unaided, he had no idea.

The little sea urchin! He could barely see her in the darkness. She was asleep. How dare she sleep, knowing she dwelled in the same house as a madman? He'd thought she would crack by now. Blast it all, she was a tough little nut! But he'd break her.

Megan Mary O'Rourke. He knew her name now, which meant her full confession and a sniveling apology would soon follow. Life was good.

Justin nearly chuckled aloud, but seeing her still form sobered him. He wished he could stomp across the distance and shake her awake. But Tia slept less than thirty feet away, just on the opposite side of the wall in the sitting room.

Lucky for him the woman slept like a log and snored loud enough to drown the blundering sounds he had made coming in. He glanced nervously in her direction. If she found him here, it would matter little that he was Tom Stearns' eldest son. She outweighed him by a good fifty pounds and was likely to tear him limb from limb and ask questions later. When Tia was told to guard a door, she guarded it, and woe to the fool to cross the line.

But little Megan needed to be taught a lesson. Blast it all! Who would have thought she would hold out so long? He had to convince her to tell the sheriff the truth and thus force Manchester to return Sure Gold, for the sooner the situation was cleared up, the sooner he could be rid of her.

He couldn't tolerate their present living arrangements much longer. When she was about he had a tendency to do and say things entirely out of character—spouting threats about enslaving her, then changing his tune with dizzying speed and taking her on a picnic.

And that picnic! Justin nearly moaned aloud. It hadn't gone exactly as planned. He had intended to wrestle the truth from her, to frighten her into a confession, but instead he'd found himself intrigued by her beauty and horrified by her past. What the hell was wrong with him? Had he lost all sense of pride? The woman had stolen his pants!

Using that memory as a sort of battle cry, Justin ground his teeth and trod silently across the floor to her bedside. Her face was just visible in the darkness.

His throat constricted. Venus. She looked like Venus—like some unearthly goddess, surrounded by flaming hair, her face all feather-soft innocence.

Justin gave himself a mental shake. What was he thinking? She was no innocent. She was a lying little swindler who thought she could get away with her crimes. But she was wrong. This time she was wrong and he was just the man to make her pay.

Dropping to his knees, he placed one hand over her mouth and leaned toward her ear.

"Beatrice." He whispered the word softly, forgetting that when Megan slept, she slept like the dead. "Beatrice," he repeated, shaking her.

She moaned in her sleep, brushing delicate fingers toward her face to rid herself of the weight of his hand.

"Beatrice," he hissed more loudly, shaking her with increased force. "It's Attila."

Her eyes opened, glistening in the pale light. She strained away from him, trying to scream, but he held her still.

"Shhh. There's a full moon." He could only hope his eyes looked half as wild as hers did. "Come out with me. We'll howl at it together."

"Mmm." She groaned through his fingers, but he shook his head at her.

"You have to be very quiet. We're surrounded by enemies. They're everywhere, but I couldn't bear being without you a minute longer. Promise to be quiet?"

She remained frozen for an instant, then nodded woodenly.

They stared at each other in the darkness. "How did you get in?" she whispered weakly.

"My charger. Shinder. He flew me up. Come." He tugged at her hand. "He waits at the window to take us down together."

"I—" She faltered. "I'm not dressed."

"Oh." Justin frowned at the sheer, pale fabric of Megan's borrowed night dress. "Hilda, my love. I'm sorry. Of course. You're not ready for battle. You're ready for love." He leaned toward her, touching her cheek with tender fingertips. "You've been waiting for your Attila." He glanced once toward the window as if wondering if his gallant steed would be safe waiting on the sill, then turned back to her with a dramatic sigh. "My army will wait, my Hilda. Tonight it shall be you and I. Move over, my love."

"I—you—no. Wait." Megan clutched the bedsheet, pulling it up just past her chin, not knowing why she whispered the words. "You can't come in here."

In the darkness Justin's body became stiff as stone. He glared ferociously at her and she cowered against the pillows. "Is there another man?" he demanded. "Tell me if there is, Hilda, and I will bring you his head as a trophy of war. Attila the Hun will tolerate none other with his woman. Is there another?" He hissed the question into her face.

"No," she whispered.

Gradually his body relaxed. He drew a deep breath and smiled. "Hilda." His voice was chiding. "I've told you, Attila doesn't like to be teased. Now move over."

She did as she was told, slowing scooting her

nearly bare bottom across the sheet while still gripping the one she held.

He followed her, placing his large body beside hers. Silently he turned to her. She looked as if she may very well drop dead from fright, Justin thought, valiantly fighting to keep his smile hidden.

"Beatrice." He sighed. "Lie down. Relax."

"But—but. . . . Tia. She's just round the corner."

"Don't worry about the enemy, my love. They cannot harm us," he assured her. "Slide down here. I have something important to tell you."

She slithered down beside him, bringing the sheet with her, eyeing him over the top of the thing. She looked utterly pathetic. Justin closed his eyes for a moment, fighting back laughter. She couldn't take much more. She'd be sorry she was ever born.

"There's a traitor in our ranks," he hissed, his face mere inches from hers.

"Wh——what?"

"A traitor," he repeated, holding one of her slim arms in his hand and shaking it gently as if to help her realize the importance of his words. "His name's Stearns, Justin Stearns."

Even in the dark Justin could see her eyes widen. It was all he could do to hold back the laughter, for her horrified expression showed her thoughts with absolute clarity. "No matter what you do, you must never admit your part in the theft of my stallion," he continued.

She was utterly silent, staring at him as if he were no more stable than a yowling ghost.

"Do you understand me, Bea? You must never

tell him the truth. Never." Justin shuddered, surprising himself with his own acting talents. "They'll take you from me. I know they will. If they ever find out the truth, they'll take you away. Stearns is that kind." Justin allowed his eyes to narrow jealously. "A do-gooder. A damn slave-lover. He thinks everyone deserves to be free. Everyone." He shook her again. "They'd send you home. I know they would. Swear you'll never tell."

She remained silent, wide-eyed, and transfixed.

"Swear you'll never tell," he hissed a bit louder.

"No. No. I'll never tell."

"You'll stay with me then? Forever?" His voice had softened to a seductive whisper. "You'll be my love slave?"

"I—I . . ."

"I won't kill you again, Bea. I promise. I didn't mean to do it. But if the sheriff found out . . ."

"Wh——where is the sheriff?" Her voice was no more than a whisper, as timid as a field mouse's squeak.

"Why?" Justin demanded, glaring suspiciously at her.

"I just . . . I just want to avoid him. I just want to be your love slave forever."

Oh God, this was fun! Justin nearly roared with laughter but kept his face sober by sheerest willpower. "You won't leave me?"

"No," she exclaimed, almost able to put some expression into the denial. "N——no."

For just an instant longer he stared at her and

then he jerked her against his chest. "Thank you. Thank you. I'll make you glad you said that. I'll make you the happiest woman in the world. Tonight I am Attila and you are my Gothic maiden, Hilda. I'll love you tonight, Hilda. The best ever." Beneath the covers, she felt as stiff as a rod. His hand slipped over her waist. It was small and tight, with only the sheer fabric of her night rail to stand guard between them. She drew away from him slightly, but he pulled her nearer, with his hand spread across her arched spine. She trembled at his touch. She acted the innocent, he thought, but he knew better. She'd wish she had never heard the Stearns name.

Slipping his hand lower, he felt the firm, soft curve of her buttocks. They were tight and round, lusciously feminine. Her breathing escalated. She'd pay.

He pulled her nearer yet, but her hand lifted now, pressing with trembling strength at his chest, touching the place where the large muscles came together. His pectorals jumped at her touch. She'd pay.

He was breathing harder. She felt as smooth as honey beneath his hands, as soft and lovely as velvet.

"My love," he whispered. Taking her restraining hand from his chest, he kissed one delicate fingertip. Her mouth opened and she seemed to pant, showing the coral pink of her tongue.

God, she was perfect. He kissed another fingertip and she trembled, sending the shiver from her warm form into his own. Taking her middle finger, he ran it ever so gently over his bottom lip, then eased the tip between his teeth, nibbling it as his tongue played against the pad.

Her gasp was a glorious sound. Her body was arched toward him and although her leg bent upwards in a half-hearted effort to ward him off, the fine, delicate limb slipped with quivering ease between his own. He had her exactly where he wanted her. She'd pay. . . . God she was beautiful! He pulled her closer and her tight thigh glided between his. The gasp he heard was his own. Her breasts pressed against the heated strength of his chest and his head jerked back slightly, his nostrils flaring at the feel of her sensuality. She'd pay. . . . She'd be his. She would. She'd be his if it took him a lifetime to win her.

A gurgling snort came from the sitting room, jerking Justin back to reality. Blast and tarnation! What was he doing? Megan lay soft and breathless in his arms, Venus come to man.

"I—" he gasped. "I forgot my sword."

"What?" Her question was little more than a sighed whisper.

"I forgot my sword." He pushed her from him as if she bore a deadly plague. "Attila can't love without his sword." He scrambled from the bed, getting tangled in the sheets as he went and making a din that seemed to echo in his own numbed brain. "I must find my sword." He stood staring down at her, thinking he truly and honestly must be out of his God-forsaken mind.

She'd pay, he reminded himself. She'd pay. "When I find it, Hilda, I'll be back, and then we can love the way you like it."

Ripping his gaze from her soft, voluptuous

curves, he stumbled across the room toward the window. The journey down was bound to be even more difficult than the climb up had been. But anything, including Satan's own wrath, was better than trying to make her pay.

Chapter 9

The sight of Justin hit Megan like a bolt of lightning. They faced each other across the fine linen of the breakfast table, each immobilized by the presence of the other. She could feel her heart pumping flaming fluid through her entire system. She trembled from her core, her limbs turned to jelly and tingling to the tips of her fingers.

He was rising from his chair, staring at her with eyes as deep and unfathomable as the ocean. Air came slowly to her lungs. She was caught in the surge of his tidal wave eyes, moving in the current with no hope of survival.

"Justin." Agatha's voice broke the trance, her tone soft but somewhat amused. "Don't just stand there, dear, offer Mary a chair."

Megan blinked twice, then turned her head slowly to note the others who were present. Both Justin's parents were there, watching her.

"Megan," Justin corrected gently. "Her name's Megan. Megan Mary."

"Well then," said Agatha, "offer Megan Mary a chair."

"I have to go." His eyes never left Megan's.

"Would you walk with me a while, Megan? Just to the barn?"

She didn't answer, but when he rounded the table to take her arm, she found she had no strength to resist.

The sky was as blue as a robin's egg, lightly dusted with popcorn clouds.

"You look very lovely today, Megan," Justin said.

She could feel his gaze on her but kept her face averted. She had no idea what to say. She had no idea what to do. Her life had gone insane. Why did her heart beat like a locomotive when she saw him? It must be fear. She had every right to fear him. Any sane person would. And yet, would any sane person wake night after night, remembering his kisses, feeling the warmth of his hands long after he had left? Perhaps it was *she* who was mad.

She lifted her face abruptly. Perhaps it was she, she thought, for he looked to be as sane and intelligent as a scholar. Their eyes caught.

"I have to ride to town for a short time this morning," Justin said. "But I wanted a moment to see you alone." He paused and they continued to walk, silent for a time. "You don't mind, do you?"

For a moment she wondered if there was uncertainty in his tone. She searched his face for it but lost herself in his eyes again, long before she could determine his mood.

The barn was just ahead, surrounded by endless paddocks and pastures that held the fine stock of Manor Royal. She could smell the

sweet, familiar scents of horses and grass, reminding her of her father.

"You probably don't want to go in." Justin
nodded toward the barn. "You'll soil your
frock."

"It's not mine." She looked up at him,
blinking a little against the sunlight. "Your
mother loaned it to me," she said, remembering
Missy's hurried alterations to the bodice. "I'd
like to go in. It smells wonderful."

"Wonderful?" Justin lifted his brows in honest
surprise and Megan dropped her eyes again.
She supposed she should be embarrassed for
her admittance, for surely the stench of a barnyard should not be attractive to her—yet it was.

"It reminds me," she said softly, "of home."

Justin studied her, knowing better than to
look at her, knowing the danger of losing himself in her soul—if she had one. "Your family
had horses?" he asked.

"Just two," she said. "And a mule."

She smiled a little and Justin felt the expression blaze a strange, burning pain across his
heart. Apparently her memories of horses were
not painful ones. In fact, he could only assume
that was her reason for smiling. It made him ir-
rationally want to march his father's whole
damn herd of brood stock out just to see that expression again.

"I think we have an Irish horsewoman
amongst us," Justin said, fighting to keep his
tone even, to keep from pulling her into his
arms.

Mother Mary, Megan thought breathlessly.
His eyes were the devil's own creation, too

tempting to turn away from. "I," she began, having no idea what she intended to say, but just then the barn's half-door was pushed open.

Justin's eyes lifted from hers, slowly, almost regretfully. "Nat," he said, addressing the black man who approached them. "I'd like you to meet Megan." His gaze dropped again to Megan's face. "Nat trains the horses here at Royal. He can do in two hours what it takes most men two months to do."

It wasn't the first time he spoke of Nat as if he were a friend, Megan noted. There was no condescension in his tone, yet no jealousy either. She turned her eyes to the slave so highly spoken of. He was several inches shorter than Justin, but broad, with a somber, intelligent face and enough muscle to pull the barn away with one arm restrained.

He nodded before turning his attention back to Justin. "Old Magic give yer papa another girl colt last night. I be just goin' up to tell him."

"Another filly." Justin laughed. "After all the years he's been waiting for a stud colt from her."

"Yup." There was the hint of some unreadable emotion on the black man's striking features. "Almost proves somethin', don't it?"

"No man can have everything," Justin finished for him.

"It's God's truth, ain't it," Nat proclaimed quietly, then grinned a little, with just a hint of mischief. "I'll go tell yer papa the good news."

They watched him go before Justin turned, bringing Megan with him. "Ever seen a newborn foal?"

"A few," she admitted softly.

"Come in. Old Magic's a sure bet for a great filly every year."

The interior of the barn was cool and quiet, wreathed with the wonderful comfort of equine company. Large, airy stalls lined both sides of the aisle they walked along. Magic occupied the fourth stall down. She stood loose-hipped and content, her head drooping over the small new-born that dozed by her feet.

"Ohh." Megan sighed, her gaze falling on the peaceful pair. "How beautiful."

The filly lay flat out, its protruding ribs rising and falling with each breath, its tiny muzzle whiskered and comical. Yet, it was a picture of purest beauty to Megan.

Justin watched her. She had a deep appreciation for the simple things in life. It was a rare quality in a woman—at least in his experience. But maybe he'd known the wrong kind of women.

"Megan," he addressed her finally, "I'm riding into town with Sonny this morning." His voice was hushed and utterly sober. "Come with us."

Her face lifted to his.

"I've told no one of your part in the theft of my stallion and that's how it'll stay if you'll talk to the sheriff. Tell him about your arrangement with Manchester," Justin urged, knowing he was acting strangely again. He was supposed to be seeking revenge for her crimes when instead he was offering her a way out. But she was so lovely, with eyes like a fawn's, and surely the games he was playing with her would only cause her to hate him in the long run. Better to let her go, before he became too deeply involved. "That's all I ask, Megan. Just clear my name." If she would do that, he could believe she cared a little, had some little bit of remorse for her crimes against him. "I won't press charges. You have my word. You can go free, today—ride off straight from Charleston."

She stared at him. Her heart felt like a lead weight, sinking slowly to the pit of her stomach. She opened her mouth to speak, but he raised his hand suddenly as if he couldn't bear to hear her words.

"I know you don't trust me, Megan. If you'd feel safer, I'll stay here. You could go alone with Sonny. He'd see you safely to the sheriff's office."

The silence in the barn stretched out around them like a chasm. His eyes were as clear and guileless as a child's. Velvet, pleading eyes.

"I don't know anyone named Manchester," she whispered finally.

A muscle jerked in his jaw and it was almost a relief when the madness reappeared in his eyes.

"Good girl, Bea," he whispered. "Don't ever tell. Never tell."

"Justin," his brother called, striding toward them. "You coming today or not?"

"Don't ever tell," Justin whispered again, not taking his eyes from her face. "Come, my love, I'll guide you through enemy territory to our camp." He reached for her arm, but she cowered away from him, pressing herself against the rough lumber of the stall. "Come, love," he repeated, sounding injured by her fear of him. "Tia will keep you safe until I return."

There was nothing she could do but go with him. And honestly, Manor Royal seemed to offer some safety, especially with him gone. Sonny watched silently as they passed him, his expression troubled.

Once again in the cool shade of the veranda, Justin turned her in his arms. "I'll be back before supper," he assured her quietly, as if he offered that news as some sort of comfort. "And tonight you'll need to wait no longer." He leaned forward to whisper his words. "I go to find my sword. Tonight you'll feel the pleasure you've longed for."

Megan paced the length of her borrowed room. He was getting his sword! He was getting his sword! Oh Lord, she was dead for certain. Or was she? Who could tell? Perhaps there was no sword. Perhaps there had never been a Beatrice. Then again, perhaps there had and perhaps he had indeed killed her with the very sword he now promised to retrieve. Oh Lord.

She had taken to chewing her fingertips some hours earlier, but now found she was past that point and had progressed to chewing the backs of her hands at regular intervals.

Somehow she had to escape tonight. Justin couldn't have had exterior latches placed on all the windows, nor could he watch every opening. Could he? She bit her hand again. He was an eerie man—and big. She remembered the way his chest felt beneath her hand. The muscles had jumped to life at her touch, almost as if awakened by her fingertips, almost as if his large form was as aware of her as she was of him.

She had to get a grip on herself. He was a madman. Insane. He was absolutely insane. He thought he was Attila the Hun, for heaven's sake. Oh Lord! She collapsed to the bed, covering her face with her hands. She had to escape or the remainder of her life was likely to be short and frightfully painful.

Supper sat before her, each dish temptingly prepared and served, but Megan had no appetite and stared at the food with sightless eyes. He hadn't returned yet. Where was he? Perhaps she could escape before he came. But she'd have to wait for Tia to fall asleep.

"Hello." Sonny entered first. "Sorry we're so late."

"What delayed you?" Thomas asked, raising his gaze from his meal for a moment.

"The usual." He grinned roguishly. "Women, wine, song."

"Sonny!" Agatha reprimanded as Thomas scowled over his chuckle.

"Sorry," Sonny apologized, seating himself swiftly. "Just fooling. I got talking to young Tolbert." He reached for the roast duck.

Megan's blood froze.

"Robert?" Thomas shook his head. "The boy spends more time in Charleston than he does on the plantation. All the boy ever does is gamble and carouse—been the same ever since he was a little spit of a thing. If he was my son—"

"If he was your son he'd be a sight more nor-

mal than the one you got." Sonny shifted his
eyes from Thomas to Megan and stopped chewing for a moment. "Your other son, I mean. You
know what he was doing today?"

"Sonny," Agatha admonished, "don't talk
with your mouth full."

"Yes, ma'am." He swallowed. "He was looking for a sword. And not just any sword. A Ro-
man sword." Sonny raised his brows as if
suggesting that they lock the man up somewhere safe. "Something Attila the Hun might
have used," he said, then grinned, shifting his
gaze to their pale, silent guest again. "I think
our Megan Mary's beauty has made him take
leave of his senses."

Megan lay stiff as a log beneath the covers.
Was Tia asleep yet? She couldn't hear any snor-
ing, but maybe she didn't always snore. Or
maybe she was wide awake. Maybe she was expecting Megan to try to escape and would never
go to sleep. Maybe Megan would be trapped
there, forever—until Justin killed her, of course.

It was that thought that finally brought
Megan from her bed. On trembling limbs she
tiptoed to the door. She shivered in the thin
night rail, though it wasn't cold. Perhaps she
should have dressed, but she hadn't dared
chance waking Tia. The cot was directly in front
of the only exit but stood several inches from it.

With eyes as wide as terror could make them
Megan stared at the still figure. Was she snor-
ing? Was she sleeping? It seemed an eternity before Megan heard the first evidence of slumber.
It was a slow, contented sound of deep sleep.

Air rushed back to Megan's lungs.

It wasn't an easy task to squeeze through the door without disturbing the cot, but Megan finally succeeded. The hall was dark as pitch, running away from her in both directions. She'd use the backstairs. Although they had more of a tendency to squeak, they were farther from the family's bedrooms.

Closing the door noiselessly behind her, Megan tiptoed down the hall, passing door after door and praying with all her might that the Stearns slept as deeply as Tia.

She reached the stairs after an eternity and panted quietly for breath. It seemed she had failed to inhale for the entirety of the endless hallway. There was no need to worry, she promised herself. They were all asleep. It was late. There was no noise and Justin's room lay near the head of the grand staircase. He couldn't have heard her. He couldn't have, she assured herself, and yet she crouched at the top of the stairs, peering into the darkness and imagining a large, dark form creeping from every doorway.

Her knees trembled as her bare foot touched the first step. It squealed beneath her weight and she jumped back, bumping into the banister and scaring herself nearly out of her wits. Finally, however, there was nothing to do but descend the treacherous staircase. Every uncarpeted stair seemed to whine beneath her feet until at the bottom of the steps she stood shaking like a windblown leaf.

It was just a little farther now. Megan stared in the direction of the door. Just around the corner. Only a short ways. Her breath stopped in her throat. Was there a light? Below that door? Her knees knocked together, seeming noisy beyond reason as they rebounded off each other.

A lifetime passed. She stood sweating and praying. It was a light. She was sure of it. And voices? Were there voices?

"Damn you, Justin!" She heard the words plain as day and froze against the wall. Sonny had spoken the words and he could only have spoken them to his brother. That meant . . . that meant *he* was there—not forty feet away.

Hail Mary full of grace, she prayed numbly. There was no hope. She knew there was none. Another lifetime passed. The voices from the room were more subdued now. She could hear nothing but a dull murmur now and then, and finally straightened from the wall. Perhaps there was no hope, but she could hardly stay where she was. How would she explain herself if they found her plastered to the wall in the morning, too weak to do more than collapse into a heap of sniveling stupidity? She had to try. She had to. It was that or death. Slowly her toes inched forward. A noise sounded from the room. She jerked back, shaking as she did so. Time passed. She tried again and this time found herself an entire two inches closer to her destination. Her eyes were focused on the corner. Perhaps she could make it. Perhaps the saints would be merciful. Perhaps she had paid her penance.

She reached the corner. The room was only a scant ten feet away now. Her fingers edged around the bend.

"You told her what?" Sonny rasped.

Megan flattened herself back against the wall, her eyes straining into the blackness.

"I made her believe I was a lunatic," came Justin's calm reply.

Megan stiffled a gasp of outrage and stayed to listen.

Chapter 10

"**W**hy in heaven's name would you tell her you were mad?" Sonny questioned, eyeing Justin's ancient sword.

Sonny was seated near the door of the library, looking perturbed and unmistakably southern, and was, Justin realized, fully prepared to fight for the lady's honor. If only the lady had some honor.

"It's a long story. Suffice it to say, I know what I'm doing."

"Oh. Certainly. Well, excuse the hell out of me. Naturally, it seems perfectly logical to you to scare the wits out of the poor gal. As if she hasn't been through enough—what with her bastard of a brother!"

"And you're so certain she had no say in the swindles?" Justin asked. It was the first time he had suggested she was less than perfectly innocent, Justin knew. But his brother's intense protectiveness for the girl made him want to rattle the boy's brains. Did no one in his family consider Megan might be guilty as sin? How had she so thoroughly fooled them? Or was their perception clearer than his?

"You jest!" Sonny scoffed. "What's wrong with you, Justin? The girl's as innocent as a babe. Anyone with half a mind can see that."

"I mean, she can't even talk, for God's sake. The horrors of her life have rendered her speechless. And here you sit, like the good Lord himself, pronouncing judgment."

"I'm not pronouncing judgment," Justin argued, wondering if Sonny's tone suggested he had more than a platonic interest in their little Megan. The thought made him clench his jaw and consider hitting something. "I'm only saying the girl's hardier than she appears."

"I can't believe I'm hearing this from my own brother." Sonny railed, raising his hands in utter exasperation. "And you always so holy about turning the slaves loose. It's not right to hold our fellow human beings in bondage, you preached. They've got their rights, just like us. Damn!" Sonny jerked himself to his feet, stomping about the room and glaring at Justin at regular intervals. "And here you are, holding a lady against her will, lying to her." He stopped to shake his finger in outraged chivalry. "Lying to her, Justin, and maybe, maybe bedding her, too. Maybe she *is* carrying your child. You've been acting mighty strange of late. Maybe you did dishonor her and now you're telling her you're mad so she'll leave and deny the child is yours."

This was too much, Justin thought. The scheming little wench had set his own brother against him. And he could hardly blame Sonny, for probably Justin himself would feel the same in a similar situation. Perhaps he should have told his family the entire tale, but in truth he wasn't ready to slander her name. Not yet at any rate.

"I explained all this before," he said coolly.

"Oh yes. Certainly. You told her you were mad, so she'd be frightened into telling the sheriff about her brother's association with Manchester. But maybe she doesn't know a thing about Manchester. Have you ever considered that? Damn it, Justin, this rivalry between you and Horace has gone far enough. It has involved innocent people now. People like—"

"Innocent!" Justin guffawed, knowing he should keep his mouth shut. "The girl's as innocent as—"

"As what? As you? Justin the saint! Justin the high and mighty! Marching about with his sword of righteousness. God damn it, man! What *is* that sword for?" he spouted in heated frustration.

"I told you. I need it." Justin hefted the rusty blade, still embedded in its crusty scabbard. "It's part of the plan."

"Part of the plan," Sonny mocked. "I swear, Justin, if you wasn't my own kin I'd . . ."

Justin was never sure whether Sonny finished his threat for in the doorway stood Megan. She was dressed in a flimsy white night rail. Her hair was uncovered and untamed, flowing out from her face in a wild tangle of flaming gold and scarlet. But it was her face that held his attention. Never in his entire life had he seen such unbridled rage.

"You lied to me!" She exclaimed the words from between gritted teeth, advancing as she did so, not even acknowledging Sonny's stunned presence as she stalked Justin. "You low-bellied son of a snake. You made me believe you were insane."

He watched her approach. If she weren't such a tiny thing, she'd be truly terrifying. But she was so small, what could she do?

"You rotten spawn of Satan! You made me tell you I loved you. Not once, but three times," she said, nodding wildly as the memory of her humiliation returned. "You made me fear for my life. And," she added, her gaze falling to the forgotten sword he held in one hand. "This sword. This sword." She reached forward to take the thing, tugging it from his grasp. "I thought . . ." She laughed, the sound eerie in the wavering light. "I thought you believed you were Attila the Hun. Imagine that. Little wonder I thought you were mad. You told me you were Attila the Hun and that this . . ." She lifted the scabbard and blade. "That this was your sword. I bet you had yourself a chuckle over that one."

"Well . . ." Justin stared at her, noting every perfect feature, highlighted in glorious rage. "It did seem rather amusing at the time."

"Oh it did, did it?" she squeaked and with her words swung the blade, aiming without fail at his arrogant head.

Why he hadn't expected the blow, Justin would never know, but he could only thank the Lord the weapon had remained sheathed, for it hit him a sound blow to the side of his temple.

She drew back, eyeing the scabbard and wondering how best to remove it for more deadly results, but Justin was not inclined to wait around for his head to be displaced.

"Give me the sword, woman," he said, rising to his feet and trying to still the echo that clanked in his aching skull.

"Why? Because Attila can't love without it? Because Attila must keep his Hilda safe from the enemy. You lying, arrogant, pile of dung!" she screeched, swinging the blade again, but Justin ducked with timely accuracy.

The scabbard, jarred from its position, was flung free and flew across the room to slam into a nearby bookcase.

"Give me the sword, Megan," Justin commanded, eyeing the thing cautiously as he straightened.

"You want the sword?" she questioned, smiling as she did so and holding the weapon in a death grip, the bare feet set wide apart. "Then come and get it."

"I'll do that," Justin said. There was a threat in his tone, but Megan was long past caring. "Put it down, Megan, before someone gets hurt."

"You lied to me."

"*I* lied?" Justin scoffed as if amazed she could even think of such an accusation. "*I* lied? And what about you? You stole my damn stallion." He advanced on her, enraged by the memory of her trickery. "I paid Manchester a fair price. How'd he talk you into siding with him? Were you lovers? Is that it?"

Megan backed away from him, watching him with narrowed, furious eyes. "I don't know anything about Manchester or his stinking stallion!" she spat.

"Don't you lie to me, you little hypocritical vixen. You took the bill of sale," he stormed, not mentioning she'd also taken his breath away, had touched his very soul with her beauty, then left him half-naked in a rented room. "You stole my bill of sale," he repeated. "Manchester took the stallion and you're going to pay. One way or another." He continued stalking her. "You're going to pay."

She was nearly backed into a corner. He saw her shift her gaze, searching for a means of escape. Her tongue darted out, licking her lips—a strangely sensual gesture. For a moment he was tempted to be rid of the damn sword and drag her to the nearest bed. But life with Megan was not so simple. While he saw the sword as a blasted nuisance, she thought of it as her only defense and waved the thing between them like a matador's cape.

"Put the sword down, Megan."

"No."

"Damn it, woman. You've been amusing in the past, but I've had enough of your tiresome antics. Put the blasted blade down."

"No," she repeated, bent over the sword like a tiny soldier.

"Then I'll have to take it from you."

Sonny stared open-mouthed, turning his head from one to the other and watching the whole affair with unblinking amazement.

"Go ahead and try, you yellow varmit."

Justin lunged for her. She swung with all her might, but he was ready. Ducking beneath the blow, he came up under her arms and caught her about the waist. She gasped at the crush of his arms, beating at his back with the hilt of the ancient weapon, but he only squeezed her harder.

"Drop the sword, Megan," he said, his face pressed against her chest as he tightened his arms by careful increments and effortlessly lifted her from the floor. "Drop the sword."

"No," she gasped, barely able to breathe.

She had bottom, Justin thought. He had to admit she had more senseless determination than any woman he had ever met.

"Drop the sword."

"No."

Her refusal was no more than a whisper. Her eyes rolled back in her head.

Blast! Justin let go abruptly, spilling her to the floor and grabbing for the blade. She made a pathetic attempt to hold on, but the sword came away in his hands.

She sat on the floor, glaring up at him with eyes mad enough to skin a cougar.

"Admit you stole my stallion," he said to her, holding the blade limply in one fist.

"You're mad," she decreed, her defiance returning with her breath.

"Really?" Justin queried nonchalantly. "And here I thought you were angry because I wasn't mad. Now admit it," he growled, glaring at her over the hilt of the blade. "Admit to your game with Manchester and I'll set you free."

"I don't know any Manchester," she croaked, her voice rising despite her windless state.

He waved the sword at her. Damned if it

wouldn't be a pleasure to cut her throat and be done with it. But. . . .

"Get up here." He tossed the sword aside and reaching down, pulled her to her feet by one wrist. "Why are you so determined to stay with me?"

She glared at him from a distance of two inches, her eyes no less angry than his. "Stay with you?" She laughed. "I wouldn't even spit on you if you paid in gold bullion."

"Is that so?"

"Yeah."

"Well, we'll see about that." With one effortless movement he swung her over his broad shoulder.

The air was once again propelled from her lungs and she gasped in outrage, wiggling wildly to get free.

"Keep still."

"You snake in the grass. You liver-bellied horny toad. You . . ."

"Oh, spare us the names," he commanded, swinging about and nearly knocking his brother flat with Megan's bare feet. "Blast it all, Sonny," he stormed. "If you can't help, at least get out of the way. Can't you see the 'poor gal's' got a paddling coming?"

Sonny shrugged, grinning lopsidedly.

Footsteps sounded on the stairs, hurried and noisy. Justin eyed his brother, saying nothing, and sure enough, Sonny came through. "Never fear, I'll tell them we were wrestling."

Justin nodded his thanks, then wasting no time, hurried his baggage up the front stairs to Megan's borrowed room. He could hear his parents' worried tones and stifled a laugh. One thing was sure. Life at Manor Royal had never been livelier.

"What'd you do to Tia?" Justin asked, pushing the door, cot, slave, and all inward. "Did you kill her?"

"I've never killed anyone," Megan protested, her tolerance for Justin's shoulder coming to an end.

"Really?" he said, sounding shocked. "How good of you. Perhaps we'll engrave that on your tombstone. Here lies Megan Mary O'Rourke. She never killed anyone."

"Put me down," she ordered, trying to pummel him with her knees.

"Gladly," he said, dropping her to the bed.

She hit the tick but remained for only a moment before she was on her feet, glaring at him with spitting eyes.

Bare feet pattered in, bringing a hastily lit candle. Missy stood wide-eyed and breathless. "What'd y' do t' her, Mass . . . Justin?" she asked, staring at Megan as if she were a rare jungle creature.

"What are you doing here?" Justin said, not taking his eyes from Megan.

"I been sleepin' next door," Missy stated simply. "T' see t' Miss Mary." She paused for a moment before restating her question. "What'd y' do t' her?"

"I didn't do anything," he denied shortly.

"She looks fit t' kill," Missy stated, lifting the candle slightly. "Y' must a done somethin'."

"You know what?" Justin gritted, finally facing the impudent little servant. "You talk too much. You've always talked too much."

"Is that so?" Missy asked, raising her round, fresh face to his. "And you always been too big fer yer britches, Justin Stearns."

"Huh," Justin snorted. "You women . . ."

"That's right," Missy interrupted quickly. "We sure is women. And if'n yer so eager t' have that one, I'd think you'd—"

"Eager to—" spat Justin. "What're you rambling on about now?"

"Don't try t' fool me. I can see right through y'. Always could. And you been struttin' like a barnyard cock ever since she showed up. You might as well admit you got an itch fer her."

Justin ground his teeth. Missy was bright and hardworking and loyal to the bone, but she could be a pain in the rear when she wanted and this was one of those times. "I'll tell you what I'm itching for," he snarled. "I'm itching to paddle her backside and nothing else."

Megan backed away a step, her bravado fleeing. Tia stirred, mumbling something in her sleep.

"That's right," Justin said, "back away, little Megan, because from now on things change. Until you can tell the truth, you'll be my slave."

Without thought Megan lifted a hand to her throat.

"That's right, my little charlatan. Think things through."

Turning abruptly toward Missy, Justin added, "If you know so much, you little gamecock, *you* watch her tonight. And if she gets away, I'll know who to blame." He stomped from the room, leaving the two women to stare at each other in wordless surprise.

"So, Mr. Tolbert, what can I do for you?" Justin leaned back in his father's leather chair, watching his visitor through narrowed eyes. It had been a long morning, and his patience was near an end. Blast and incinerate Megan O'Rourke and her endless stubborn streak.

"Well," began Tolbert, taking a seat not so far from Justin's. "It's not what you can do for me, but perhaps what I can do for you."

He gave a smug smile, and Justin stared at him, wondering if he were going to explain or if he'd need to be urged. He didn't feel like urging the man. In fact there was only one thing he did feel like doing. But since his family would not condone his strangling Megan, he sat silently watching his guest until he continued.

"I got a chance to talk with Sonny yesterday in Charleston."

Justin nodded, saying nothing.

"I heard you've had a bit of—excitement."

Silence fell again. Justin didn't like Robert Tolbert—ever since they were boys and Tolbert had hosted midnight games of chance at the old Burdock house. Justin scowled, remembering the thrashing he'd received when Thomas had caught him sneaking from the house to join the other boys.

"Can you get to the point, Mr. Tolbert? I've got things that need doing."

"Yes." Tolbert laughed. "I would suppose she keeps you busy most all the time."

Justin clenched his jaw and scowled, leaning forward to lean on the heavy desk. "And who would you be referring to, Tolbert?"

"The girl, of course." Tolbert raised his hands, palms up. "Mary, wasn't it?"

"Yes." Justin watched the other, wondering at his game. "Megan Mary."

Tolbert's grin was smug. "You know that's strange cuz you see Sonny told me all about what happened. Told me about the girl and her brother and I'm willing to bet it's the same pair I met. Only her name wasn't Mary or Megan."

Damn Sonny and his big mouth.

"Your brother seemed quite taken by the girl and was convinced she's innocent of any wrongdoing." Tolbert laughed. "But I can tell you one thing for sure." He leaned back in his chair. "She's a far cry from innocence."

Justin entwined his fingers and tilted his head, keeping his expression bland. "And how did you decide that?"

"Well, you're not the first man she's sidled up to. It's obvious she's looking for a rich gentleman and what better way than to awaken our sympathy for her?" He leaned forward suddenly, his eyes alight. "She comes around, looking abused and mistreated, and what does any decent man want to do? He wants to protect her. Only she don't really want protection." He smiled again, slowing his speech. "She wants the good life. Maybe a little house of her own and a man to ... please her now and again."

Justin's fingers tightened against each other. Perhaps it was all true. So why did he want to throttle the man? "Why are you telling me this, Mr. Tolbert?" he asked evenly, his eyes narrowed.

"Because she tried the same on me. Tried to stir up my sympathy and offered me—well, let's just say she offered . . . a good deal."

"Are you saying you bedded the girl?" Justin asked in a deadly even tone.

"Well now . . ." Robert entwined his fingers. "I don't think a gentleman is at liberty to say. But let me say this. She's a hard morsel to resist."

"Yes." Justin erupted from his chair a bit faster than he'd planned, trying to slow his movements and calm his breathing. She was hard to resist, just as hard as it was to resist walloping the tar out of Tolbert's smug little form. "She is indeed hard to resist. But why are you telling me this?" he asked, rounding the corner of the desk to lean a hip against the level edge.

"Because it's my duty," Tolbert said quickly, then sighed and dropped his hands. "The truth is . . . I was real taken by her. Thought about marrying her even—until I found out she was a—a wanton." He clenched his fists, congratulating himself on his own acting ability. "I was terribly distraught at first of course. But now . . ." He dropped his hands and shrugged. "Now I see things as they are—and I'm willing to take her off your hands."

Justin stared in absolute amazement. Whatever he'd expected from Tolbert, it hadn't been this. "Take her off my hands?" he asked slowly.

Tolbert shrugged again, grinning a little. "You

set the stakes, Justin," he said. "I'll buy her from you—for twice the price you paid."

"Buy her?" Justin asked softly, gritting his teeth and keeping his temper in check.

"Well, after all," Robert said quickly, "her own brother sold her. I'll vouch her mother was a quadroon doxy if you will. Who's to be the wiser? And it's not as if she doesn't deserve it. She's just a little—"

Suddenly Justin was gripping Tolbert's shirt front in his calloused hands. "Just a what?" he snarled into the smaller man's face.

Tolbert wriggled in his grasp, fighting for breath. "Let me go," he squawked.

"Just a what?" Justin repeated, giving the other a sound shaking.

"Hey! You know what I mean," Robert said, his hands clawing at Justin's.

"I'll tell you what I know ..." Justin drew a deep breath. He was acting the fool, he thought raggedly, but damned if it wouldn't feel good to slam the little weasel up against the wall. He let go his grip reluctantly and Robert smoothed his hand abruptly down his rumpled shirt front. "I know you're bad-mouthing my guest," Justin said more rationally. "And I ..." He shook his head and refrained from shaking a finger at the other. "I don't take it kindly. You understand me?"

Tolbert nodded once, his eyes bugging from his head as he tilted his face up to Justin's.

"One other thing," Justin added gently. "I don't like gossip. If I hear any more gossip about my guests, I'm likely take it personally.

I'm likely to come and find you. You take my meaning?"

"Y——yes."

"Good," Justin said with surprising calm. "That's a good boy." He reached out, helping to smooth Tolbert's shirt back in place. "Now, you'd best leave. I have things to attend to."

Justin strode down the hall with long, rapid steps. Arriving at Megan's door, he hesitated not a moment but swung the portal inward.

She stood at the window, dressed in an understated, borrowed gown that hugged her bosom while her hair framed her face in glory.

"Leave us alone, Tia," Justin commanded.

Tia straightened, her extra chins tucked tightly against her neck as she scowled her disapproval. "You feverin' again or you just not thinkin'?" she challenged. "What you doin' in Miss Megan's room? You get yourself gone afore I tell your Pa."

"I'm in no mood to argue," Justin replied. Blast it all, Megan had sneaked past the woman in the dark of night, when Tia was set to guard her, and now Tia stood like a great black pillar of wrath, defending the girl as if she were some fresh-faced debutante. "Go out in the hall and wait. I won't hurt her," he admitted regretfully.

Tia lifted her chins proudly, glancing at Megan as she did so. "I'll be in the hall if you needs me, Miss Megan. Don't you be lettin' him bully you, y' hear?"

The door closed behind her bulky form.

The room was silent as a tomb.

Justin crossed the floor slowly, then stood not two feet before Megan, eyeing her evenly. "I have just one question. Did you bed Tolbert?"

Megan scowled, unable for a moment to recognize the name. "Who?" she asked shakily.

"Tolbert," Justin repeated. "Have you pleasured so many men you're unable to keep them straight? Robert Tolbert. Did you bed him or not?"

"Tolbert?" she whispered fearfully. She knew she sounded beaten but found she had no strength to be brave. "Robert Tolbert? Oh," she said as the man's image appeared in her muddled brain. "Tolbert."

"Yes. God damn it!" Justin raged, finding himself lathered by the wait. "Robert Tolbert. Did you lie with him or not?"

"No." She shook her head, thinking she should refuse to answer.

Justin watched her eyes, trying to learn the truth in those large, emerald orbs. Silence gripped the room. They stared at each other.

"Damn it all." Justin drew away first, pulling his gaze from her wide, honest-seeming eyes. "I should throw you out on your pretty little fanny," he ranted, pacing past the canopied bed and back. "I should throw you right out." He stood before her again, glaring into her face. "But you'd like that, wouldn't you? Sure, that's what you want." He nodded cleverly, confusing Megan with his twisted reasoning. "So I'm not going to. I'm taking you home. That's what I'll do. And then we'll see who has the last laugh. We'll just see."

The door slammed behind him and Megan sunk slowly to a chair.

Chapter 11

"**M**istress Agatha says to make you especially beautiful," admitted Missy as she fussed with Megan's hair.

It had been lifted away from her face and neck and propped atop her head to fall in ringlets that cascaded to her shoulders. Megan stared at her reflection. Her borrowed gown was an ivory tone with sleek, simple lines that hugged her body with silky fingers. Her hands shook as she touched the fabric of the skirt.

"Did . . ." Megan bit her lip. Surely no thanksgiving goose had ever been more carefully prepared for slaughter than she had been. "Did she say why?" she asked in a weak voice.

Missy patted a last curl in place. "I think . . ."

The women's gazes met in the mirror.

"You think what?" Megan urged, her eyes wide, her composure gone.

"I think she likes you," Missy said quietly.

Megan let her gaze drop. "No. I fear she doesn't." She shouldn't care. She shouldn't care what they thought—but she did. "I fear they know me too well," she whispered.

Missy was silent, reading the emotions and

understanding the pain with stunning clarity. "The Stearns's is a strange lot," she said gently. "They been hard on the boys sometimes. 'Specially Justin, but they care a whole lot."

Megan was quiet, not understanding the inference.

"They been worryin' bout Justin. Thinkin' he needs him a woman." She shrugged, narrowing her eyes. "They think you might be the one."

Megan blinked. The one what? she wondered dimly. The sacrificial lamb he would burn at the altar?

"I know Massa Justin been actin' mighty ornery lately. But he ain't usually like that," Missy said, biting her lip and looking concerned about her own bold words. "He's most often real considerate. You can ask any of us black folk. He's got a real good heart. He just—well, he just forgets the fact sometimes, I suppose." She dropped her eyes to smooth a fold in Megan's ivory gown. "I don't know what's gone between the two of yahs, but I can see you got yourselves some problems. There's talk that you's his slave. But, you know, Justin—he don't take t' slavin'. So I don't understand how things be. Still . . ." She scowled, thinking aloud, "it seems t' me you ain't much more free t' choose yer life than I is t' choose mine.

"I know it ain't my place t' speak up like this and I guess Massa Justin was right when he says I talk too much. Him and Nat been tellin' me that ever since I been old enough t' foller them about."

"Nat and Justin are . . ." Megan paused,

knowing her statement was strange. "They're friends, aren't they?"

Missy lifted her gaze as if looking at something far in the distance. "Massa Justin and Nat—they're the same kinda men, under their skin." She lifted her loose fist to her chest. "Inside. They're both good—way down good, but they . . ." She paused again, shaking her head. "They sure enough can be ornery. Ornery through and—"

The door opened behind them.

"Are you ready?"

Megan jerked to her feet at the sound of his voice, her heart tripping clumsily in her chest and her breath began coming hard. He was dressed in dark britches, a white shirt, and a vest. His expression was somber. She pulled herself into a straighter line.

Justin watched her. She was beautiful! More beautiful than he'd known it was possible for a woman to be.

"Where'd you get the gown?" His voice sounded gruff to his own ears and he could only hope she couldn't guess the cause. Would not know that the sight of her made him struggle to be strong.

Megan couldn't speak. Somehow she'd entirely lost that ability.

"Your mama gave it to her," Missy said abruptly, straightening her own back and seeming to step directly into the line of fire. "She said . . ." Missy paused, reading Justin's expression with more accuracy than Megan was able and grinning a little to herself. "She said for me to make her especially beautiful."

Beautiful! She was that, Justin thought. That and more. Lord help him! What was he doing?

"Do you have her things packed?"

"Yessah."

"What for?" Megan found her tongue.

Justin scowled at her. God save him from his own stupidity. "We'll be leaving for Free Winds. Immediately."

"Free Winds?" she asked, the words strained.

"My home," he said bluntly, offering no more explanation.

"But," Megan whispered, barely able to force the words past her frozen lips, "I thought you lived here."

"You thought wrong. Missy, see that her belongings get into the carriage."

"Yassah."

His gaze shifted back to Megan, who stood as stiff and immovable as before. "Are you ready then?"

No answer was forthcoming. Justin scowled. "I'm not going to beat you, girl," he said, stepping forward to take her arm. "Come along."

It was only a matter of minutes before they were in Royal Manor's carriage, closed away on the dark, soft leather of the upholstered seats, with Nat perched up in front.

Agatha gripped her husband's arm and tried to smile. Her first born son was taking a woman into his home—a woman he had bought from her own brother, a woman whose only chaperone would be the neighboring Mrs. Miller. It was highly improper, but Justin had never followed the beaten path. He'd always pressed the limits, daring to flaunt his individuality. She wished now that her sons were mere boys again. She wished for the days when she could steer their lives. But those days were long past. They now made their own decisions and if she knew anything about the Stearns men, she knew Justin would not be dissuaded from his present course—whatever that course might be. She sent up a silent prayer.

She had hoped if she dressed Megan like a lady that perhaps Justin would see her as a person of some position and not as a possession. After all, the girl was certainly white and even if she weren't pure of blood—did it matter? It wasn't clear what Justin thought of her but it was obvious his feelings were deep. And couldn't those deep emotions grow into something more?

She didn't know. There were so many unanswered questions. Agatha had once hoped Justin would take a southern wife and live as his parents did. She knew better now. Justin was a different breed than his father. The same—yet different.

"Come back and visit us soon," she said, struggling to keep her tone light. "Both of you." She waved and the conveyance rolled away, allowing her to reach for Tom's arm with her other hand. His arm bent to hug her.

"There now, Aggie," he said softly. "It'll all come right." He lifted his face and shook his head at the retreating carriage. Blast Justin for being so stubborn. So like his old man.

Inside the conveyance, Justin stared out the

open window. Blast and damnation, he fumed. How in heaven's name had his little scheme gotten so out of hand? And why had he decided to take the bewitching little troublemaker to his home? What was he hoping to accomplish there? Confession produced by terror?

He glanced toward her. It might work, he thought dryly, for she looked frightened enough to faint dead away. But, he sighed mentally, it was probably a trick. Instead of being cowed, the girl was most likely planning a way to steal the carriage right out from under his—

"Is it far to Free Winds?"

Megan's question sounded weak enough to have been issued from a half-starved street urchin but Justin was not about to be fooled by her beaten attitude.

"Not far," he said, refusing to soften his attitude toward her and turning back to the window.

The silence was as deep as a well.

"What ..." She paused, biting her lip as he faced her again. "What am I to do there?"

Justin gritted his teeth and leaned back against the upholstery. She looked as if she might burst into tears. She looked like some damned downed angel, awaiting the horrid visitations of man.

"What *can* you do?" he asked, leaning against the wall of the vehicle.

Megan's mind scrambled. What indeed? "I'm a fair hand with a horse," she said suddenly.

Justin all but laughed. How was it she continued to surprise him?

"With horses?" he asked, leaning toward her slightly.

She nodded in return, looking so blasted sincere Justin could not stop his words.

His hands slipped out of their own accord, clasping one of hers between his own. "I believe I can think of something more appropriate than that."

Sparks snapped from her hand and sprinted up her arm. Her mouth fell open. She had not a shadow of a doubt what he meant.

"I . . ." She jerked her hand from his with an effort. "I'm quite strong."

His brows rose sharply. "That's—very comforting." He grinned a little. "I like endurance in my women. It makes the nights so much more—entertaining."

Megan pressed her back against the seat, feeling the blood seep from her face. "I can dig a straight furrow," she spouted. "My pa said so."

"Well, love," he crooned, warming to the game. "If I ever want to do my plowing in a furrow, I'll let you know."

She clasped her hands suddenly in front of her chest as if those small fists might ward him off.

"I'll work," she whispered. "But I won't—lie with you."

Anger infused Justin's system. "So you'd offer yourself to Tolbert," he spat, suddenly gripping her arms in rough hands, "but you'd rather plow the fields than lie with me?"

She shrank against the cushion.

"Well?" He shook her slightly. "Is that so?"

"No," she whispered fearfully.

"No what?" he ground out, but the carriage was slowing now, signaling their arrival.

His hands dropped away.

"Are we here?"

"I fear so," Justin answered, his mood as dark as night.

Pushing open the door, he stepped down, then turned to her.

Megan didn't move. Terror held her to her seat.

"Come here," he ordered in exasperation. "Nat'll think I beat you daily."

Megan shuffled forward and he caught her by her waist, lifting her down.

Sparks fled upward from his fingertips. Her breath caught in her throat. Time ground to a halt.

"Well . . ." Justin let her feet slip to the ground. Her waist was tight and small beneath his hands. "This is it." He hadn't meant to say anything, but the shock of touching her seemed to need some distraction. "Such as it is."

Megan stood stiffly, forcing her gaze from his face. It was not quite dark, allowing her to see the dim exterior of a field stone house, accented by several large, white shuttered windows. There was a fence surrounding the place, constructed of the same aged stone as the venerable home.

A pond was just to the south, and off to her right, Megan could discern the dark shapes of large animals behind the irregular, triple rails of fencing.

Justin watched her for a moment, scowling at her expression. She seemed to have forgotten him for a moment, lost somewhere in her own thoughts. He paced up to Nat, speaking to him quietly, but Megan failed to notice.

There was no mansion here! The evening air was cool against her face. She took a step toward the house, drawn there somehow.

Behind her, Justin's words ceased as his eyes lifted to watch her. She was slim and lovely and looked like an angel afloat in the night.

"I'd best see to the girl," Justin said. Drawing his thoughts together, he took the single clothing bag from Nat and strode away.

Behind the pair of horses Nat smiled. If Missy was right about Miss Megan, Justin had finally met his match, he thought. It would be nice to stay with them—to watch them work out their troubles, to help them make Free Winds prosper, but Nat belonged to Manor Royal and had no say in where or how he lived his life. Lifting the lines, Nat silenced his discontent and headed back to Royal.

The path that led to the house was paved with well-worn rocks. There were two steps leading to the front door and Justin ascended those steps, pushing the door inward and reaching for a lantern hung just to the right of the hefty portal.

"Come in," he said and she followed, stepping in with hands folded in quiet uncertainty.

It was dark inside but it took only a moment for Justin to set a match to the wick. Light spread outward, touching each homespun item with golden firelight.

Megan absorbed the view, watching as the glow set the place to life.

"Don't be afraid, Megan." Justin said the words against his will, for wasn't his purpose to frighten her? "I'll not harm you. Feel free to look about."

Megan said nothing, not knowing whether to believe him, but drawn for a moment into the quiet beauty of the house. There was an ageless, unshakable strength here. Against her will she felt herself relax and seeing the stone wall of the large fireplace through an open doorway, she walked the few steps to peer into the kitchen.

The life of the place seemed to be there, in the innumerable copper and castiron pans that hung above the hearth.

Megan smiled unconsciously but suddenly the quiet of the place struck her. "No—slaves?" she asked softly.

For a moment he was tempted to say she was his first and only, but she looked so utterly fragile just then, so lovely and soft. "No," he answered simply. "None."

She nodded, biting her lip. "And you live here—alone?"

Silence held the place in a gentle grip.

"Are you afraid?" he asked quietly.

"Yes." Her answer was no more than a whisper and for a moment Justin wondered what would happen if he kissed her. What if he abandoned all caution and took her in his arms?

"It's nothing grand," he said finally, gripping

his good sense with all his waning strength. "But I'll show you what there is, if you'd like."

She nodded once and he stood for a moment, trying to read her mind, but it was no use. Lifting the lantern, he led her through the kitchen to the small dining area. He paused in the doorway, but Megan continued further, stopping before a well-scrubbed table to run her hands lightly across the open grain of the ash. He didn't hurry her but watched her roam to the stone wall at the far end of the room where the baskets hung awaiting use.

The simple tour continued through the small family area to the private office where Justin kept his books. Megan peeked in for only a moment, then followed Justin up the stairs to view the three bedchambers.

The first was unfurnished, and while the second was small it boasted a neatly made bed and a small commode where a ceramic pitcher and basin stood. The bright, patterned coverlet matched the braided rug and tied back curtains, and Megan stopped, absorbing the warmth of the place.

The final room was obviously Justin's. It had a masculine feel, blended in the cinnamon browns and cozy tans of the place. Upon the walls were pictures of livestock. The long-legged horses of the artist stared at her with baleful expressions and Megan stepped in a ways to stare back.

"Did you build it?" she asked, seeing no need to qualify her question.

"The house?" Justin asked, frowning a little. "No. A mason built it some eighty years ago, when Charleston was still called Charles Town. Do you like it?" He hadn't meant to ask. He hadn't!

Megan lifted her face quickly, biting her lip. If circumstances had been different she would almost be able to believe he cared about her answer. She could almost believe there was vulnerability in his voice.

"It's beautiful," she said, wishing her tone didn't so completely give away her emotions. "It's a—a real home."

A real home? Justin stared at her. How was he supposed to read her? She seemed as soft as a kitten, so utterly taken by his humble property. It was a strange thing, for during her stay in the luxury of Manor Royal she had not said a word about the loveliness of that place. Perhaps she had finally realized the precariousness of her situation. Perhaps she finally understood the damage he could do to her, especially now that they were alone. That was it. She was scared and simply hoped to flatter him. But it was too late for that.

He had vowed to make her pay. He deserved revenge. After all, she was a lying little schemer. A cheat!

But her eyes were as green as springtime, as large and innocent as a frightened doe's. Her form was firm and delectable and womanly.

But, he remembered raggedly, she'd stolen his pants. She must pay.

"Megan," he said gruffly.

"Yes." Her face lifted to his again, her expression frightened and guileless.

"I . . ." He faltered. "You sleep here tonight. I'll be in the next room if you should need me." Turning quickly, he strode down the hall.

Chapter 12

J ustin roamed about the dining table once
again. She was up there—in *his* bed. He
drummed his fingers against his thigh and
pursed his mouth as he stared angrily toward
the stairs. Why was he down here? Chivalry?
Chivalry was dead—killed by the likes of her,
women who toyed with the sensitivities of true
gentlemen. He circled the table again.

He should have gone through with his original plan to ravage her. It was a good plan—
solid, very manly. He'd liked that plan, but then
she'd had to spoil it by looking at him. She had
the most fascinating eyes, like something unearthly. Angel eyes maybe. And she'd been so
taken by his house.

Justin ceased his pacing, stomping down the
emotional euphoria raised by that memory. She
was an actress, he reminded himself. She didn't
really care for his utilitarian home, but only
hoped to save herself from the punishment she
so richly deserved. And it had worked. All one
had to do was look at the circumstances to realize she had won another round. After all, she

was comfortably tucked into his bed, while he paced the floor like some untamed beast.

But no more! Stopping at the bottom of the stairs, Justin slammed his fist on the top of the banister. No more! She was a vixen, a demon, a scheming little sea urchin and Justin Stearns was not going to be taken in by her pretty face and tempting little figure.

He took the steps three at a time, then stormed down the hall to throw the door wide. The portal hit the stop with reverberating force, shaking the wall slightly. But the small figure in the bed didn't move. He glared at her.

She was sleeping. Justin stood only inches away, scowling down at her with scalding anger. How dare she sleep while he paced?

"Megan," he called gruffly. "Wake up woman."

She didn't so much as move. God, he hated sound sleepers.

"Wake up I say." He leaned forward, shaking her shoulder but it did no good for Megan had gone too many nights in the throes of fear-induced insomnia.

He shook her again but it took him only a moment to realize she was dead to his presence.

Blast! He stomped about the room, enraged by her fatigue. What was he to do now? Ravaging a sleeping woman held little appeal.

"Go ahead and sleep then," he snarled finally as he nearly tore the buttons from his shirt in his haste to remove the thing. Perhaps he couldn't waken her but that hardly seemed a reason for him to avoid his own bed.

One article of clothing followed the other until Justin stood naked. Planting his fists on his lean-muscled hips, he scowled down at Megan before snorting his disgust and tossing aside the covers.

She was dressed in the night rail his mother had lent her with her hair spread about the pillow in flowing waves.

Justin soaked in the sight of her. She was beautiful, a veritable angel. Yes, it appeared the dreadful little vixen had once again fled, leaving this little bit of fluff in her place.

What could he do? Placing himself beside her with a sigh, Justin drew her gently into his arms.

"No," she whimpered weakly, lifting a feather-soft hand as if to ward him off, but Justin only chuckled as he settled her against his shoulder.

"Oh keep still, you little demon," he demanded.

Morning dawned without fanfare. Things seemed little changed from the day before except that in Justin's bed slept Megan—the woman he had vowed, and failed, to punish.

He stared at her, trying not to smile. She truly had a gift for sleeping. There were few who did it better. In the morning light she looked incredibly young, little more than a child, despite the luscious curves hidden beneath her wear-softened night rail.

He lay facing her, resting one hand on her narrow waist. How had it all come about? It seemed a strange tale, and an unlikely thing that the two of them now shared a bed when she had only so recently reentered his life.

Who was she? And where had she come from? Was she the put-upon young innocent he had first thought her to be or was she the swindling vixen she sometimes seemed? The question plagued him, making him scowl, but he sighed finally, thinking it made little difference.

The fact was, she was his, bought and paid for, and whether it was a legal purchase or not was a moot point for she was here and he would care for her.

That thought caught Justin off guard and he paused to consider it. He hadn't planned to care for her, after all. But here she was, in his arms, in his bed, in his care.

"Good morning."

Her eyes opened slowly, then widened to enormous widths as her small hands scrambled for a grip on the bedlinens.

"I—I thought you were to sleep in the other room."

"I had planned to, but my own humble bedchamber was too tempting. Did you sleep well?" He smiled against his will.

"I—I . . . yes."

"Good. Me too. Surprisingly so."

He stared at her, resting on one elbow as the minutes ticked away.

"Megan."

"Yes," she answered hurriedly, jerking at the sound of her name.

"I've been giving our situation a good deal of thought." He paused, watching her, feeling his own tension. "I've never meant to hurt you,

Megan. In fact I'd hoped for the opposite. But I confess I've wanted to convince you to tell the truth."

Silence again. Both persons now lay in the bonds of tension.

"You've denied having any knowledge of my stallion," Justin continued, then lifted his hand quickly, placing a finger to her lips as if to stop her words. "I was thinking, perhaps it wasn't you who caused my stallion to be taken." He scowled, concentrating on her expression. "Perhaps it was your brother."

"Michael?" she whispered.

He nodded and she stared at him. His fingers had fallen from her lips and now lay unmoving against her throat.

"I don't believe he had any knowledge of your stallion."

Justin watched her for an instant longer, but it was so difficult to keep his attention riveted on their conversation when so many more interesting items remained untouched. "Are you certain?" he asked as his fingers roamed leisurely along her ivory throat, pushing the bedlinen aside as he went.

"He's my brother," she explained as she attempted to tug the wayward sheet back into place.

"I realize he's your brother, Megan, but sometimes it's difficult to recall. You're so much more appealing than he." He lifted his eyes to the bright emerald width of hers. "Why do you suppose that is?"

She shivered beneath his touch. "I—I don't

know," she replied, wondering if she would ever quit stammering in his presence.

"Listen, my love," Justin continued, realizing he was fast losing his concentration. "This seems a terrible time to discuss such a thing . . ."

"No!" Megan argued, holding the bedsheet with white-knuckled strength. "This is great—a great time, I mean—great."

Justin couldn't contain his chuckle. She looked so utterly innocent—as if she had never been in a man's bed before. "Well, I can think of much more enjoyable things to do so long as we both happen to be in the same bed at the same time. So I would ask you a favor."

She nodded woodenly, though her eyes only seemed to get wider with the gesture.

"Think about my words. Perhaps there might have been some sort of alliance between your brother and Horace Manchester." Justin's fingers slipped down her arm, where the sheet revealed the delicate white of her flesh. "All right?"

She nodded again, even more jerkily than before, and Justin smiled.

"Thank you. Let's forget about the entire issue for now," he whispered, drawing nearer.

Megan drew back into the pillow. He was so large, and he smelled wonderful, like. . . . Mother Mary, but he smelled good. And he looked good—like a marble statue come to life.

She had to get a grip on herself. She was in the enemy's bed. Despite his gentle words, he was still the enemy. He had accused her of terrible things and was now accusing her brother. He was just trying to seduce her. She knew it.

"You're very beautiful," he whispered softly, touching her face gently. "But I suppose you've heard that a thousand times."

She shook her head, staring at him.

"No?" he questioned in disbelief. "A hundred?"

She shook her head, tense as a bowstring.

"Fifty?"

"I've—no one's ever told me that," she admitted, then bit her lip, as if scolding herself for conversing with the enemy.

"What?" Justin drew away abruptly, scowling at her. "You're fooling me."

"No." She swallowed, then cleared her throat as she dropped her gaze to the sheet. "I've always been like my Ma."

"And how's that?" He studied her closely, noting how her rose-hued mouth puckered slightly in thought.

"Plain."

He wondered vaguely if he looked as surprised as he felt, but she didn't raise her eyes to notice. "Don't they have mirrors where you come from, Little One?"

She scowled at the bedsheet. "Well, yes, of course."

"Then you're fooling me."

She blushed to the roots of her hair. He was so very close, staring at her with almost painful intensity. "I'm not. I've just always been plain. But my Pa always said it didn't matter—that I had horse sense and that was enough."

Justin was silent for a moment, noting the tiny freckles that dotted her nose. "Did your father say many such nonsensical things?"

She giggled. She couldn't help it. It just swelled up in her throat and pushed from between her lips.

Justin could feel his breath being taken. She lit up like the morning sky when she laughed. He'd never seen her laugh before, not an honest gesture of humor or happiness, and it startled him. There was so much life in her, so much . . . everything.

He lowered his head, eager to kiss her.

"My . . ." Megan gasped, not knowing what to say but knowing she must do something to keep him at bay. "I'm very sorry about your stallion," she whispered.

Justin drew back slightly. She looked utterly sincere.

"Was he . . ." She gulped. His expression was somber, his hair dark and ruffled by sleep. "Was he very valuable?"

"Yes." He refused to move away for she felt like heaven nestled against him. "Very valuable. And very beautiful—like you."

He lowered his head again.

"And—" she squeaked, grasping at straws. "And you had just bought him—that night?"

Justin grinned against his will. Her ploy to keep him at a distance was ever so obvious and very interesting, for if she were indeed a wanton woman, why would she care if he kissed her? Unless she were afraid of becoming involved with him. He leaned backward slightly at the thought, not admitting how it eased his mind.

"Yes, little Megan," he said, abandoning the idea of a kiss for a moment and touching her cheek with his fingertips. "I had just bought him. Paid a small fortune."

"I don't understand how you lost him," she said in a small voice.

Didn't she? Was she pretending? And would it hurt to explain it? If the truth be told, the story failed to make him look incredibly intelligent or even completely honest, but perhaps this was a good time for truth.

"Horace Manchester was a childhood—friend," he began quietly, thinking out loud. "His father built a plantation not so many miles to the south of here and we would see each other quite often. But as we grew we became increasingly competitive."

"Competitive?" she asked. "Over what?"

Justin studied her in silence. Would she care if she knew of the women they had sparred over? Did he want her to?

"Everything," he said. "It made little difference what it was. We enjoyed the rivalry. Then when we grew older our clashes merely took different avenues.

"The Manchesters raised fine horses. Some of the best in the county. When Horace Manchester took over the plantation, he improved the stock, breeding a walker stallion of outstanding bloodlines and quality. I had heard that stallion was finally up for sale."

"So you bought it." Her tone was utterly matter-of-fact, Justin noticed. It would be simple to let her believe the entire process had been perfectly above board, but would they ever clear the fog between them if they let misconceptions linger?

"I did buy him, but not outright. Instead I sent an employee to make the purchase." He paused, realizing she wasn't the only one who had schemed. "We never told Manchester the horse would be mine."

Megan was quiet for a moment, thinking. "But the price was fairly paid."

"Yes." He found to his utter amazement that he had been anxiously awaiting her response, that he cared what her reaction might be.

"Then the animal should be yours."

What would it hurt to kiss her? "My bill of sale was in the pocket of the britches you took." He said the words dryly, without accusation, but her face reddened nevertheless.

"Oh."

"And somehow." He twirled a strand of her red-gold hair about his finger. "Somehow Manchester knew I had no receipt. Perhaps," Justin whispered, "your brother told him."

Megan held her breath. The truth was she knew nothing about the stallion. The truth also was that it seemed she was inadvertently responsible for his loss. Would she be as patient as Justin if the circumstances were reversed? If the horse had been hers?

"Do you think it's possible?" Justin asked, leaning nearer, barely remembering his line of thought.

Megan could feel his light breath on her face. "What?" she whispered dizzily.

"Do you think your brother might have been a cohort of Manchester's?"

"My brother . . ." She was having difficulty remembering who her brother was much less what he'd done. "My brother is not ... altogether ... honest." She pulled her shoulders up, causing the glorious mass of her hair to press around them and looking utterly small and helpless. "I'm sorry," she whispered, "for the trouble we caused."

Justin couldn't delay the kiss any longer. Vaguely, somewhere in the back of his consciousness he knew he shouldn't do it. It was dangerous. *She* was dangerous. But she was also Megan.

She panted beneath his lips, trembling against him. Somehow the traitorous bedlinen had disappeared, and in its place was his body, pressed against hers with breathtaking intimacy.

"Justin," she gasped against his kiss. "I ..."

"Yes, my love?"

"I—this isn't right, you know."

"I don't know," he whispered, letting his lips trail sensuously down the smooth flesh of her throat.

"It's—it's immoral," she said. "A sin."

"Are you certain?" he whispered, but she failed to answer for his tongue had touched the flesh of her neck, stopping her thoughts and causing gooseflesh to erupt along the entire length of her quaking form. "Did you know you have the most incredible body I've ever seen, Megan?"

"Have—have—have you seen many?"

"A few." He chuckled, feeling her tremble beneath the word. "But not like you."

A woman could drown in his charm, Megan thought desperately. Or expire. What would happen if she simply dissolved beneath him?

Her body was already in flame. What if she melted?

The sound of a door slamming below jarred them apart. They stared at each other, almost seeming surprised to see the other there.

"Who's that?" Megan asked, finding the recalcitrant sheet and pulling it tightly to her chin.

"Miller," he explained dryly. "It's Mrs. Miller."

"She—she," Megan stuttered, trying to find her bearings.

"She cooks for me," Justin explained, then took a trembling sigh, pushing his fingers through the thick waves of his dark hair. How had he been so easily seduced by her presence? "It must be later than I realized. I'd best get to work. I've been a slacker long enough."

He delayed a moment longer but sat up finally, dropping his long-muscled legs over the edge of the feather tick.

Megan glued her eyes to the bedlinen as he moved about the room. Was he ... was he naked? Had he no modesty whatsoever? She darted a fleeting glance upward, then adhered her sight to the bedlinen again as she flamed with embarrassment.

He had no clothes on. Not a stitch, not a thread. She couldn't look. She couldn't. But she did. He was facing the chiffonier and had already donned a fresh undergarment.

His back was a deep golden tan, as were his arms. Even the back of his broad, masculine neck was dark. And every inch of him looked strong. Muscles crisscrossed his body with the smooth grace of hunting beasts. They flexed and darted across his back as he reached for his pants.

He turned toward the bed, causing Megan to jerk her gaze back to the bedsheet as he stepped into his breeches. "Daphne will prepare whatever you like for breakfast," he said, finally pushing his heavily muscled arms into his sleeves. "Within reason that is. I'm afraid my larder isn't as extravagant as my father's."

Buttoning the final button, he turned toward the door.

"Justin," Megan called softly, then bit her lip to stare at him above the bedsheet. "What is expected—that is, what should I do with myself?"

Justin scowled at her question. Was she his slave or was she not? The fact seemed pathetically clear that he was going to have a hell of a time making her his mistress, for as much as he ached to have her, he couldn't force her and certainly, no matter what the extent of her sexual experience, she needed time to adjust to the situation.

"Everyone on Free Winds works, Little One. Daphne takes care of the house and my men and I handle the horses." He paused for a moment, then added, "There's a garden, a big, neglected piece of land just to the back of the house. I'm afraid none of us have found time to care for it. It's yours if you care to try your hand at it." He touched the door latch then paused for one final glance at her. "Have a care though. Carolina weeds are a hardy lot and may eat up a little ragamuffin like you."

Megan stared at the door as it closed behind

him. A garden. Of course he had a garden. She
was out of bed in a moment and in another instant found the small carpetbag Justin had de-
posited in the room sometime during the night.
Dragging out a loaned, faded gown, she pulled
the thing over her head, twined her hair into a
heavy braid, and hurried downstairs.

"Hello." Megan stood in the doorway of the
kitchen, smiling at the housekeeper. She was a
handsome woman, immaculately dressed and
elegantly coiffured. "You must be Mrs. Miller.
I'm . . ."

"I know who you are." The woman didn't
look up. "You're Mr. Stearns' new—friend."

Megan stared in dumbfounded misunderstanding. "I'm his . . ." In truth she didn't know
what she was. "His . . . servant."

"Of course." Mrs. Miller looked up, smiling
wisely.

Megan's breath caught in her throat. Shame
burned her face. She was no whore, she wanted
to scream, but it was impossible to tell what she
would become in Justin's arms. She'd done a
poor job of fighting him off.

"I was just planning the meals. Will you be
here this evening or will you be gone already?"

"Gone?" Megan asked numbly.

"Well . . ." Mrs. Miller shook her head, as if
sorry to have to impart bad news. "I fear Mr.
Stearns is—well—easily distracted, should I
say? And there are so many beautiful women to
choose from. Women who—" She let her gaze
ease slowly over Megan's casual attire. "Women
of his own class. Women not found on the auction block."

Megan backed away, her face tight with emotion. Who was this woman? And what did she know about Justin or herself? She could think of nothing to say, and turning abruptly, hurried from the house in search of air.

The garden was easy to find. It was the huge, fenced area where the weeds jostled each other for a better view over the enclosure. Megan eyed the gargantuan plot. It was a farmer's paradise, but Daphne Miller's snide words ate at her, dulling her enthusiasm for the rich soil beneath her feet.

Still, it was there that Justin found her some hours later. She wore a somewhat battered hat that drooped over her face, shading the spot where she worked.

No delicate flower was she, he deduced, watching her as she tore into the weeds with fervor. In fact she moved with the robust energy of a Missouri mule at feeding time. He smiled—an enigma was little Megan.

"It's time to eat," he said, leaning against the fence to get a better view of her.

Megan jumped, abruptly lifting her face from her task. "Oh—I'm not hungry."

"Not hungry?" Justin questioned doubtfully. "You've dislodged enough weeds to cover all of Dixie. You must be hungry."

Megan bit her lip, studying him. If the truth be known she was hungry enough to eat her weight in sawdust. Her stomach rumbled painfully.

"I suppose I can stop for a while."

"Thatta girl."

She rose to her feet and Justin hid a smile.

Dirt stained the front of the borrowed frock and a vengeful weed had planted itself behind her left ear. Her hair was braided into a thick, honey-hued rope that slipped beneath the frayed edge of the seasoned hat and the back of her hands were tinged with pink from exposure to the sun.

She was lovely, utterly and undeniably beautiful.

Justin's hired hands joined them for the meal, making a total of six around the trestle table. Benjamin Ezekial Willard was a small, lean man who insisted she call him Zeke. He had a fire-quick smile and unquestionable pride in the three young men whom he introduced as his sons. The three lads were not only spitting images of each other and their sire, but were, by Justin's admission, as talented with horses as was Zeke.

Megan avoided eye contact with Mrs. Miller and tried not to recall her words. But the uncertainty of her own future nagged at her.

"I'll be returning to the garden," Megan said, rising from her seat and smoothing her worn gown with nervous hands.

Four men rose with her, as a salute to her gender.

"There's no hurry," Justin said. "There's always tomorrow."

Their eyes met for an instant but Megan drew quickly away from the visual contact, glancing nervously toward Daphne who stood smiling smugly behind Justin's back.

Would she be there tomorrow? "I enjoy the

work," Megan said, and turned quickly from the house.

She was busy in the garden once again when Justin found her some hours later. What she had been before her brother had chosen to care for her, he couldn't know for sure, but it seemed likely enough she had told the truth about being farm reared. He watched her for a moment, then pushed the gate inward to tread between the rows toward her.

"Megan."

She straightened from her work, hopelessly rubbing the dirt deeper into her gown and blinking against the sunlight.

"I brought you some gloves," he said, extending a worn, oversized pair.

"Oh." She eyed the things but failed to take them. Instead she held her palms pressed against her skirt as if she were ashamed to show them.

"What is it?" he questioned, scowling at her. "You've overworked, haven't you?"

She shook her head like a recalcitrant child but he refused to believe her and stepped forward to lift her hands from her sides. The palms were reddened and chafed, stained green and black, and painful looking.

"Megan," he scolded gently. "Look what you've done. You've blistered your hands." He lifted his gaze from her palms to her face. "And such pretty hands."

Her breath stopped in her throat. Why did he look at her like that? Didn't he realize she couldn't breathe when he did that? Didn't he know her heart was likely to stop dead in her chest and refuse to beat again?

"See what you've done now?" he asked, chiding softly. "You've distracted me from my work. Now there's nothing else to be done but take care of you, I suppose." He sighed as if greatly put out, then smiled, with just the corner of his lovely mouth and his eyes. "Come with me, Little One. I suppose if you insist on neglecting yourself, I'll need to look after you."

He led her from the garden by the hand, then gently tugged her along toward the corrals where a barrel of fresh rain water stood in the shade of the barn.

"Pull up your sleeves," he commanded, but when she was slow to comply, he set his own fingers to the task of unbuttoning the cuffs. "You Irish!" he scolded as he shook his head and pressed her sleeves up her slim forearms. "Set you to work and there's no stopping you. Zeke's Irish, you know. But not redheaded."

His eyes sparkled. Never in all her life had she seen eyes like his. They were a myriad of colors and expressions, and she fell with hopeless abandon into their depths.

"And not so pretty," he continued, sensing her watch him before pushing her bruised hands into the cool water. "It's quite a hardship, you know—working with the Irish." He scrubbed gently at her hands, then pulled them from the water to examine them before dousing them again. "Trying to keep up could wear me thin, especially with someone like you." Taking her hands from the water again, he kissed the back of each, then turned them over to gently kiss the scathed palms.

His touch was feather light and Megan watched breathlessly, feeling there was nothing she could do but be absorbed into the pleasure of his touch. His kisses wandered upward, over her bared wrist until he reached the delicate, ultra-sensitive crease of her elbow. She trembled and he lifted his head, looking shamelessly roguish.

"I imagine I'll need to work night and day to satisfy a woman like you." He smirked, holding her arm gently. "But a man must do what a man must do." He kissed the delicate crease again and she jerked involuntarily, causing him to grin outright and caress the velvet-soft flesh of her arm with his fingertips, setting her to tremble anew. "What do you think, love?"

"I—oh!" Megan exclaimed, finally jerking her arm free and gazing at him with eyes wide enough to become lost in. "I'm feeling much better. Thank you."

Justin smiled, straightening slightly. "My pleasure."

"I—I should get back to work."

"No you shouldn't."

"What?"

"You shouldn't go to work. You should go to bed."

She became incoherent at the mere thought of his bed.

"Me too," he teased, "but I can't just now. So you hike yourself upstairs and rest. You're not used to the hot sun. You looked fairly flushed."

She realized he knew the heat of the sun

wasn't the problem, but what could she say without revealing the emotions that boiled inside her?

"I don't think Mrs. Miller likes me very well," Megan murmured, doing her best to avoid his eyes.

"Miller? Not like you?" Justin asked in genuine surprise. "How could anyone not like you? Except me of course. You stole my stallion. I'm not allowed."

She stared at him. Who was he? And why in heaven's name was he so charming?

"Come along." He tugged her along toward the house. "Daphne's already gone anyway. But she left us some supper. You get yourself something to eat and then take yourself off to bed. All right?"

"All right," she agreed quietly.

"Good girl," he said, patting her behind, then grinning boyishly at her shocked expression. "Rest up, love. You'll need it."

Megan lay between the cool linen sheets. She shouldn't be here. In fact, she should be running from here so fast it would make her head spin. But the only thing spinning her head was Justin. She closed her eyes at the memory of him, then trembled a little. What was she going to do? He was being so kind, or so something. And why? What was he planning? He still believed she was responsible for the loss of his stallion, or so he implied. And in a way she was.

Holy Patrick, she couldn't bear to think about it any longer. Curling into a ball, Megan closed her eyes and drifted off to sleep.

Justin entered some hours later. He watched

her solemnly. What was he going to do with her? He couldn't make love to her, regardless of his words earlier.

He had vowed to make her tell the truth, to apologize for her crimes against him, and that's what he planned to do. There was no room for love in this relationship. No room at all.

Chapter 13

"**H**ello, Megan," Justin greeted her quietly, resting his forearms upon the top rail of the split oak fence. He had awakened alone some ten hours earlier. And after scrambling wildly about for his clothes and for thought, he had found her just where he found her now, in the garden, against the riotous backdrop of bunched flowers. He hadn't disturbed her then but he could wait no longer. She haunted his every minute, whether awake or asleep. Megan in the garden, Megan in the kitchen, Megan in his bed. "Have you been avoiding me, Little One?" he asked, studying her across the barrier of the fence.

"No!" She knew herself to be a poor liar even in the best of circumstances. And this was hell and gone from the best of circumstances.

Justin chuckled wryly, wondering how she had survived as a swindler for so long years. Michael, he deduced, must take credit for most of their dishonest success.

"Will you come out to the barn with me?" he asked, showing none of his thoughts.

"I—ah. I wanted to finish with the raspberries," she murmured, fiddling with the soil and refusing to meet his eyes. Being near him was too pleasantly painful to give in immediately to his request and yet, when she finally looked up at him, Megan found that awful weakness in her again, that terrible breathtaking eagerness to do whatever he asked.

Inside Justin's barn was the same cool, quiet atmosphere present in most equine barns. Megan breathed the heavy scents of the place and felt a bit of tension slip from her shoulders.

"Right down here," Justin said, leading the way to an end stall.

It seemed to Megan that she had lived this moment before, as she stood before the quiet pair of horses. The mare was black, as had been the mare at Manor Royal. The foal was newborn and delicately priceless.

"Remember the filly at Royal?" Justin asked quietly. "This mare is the daughter of old Magic, the mother, and this foal is the first grandson we've raised from the grand old dame." He chuckled, not sharing his thoughts for a moment, but finally explaining. "Father will be green with envy. He's been wanting a horse colt of these bloodlines for as long as I can recall. I'll be sending him a message to come and see the pair." He paused, watching her. "Do you ride?" he asked quietly, realizing his thoughts were somewhat erratic.

"I . . ."

"Certainly, you do," Justin answered for her. "How could a good Irish girl not ride? And besides, you told me yourself you were a good hand with a horse. Of course . . ." He leaned

closer, grinning a little. "I suspect you were trying to convince me you were worth more out of
my bed than in it at the time. A theory I'm not
likely to agree with, by the way."

She blushed bright red and he laughed, loving
the fact that she was so easily embarrassed.
Surely that said something about her previous
experience, or her lack of it. Didn't it?

"Come along," he said. Lifting her hand, he
led her to the opposite end of the barn where
two horses waited in adjoining stalls. "I'll show
you Free Winds."

It took only minutes for him to saddle the
pair of mounts. For himself Justin had chosen a
large liver chestnut stallion that pranced as he
mounted and tossed his charming head at the
mare Megan rode.

"What's her name?" Megan asked, settling
herself into the padded sidesaddle.

"Cherry," Justin answered. "And this is
Rum," he said, nodding toward his mount and
noting how she held her hands with the steady
delicacy of the born equestrienne.

They went along leisurely, side by side. The
lane down which they rode was red-toned and
mostly untraveled. Along both sides were pas-
tured the horses of Free Winds, well-bred, elegant animals that grazed upon the lush hills of
Justin's property.

"How long have you lived here?" Megan
asked, noting how the horses appeared as
dreamlike silhouettes against the multi-colored
sky of early evening.

"Nearly ten years." He studied the land
around him, remembering the struggles it had

taken to build his property to what it now was. "When I was seventeen my father and I had a dispute over the issue of slavery. He believed, as he does now, that slavery is a gentleman's way of life, and that, in order for the south to survive, there's a need for human bondage." He shrugged, his face sober, not looking at her for a moment. "I disagreed and when he challenged me to prove otherwise, I began looking for a place to do just that. And so . . ." He lifted a hand to indicate the sweeping acres around him. "Free Winds.

"There," Justin said, pointing to a pasture not far in the distance. "That's my herd of youngsters. I put them out there to mature. Yearlings, mostly."

Megan watched the herd as they approached. They were fine stock, long-limbed and full of lively potential. She smiled as they cavorted about the field, shaking their elegant heads and staging playful battles for any onlookers.

"And the black gelding?" Megan asked as they drew close enough to distinguish each individual horse. "What about him?"

"I'm beginning to believe you didn't overstate your knowledge of horses, little Megan," Justin said, watching her carefully but then turning his attention to the aged gelding she had mentioned. "That's old Badger. We keep him out here to add some sense to the young 'uns."

"He's seen a few years," Megan said matter-of-factly.

"That he has." Justin nodded. "My father gave him to me for my ninth birthday. He was a handsome animal then. I rode him everywhere. I thought I owned the world when I rode Badger." He chuckled aloud from deep in his throat and at Megan's curious expression, explained. "When I was, oh, ten or eleven, my father built an addition on to Manor Royal. The house used to be much smaller than it is now. The old brick structure—the part you climbed down," he added, unable to ignore the memory of her hanging like a monkey from the weaving vines, "is the original building. In fact, that's not altogether true. Manor Royal was first built south of where it now stands. It was destroyed by fire. But"—he shrugged watching her closely. She had an undeniable quality about her, a fresh, unforgettable loveliness that drew his soul. "We Stearns have a habit of making the best of a bad situation. Father simply built anew. Bigger than before." Urging his stallion forward, Justin followed the fence line, with the entirety of the young herd coming along behind. "I remember when Father built that huge veranda and then put in the double doors. I couldn't understand why anyone would need two doors in the same place." He laughed at himself. "I guess I'll always be a peasant at heart.

"Anyhow, I told Sonny one door should be enough for anyone. I bet him I could ride old Badger through one door without opening or touching the other."

"You didn't try it, did you?" Megan asked, urging her mare along beside.

"Certainly I did," Justin disagreed, turning in his saddle to smile at her. "A bet's a bet."

She laughed and the silvery tone wafted out

on the gentle breeze and into Justin's soul, like a balm on his worn nerves.

"So what was the outcome?" she urged.

"Well," said Justin, stopping his mount to look at her, "I got the old boy up the stairs sure enough and we got through the door without touching the other, but when I was about to turn Badger around, one of the house Negroes saw us." He shook his head at the memory. "You would've thought she'd lost her hair to red Indians, the way she screamed. Old Badger knew we were in a pile of trouble and lit outta there like a rifle ball, with me just hanging on for the ride."

"So you won the wager," Megan deduced, laughing appreciatively.

"Well, I won the bet, sure enough," Justin admitted, smiling at her laughter. "But Mother lost her azaleas when Badger launched himself from the veranda and into her flower bed. And me, I lost a good deal of hide when Father found out."

"Oh no!" Megan frowned suddenly, seeming disappointed by his father's lack of humor. "Honestly?"

"Well, perhaps I didn't actually lose any flesh, but I wasn't so eager to ride for a while, or even sit, for that matter." Justin studied her compassionate expression for a time, then asked, "Don't you think young scallawags should have their hides tanned in such circumstances?"

Megan was quiet for a moment, her brow puckered in thoughtfulness. "It seems sometimes," she began slowly, "that if you're lucky enough to have a family and a home you shouldn't waste time on anything but enjoying them."

Justin watched her. There was so much more to her than met the eye—a wealth of emotions.

"I think you'd make a very amusing mother," he finally said, smiling a little.

She smiled in return, dropping her gaze to her mount's mane. "Amusing," she said. "I'm not certain that's a compliment as far as motherhood is concerned."

"I'm certain it is," Justin argued, appreciating the hint of a blush on her cheeks. "I think laughter can heal many wounds." He paused. "And you make me want to laugh, little Megan— along with wanting other things."

He was too attractive, too close, too charming.

"So," she said nervously, not lifting her eyes from her mount's copper-colored mane, "you learned not to wager, I suppose, after Badger demolished the flower bed."

"Oh, hardly that," disagreed Justin, allowing her to escape behind her question, but watching her closely nevertheless. "I'm always ready for a good bet. As a matter of fact, how about a simple wager right now?"

Megan raised her gaze quickly, finding his honey-warm eyes on her. "Of what nature?" she asked uncertainly.

"A short race," he challenged.

"What?"

"Sure." He watched her as he spoke. Her bonnet had been left in the garden, allowing her untamed hair to feather out about her oval face and fall in sun-sparkling tendrils toward the wonderful curves of her delicious little body. "You ride Cherry very well."

Megan bit her lip, glancing down at the mare then up at Justin's expectant face. "I think you'd have the advantage," she stated.

"Now there you go," laughed Justin. "You're underestimating poor Cherry. She's quite fast really. You might be surprised."

"It's not Cherry that I doubt," Megan argued loyally. "But your stallion's much larger. It'd hardly seem fair."

"That's true," said Justin practically. "He also carries double the weight, however. But, if you're unsure, I'll give you a three lengths lead."

"Oh no, you don't." Megan scowled, immediately angered by his condescension. "When we O'Rourkes race, we start even or not at all."

"All right then." Justin hid his grin. She had more fire than any woman he'd ever known, and it was that fire that seemed to have sparked a flame in his own parched body. "We ride even."

"Now not so fast," she argued quickly. "For what do we wager?" she questioned, cocking her inquisitive little face at him.

"What do you wish for?" he asked. There was a quiet intensity in his question, as if he truly needed to know.

She hesitated. What did she truly want? There was no need to look at him, for she had memorized his every feature and mannerism, his dark, rugged face, his long, wonderfully muscled body, the gentle way his hands held the reins.

"I want to go home." She whispered the statement as if she feared some unbidden words might escape. "I want you to let me go."

Silence lay between them—silence and hurt, possibly unhealable hurt. He wasn't sure. "I lost my most valuable stallion," he reminded himself softly. "Because of that I'll miss this breeding season. You deny any dealings with Manchester but how can I let you go when circumstances make it so hard to believe you? Your confession could force Horace to return Sure Gold to me. I'm not a wealthy man, Megan. I've worked hard to achieve what I have. I can't afford to forfeit next year's crop of Gold's foals—not after what I paid to purchase him."

Megan dropped her eyes. They sat on their mounts, unmoving.

"I'll agree to your request, Megan," Justin said finally, his tone deep and strained, "if you'll agree to mine."

She raised her gaze, looking as frightened as he remembered her at Manor Royal, but it was no longer amusing, only sad, as if the sun was hidden without her smile.

"What do you want?" she murmured, her eyes wide, her rosy mouth small and puckered.

"I want you tonight, willingly." His expression and body were tense and marble-hard.

Her jaw dropped and she blinked twice, caught off guard by his blatant request. "But I couldn't do that. It'd be wrong."

"It's a little late to worry about right and wrong, isn't it, Megan?"

She blinked. Belatedly, Justin realized his unintentional insult. He hadn't meant to criticize her, but rather himself, for he realized suddenly that he was far past caring what was right and what was wrong. He wanted her! That was all!

Megan hid her hurt behind a silent mask. He thought nothing of her honor. Indeed, he thought she had none.

"And if I win, you'll set me free?" she asked. Her chest ached from his jibe, but she kept her tone cool and distant.

"Yes."

Megan set an unsteady hand to the mare's shoulder, assessing the power hidden beneath the glistening hide. "All right." She lifted her face abruptly, believing she could win. "If I set the course."

Justin studied her, seeing the hurt behind her emerald eyes. But there was something else— excitement maybe, the thrill of the challenge. "You set the course," he said finally, his tone revealing nothing.

She nodded, her face taut with tension, then urged her mount back to the road they had left not so many minutes before. Justin followed, watching the fluid way with which she handled the mare. She was no novice, he deduced. She possessed a good deal of equine knowledge. But more than that, she was a woman born with a God-given understanding of horses—an unusual connection with the equine species. A strange emotion swelled in him, an odd airy feeling that seemed to fill his chest as he watched her.

"There," she said, pointing down the road in the direction they'd come. "See that copse of trees we passed? We'll race to them."

Justin drew his gaze from her flushed face to look in the direction she indicated. The stand of trees was a good ways off. "A mile, a mile and a quarter, maybe," he said, narrowing his eyes to consider the distance. "It's a long course." He studied her again. She knew what she was doing. The longer the course, the greater his disadvantage. "All right. It's a bet then?"

"It's a bet." She nodded solemnly and in that instant he realized he'd never met a woman who made him ache in the core of his soul.

They placed their mounts side by side, both riders taut and ready. The big stallion reared with energy while the mare merely waited, her ears pitched forward as if she understood the task ahead of her.

"Go!" Megan yelled the start.

The animals launched from their positions. Powerful haunches bunched to grip the wet earth beneath them. But the stallion was too impatient, wasting his energy and plunging out of the most direct path.

Cherry's powerful legs churned beneath her. But Megan rode with a handicap, for her balance was not its best, perched sideways as she was in the stylish saddle.

"Run!" she screamed into the speeding wind, glancing back over her shoulder to the stallion that strained just behind. "Run!"

The first quarter mile sped beneath the horses' pounding hooves as the striving mounts held their positions. But around the bend Megan sensed the stallion's gain.

Streamers of red-gold hair blurred her vision as she looked behind again. He was gaining.

The stallion's nostrils were flared wide, drinking in the air in great gulps as he poured his heart into the race. Turning her head, Megan bent low, considering the distance left, knowing her handicap well. Then, abruptly decisive, she swung her leg over her mount's lathered neck to hug the heaving sides with her thighs.

Stirrups were only a nuisance now and flapped uselessly as Megan's thighs gripped high to the withers. Her skirt pressed upwards, exposing the gripping muscles of her upper legs, but she no longer cared for modesty. Her ancestral blood flowed hot and fast as her steely, competitive spirit screamed within her breast.

They were nearly there. She could see the trees well, just ahead, and the lead was held steady. Just one turn and she'd be free.

But the earth was damp, the mare tiring. Megan leaned into the curve, mentally cursing the interference of the ungainly sidesaddle. The mare's strength was ebbing. Megan felt her lurch as one foreleg struck the other. Cherry made a valiant effort to recover, but the impact was too great and her knees hit the earth with shocking force.

The ground flew up toward Megan. She tried to hold it back with her hands, but it came too fast. Her head struck the red Carolina soil with a resounding thud and blackness came, settling in around her with muffling quiet.

Chapter 14

⟋⟍⟍⟋⟍

"Megan." Justin's voice seemed to come to her from a great distance, calling from a cool fog.

Her eyes opened slowly to rest on Justin's dark, chiseled features.

"Are you all right?" His fingers were light and gentle as they brushed away a splotch of mud from her upturned nose.

"I think so," she answered weakly, caught in the warm, cider depths of his eyes. They looked worried, she thought distractedly, and dangerous, with that lovely expression of concern embedded deep in the soft, flecked irises. She attempted to rise, but he kept her steady, pressing gently against her shoulder.

"Relax for a moment, love, until your head clears," he urged. Taking her arm between his large hands, he massaged it, feeling for breakage. Then, with a glance at her face he set the limb aside, lifting the other to test it in the same manner. Finding nothing wrong, he kissed her upturned palm, then disappeared from her limited view to search for breakage in her half-exposed legs.

Megan lay without complaint. She should be embarrassed, she reasoned, especially since she was accustomed to wearing very little under her gowns. In fact, her legs were bare below her knees, but embarrassment seemed such a worthless emotion when his hands felt like tangible sunlight against the flesh of her calf.

They moved upward, easing past her knee to the femur, then down the opposite leg to her ankle. Warmth followed in the wake of his massage and she felt a twinge of guilty disappointment when the movement ceased.

"You seem unbroken." He appeared before her, searching her face for signs of pain. "Do you feel whole?"

Megan could find no words as she stared at his rugged beauty. There was no hostility there now, no distrust, only a sort of flattering worry—and maybe something more.

She had never been afforded such an opportunity to examine him at close proximity and used her time well now, noting each sculpted feature. There was nothing about him she could fault. Every inch of him seemed to personify masculinity and she stared in open wonder.

"Are you whole, Megan?" he repeated with a scowl.

She said nothing, trying to straighten the facts in her own muddled mind. Was she whole? She searched the solid squareness of his face, looking for the answer there. Could any woman be whole and not wish to touch the masculine beauty of his face?

She reached up hesitantly with one smudged

hand, to rest her fingertips on the rough-bristled skin of his cheek.

"Megan?" he said, sounding truly worried by her strange behavior.

"Yes?" She smiled a little, drawing her fingers away. "I'm sorry. I think I can ride."

She attempted to rise, but he scowled her down, pulling her against him with gentle strength and slipping one arm beneath her bent knees. He rose to his feet, barely noticing her weight as he lifted her.

"I—I'm sure I can ride," she stammered, glancing nervously about for her mount.

"I'm sure you can ride too, like a little centaur," Justin said, still scowling his worry as he strode toward Free Winds. "But Cherry was in a hurry to get home, with or without you. And Rum has always liked a gal who plays hard to get. I fear he followed her back to the barn." He smiled.

"I think I could walk. I think, you know . . ." Any semblance of coherence had fled with her fall, it seemed.

"Don't be silly."

"Truly," she insisted, feeling the heat of her face with painful awareness.

"Why do I make you so nervous, Megan?" he asked gently. "I've never hurt you."

She was silent for a long while, then whispered, "But you promised me you would." She bit her lip, raising her eyes finally to his.

"Megan," he began, scowling at her, "why don't you tell me the truth? You had my bill of sale. It was in my pocket when you stole my breeches. Manchester came to accuse me of stealing the horse I had rightfully bought. He knew I no longer had the bill of sale. Logic says you were the one to tell him."

"I don't know any Manchester," she whispered.

"But you do know of the bill of sale," he urged.

She stared at him, wishing she were someone else, someone who didn't evoke such hatred in him. "No," she answered simply. "I don't."

He was silent and his jaw flexed. She could see the anger in his face. The house was just ahead now and he carried her the final steps before pushing the door wide and carrying her up the stairs to the bedroom they had shared.

"I'll fetch some water and catch the horses." His tone was clipped. "Will you be all right until I return?"

She nodded and he watched her for only a moment before turning to leave.

Megan lay against the cool sheets and closed her eyes to her unnerving emotions. Her fall had upset her, that was all, she told herself but in the quiet place in her mind she saw his face, dark, smiling, so full of masculine allure that it took her breath even now.

"How are you?" Justin came through the door in only a matter of minutes, carrying a wooden, leather-strapped bucket of water.

"Fine." She didn't look at him. "How's Cherry?"

"A bruise on her right tendon. She'll mend."

Megan bit her lip, feeling the tension. "I'm sorry I caused her fall."

She could feel his gaze on her face and

wished she could hide beneath the covers as she had as a child.

"It wasn't your fault, Megan. I shouldn't have challenged you, especially on a horse you're unfamiliar with." He eased his weight onto the bed beside her, studying her. "Do you hurt a great deal?"

"Some," she admitted softly.

"Where?"

Megan frowned. How was she supposed to discuss body parts with this man when his were so near and large and. . . . She blushed from the roots of her hair to the tips of her toes.

"I—I'm fine," she repeated rapidly, refusing to raise her eyes and wishing her assurance of well-being would send him strolling from the room with a whistled tune.

"Don't be childish, Megan," he scolded, but beneath his frown was the suggestion of a grin. "Tell me where it hurts the most."

Her lower lip felt raw and mangled as she bit it again. "My hip, I think."

"Truly?" he asked, sounding suddenly cheerful. "How lucky for me."

Megan scowled at him but refused to ask for clarification.

"Well," he said more soberly, watching her watch him. "Let's have a look at it."

"At what?" she asked suspiciously.

Justin chuckled, the sound low and soft. "At your wound, of course."

"My—No!" Megan argued, shaking her head vehemently. "It's fine."

"It is not fine." He chuckled, placing his hand on her skirt and pushing it firmly upwards, but suddenly Megan's small hands were in the way, resisting the movement.

"It doesn't hurt anymore," she lied, her face flaming.

Justin laughed outright and removing his hand from her gown, settled back for a moment. "Megan, it is not miraculously healed. Now quit being a child and let me have a look."

"I'm not a child," she argued, her expression ferocious, her hands unmoved.

"I know you're not, love." His tone was ultimately sincere, his eyes as warm as heated cider. "Now let me see." He waited only a moment but when his hands moved to her skirt again, she failed to resist him, though her own fingers followed the skirt upward.

She wore pantalettes beneath the faded gown, but they were a strange, shortened version, and Justin frowned as he inspected them in silence.

Megan knew his thoughts and wished she had worn a full suit of armor beneath the simple gown. "I was hot," she said defensively.

"I see." His face showed no expression. "That's very practical of you, little Megan," he said solemnly. "It's rare," he added, "the combination of beauty and practicality."

Gently he pulled down the soft fabric of her pantalettes and she winced, whether from pain or from his nearness, she wasn't sure.

"It's quite swollen," he said, examining the purpled flesh and aching with his own blood-infused swelling. "But the skin's unbroken. I think it'll heal fine on its own." He was speechless for a moment, then added in a stilted voice. "How disappointing."

He grinned with a deadly boyish charm that stopped her heart.

"I was hoping it would need long and extensive care." He shrugged, holding her gaze warmly. "But I can't have everything, I suppose. I should be grateful to you for being injured in such an interesting area in the first place."

She stared at him, feeling the blush seep through to her bones and knowing if she spoke she would humiliate herself completely.

He laughed softly. "Is there anywhere else that needs my administrations, little Megan?" he asked gently. "Higher maybe?" He glanced upwards, his eyes caressing the graceful swell of her breasts. "Or lower?" His gaze fell to her hips where the bunched fabric of her skirt revealed the soft linen of her abbreviated pantalettes. "I'm easy to please."

"N——no. No," she said hurriedly, pushing her skirt downward, though his hands remained where they were and became hidden beneath her gown, a condition that only increased her nervousness.

"You're not dizzy at all?" he asked, raising his eyes to her heated face. When she shook her head negatively he added, "Strange. I feel terribly unsteady myself."

The world around them was held in a terrible quiet. Megan was certain she could hear the frenzied beating of her heart and scrambled for some coherent words to drown the sound.

"Listen, Justin," she babbled. "About the bet . . ."

"Yes, love?"

"I——I should never have made such an improper wager. It was terribly wrong of me. I regret it now. Truly I do."

The warmth of his fingers beneath her skirt made her question her own words but she hurried on nevertheless. "I feel badly about it. I do. Really. But of course I can't go through with it. It would be immoral. And I have no money to see the wager fairly paid. But . . ." She stopped for a moment, wishing she could guess his thoughts. "I do have a mare. She's a wonderful animal. Really. Exceptional. I left her in Charleston before going to Manor Royal."

His face was as inscrutable as a granite wall.

"She'll still be there, at Matt Teaker's livery," she stumbled on. "I would give her to you, in lieu of what I wagered."

Why didn't he say something? Megan wondered desperately. Why didn't he give some indication of his thoughts instead of simply staring at her as if she were some strange phenomenon?

Time ticked away with the slowness of a dirge. And with each second gone, Megan was certain her pulse escalated until she felt sure her heart would jump from her chest.

Say something, she wanted to scream. Do something!

"So you're saying you've changed your mind," Justin deduced quietly, "and have decided not to pay the debt honestly?"

"No," she argued quickly. "I'll give you my mare, like I said. She's a fine animal, fine—certainly much more valuable than . . ."

"Than what, Megan?"

"Than—than . . ." she faltered, finding it impossible to meet his gaze.

"More valuable than a night alone with you?" he asked quietly. "How would you know how much value I place on one such night?"

"It's just . . ." She was panting, still pressing her gown over the bruised flesh of her hip, entrapping his hands beneath. "I shouldn't have made the wager. I shouldn't have."

"And so you hope to make it right by breaking your word, Megan?"

"I'm not breaking it; I'm offering you Rainstorm. I'm offering you something very valuable."

He stared at her, his mahogany gaze burning her face for what seemed to be a lifetime.

"I don't want your mare, Megan." Slowly he drew his hands from beneath her gown, pulling himself to a standing position at the edge of the bed. "I don't want anything from a liar. I see now that it's impossible for you to be honest in any of your dealings."

His expression showed a coldness she hadn't seen since their first meeting, an artic disdain that froze her to the mattress. The world ground along on its slow course. Megan saw him turn, saw the finality in the gesture, and suddenly, seemingly of its own accord, her hand reached out.

She tugged at his sleeve with the uncertainty of a child, looking up at him through wide, frightened eyes. "I'm not a liar," she whispered.

"No?" There was no cynicism in his tone, but rather a breathy sort of hopefulness, a longing to believe.

"No," she repeated. She pulled at him.

His broad knee touched the mattress and then he was above her, the breadth of his chest covering her.

"Then I want you Megan. More than I've ever wanted anyone," he whispered.

His lips touched hers with shocking tenderness. The warmth spread downward, searing a path to the farthest extremities of her quivering form. He brushed her hair gently from her throat and his kisses followed his hands, burning her flesh, branding her with a luscious, heart-throbbing heat.

"Megan," he whispered. "You make me forget the past. You make it seem inconsequential." His fingers touched the top button of her simple gown. "You make it all unimportant, love. You make me a fool."

He drew his dark head back for a moment, studying her. She could feel the heat of his breath, could feel the hard curve of his long, lovely body, pressed intimately to hers.

"And the horrible part," he continued softly, easing her button from its hole, "is that I don't care. Not tonight. Tonight I'll gladly be a fool."

Buttons slipped open beneath his warm fingers and she pressed her head back in the pillow, drawing deep breaths through her opened mouth, breathing in the moment in great, trembling gasps. His lips touched her breast, just above the lace of her chemise. She jumped at the burning sensation, jerking her head from the pillow to gape at him. Never in all her years had she felt such intensity, such burning, aching desire.

He lifted his head from her breast, his eyes finding hers. "What is it, love?" he asked huskily, his sensual lips curving into a smile. "You like that?" With tantalizing slowness he lowered his lips again. But now his tongue touched her flesh, burning a tender trail along the upper extremity of her lacy undergarment.

She couldn't speak, but jerked beneath him, pressing her shoulders into the pillow and letting her eyes fall closed. A strap sighed from her shoulder. His kisses moved from her breast to the tender flesh of her upper arm. She pulled the limb tightly to her side, but his fingers encircled her wrist now, urging it to straighten. She could feel her sleeve being pulled from her arm but dared not look, for behind the sleeve came his kisses, burning down the quivering flesh of her arm. The second sleeve followed in a moment and now she lay beneath him, her upper body covered only in the frilly cloth of her chemise.

He was watching her. She could feel his gaze on her and opened her eyes slowly. He was resting lightly on his palms and one hip, holding his weight easily from her wound. His nostrils were slightly flared and for the first time Megan wondered if he wanted her as badly as she did him. The thought came like a revelation, and she lifted her hand to gently touch his chest. His intake of breath was no less loud than hers had been, shocking her with its intensity, making her bold and inquisitive.

His white shirt billowed away from his body, the buttons drooping toward her slightly and she found them with tentative fingers, peeling them open one after another.

The tight mounds of his chest were visible now and she lifted her gaze from them for a moment to find his eyes with hers. They looked hot and eager, with his face as tense and still as his body.

Slowly, she moved her hands from his button to smooth her palm across his sun-darkened chest. The muscles jumped beneath her touch and despite her inexperience, she smiled. "What is it, love?" she mimicked innocently. "You like that?"

A growl grumbled up from his chest and suddenly she was locked against him and rolled to the top.

"I like it," he snarled. But now her breasts were exposed to an even greater extent, pulling his attention from her face.

The sensation of his lips against the upper regions of her breasts was even more shocking now and she gasped aloud. "That'll teach you to tease me, Little One," he murmured against her flesh, but the impediment of her clothing was too much to be borne now, and he pushed her back onto her knees.

The rosy light of sunset filled the room, bathing them in pink shades of glory as Justin gently pushed the bothersome garments from her body. She shivered under his touch, lowering her eyes shyly. But when the final bit of fabric had been pushed to the bed, he raised her chin with tender fingertips.

"Look at me, Megan," he pleaded.

It took her a moment, but she raised her eyes

to his, which he met with his own. "You're even more beautiful than I imagined," he whispered. He paused for a moment before the corner of his mouth lifted to a grin. "And believe me, I've spent a good deal of time imagining."

Her eyes shifted downward, away from his face. She was naked, trembling and impatient.

"Megan," he said again, his voice even softer now. "You were right, Little One. It was a foolish bet." Time stood still. She could hear her breath mingled with his. "If you choose, we'll stop now." The room was as quiet as nightfall. "I'll call the bet duly paid."

Her eyes raised abruptly, in disbelief. She had been wrong, she thought suddenly. He didn't want her nearly as badly as she wanted him. She should withdraw now. She should gather her clothes about her and flee the room. She should....

Her fingers slipped into his shirt, touching his side where his lean-muscled ribs slanted inwards toward his taut belly. Crisp, dark hair grew more densely there and she ran her hand toward the thickest forest.

He inhaled sharply and she lifted her eyes to his face, realizing suddenly that he hadn't been breathing. Perhaps.... She bit her lip sharply, trying to control her excitement. Perhaps she had been wrong again. Perhaps he did want her.

"Don't play with me, little Megan," he warned gruffly, "unless you're ready to finish the game."

He looked utterly harsh and masculine, and yet under the pads of her fingertips she felt him quiver, a long, luscious shiver that quaked his

large form. She smiled again, although she tried
not to, and then slipped his shirt open and ever
so slowly pressed her bare body to his.

It was more than he could endure. For a moment he closed his eyes to the ecstasy of the
feeling but in an instant he pushed her away,
stepping from the bed to hurry from his clothing.

She tried to look away, but it was too difficult.
He was too alluring. His body was made of the
most incredible muscle, molded in long, fine
masses that quivered as he jerked his arms from
the sleeves and unbuttoned his pants. Her face
flamed, but she kept her gaze on him as he
pulled his boots free and finally pressed the last
of his clothing from his endless legs.

He came to her in a moment, wrapping her in
the wonderful strength of his arms, and suddenly Megan wondered if this was sin or if perhaps this was heaven itself. Justin eased her to
the bed and they lay side by side, saying nothing, unmoving.

She could feel the dynamic heat of his manhood, hard, swollen, and impatient, pressed up
against her thigh and she shivered. She knew
little of men, but had always equated the act of
intercourse with the hurried animal matings
she had seen in the barnyard. She hid her face
against his neck and shivered again, but now
his hands were moving, stroking her back in
long, fluid movements that pressed her even
more tightly up against him. His kisses were
confined to her shoulders and throat, although
his hands became more bold and roamed down

her spine to the curve of her buttocks, squeezing gently as they went.

In the warmth of his caresses, she relaxed, dropping her eyelids and luxuriating in his touch. His kisses dipped downward, smoothing between her breasts and over her belly. She felt his face brush her triangle of golden hair and then his lips were on her thigh, kissing, licking.

She squirmed beneath him. Never had she imagined it would be like this. Never had she thought she would burn where he touched her. But burn she did, with an ever-increasing flame that arched from her thighs to her breasts to her brain, filling her with electrifying excitement that left her panting and breathless.

When he pushed her thighs apart she did nothing to resist but instead wrapped her arms about his broad back, pulling him more tightly to her chest.

"Megan," he whispered throatily. "I can wait no longer," he apologized. "You're more than I can resist."

There was no pain when he entered, just a warm pressure, a satisfying fullness. She rocked her hips up against him, feeling the primitive call, but there was a barrier.

"Megan," he whispered again, but now his tone expressed a new emotion, an awed disbelief. "I didn't know," he rasped. "Why didn't you tell me?"

She had no idea what he meant. But neither did she care. She was poised on the edge of ecstasy, just an inch from euphoria and pushed on, impatient with his talk.

"Love," he moaned, trying to hold himself

from her, to spare her the pain, but his will was insufficient to deny her. The entrance to her core broke free.

Megan stiffened in his arms, surprised by the spark of pain, but it passed in a moment and now she was free to press up against him with all her trembling strength.

Their lovemaking was like the rhythm of the seasons, so natural it seemed to overtake them, raising them to a plateau that took them out of themselves and bound them together in dancing euphoria.

The tempo increased, building to a crescendo until it pushed them over the edge, and they tumbled into feather-soft satisfaction where they lay in each other's arms, breathing in unison.

Justin held her gently to him and in the moment before he found sleep, pushed her damp curls aside to kiss the sweetness of her neck.

Chapter 15

Justin woke to the quiet of predawn, the time when the world waits for the coming of the light. It was dark in the room. Megan lay beside him. He could sense her presence almost as easily as he could see her. She was sleeping. In the dimness, Justin could just make out her features. Her lips were slightly parted, her youthful face untroubled and wreathed by the splendid glory of her tousled hair.

Justin drew a deep breath, calming his emotions. How had it all come about? How was it that such an angel had landed in his bed? True, she was volatile and unpredictable, but somehow those qualities only seemed to enhance the uncontrollable attractiveness she had for him. Even now, with their lovemaking only hours old, her allure drew him closer.

With slow gentleness he touched a curling lock of her red-gold hair. It was soft, like her; fiery, like her; and it seemed to caress his hand much as she had caressed his body.

He drew his hand away quickly, realizing his weakness. He needed time to think, to be alone, and if he touched her again there'd be no turning back. If he felt the thrill of her body against his. . . .

Justin drew a shuddering breath and moved slowly away from the woman in his bed. Desire already raged within the deepest core of him and if he stayed, he'd not take time to sleep.

Megan woke late, opening her eyes slowly. It took her a minute to get her bearings as her gaze skimmed the room. But in a rush the memories came.

She bit her lip, staring at the empty spot beside her. He was gone. An ache came with that realization, a slow, burning pain somewhere deep inside. She closed her eyes to the feeling.

Footsteps sounded in the hall and she jerked her eyes open, pulling a blanket tightly to her chin. Her breath came with an effort, and her body felt painfully tight as she waited for him.

The door swung open. Daphne stood in the hallway, dressed in a bell-shaped satin gown, and looking as if she were ready for a promenade, rather than daily housework.

"You're still here." Her sticky smile was firmly in place. "I thought perhaps you'd be gone by now. But I see Mr. Stearns is being generous. "Or . . ." She scowled as if an unpleasant thought had occurred to her. "Perhaps he figured he'll get more money for you if he trains you for your duties." She paused, observing Megan's expression of horror. "I'm sorry, my dear, but it's best to be aware of the truth—to be prepared."

The door closed behind her.

Megan lay in silent terror. Daphne was probably right. Justin was using her for his own purposes.

Regardless of the intensity of her feelings last night, they had spoken no vows, she reminded herself. Indeed, not a single word of love or commitment.

How could she have allowed herself to be seduced by him? How could she have been so foolish? And where was Justin now? Had he gone to the sheriff? Perhaps he had gotten what he wanted from her and was now prepared to turn her in. But he had no proof of her crimes. Did he? And if all he had wanted from her was one night, why had he waited so long? He could have forced her days ago.

Megan squeezed her eyes tightly against the rumble of thoughts, trying to shut out the memory of his hands on her body. He had been so warm, so fine and strong beneath her touch. His muscles had felt like wondrous silken ropes, binding her with their magic.

She should leave. She knew it. But how could she leave now, after last night? She couldn't simply walk away. Perhaps he had used her, but perhaps not. Maybe he had felt some of the same magic she had.

She had to know the truth. Stepping shakily from the bed, Megan dressed quickly, donning one of the simple, worn gowns Agatha had loaned her, then slipped down the stairs, avoiding the kitchen.

There was no one in the barn. Hurrying around the corner of the building, Megan strode to the training corrals. Zeke was there, riding a tall chestnut in the circular pen while a young man stood brushing a bay tied to a hitching rail.

"Miss Megan," Zeke called cheerfully, drawing the chestnut to a gentle halt. "I been wonderin' if y' might come on out." He dismounted quickly to approach the rail at a bandy-legged gait.

Megan bit her lip, wishing now she had at least taken the time to fetch a bonnet. But Zeke already stood at the rail, smiling at her over the top timber.

"Don't you look purty this morning, Miss Megan. Bright as a flower. Justin, he said you might be comin' out. Asked if I'd dislike showin' y' around till he gets back. And I said, no-siree, I'd be happy as a pig in the mud. And I would, too." He nodded, delaying his speech for a breathless moment. "Can't think of nothin' I'd rather do than get t' know y'."

"Hey. Malici," Zeke yelled to the boy with the bay. "Come take Cinnamon here, will y'. I'm gonna be busy fer a spell."

Megan frowned slightly. "Is Justin gone then?"

Zeke studied her for a moment, then wrapping the gelding's reins about a rail, slid nimbly between them to stand beside her. "I'm afraid he is, miss," he said. "But that ain't no reason t' took so glum. He'll be back soon enough."

"Oh, I'm not glum," Megan disagreed quickly. Apparently her expression had shown too much. "I just needed to talk to him for a moment."

Zeke watched her again. His eyes were a deep, twinkling blue. Wrinkles radiated out from them in irregular furrows. There was humor in those eyes—and friendship, offered freely. "Y' don't need t' tell ol' Zeke nothin' more," he said easily. "I'm sorry if'n Justin went off without talkin' t' y' first but young men don't sometimes think proper when there's a purty girl involved. It was the same with me when I met my Sara."

"Where'd he go?" she asked softly, feeling foolish, despite the man's kind understanding.

" 'Fraid he didn't tell me that, miss. But he said he'd be back home again before we was done fer the day."

"Do you want me t' put Cinnamon away fer y', Pa?" asked the boy who had hurried toward them.

"This here's my son, Malici," beamed Zeke, with a pat for the boy's arm.

Megan stared at the skinny lad. He looked identical to several others she had met since her arrival at Free Winds and yet she was certain none of them had been named Malici.

"Hello Malici," she said and Zeke laughed aloud, reading the uncertainty on her face.

"It's a mite confusin' at first, miss. I admit they all look a tad alike. But you'll catch on soon enough," he assured her, then turned to the boy with a pause.

"Yup, put him up fer me, will y', boy. I'm gonna be showin' Miss Megan round."

Megan's morning was spent in the leisurely introduction to the broodmare herd. Zeke, it seemed, not only possessed extensive knowledge regarding each animal but also knew a great deal about the lineage of every horse kept on Free Winds property. And despite her preoccupation with her own thoughts, Megan found herself drawn into his stories and anecdotes, asking questions and expressing some of her own opinions on the care and breeding of horses.

"Well, Miss Megan," he said finally, "my stomach tells me it's high time fer dinner. I'd be right honored if you'd accompany me, seein's how Justin ain't made it back yet."

"Oh." Megan scowled, not wishing to encounter Mrs. Miller again, especially on her own turf. "I think I'll not have dinner today. I'm not very hungry."

"What's that?" Zeke asked, scrunching his weathered face at her in disbelief. "No dinner?" He was silent for a moment, studying her with an inscrutable expression. "You ain't letting ol' Miller buffalo y', are y', gal?"

"Mrs. Miller?" Megan asked, doing her best to sound surprised. "No. I . . ."

"Now, Miss Megan," Zeke interrupted, scolding lightly, despite her denial, "don't y' let that old bat under yer skin. She ain't worth the trouble."

Megan studied the toes of her worn shoes, biting her lip and trying to calm her thoughts. "What do you know about her, Zeke?" she asked, not meeting his eyes.

"Well, I know she's been a thorn t' me and my boys since the first day she set foot on Free Winds."

"How long ago was that?" Megan asked, finally lifting her face to his.

"Well now, it seems t' be a lifetime or so, but if the truth be told it ain't been more than three months, I 'spect. My missus used t' do the cookin' for us. But when she got further along with the baby, Justin said he couldn't have her workin' so hard no more. So he ups and puts the word out that he needs a cook. But we sure as shoot didn't expect no one like ol' Miller t' come along." He paused for a moment, looking toward the stone house on the hill.

"Why's that?" she asked, following his line of view and scowling a little.

"Well, it's like this here. Miller married herself a rich old gent some ten years ago and when he passed on, he left everything he owned to her. She don't need to work, and she never has neither, not till she hears 'bout Justin needin' help." Zeke canted his head, squinting his eyes slightly at Megan. "If you ask old Zeke," he said quietly, "I think she had a weddin' in mind."

"You mean her and—Justin?" Megan felt her heart sink. Mrs. Miller was a very handsome woman who possessed more poise and regal bearing than Megan believed she ever would. It was possible that Justin would be interested in her, would see her as his peer.

Zeke took Megan's elbow in one calloused hand, leading her toward the house. "I can't tell y' how happy I was to meet you, little lady," he said with feeling. "Now Justin's mama didn't raise no fool, but y' never can tell for certain. A man can get mighty lonesome without a woman t' care for him. And Mrs. Miller, she can act right sweet when Justin's about—and she ain't the homeliest thing I ever laid eyes on. Not that looks is the most important thing in the world. But a hot-blooded young fella like Justin might ferget that. He might ferget he needs him a woman who believes in what he believes in— a woman who believes in hard work, a woman who knows her horses. An Irish woman." He grinned. "Like you. A woman's whose beauty goes clean through to the bone." He smiled into Megan's paled face, then shook his head gently. "Yup, I ain't never been happier than when I seen that you'd stole Justin's heart."

Megan turned her eyes away. She'd stolen from Justin, all right, she thought. But she'd never gotten anywhere near his heart.

In the end Zeke nearly forced her to the dinner table, refusing to allow her to go without a meal. Megan sat between Zeke and his fifth son, who looked to be identical to the other two boys present, only smaller.

The meal seemed endless, for while Mrs. Miller said nothing to insult Megan, the woman failed to hold her tongue in front of the Willard family. Even little Malici, who Megan found utterly charming, was bitten by Miller's bitter words.

"Well, Miss Megan," Zeke said, immediately after taking his last forkful, "It's time I show y' the remainder of the place, I 'spect."

Megan smiled her gratitude, certain he realized her need to escape the house. "Yes," she said with an enthusiastic nod. "That'd be wonderful."

Rising nimbly, Zeke stepped behind Megan's chair, then lifted his gaze over her bright head to Miller's scowling countenance. "Ain't it nice to have Miss Megan here with us, Daphne?" he asked, using her given name and causing her to scowl even more darkly. "Ain't nothing like having a purty young face about, aye."

Hiding his smile, he pulled Megan's chair back. She rose to her feet, feeling Miller's anger like a tangible thing, and wondering how to break the tension.

"I'd best get a hat, Zeke," she said as his sons hurried from the house and Daphne's stifling presence.

"All right, miss," Zeke agreed, his eyes twinkling with mischief. "We sure wouldn't want y' t' burn your purty face." He spared a glance for Daphne, whose face looked to be burned to a dark hue of angry red. "I guess I'd best be goin' while I'm still healthy. But you come on out whenever you're ready."

It took only a minute for Megan to find her straw bonnet and hurry back down the stairs.

"That's right." Daphne stood at the bottom of the steps, smiling up at Megan with a syrupy expression. "You're wise to keep the sun off your face, dear. You don't want more of those unsightly freckles. Best to do what you can to maintain your position here—no matter how degrading that position is."

Megan scowled, but stopped herself from gazing down at the worn calico of her borrowed gown. "What makes you hate me so, Mrs. Miller?" she asked suddenly, refusing to lower her eyes from the other woman's.

"Hate you?" Daphne asked, forcing an astonished laugh. "I don't hate you, my dear. I just don't want you to get hurt any more than necessary. It would do no good for you to get to thinking you might be staying."

"And how do you know I won't be?" Megan whispered.

"Well"—Miller laughed—"everyone knows the Stearns are a very proper family. The old man would never allow his son to become involved with . . ." She let her eyes skim up and down Megan's stiff form. "Well, it's simply unheard of. I know about you from Robert Tolbert, you see. It seems the Stearns have been taken in by your innocent act, but when old man Stearns learns the whole story about your sordid past . . ." She shrugged. "Justin would be stricken from the will if he became serious about a woman like you."

Megan's mind spun. She needed to get away, to breath clean air. Pushing past Daphne, she hurried down the final steps, but Miller grabbed her arm, holding her sugary expression with tenacious spitefulness.

"If you're as smart as I think you are, Miss Welsh," she said, using the name Robert Tolbert had known her by, "I suggest you leave while you still can. You could probably find another man to take you in."

Megan didn't stop or turn, but faltered for a moment before hurrying from the house, her heart pounding madly in her chest.

Running to the barn, she willed back the tears. She didn't cry. She hadn't cried for over three years and she wasn't about to start now. "Oh! Zeke!" she gasped, running squarely into the man's chest as he exited the barn.

"Miss?" he questioned, seeing the strain on

Megan's face. "Why, you been cryin'," he said in dismay.

"I have not," Megan argued staunchly. "I never cry."

"Well, then you been mighty upset," corrected Zeke, his expression dark enough to show his concern. "What'd that old bat say to y'?"

"She . . ." How could she explain? What would he think of her if he knew of her past? She'd been such an idiot. She should never have agreed with her brother's plans. She should have spit in his eye and run for cover instead, but. . . . And she should not have lain with Justin. She was nothing more than a prostitute to him—a woman bought to warm his bed. "It's nothing, Zeke," she said weakly, trying to hide her pain. "I'd like to see the rest of the livestock, if you have time."

Zeke Willard scowled and Megan tried a tremulous smile, realizing the extent of his anger. "Do you know?" she asked softly, placing a gentle palm on his weathered hand, "I've never had a friend, before you." She paused, suddenly nervous with her own words. "I mean I . . ."

"I'm yer friend, miss," Zeke said softly, and for a moment Megan wondered if his eyes looked suspiciously moist. "Justin's been mighty good to me. Y' see, I've done some things I ain't real proud t' admit. But a body'll do most anything when he's up against the wall. Anyhow, Justin, he understood." Zeke paused, looking solemn. "I'd do most anything fer him, miss. I want only the best. And you . . ." He smiled. "You're the best—fer him anyhow.

And just the gal to keep him out of old Miller's clutches."

"No, Zeke, I'm—" Megan began but Zeke shushed her.

"There ain't much I know, miss, but I know folks. And Justin, he sees clear, too."

They stared at each other for a moment. "Well." Zeke cleared his throat noisily. "It ain't likely t' be light all day, and we got us a bunch of animals t' see yet."

In the next few hours Megan learned names, pedigrees, and endless lessons about horses and training. And even though she was truly interested in all the information Zeke shared so enthusiastically, she couldn't keep her gaze from straying to the road down which Justin would eventually come.

"Well, miss, I'm sorry t' leave you here alone," Zeke said, leaning forward on the hard seat of his rickety buckboard. "But with my missus so close to birthin' I can't hardly be stayin' no longer."

"I'd be happy to stay with you until Mr. Stearns returns," Daphne said, strolling from the house. "We'd have time for some girl talk."

Megan opened her mouth to respond, but Zeke was the one to object.

"I told Justin I'd bring y' here each morning and take y' home each night, Miller. And that's just what I aim t' do," he said, frowning darkly at the woman. "So get yerself in the buckboard."

Daphne's smile dripped with crystallized sugar. "Isn't that sweet? I think you've found yourself a protector, Megan. But then I suppose your kind has got to stick together. White trash . . ."

Two horses came down the lane. All faces turned to watch the arrival, but the sun was sinking toward the western horizon, making it impossible to identify the newcomers.

Seconds ticked away. Megan could feel her throat constrict, could feel her heart hammering, heavy and binding as sand. Had Justin brought the sheriff? Had he spent one night with her and decided to turn her in?

The horses passed from the sunlight into the shadows and Megan's jaw dropped. Voices rumbled around her but she failed to identify the words.

It was Justin! Beneath him his bay mare cantered easily and behind him, following with elegant grace, came Rainstorm.

Chapter 16

Justin watched Megan as he rode in. All day he had berated himself for leaving, thinking she might disappear while he was gone. But she hadn't left. The realization washed relief over him, taking the tension from his shoulders. The sinking sun shone under the curved brim of her aged bonnet, setting her hair to flame and lighting her small, oval face with a rosy glow. She was dressed in nothing more elegant than her faded calico and though Daphne Miller stood behind her wearing her usual finery, there was no comparison between the two.

Megan shone with her own light, holding his gaze like a candle in the darkness. Lifting the reins, he slowed the two animals to a trot, approaching the buckboard at a slower rate.

He could see the surprise on Megan's face. Her lips were slightly parted, her large, emerald eyes alive with an emotion he was almost afraid to read.

"Mr. Stearns," Daphne called, slipping forward as he pulled his mount to a halt. "We were worried about you. I'm so glad to see you're safely home."

Justin was pulled into Megan's eyes. They were as deep and mysterious as Sutter's Bay on a June morning.

"What a lovely horse," Daphne continued, holding her sugary tone. "He must be new."

There was something in Megan's eyes, something hidden and yet almost reachable, Justin thought. If the world would just give him time, he'd find it. He'd reach her, touch her soul.

"Justin," Daphne crooned more loudly, using his Christian name. Her patience was ebbing. "Did you just buy him?"

"What?" He scowled at the woman. Why was she jabbering at him? "Oh. No." His eyes returned to the emerald stare beneath the battered bonnet. "She's Megan's."

Zeke looked on, reading the signs with unfailing accuracy. "I'm leaving, Daphne," he said in a low tone, as if not wishing to disturb the couple's reunion. "Are you coming or no?"

"No," she snapped, momentarily forgetting herself as she too observed the intimacy.

"Have it your way," Zeke said, lifting the lines with a single nod. "But it looks to me like you'll be walking home cuz there sure ain't no one here's going to give you no ride after we's gone."

She glared at him and opened her mouth to disagree, but one more glance at Justin's preoccupied expression changed her mind. Lifting her elegant skirt with a sniff, she climbed unaided to the wooden platform. There was a clicking, a rattle of metal, and they rumbled off.

The world was quiet. Megan looked as young

and vulnerable as a doe, with her face tilted up toward Justin's.

"I found her at Teaker's Livery," he explained, searching for words and finding them with great difficulty. "It seemed a terrible shame, leaving her there." He watched Megan's eyes, to read her thoughts. "So I brought her here for you."

Justin lifted the mare's reins slightly and Megan stepped forward to take them.

"Rain." She whispered the name, touching the delicate face with a hand that trembled slightly.

The mare nickered low in her throat, a warm note of homecoming, and pushed her broad forehead against Megan's chest.

"Rain," she whispered again, her voice breaking.

There were tears welling in her eyes. Justin could see them plain as day, the sunset making them as bright and translucent as diamonds. And suddenly his journey seemed worth every mile, every minute of mind-numbing worry.

"Thank you." Megan's words were no more than a whisper, spoken against the mare's lowered head. She stroked the dappled neck and upon her faded sleeve a diamond teardrop fell.

"You're crying," Justin said in soft amazement.

"I don't cry." She sniffed, hiding her face against the gray's.

He stepped from the bay and touched her arm but she refused to lift her gaze.

"Why didn't you tell me what she meant to you, Megan? I could have gotten her sooner."

She was quiet. Evening settled in around

them in a hush of nightime noises. "I . . ." she began finally, "I'd like to give her to you."

He stood immobile, straining to hear her.

"I'd like you to take her, in payment for what we took from you on that first night."

Justin remained silent, watching her, and finally his gaze lifted to the mare as if he was considering her proposal. "She's a special animal, Megan. I see that. Too special for me to take."

"Please." Her eyes lifted abruptly. Her tone held a strange, parched note of pleading. "Take her."

Her eyes were as deep as the sky with a universe of emotions sheltered behind the emerald irises and for just a moment he was tempted to tell her the truth—that the hours without her had been endless. That the sky had lost its color. Life had lost its purpose.

"It seems a terrible thing, you offering the mare to another." He noted how the dappled head still rested against Megan's tender breasts. "She's used to having you about, Megan. It would be difficult for her to be parted from you after coming to cherish you."

It was the closest he came to voicing his own true feelings and the silence that followed emphasized his words.

"Thank you," she whispered finally.

He wanted to lift her into his arms, wanted to pull her against him and promise her love and happiness ever after. He cleared his throat. "It's been a hard ride. The horses are thirsty. I'll get them watered and fed."

"No," Megan said quickly, then bit her lip

nervously and dropped her eyes. "I'll see to Rain."

Justin watched her solemnly, loving her possessiveness. "All right."

She allowed the horses a small drink before pulling their muzzles from the trough and leading them side by side down the tree-lined lane.

"Why did you do it?"

"Maybe I wanted to know if you told the truth," Justin suggested, watching her in the dimness. "Maybe I thought there really was no mare to pay for the wager you lost."

She was quiet for a moment, then said, "Is that it?"

"No."

Megan stopped the mare, forgetting the purpose for her walk. "Then why?"

Even in the darkness Justin could see the intensity on her face, as if she struggled to understand him. "Maybe I wanted to see if you could cry."

"I don't cry."

He smiled slowly, lifting a corner of his sensual mouth and against his will, raised a hand to touch her cheek. "Maybe I needed your gratitude," he suggested softly.

She stared at him. Her lips parted as if to say something, but then she turned, leading the mare back to the barn.

Justin watched her go. She was so unpredictable, so changing. How would he ever understand her when she kept hiding behind her fear? Scowling into the darkness, he continued down the road.

* * *

His room was empty when he entered it. Where was she? For a moment panic struck him but he pushed it back, hurrying down the hall and into the smaller bedchamber.

She was there, a small lump beneath the light covers.

"Megan." He squatted beside the bed, his face even with hers, and her eyes opened.

There was no wariness, no sleepiness. He touched her face with his fingertips, nearly shivering at the feel of her skin.

"Why didn't you tell me, Megan?" he whispered.

She stared at him, not understanding.

"Why didn't you tell me you were a virgin?"

He could hear her intake of breath and for a moment thought she might draw back behind the curtain of her eyes. But she didn't.

"I—couldn't . . . it didn't seem quite . . . proper."

He stared at her, confounded for a moment, and then chuckled. "You could have tried."

Her face turned a lovely shade of pink and he watched her, surveying her mood.

"It was an idiotic bet," he said seriously.

She made no response.

"But I don't regret it," he added softly. "Idiotic or not, it was the best wager I ever made."

"I'm sorry I hurt Cherry," she whispered, lost in his eyes.

"She'll heal well, Little One," Justin breathed, "and from today on you'll ride your own mare—if you like."

Megan lowered her eyes. "She should be yours," she whispered.

"Why?" He caressed her cheek tenderly and she drew her breath between her teeth, startled by his touch.

"It seems," she said quietly, "that I'm to blame for the loss of your stallion."

"But look what you've given me." Justin stared at her. How could he ever have wished to punish her? She was so delectable, so small and lovely and defenseless.

"What I've given you?" she whispered.

"Yourself," Justin answered, letting her fingers gently sweep the tender satin of her throat. "You've given me yourself, love."

Their eyes met—hers wide and innocent, his warm and deep.

"You truly don't know your value, do you, Megan?" he mused. "You've no idea what a man would give to touch your beauty."

He kissed her with a tenderness that made her shiver. "I myself would give most anything," he whispered. "For this." He touched her cheek, then kissed that spot. "Or this." His fingertips burned a trail down her throat and kisses followed, scorching that trail to cinders. "Or this." His touch eased down, caressing the taut peak of one breast and Megan gasped, pressing toward him.

"Justin!" His name escaped her as little more than a savage moan and now Justin shivered, pulling her closer, wrapping her in his arms.

"Let us share the treasure of your person," he murmured huskily.

She did nothing to resist as his fingers tugged open the ties that held her night rail. Hot kisses torched her throat, her chest. She arched nearer the flame, clasping him in her arms but the gown was a traitorous nuisance, inhibiting their pleasure and Justin reached for the hem, smoothing it over her rounded buttocks and finally pulling it from her completely.

She lay naked and shivering beneath him and he leaned back for a moment, made breathless by her beauty.

"Priceless," he said and she was lost, knowing she shouldn't, knowing it was wrong, yet aching for the pleasure he had taught her.

She could feel the hard length of his desire pressed against her and failed to find adequate reason to resist.

"I . . ." She lifted her eyes to his, her face hot, her body goosefleshed. "I . . ." she said again, then reached out to clasp his shirt front in one small hand. "What are we waiting for?" she breathed.

Chapter 17

Megan felt him leave the bed. It was early yet, just before dawn, and she didn't open her eyes. She couldn't. The feelings were too fresh, too intense and raw. She could still feel the touch of his hands, could sense his presence as easily as she might reach out and touch him with her fingers.

She had given herself to him. She should be ashamed. What Daphne had said was true. She should leave while she could. But . . . there was no shame. In fact, there was a lightness within her that defied explanation.

She opened her eyes slowly, watching him in the dimness. He moved with the grace of a hunting beast, as quiet and smooth as a large cat. Hair partly covered her face and she hid behind it, watching without being watched as he searched for his clothes in the darkness. There was no way to distinguish his every feature, but even the shape of him seemed to touch her within, somehow quickening her senses.

He found his shirt and soundlessly pushed his heavy arms through the sleeves, then moved to the bed to search beneath the tick for his pants. His shirt hung open, baring the hard, mounded muscles of his chest as he bent double. Megan smiled in the dimness.

He was a thing of beauty. Like a tree or a cloud, or a stallion. That was it. He reminded her of a stallion, a dark, heavy-maned animal that defied the world with its strength and self-worth.

Justin straightened and Megan snapped her eyes closed. He stood motionless beside the bed and feeling his gaze upon her she wondered what he was thinking. He moved from the bedside and she opened her eyes again, watching as he pulled his pants over the endless mass of his legs.

It was only a few moments longer before he left. In the darkness Megan took his pillow from its spot beside her and pulled it to her body, cradling it against her naked breasts and falling back into the feather-soft folds of sleep.

She awoke to Daphne's offensive presence once again.

"Sleeping alone so soon, Megan?" she crooned.

Megan scowled at her. Her dreams had been tender and refreshing, making Daphne seem even more abrasive.

"What do you want?"

"I just wanted to see if there was anything I could do to help, my dear. There's no need for you to be so defensive."

"Help me with what?" She felt vulnerable and naked, both of which she was.

"Help you prepare to leave."

Megan's breath stopped.

"Oh dear!" Daphne said, shaking her head. "He didn't tell you?"

"Tell me what?"

"About selling you to Robert Tolbert. Surely you know Robert went to Manor Royal to negotiate the sale." She shrugged. "I thought you were bright enough to figure it out. Mr. Stearns simply needed a few days to ..." Daphne smirked, dropping her eyes to the sheet Megan clutched to her breasts. "To get to sample your wares before letting you go. I'm so sorry. He asked me to pack your things."

Cold fear gripped Megan's heart.

He had spoken of her worth—her value. But she hadn't thought. ... Dear Mother of God! She had wanted to believe he cared for her, not that he intended to sell her like so much chattel.

"Robert will be here shortly," Daphne said. "You'll want to make yourself presentable. He's not so tolerant as Justin. But he's not so terrible although a bit rough—with his slaves."

Megan's mouth opened in soundless misery.

"Or ..." Daphne's voice lowered. "You could leave—while you still can. Justin's gone. There's time."

Megan's world crumbled. The door closed behind Daphne, but she failed to notice.

What could she do?

There were no options. She'd leave. Immediately! It may be her only chance.

Rainstorm waited in a small paddock and nickered a greeting. From the corner of her eye Megan saw Zeke in the distance and and mur-

mured a quick, silent prayer that he wouldn't
see her. Something wet and burning bleared her
vision. Her hands shook.

It took only a moment to bridle Rain. She
swung to the bare, dappled back. With a touch
of her heel the mare turned toward the door.

"Megan!" Justin stood in the doorway, his
mount behind him. "Where are you going?"

Suddenly Megan's fear dissipated, the sight of
him driving it away to be replaced by—rage!
Sell her, would he? She'd die first! And so
would he! "Get out of my way," she ordered.
Scattered tendrils of her tousled hair obscured
her view, but she was certain she could hit him
square on if he remained where he stood.

"Megan, what's wrong?" he questioned, taking a step forward.

"Move!" she shouted. "Unless you wish to die
young."

Justin scowled his confusion. He'd planned a
visit with the sheriff, for he'd awakened to the
petrifying fear of losing her. What if someone
actually believed she was part Negroid and insisted she be enslaved? It had happened to others and would be no one's fault but his. There
was no time to waste to clear up the mess. But
half a mile down the road he'd decided it would
be best to take Megan along. Her fair complexion would be the most convincing evidence of
her own heritage. Now, however, her face was
dark with anger.

"What's the trouble?" he asked. "Get down
from that horse."

"Not if you paid me in blood," she retorted in
a low, feline growl.

Placing his hands on his hips, Justin tried to puzzle out this new mystery. "Blast it all, woman. What's come over you? You seemed content last night."

"Last night?" she rasped out, tossing her head to clear the wild, gold strands from her vision. "Last night I didn't realize you deserved to die by slow increments."

"What's come over you?" Justin asked, scowling as Rainstorm's fidgeting became more animated. "Get down off that horse before you get yourself killed."

"Get out of my way," she warned.

"Get off that horse."

"No!"

"Then I'll take you off."

"Take one step closer and they'll have to dig you up with a spade."

"Blast!" he said, cautiously stepping into the dimness of the barn.

"Stay back."

"I'm taking you off."

Megan watched him cautiously as he neared. She had to get away. There was no other exit, but the one he guarded. With a momentary hesitation, she put her heels to the mare's sides.

Rainstorm took the cue like a well-trained racehorse and plunged forward, but Justin held his position. Megan tensed, leaning toward the gray's neck, ready for the impact.

But none came. He waited until the last moment, then, leaping to the side, Justin reached out and grabbed Megan's arm in a bulldog grip.

Rainstorm skidded to a halt. Megan fought with all her might, trying to wrestle her arm from his grasp, but she was no longer a moving target and Justin had the great advantage of strength.

"Let me go!" she shrieked.

"Release the reins," Justin said, fighting for a grip on her waist.

She wriggled in his hands, kicking wildly. He held on with tenacious strength but Rainstorm shuffled nervously sideways, knocking him off balance.

"Let go," Megan screeched, fighting to remain astride. But it was already too late and she was falling.

She landed squarely on his chest, her small sharp shoulder knocking the wind from his lungs. She heard the whoosh of his air and taking no time for apologies, popped to her feet. She was running before he knew what hit him.

Justin grimaced with pain, then swiping the swirling stars from his numbed brain, pushed himself to his feet with a growl. Blast her and her infernal temper.

It took less than twenty yards for him to overtake her, but when he did their landing was less than gentle.

"Leave me be," she gasped, scrambling to escape on all fours, and kicking at him with her pistoning feet.

"Damn it, Megan," he swore, losing his grip as one small foot hit his nose dead center.

She was up again, but he caught at her dragging hem and pulled her back down. He was on top of her in a second, covering her small body with his.

They lay like mating chickens in the dirt, too

breathless to move or speak, but Justin finally straddled her, supporting his weight on his knees and turning her over to face him. Her eyes spit at him from her mud-streaked face while her fingers formed claws, pinned to the ground by the overwhelming strength of his hands.

Vaguely, he was aware of Zeke and his offspring, gaping from a safe distance, but he had no time to explain.

Last night he'd thought her small and defenseless. Would he never learn? "What's this all about, you little she-devil?"

"As if you didn't know!"

"I don't know!"

"Huh!"

"Blast it all, Megan. I spent all yesterday riding my tail off to retrieve your mare. I don't need a raving lunatic to make me think my time was wasted."

She glared at him through her scattered hair. "You're the lunatic," she said, "if you think I'm going to wait around for you to.... Ohhh!" she growled, wrestling to be free.

Justin raised his head slightly, scowling at her as if she truly had lost her mind. "Waiting for me to what?"

Megan bucked beneath him, incensed by his feigned naivetè, and almost managing to dislodge him.

"Damn it!" He scrambled to keep his balance atop her. "Lie still," he ordered, settling himself more firmly above her. "You seemed happy last night."

She glared at him in silence.

"Tell me what set you off."

More silence.

"A-hum." Old Zeke cleared his throat nervously, then ventured a guess. "I think it could be Mrs. Miller upset her a mite."

"Mrs. Miller?" Justin questioned, his eyes not leaving Megan's steaming face. "What's she got to do with it?"

"She told me!" Megan growled.

Justin shook his head slowly. How had life become so complicated? He was a simple man. Was it too much to wish to live out his days without being murdered for reasons he couldn't even fathom?

He was tired. Blast, he was tired. The strain couldn't be good for him. He felt himself age each time Megan scowled. Contemplating death did that to a man. "If I let you up, will you promise not to run off?"

"No!"

"God damn it, Megan, I don't mind a little dispute now and then," he said quietly, "but do we have to provide daily entertainment for the entire county?"

It seemed to take a moment for her to become aware of the situation. It was entirely possible, Justin thought, that her rage had made her oblivious to their audience, who stood not twenty feet away.

"Let me up," she said, her tone muted, her face red.

"You won't . . ."

"I won't run."

Justin eased himself slowly to his feet, not entirely certain he could trust her. She followed him slowly, keeping her eyes on the ground.

"Let's go to the house and talk," he suggested.

"No!"

"Blast it, Megan, you . . ." he began but could think of nothing to say to complete his sentence. "All right then. Will you talk in the barn?"

She nodded once and he mentally breathed a sigh of relief. Glancing once at Zeke's wide-eyed expression, he turned his back and followed her there.

Inside the cool of the stable Justin directed her to the tack room where two narrow benches were aligned against the rough hewn walls. He motioned her to a seat next to a row of saddles, but she ignored him and stood stiff and sullen beside the door.

There seemed no easy way to figure his course and so Justin stared at her for a moment, wanting to read her mind. "What happened, Megan?" he asked simply.

"Nothing." Her answer was quick and childish and for one lovely moment Justin considered ringing her neck.

"Something happened," he tried again, gritting his teeth and searching for patience. "What was it? Did Mrs. Miller say something to offend you?"

Her gaze met his with burning ferocity. It took no scholar to see he had hit the mark.

"What'd she say?"

"The truth."

Life would be so much simpler if he could strangle her, or drown her in the sea. Now there was an attractive option. He could drown her. Who would know?

"And what is the truth?" he asked, stuffing his scandalous thoughts into the deepest recesses of his mind.

"What?" she asked sarcastically, her face lifting abruptly to his. "You don't know the truth?" She laughed, her muddied face looking rather comical above the filthy calico gown. "Forgive me, but it's rather difficult to believe you forgot your own intentions. Especially since your plan should be so lucrative."

"Lucrative?" he asked wearily. "What are you talking about?"

"Don't act stupid with me," she hissed. "I know you're not."

How she managed to make the statement sound insulting he would never be certain. "Then humor me," he suggested. "Just give me a hint."

"I'm talking about . . ." She found she could not even verbalize the possibility of being sold. It was too degrading. "Robert Tolbert!" Megan snarled, jerking her head toward the house.

"Tolbert?" Justin immediately stiffened with jealousy and uncertainty. "What about Tolbert?"

"Deny you met with him at Manor Royal!" she challenged.

"How did you know that?" When had she seen Tolbert? Perhaps they'd had a private tryst while he'd been in Charleston.

"You admit it then!" she shrieked, but Justin's own anger was heated now.

"How did you know?" He gripped her arms.

"What does it matter?" she railed.

"How?" he bellowed, enraged by the thought of her with another man and tightening his grip on her arms.

"*She* told me," Megan roared back.

"She? Miller?" he asked in amazement.

"Aren't you the smart one? Who else would you have told?"

"You stay here!" He shook her. "Do you hear?"

"No!"

"Blast and incinerate it! You will stay," he roared.

They glared at each other, each ready and eager to tear the other limb from limb, but sense finally dawned on Justin. He had only one choice.

"Very well then," he stated through stiff lips. "Have it your way."

He turned his back and stalked out, slamming the tack room door behind him. From outside the room Megan heard a cacophony of banging, followed by the gravelly sound of something heavy being dragged before the thick portal.

He spoke no word, but she could imagine him standing, hands on hips to survey his handiwork with a smug expression. The sound of footsteps came finally and she knew he was retreating. Going where?

Pivoting about, Megan hurried to the room's single window. He was going to the house. His broad back was straight, his strides long.

This was her chance to escape! With a feral snarl, she spun stiffly on her heel to attack the door.

It was two inches thick, made of rough-cut

plank and hammered, iron hinges. No hope there. She kicked the offensive portal, then turned again, her gaze flitting about the narrow space. No other way out.

Think, think, Megan told herself, her narrowed gaze skimming the room again. It was impossible to tell how long he'd leave her alone, but one thing was certain, she had no intention of being there when he returned.

Or did she? Suddenly her eyes fell to the large, wooden box that occupied one corner. She sprang to the thing, wrestled up the metal hasp and stared inside.

Horse liniment! She lifted the narrow bottle reverently to her chest and smiled. God was gracious. He had forgiven her past transgressions and was about to send her home.

Chapter 18

"Megan," Justin called. His tone was considerably softer than it had been earlier. His temper had cooled, allowing guilt to congeal somewhere in the recesses of his molding conscience. He shouldn't have left her so long in the small, airless tack room, but his options had seemed limited. Dragging away the huge box he had placed before the door, he called again, "Megan."

There was no answer and for a moment panic surfaced. He calmed himself quickly, however, almost chuckling at his own gullibility. She was probably hiding behind the door, he reasoned, ready to carve him into bite-sized morsels with a hoof-knife.

Opening the door cautiously, he peered inside.

Megan lay sprawled upon the cool dirt of the floor. Her face, turned toward the ceiling, was damp with perspiration, as was her hair, which was pushed back from her neck and lay in a tangled heap beside her.

Blast it to hell! Justin paused for a moment. She was an actress, he reminded himself, a deceiver. And yet he hurried across the floor, his face set in deep lines of worry.

"Megan," he said gruffly, squatting beside her and half-expecting to be stabbed through the heart with some impromptu instrument of death.

Her eyes opened groggily and seemed to swim a bit in her head, but the sight of him revived her somewhat. "Leave me be," she ordered, pushing herself to a sitting position with great difficulty. "Don't touch me." Her words were slurred.

"Megan." He placed a hand to her forehead. It was sticky with mud and sweat and he scowled his guilt. "I'll get you out of here." The place was an oven. He'd been gone longer than he'd planned and had failed to realize how hot the room would become in his absence. He pushed his arms beneath her, but she pressed at him again, irritated by his presence.

"Leave me be, I said," she mumbled.

He scowled at her, ignoring her words and gathering her to his chest. Outside the breeze touched their faces. Megan lay as limp as a rag doll in his arms.

She murmured something incoherent and he leaned his head closer, trying to understand her words.

"Let me go," she breathed and he scowled again, uncertainty gripping him with shaking hands.

"I'll take you to the house. Get you out of these clothes." He watched her as he said the words, awaiting a reaction.

"Don't you dare." Her response was no more than a pathetic whisper.

Good God, perhaps she truly was too ill and too weak to become incensed by the removal of her clothes. The door to his home slammed against the wall and once again he ascended the stairs by twos.

He lay her on his own bed, then backed away a step, scowling into her face.

"You can drop the act now, woman," he said. "I sent Mrs. Miller home with the Willards. We're all alone. There's no one to appreciate your fine performance."

"I won't stay here with you," she gasped, standing shakily. "I won't be your whore."

"Get back on that bed," Justin said, giving her a gentle shove that toppled her onto the coverlet. "You're overheated and you're going to stay put until I tell you to leave."

"No, I'm not," she murmured, but her strength seemed insufficient to move her from a seated position and she remained as she was, only her eyes sparking defiance.

"Tarnation, Megan," he snapped angrily. "I don't pretend to know if you're acting or not, but one thing's certain. You'll stay here until I tell you to leave. Is that clear?"

She said nothing and for a moment he wondered if she might faint.

"I'm going to get some water," he said in a gravelly tone. "You dare leave and I'd catch you, tie you to the bedpost with harness leather, and keep you here till your ribs stick out like bristles on a boar. Do you hear me?"

No response came. Her eyes had closed sometime during his harangue and he turned away with a curse, hurrying down the stairs to the well.

Megan opened her eyes with a snap. He was gone! She'd done her best acting ever. Jerking up her skirt, she grasped the neck of the small liniment bottle and pulled it from her pantalettes. What if he'd undressed her? Pulling the cork from the bottle, she sniffed the astringent odor, then shuddered. It was a horrid situation, but her choices were few.

Splashing the liniment into her hand, she rubbed it roughly onto her face, letting it dribble down her neck and onto the upper portions of her chest. Pulling up the worn sleeves of the calico gown, she dribbled the bracer onto her arms. The hairs along her forearms raised at the feel of the cool liquid and she wrinkled her nose, shivering at the memory of her childhood experience with the stuff. But freedom was well worth the misery.

She capped the bottle with trembling hands, then, jamming the thing beneath the bed, scrambled back onto the mattress to resume her former position.

Justin entered less than a full minute later, his steps hurried, his expression dark. "I brought water," he said, entering with the same bucket he had carried only two days before. "Are you feeling any better?" He approached the bed and stopped abruptly. Well water splashed down the front of his pants legs. "Megan," he said hoarsely. "What happened?"

Welts covered her face, spreading up from her chest in an awful tide of red, bumpy flesh that threatened to rise above the tip of her upturned nose. She stared at the ceiling with wide, seemingly sightless eyes, her head pressed back into the pillow, her arms stretched out on her sides in immobilized pain. Only her fingers moved now and then, clawing desperately at the blankets. Her mouth was slightly open and now and then she would draw a tortured, rasping breath.

"Megan," he said desperately, still holding the bucket in a deadly grip. He had seen enough sickness, had felt it himself. "I'll get you to a doctor." Finally realizing there was no time to waste, he splashed the bucket to the floor and reached for her.

Megan's scream was like that of a tortured animal's and he jerked his arms back. "It hurts," he deduced wildly, his mind spinning for ideas. "It hurts when I touch you. Where does it hurt, Megan? Where?"

There was no answer, only an increase in her awful gasping for breath. He couldn't chance touching her again. He'd have to leave her there and pray she'd survive until he returned.

"I'll get help." He reached for her hand. It was burning hot and bumpy. "I'm sorry." He leaned over the bed, staring at her terrible agonized countenance. "I'm sorry for everything. Hold on." His voice sounded choked with emotion. "Don't die. Don't die. I'll be back soon. Hold on." He turned, running from the room with long strides.

Was he gone? Megan lay as stiff as a board upon the bed, her hands still forming claws, only moving her eyes sideways to study the door. She waited, grinding her teeth and count-

ing backward from one hundred to keep from
rubbing the skin from her body. Hoofbeats
sounded in the yard below. She sprang from the
bed like a hare before hounds, racing across the
floor to peer from the window.

Justin was swinging onto Rum's back. There
wasn't a heartbeat of hesitation, not a moment
of delay. He leaned over the black mane, setting
his heels to the animal's sides. And they were
off, racing down the road toward the south.

Megan screeched a quiet yelp of victory. He
was gone! And soon she would be too. There
was nothing she needed but Rain. She thun-
dered down the stairs, scratching her arm with
craven zeal. Outside, the sun beat down upon
her tortured flesh, stinging with its heat. But
Megan ignored the agony and lifting her skirt
high, sprinted across the yard.

There was no time to waste, but the rain barrel stood to the side of the barn. It was too
tempting to resist. She raced to it, then dipped
her raging arms into liquid heaven. She closed
her eyes to the ecstasy and then, placing her
hands on the barrel's rim, thrust her head into
the water in a frenzied attempt to ease the pain
there.

She came up in a moment, swinging her
soaked hair onto her back. Water dripped from
her enflamed face in rivulets. She blinked it
away.

It was time to go. There was no way of knowing how soon he'd be back. Running down the
aisle of stalls, she searched for her mare.

She wasn't there. Megan's panicked gaze
swept the barn again, but no dappled head

peered over a door. Racing outside, she searched the paddocks.

The gray stood not far out, grazing in a pasture of mares. Megan's heart thumped heavily with relief. In a moment Rain was through the gate. There was no time for a saddle but she found a bridle in a moment. Slipping the bit into Rain's mouth, Megan pushed the slipper-shaped ears beneath the headstall and turned to leave.

"Feeling better, Megan?" Justin stood in the doorway, big as life.

"No!" She shrieked the word at him.

"Oh yes," he argued gently. "Here we are again."

"Leave me be," she screamed, but he only smiled, his expression as cold as the devil's.

"Not on your life, Little One." He took a step forward, bringing his mount with him. "You know how I knew?"

She didn't answer, but backed away, bumping into Rain's shoulder.

"It was the smell of the liniment." He nodded. "It took me a few minutes but then I remembered. When I was a boy we put the stuff on a neighbor's pig. It pimpled up just like you."

"Are you comparing me to a pig?" she snarled.

Her hair was snarled into a tangled rat's nest and hung in a sodden mass about her face. And her face ... it was nearly unrecognizable, blotched and tortured like sun-blistered paint. Her eyes were bloodshot and seemed to have sunk into her face as the edema overtook her sockets. Her borrowed, calico gown was filthy and the buttons had not been correctly aligned so that the entire garment hung askew.

"Yes," he answered finally. "Actually, a pig doesn't seem an unlikely comparison."

"How dare you?" she hissed in outrage, not realizing the fantastic extent of her ugliness.

"It's not difficult, really. Put the mare away and come with me."

"You'll have to kill me first."

Justin shook his head slowly. "Don't tempt me with your melodramatics. It just so happens I've thought of ten very entertaining ways to do just that and it wouldn't take much to convince me to employ any one of them."

"Try it," she sneered.

He nearly rolled his eyes toward the ceiling. The girl had a wish to die.

"If you don't put that horse away and get your fanny over here, I swear, Megan, I'll lift your skirt and give you the paddling you've deserved for too long."

"You wouldn't dare."

He took a step forward. Megan stepped back, crowding Rainstorm behind her.

"Put her away, Megan," he warned.

She scratched frantically at one arm, eyeing him, and then, to his utter amazement, she sent the mare into a stall and pushed the door behind her.

He must look even meaner than he felt, Justin deduced dryly. Putting the stallion in the opposite stall, he swung the door closed and crossed the aisle.

Megan stood staring at him with blood-streaked eyes. Her hair was drying somewhat and frizzed out from her head in wild disarray.

"You look like hell," he said matter-of-factly. "Come on." Taking one swollen hand, he tugged her along behind him.

"Where?" she snapped.

He didn't answer.

Behind the house flowed a stream and Justin pulled her in that direction until they stood on the pebbly bank.

"Take your clothes off."

"I beg your pardon," she said haughtily, raising her brows at him like an unthroned toad princess.

"Take your clothes off, woman, and get in the water before that stuff blisters you to the bone."

"It won't blister," she countered crossly. "I tried it when I was a child and it didn't then."

"You're still a child," he countered wearily. "And if you think I want to take a chance on living with a bumpy-faced hag, you're sadly mistaken. Now take off your clothes." He still held her wrist and backed up his words with a gentle jerk.

"T——turn your back."

"You jest," he said.

They stared at each other. A bluejay screeched from the top of an oak tree and two horses lifted their heads to stare across the fence at such silly human antics.

"I can't undress in front of you," she stumbled, honestly feeling she could not.

It was impossible to tell if she was blushing, Justin thought, for the horrid rash muffled all expression.

"Then I'll help you." He was behind her before she could speak, and although she jerked at his touch, his fingers slipped the buttons from their mismatched loops with ease. He stepped before her to tug at a sleeve and she winced as the fabric scraped her arm.

Justin lifted his gaze to her face, scowled, then pulled more gently, guiding the garment from her body. She stood in shortened pantalettes and her frilly chemise. "Now take off the rest."

Her mistreated arms crossed her chest, trying to hide her more private parts from him. She moved her mouth to speak but no words came.

Justin stared at her. Where on God's earth had the little she-devil fled to? One moment she was screaming like a banshee and the next she was too meek to speak. Who could figure such a woman?

"Oh, very well then," he said. "Leave them on. Just get in the water."

He didn't have to tell her twice. The feather-soft waves felt heavenly against her abused flesh. She crawled in on hands and knees, letting it soothe her aching arms.

"Here." He squatted beside her, allowing water to flow halfway up the fine leather of his boots. "Let me wash your face." He scooped liquid coolness into his hands, splashing it against her face, and she sat back on her heels, closing her eyes. "We need a cloth." He glanced around, looking for an answer, scowled, then set his fingers to the buttons of his own shirt.

"Wh——what are you doing?" Her eyes hade snapped open and she stared at him distrustfully.

"I'm taking off my shirt," he said gruffly, as if even she should be able to determine that much. Pulling the tail of the garment from his waistband, he slipped his arms gracefully from the sleeves.

They were beautiful arms with muscles that bunched and flexed with each movement he made. Megan bit her lip and for the first time was aware of the awful condition of her face.

He immersed the shirt in the sparkling water, then pulled the garment out to apply it to her cheek. It felt achingly wonderful and she sat without moving, letting her eyes rest on the sloping glory of his dark chest. It was smooth and broad and for one agonizing moment she was tempted to touch it where his pectorals met in the center of his being.

"Feeling better?" His voice had lost some gruffness and she nodded.

Justin drew a deep breath, watching her face. The awful rash was already receding, he realized with relief. "What did Miller say to you?" he questioned softly.

It had taken several minutes, but Justin's words now dawned on her. He said he didn't care to live with a bumpy faced hag. Did that mean he wasn't selling her? Megan tried to think. But the ache of the rash obscured reason. "What . . ." she said softly.

"What did she say to you?"

Megan looked up at him with tortured eyes and he returned her gaze with silent thoughtfulness. Below her welted throat the high portions of her breasts were visible above her chemise. It seemed impossible that the sight of her thus could heat his blood and yet.... He held his gaze steady on her face, trying to concentrate on their words or her welts, on anything that would keep his desire at bay.

"She says you've hated her from the first day you came to Free Winds," he admitted gently. "She denies saying anything to upset you."

Megan was silent. Her eyes dropped to the glistening water as it hurried across the shining pebbles. "She said ..." Megan closed her eyes, feeling nauseous. "She said you were selling me—to Robert Tolbert."

Justin's breath rasped through his teeth and he stared at her in silence. Was she lying? Was she staging an excuse for her frenzied attempt to escape?

"Why would she say that?" he asked, narrowing his eyes and thinking aloud.

"Is it true?" she whispered, unable to raise her eyes, but suddenly her arms were clasped in Justin's tight grip and he pulled her toward him.

"What do you think, Megan? You think I'm the kind of man to take your virginity then sell you down the road?"

Megan stared at him in mute horror.

"Do you?" he stormed, shaking her slightly.

"I don't know," she whispered fearfully. A tear escaped, rolling down her tortured cheek.

Justin's anger dissolved. Pulling her to him, he wrapped her in his arms, holding her to his chest. "I don't know if you're lying, Megan." His own eyes were closed, his body taut against hers. "I don't know. But I swear to you, I'd never attempt something so awful as to sell you to another."

Megan sat numb and aching in the water. She believed him. God help her, but she did. And if he were being honest that meant. . . .

"Sell you?" He shook his head, pushing her away from him and catching her eyes with his own, his face somber and strained. "I haven't the strength to let you go, Megan. Much less the strength to send you away."

Megan's head felt light and her heart ached—symptoms she hadn't experienced during her last bout with the liniment. Symptoms of his words, of his nearness. He must be telling the truth, she reasoned joyously. He must be. And therefore Daphne lied. And if Daphne lied it was for the express purpose of having Justin for herself.

Somewhere in Megan's being a primitive possessiveness stirred.

Daphne lied, she thought soberly. And Daphne would pay.

Chapter 19

Megan stalked the length of her room, bit her hand, stared from the window, then stalked again.

It had been two days since Justin had sent Thomas Stearns an invitation to see Magic's colt. Zeke's seventh son, Jeremiah, had taken the message and returned with the news that Justin's father would be coming on Thursday.

It was Thursday now. Megan looked again from the window, watching as Daphne lifted her fine skirts along with her patrician nose and climbed onto the irregular floor of Zeke's old buckboard. They were going home. Megan licked her lips nervously, reviewing her scheme and smoothing the skirt of her finest borrowed gown.

Swallowing her pride, she had asked for Zeke's help. And Zeke, true to their quickly formed friendship, had agreed with enthusiasm. She'd found Justin's note to his father on his desk, and with only a spark of guilt, had practiced forging his handwriting. She'd penned a note to Daphne, signed Justin's name, and placed it carefully in the large, copper pan the woman used daily.

All day Megan had worried that this might be the one day the woman neglected to use that pot, but God had once again been merciful. She *had* used that pot and so must have found the note. She must have.

Biting her lip, Megan scowled at the scene below her. If Daphne had received the note she certainly gave no indication, but then, she was no fool. Perhaps she knew the handwriting was not from Justin; perhaps she was suspicious. Perhaps she would be too proud to cooperate. But, Megan thought, recalling Daphne's nasty attempts to force Megan to leave—perhaps not.

Minutes passed with painful slowness. The buckboard moved from beneath the shadow of the elms, traveling down the road and out of sight. The door opened beneath her, and Megan jumped at the sound. Justin was in for supper.

She paced again. She had barely seen him in the past two days, had carefully avoided him during the day, and each evening had ferreted herself away in the small bedchamber that adjoined his.

There was no lock on the door. She'd lain awake for hours wondering what she'd do if he came, then lain awake longer trying not to think about what she'd do if he didn't.

How long would it be before their guest arrived? It would be dark before long.

Time passed and Megan paced, watching the window for the first signs of darkness and chanting a continuous litany of silent prayers as she stalked the room. It seemed an eternity before she heard hoofbeats.

Two horses stood beneath the ancient elm and she scowled as she recognized Tom and Sonny Stearns.

Megan stared from the window, watching as both men dismounted and tied their horses to the short rail beside the elm. The elder Stearns had an air of rigid propriety to him, a stiff formality that his sons had not inherited. And yet there were many similarities between Justin and his father. Tom was a big man, like Justin. Strong-willed, attractive, and endlessly proud—like Justin. Megan noted how he walked. There was a resemblance there also, a sure, self-confident ease. She bit her lip. Justin would age like that, she thought, and suddenly found herself wondering what it would be like to grow old with him—to bear his children. . . . But she was being foolish. They were held apart by heritage and class. She should leave—should escape while she could. But to leave him to another woman. . . .

Jealousy roiled within her. She clenched her fists and jerked away from the window. What in the name of Saint Patrick was she thinking? How could she care about him after all they'd been through? The man had humiliated, threatened, and bullied her. He had pretended to be insane, had accused her of heinous crimes, and had locked her up. Thus far it had hardly been a flawless relationship. Still there was the thought of his touch, of his smile, of the deep timbre of his voice in the morning. She couldn't leave. Not yet.

But neither could she accept the company of a woman who coveted Justin for her own. Lifting her chin, Megan took a deep, fortifying breath and descended the stairs.

Sonny leaned against the wall while Tom stood near the doorway.

"Megan." Tom's voice held surprising warmth. "It's good to see you."

He held his hat in his hands and smiled, and suddenly Megan felt he actually meant the words. Guilt invaded her. It was, after all, not a perfectly proper scheme she had planned.

"I'd heard you were feeling better," Tom continued. "Young Jeremiah told us you were doing well." His gaze noted Megan's healthy complexion and lovely eyes. "We thank God for the recovery of your speech."

Megan nodded numbly. She'd forgotten they had believed her to be mute.

"It's a miracle," Sonny said blithely, hiding a grin with a courtly effort. "A miracle."

She felt herself blush. Why had Sonny come? Sonny, who had witnessed the humiliating scene with Attila's sword.

"I hope Mrs. Miller has served as an adequate companion," Tom continued. "Where is she now?"

Megan merely stared. A companion? Daphne?

"She left for a few minutes," Justin lied speedily. "But she'll be back soon."

"Good." Thomas nodded. "Agatha would age ten years if she thought Megan was here unchaperoned."

Megan blanched. Agatha would drop dead on the floor if she knew the truth, for apparently

Justin had indicated they'd not be alone here at Free Winds. Which perhaps meant he cared somewhat for her reputation. Or—perhaps not. Daphne had said Thomas would disinherit Justin if there was any impropriety. Perhaps Justin only hoped to save his inheritance.

She glanced toward him. He was watching her, his eyes deep and unreadable, and she looked away, wondering if he could see into her soul.

"Can I get you something to drink?" Megan's voice was soft, her sweaty palms pressed tightly to her peach colored skirt. "I could make lemonade."

Justin's expression was cautious. She'd been so quiet for the past few days, avoiding both himself and Daphne and he'd left her be, afraid he might drive her away. If what she said about Daphne was true, she had a right to be angry. But how was he to know? And was it fair to terminate Miller's employment when he was uncertain about her role in the situation?

"We don't need anything," Tom said. "Please don't let us trouble you."

"It's no trouble," she assured him. It wasn't quite dark. It was still too early. She needed time. "Why don't you sit for a spell? I'll only be a minute."

All three men watched her. She felt as nervous as a treed coon but resisted fidgeting as best she could.

"Some ade would be wonderful." Tom smiled. "You don't mind waiting, do you Justin?"

"No." His answer was quick enough though

his eyes didn't leave Megan's face. "Come on in."

Left alone in the kitchen, Megan glanced about uncertainly. As a child she'd spent most of her time outdoors with her father. Household chores weren't exactly her specialty, but making lemonade seemed an easy enough task. It took her some time to squeeze the juice from the fruits, but she was in no hurry. Darkness was just now settling in, increasing her nervousness.

It was just about time.

"Lemonade." She brought three glasses in on a cherry tray and after offering a drink to each of the men, seated herself on Tom's right.

The conversation continued, mostly centered around livestock and agriculture, and Megan listened with half an ear. Time was passing. Who knew how long Daphne would wait, if she was indeed waiting at all?

"Megan?"

"What?" She jumped at the sound of her name.

"I said, we'll be going to see the colt now. Would you care to accompany us?" Justin asked, watching her with the same wary intensity she had noticed earlier.

"Oh! No!" She sat as stiff as a rock. "Thank you."

"Come with us, Megan," Sonny urged, a roguish grin just below the surface of his expression.

"No, I—I ..." she stuttered, wishing Sonny didn't know her so well and searching for an excuse, but Justin interrupted smoothly.

"Come along, Megan." It seemed more of a

challenge than an invitation, she thought, and turned her gaze to his. "Why not?" he asked. His tone was casual, but she sensed his suspicion.

What did he suspect? "Very well." Megan's own gaze remained riveted to his. "I will."

Outside it was cool and dark, with only the light of Justin's lantern to find a path by. A horse whickered to its companion, bullfrogs sang their night songs, and locusts hummed. The latch on the barn door creaked as Justin lifted it and Megan prayed for grace and held her breath.

The foursome stepped inside. The horses lifted their heads, blinking against the light, but there was only a moment to notice the horses.

A shriek split the restful quiet. A frantic scrambling sounded from above, another shriek, and a falling body.

The foursome stood in dumbfounded awe, staring at a naked Daphne who lay sprawled upon a generous mound of straw.

"I was pushed," she gasped indignantly, as if expecting some gallant to march up the ladder to seek revenge on the accused villain. "Someone pushed me," she sputtered, but the foursome could only stare.

"What's the meaning of this?" Tom demanded, finally tearing his eyes from the naked woman and finding his voice.

"Justin asked me to meet him," Daphne said, frantically trying to cover her generous proportions with her large limbs.

"What?" Tom growled, turning his angry gaze

from the woman to his son. "What's this all about?"

Justin lifted his eyes with slow suspicion to settle on Megan. "I'm not certain."

"You're not certain?" Tom roared in return. "Are you telling me your serving woman— Megan's poor excuse for a companion—falls naked out of your loft at all hours of the night and you're not certain why she's there?"

"I'll find out." Justin's gaze burned Megan's face.

"You'd damn well better find out, boy! But I'll tell you something. I want to hear you are going to dismiss this woman immediately. Do you hear me?"

"Yes." Justin drew his gaze slowly from Megan's wild-eyed stare. "I might just as well. It seems the only prudent thing to do."

"And until you find a *decent* companion for Megan, she'll stay with us at Manor Royal."

Justin's face showed no expression. "She'll stay with me," he said in low-voiced certainty.

"See here, Justin," Thomas exclaimed. "You'll not tarnish the girl's reputation more than it has been. She's been through enough, what with her brother's nefarious dealings."

"It's her brother I'm thinking of," Justin replied. "Far better some prune-faced, big-nosed belle spreads gossip than have her brother come and steal her away." He glowered at his father from a three-foot distance. "She'll stay with me!"

Thomas drew himself up. "Have it your way, then. But if I hear any complaints from the girl, I'll come and rescue her myself. Hear me?"

Justin nodded and Sonny grinned, dropping an arm around Megan's waist for a brotherly hug and a private whisper.

"You're a peach, Meg." He raised his brows at her. "Thatta way to keep him hopping."

"What're you yipping about?" Thomas demanded.

"Ahhh, just said she should tell us if old Justin gives her any trouble," Sonny lied.

"You tell us, all right," Thomas agreed. "He's not too big for me to tan his hide." He turned toward the door, but a squealed voice stopped him.

"Hey!" Daphne raged, beating the straw with clenched fists. "What about me?"

"Don't come back!" said Justin and Thomas in unison, and Megan scurried from the barn.

Chapter 20

⟨ഗ൦⟩

Justin stared dismally at his platter of food. It had been three days since Daphne's departure and three days since he had tasted anything edible.

Burned potatoes, half-cooked turnips, and something that appeared to have once been meat of some sort. He was starving to death.

"Megan!" He roared the word, lunging to his feet and toppling his chair in his haste.

There was no answer and he growled low in his throat. "Damn." Blast it all, he'd had it with the little swindler. It was high time to teach her who was boss and he was just the man to do it. "Megan!"

She wasn't coming. He glared toward the empty stairway, realizing she wasn't about to come running at his command. He took the steps three at a time, slammed open her door, and stopped in his tracks.

Megan stood by the wash bowl, her pink mouth agape as she frantically clutched her gown to her bared chest.

Justin took a deep breath, steadied his nerves,

and kept his voice low with an effort. "I want to talk to you."

Her eyes looked enormous in the candlelight, her skin as smooth and clear as a child's.

"Wh——what about?" She pulled her gown closer to her breasts, hunching her shoulders and trying to cover any parts that might still be visible.

"Why'd you get rid of Daphne?"

"I—" she began, but he shook his head, warning her not to continue.

"Don't bother saying you had nothing to do with it, Megan. I've been eating dog scraps for meals and I'm in no mood for your games."

She lifted her chin slightly. Candlelight glimmered on her damp skin. The sight of it warmed him, lighting a spark somewhere deep inside.

"I didn't ask to do your cooking," she said haughtily.

"But you had Miller tossed bare-assed out of the hay loft. Why?"

Megan drew herself up, anger seeping into her consciousness as she remembered the woman. "She said you planned to sell me," Megan said evenly. "Was it a lie or was it not?"

"It was a lie, God damn it," Justin said. "But that hardly seems a reason to throw her—"

"I think it's a very good reason," raged Megan in return. "She was a bitter old witch."

"And you're no saint, Megan," he responded evenly. "I think there's far more to it than you say."

"I don't know what you're talking about."

"Don't you?" His tone was soft now, his face

tense and still, his body immobile. He was the picture of intensity, like a hunting predator, as lithe and sensual as a cat, as tough and arrogant as a stallion.

"No," she whispered.

Something sparked between, a shocking current that whipped from him to her.

Megan's breath came in deep gulps. She could feel herself breathe, could feel the need for more air. He came toward her and she watched him hopelessly, her lips slightly parted.

"You know what I think?" He stood near enough for her to see the golden flecks in his eyes. "I think you were jealous." He reached out with aching slowness, his fingertips touching her cheek. "I think you believed she might take your place in my bed."

Her head fell back slightly. Her throat hurt, her skin tingled. "It's not true." Her words were forced past dry lips.

"It is." His hand slid lower, touching her shoulder, then skimming along her collar bone to rest at the pulse in the hollow of her pale, delicate neck. "Daphne was a handsome woman. A woman who needed a man. You thought she might get me."

"I couldn't care less," Megan whispered unconvincingly. She was drowning in his eyes, slipping under his spell. Justin bent his neck. His lips touched hers.

She trembled. Her eyes fell closed but her mind would not quit. Daphne's memory invaded her consciousness and she jerked her eyes wide, imagining the woman in Justin's arms.

"Don't!" She pushed at his chest, still holding the gown and exposing the upper regions of her lovely breasts.

They were pale and smooth, pressed upward by her arms and more inviting than anything he could have imagined. Justin's breath caught painfully in his throat. He stared at her beauty, mesmerized by it, drawn to it.

"Megan." His voice was hoarse. His entire body ached for her with a burning heat that refused to be ignored. "Let me touch you. Let me love you."

She shook her head, as if not quite able to convince herself to disagree. "What do you think I am?" she asked raggedly. "Am I your slave, your servant?" Her heart pounded like a thousand running horses. "Your whore?"

"You're . . . beautiful," he said, not understanding her pain, her need to know her status.

"I'll not stay and be your mistress," she said, wondering if she was lying. Wondering if she had so little pride that she'd stay with him, whatever the circumstances.

"I have no need for a mistress," he said, his nostrils flared.

"Then why am I here?"

"Because I want you."

"What does that mean?" she asked, fists clenched.

"I want you to stay, Megan."

"But I can't!" Don't you see?"

"Why?" His voice rose. "Because of what others might think?"

Megan straightened her back. "I'm far past caring what others think," she said, knowing it was true. She gave little thought to the populace at large, so why did it matter what he thought?

"Then stay as my friend," Justin whispered, "until we know what we are to each other."

"But I'm—" she began weakly.

"You're the most captivating woman I've ever known. And I need to touch you, to learn about you. To know who you are. . . . Come to Charleston with me, Megan."

"What?" She stared at him, dizzied by the suggestion and his words of need.

"Come with me." He didn't touch her, though he ached to do so. "You're a unique woman with many talents, but I see cooking is not amongst them. We'll find someone to do the house duties so you can . . ." He paused. "You can do what you like here, Megan. Work with the horses, maybe." His gaze fell from her enormous eyes to the bright mass of hair that lay against her shoulders. Slowly he reached out, slipping the multi-hued curls between his fingers. He lifted a single lock and she watched as he stroked it against his lips. It was an utterly sensuous motion, as stimulating as if his lips had touched her flesh. "Or maybe not." He grinned, one corner of his mouth lifting slightly. "Maybe you'd prefer to stay in bed . . . all day."

His gaze rose to her face again and he replaced the lock beside her throat, then gently brushed the firelit tendrils behind her shoulder. Drawing nearer, his head slightly tilted, he touched his lips to her neck, just where the hair had been. "What do you think, Megan?"

"Think?" she gasped, trying to catch her breath.

"Come with me, love," he said again and she was lost.

Megan stood beside Justin in the lobby of the Charleston Inn. It had been a leisurely trip. She'd dressed in her mauve gown and ridden Rainstorm sidesaddle, while Justin had taken a young, green-broke mare. Nothing had distracted him, not the mare's skittish nature, not the beauty of the scenery, not Megan's nervous chatter.

His eyes had rarely left her, it seemed, and on the one occasion when his hand had touched hers, it had felt like the kiss of the sun on a winter's day, as warm and caressing as spring.

"We'd like a room for two," Justin said, addressing the thin, spectacled man behind the desk. But the inn's employee failed to reply as he stared past Justin's shoulder toward Megan.

"Excuse me," Justin said a bit louder, immediately annoyed by the man's infatuation with her. She was unusually stunning today, he admitted to himself, even for her, but that was hardly a reason to ogle the girl. "Is there one available or not?"

"I beg your pardon." The thin man's adam's apple bobbed as he recognized his patron's irritation.

"I'm inquiring about a room for two," Justin explained irritably.

"Oh, yes sir. Certainly, sir. For yourself and the lady."

"For myself and my . . ." He paused, glancing at Megan and stifling a grin. "Wife," he said evenly. He hadn't planned the lie, but he could hardly introduce her as anything but his spouse and he was not prepared to rent two rooms. Not when she looked as she did—like a goddess come to man.

"Yes, sir. You and your wife, sir." The man's pale green eyes lowered quickly to skim the pages of the heavy ledger. "Your husband's a lucky man," he proclaimed, raising his watery eyes to smile at Megan, who smiled wanly back. "We still have number seven open. One of our best."

"Very well." Justin reached for the inn's log but found the man had it in a firm grip as he stared, bedazzled at Megan. The weasel-faced little polecat, Justin fumed, jerking the log from the innkeeper's hand and scowling over the book at him.

"Did you come for the horse auction?" asked Mr. Spectacles, not taking his eyes from Megan's bright, enchanting face.

"We're in town to find a housekeeper," Justin answered noncommittally.

"Ah, a housekeeper," Mr. Spectacles said. I fear I can't help you there. I wish I could." His gaze wandered to Megan again, giving Justin the impression that he would have given his arms to be more helpful.

"Perhaps you can help me in another area then," suggested Justin. "My wife's in need of some new gowns. Is there someone in the city you might recommend?"

"New gowns?" Mr. Spectacles asked, seeming lost in the vision before him. "But I think she looks ever so lovely in the pink . . ." He caught himself just in time and reddened from his ears to somewhere far below the top button of his shirt. "A seamstress, a seamstress," he muttered, frantically avoiding Justin's enflamed face. "Ah, I know just the one. Widow Butler. She has a little shop down Cypress Street. I've never heard a word of complaint about her work."

"Mrs. Butler," Justin repeated gruffly. "On Cypress."

"Yes. Just a bit of a walk from here. In fact, I'd be ever so happy to make certain your wife gets there safely if you have other things to do."

It was the final straw. Justin slammed the heavy logbook shut, startling Mr. Spectacles as he glared into his face. "I think I'm capable of seeing my own wife safely there. Thank you."

"Yes, sir. Of course, sir," he corrected quickly, but Justin had already turned his back, taking Megan's elbow in a firm grip and marching her away.

Once inside their room, Megan wandered nervously about, fiddling with a curtain, staring from the window, and finally untying her bonnet to slip the thing from her head. Justin watched her, letting his tension ease away. He could hardly blame Mr. Spectacles for being obsessed with her. There was a quality about her, a fresh, clean beauty that forever drew eyes to her.

She turned a little, holding the bonnet in one hand and looking tense. "People will know I'm not your wife."

"Justin crossed his arms over his chest and leaned against the wall. "How will they know, Megan? Because I'm so obviously taken by you?" He smiled, tilting his head. "Isn't a man allowed to be enamored of his wife?"

"People know you," she said in frustration.

"It's a big city, Megan. It's doubtful I'll see anyone I know."

"But what if you do?"

"You're absolutely right," he said. "I suppose we'll have to spend our entire time locked away in this room."

Megan's eyes seemed to widen. Her lips parted. Justin pushed away from the wall, stepping nearer.

"It'll be a hardship, love," he murmured. "But I suspect I can think of something to keep me busy here."

"But ..." She backed away. "You have to ... look for a housekeeper. You said so."

He shrugged, stalking her. "I've changed my mind. Besides, there seems little point in my choosing someone, for surely if you don't like her you'll plan some awful demise."

"But I ..." She was backed against the wall. "Listen, Justin ... I shouldn't be here. It's wrong ... immoral."

"Immoral?" He stepped in front of her, placing his hands on the wall beside her. "Immoral to give someone pleasure? To get to know another's soul before ..." He stopped abruptly, his face becoming sober. The room was quiet. "Perhaps it's a far greater sin for a man to marry a woman he will never love, a woman he will leave for the bed of another. And perhaps it would be better if he abandoned propriety to marry the woman who ..." He paused again, lost in her eyes. "The woman who captures his heart."

Megan remained immobile, her heart thudding. What was he saying?

"I'm not a man to believe in following custom just for custom's sake, Megan. Not when there is so much wrong in our society."

He had depth beyond her comprehension, a wealth of knowledge and integrity, but it was a different kind of integrity than that of most gentlemen. It was real and far-reaching.

"Why do you live here, Justin?" she asked softly. "When you disagree so with the customs?"

He drew a deep breath, then shrugged. "Some aspects of the south are very good, while some are a disgrace to humanity. Still, Carolina is my home." He drew his hands from the wall, touching her cheek. "Could it be yours?"

Her lips parted. No words came.

"Could it, Megan?" he murmured.

"What are you asking me?" she breathed.

Time stood still.

Justin straightened. "I'm sorry." He drew away. "I've no right to ask that. Not as things stand."

How did things stand? Megan wondered dizzily. What was he asking? And why did her chest ache when he was near?

"We'd best see Widow Butler about those garments," Justin said, stepping away.

Megan remained where she was, feeling pale and weak. "There's no need to buy me any gowns," she said.

"I think there is." Justin turned to look at her,

drawing a silent breath and finally smiling a little. "Not all men have my self-control so I can't allow you to go traipsing about Charleston in that pink thing you're wearing. It would be foolhardy."

Her blush only enhanced her beauty. It was a marvel to him, that she could be more attractive, and he watched her carefully.

"It's very lovely on you, Megan," he continued. "But I've been wondering why you wore it." He leaned casually against the wall, canting his head a little. "Perhaps you're trying to seduce me."

"I—I'm doing no such thing." Her blush deepened and he chuckled.

"There's no need to be ashamed, love," he teased gently. "In fact I'm very flattered. I haven't had a woman try to seduce me for. . . . Oh, let's see. Well, since the night in the barn, when Daphne mysteriously fell from the loft."

Megan turned away stiffly, hiding her expression.

"I'd like you to tell me something, Megan," he said with a hint of humor. "Who did you get to do the pushing? Was it Zeke?"

Megan said nothing.

"It's all right. I don't mind. It was quite entertaining, really. And good to know you've made a friend—whoever it was that did the pushing. And . . ." His expression grew more serious. "I'd like *you* to choose the woman to do the housework."

"Me?" Megan blinked. "But I don't know . . ."

"What would you think of Missy?" he asked quietly, watching her intently.

"Missy? From Manor Royal?" Megan frowned. "But you don't keep slaves."

"No," he said simply. "I don't."

"Then you'd . . ." Megan stepped away from the wall, her eyes alight. "You'd set her free?"

"How would you feel about it if I did, Megan?" he asked. "It's not a well accepted thing to do. We'd be frowned upon by some."

"You'd set her free?" Megan asked again, smiling now. "And she could live at Free Winds?" She had felt a kinship with the beautiful slave, a similarity of spirit.

"You wouldn't mind?" Justin asked solemnly.

"Mind?" Megan watched him. "I would think you were . . ." Mother Mary! She couldn't allow herself to fall in love with him! It would be foolish! Dangerous! "I would think you were very kind," she said, trying to hide the depth of her feelings.

"And you wouldn't resent being in a household with a freed slave?"

"I am a slave," she said, then tilted her head at him. "Remember?"

"Ah, yes." He smiled because he couldn't help it. "I forgot," he admitted, then stepped forward to slip his arms about her waist and kiss her gently.

Megan felt the caress burn her lips and closed her eyes to the feeling, but he drew away in a moment, seeming to employ the entirety of his self-touted control.

Perhaps she was his whore, Megan thought dizzily. And perhaps she didn't care.

She raised her palm to his chest, feeling the

rapid beat of his heart through the fabric of his shirt.

"Daphne said you'd lose your inheritance if your father learned of any improprieties." She couldn't bear to hurt him, not now. Not in any way. "Is it true?"

Justin watched her carefully. "I've already disavowed my inheritance, Megan. I have great respect for my father, but I don't believe slavery is just and I refuse to gain from it." He paused, his eyes unfathomable. "I may never have more than I do now."

Silence came, followed by Megan's whisper, pulled from her as if against her will. "I don't want more."

Justin drew a deep breath, pulling her back into his arms to squeeze his eyes shut above her head. She felt like a small piece of heaven pressed against his chest—like a promise of happiness waiting to be discovered—but finally he pushed her gently from him. "We'd best go. Before my virtuous self-control disappears completely."

Chapter 21

The seamstress shop was small and warm, spread with endless bolts of fabric and lace. Mrs. Butler was an aging widow lady with a quick eye and an intellect to match.

"So you want something for the lady to ride in?" she questioned, cocking her head in a birdlike gesture.

"That's right," Justin said. "But I want a special garment, something suitable for riding astride."

"Riding astride?" Mrs. Butler asked quizzically.

"That's not necessary," Megan said hurriedly.

"Oh, but it is," Justin disagreed gently. "What if you feel a need to prove your riding skills in public?" He raised his brows at her, remembering the dazzling display of her bare thighs as she swung her leg across the straining neck of his mare. "You don't imagine I want anyone else to witness what I did, do you?"

"Justin," she whispered, withering with embarrassment, but he only laughed, winking to the little seamstress and loving the memory.

"Well, let's get at it, Mrs. Butler."

274

The widow turned hurriedly and Justin followed, leaving Megan behind to be consumed by embarrassment.

Outside the shop, the sky was pinkening toward evening. Megan placed her small foot in the stirrup and gathered her mare's reins. "There was no need for all those gowns," she said. "I'm certain there are other things you could buy with that money."

"Yes." Justin said, settling in his own saddle to smile at her. "But nothing that gives me so much pleasure." His eyes rested on her, warm and suggestive. "Let's get some supper, Megan. Watching you being measured and turned has made me work up quite an appetite."

They found a small eating establishment where they were seated in a garden area. Not another patron was in view. Exuberant clusters of blossoms jostled in the breeze, filling the air with a sweet, heady perfume.

"Will there be wine tonight?" A conscientious waiter half-bowed before them with a smile that suggested he had nothing better to do than see to their every whim.

Wine, Justin thought, watching Megan's nervous expression. Wine was just the thing. "Yes." She was exceptionally lovely tonight with her emerald eyes as bright as an angel's.

"Very well, sir," said the waiter, then disappeared with a haste Justin much appreciated.

Justin's gaze held on Megan's face. There was a magical quality about her, a sweet freshness that seemed intensified by the blooming color around her and he sat transfixed by it.

Megan stared back but unable to bear the intensity of his gaze, turned her head quickly. "Such beautiful flowers," she said nervously.

"Very beautiful," he agreed, not taking his eyes from her.

"My mother used to raise flowers," she added, unable to watch him watch her. The memory of his touch and the warmth of his gaze made her feel fidgety and tense.

"Up north," Justin added, remembering that small bit of information she'd trusted him with.

"Yes." She toyed with the lace on her gown, trying to find a place to rest her gaze.

"It's said that Charleston boasts the world's most beautiful women." His thick forearms rested on the table and he leaned toward her slightly. "But it was untrue—until now."

It was so warm, Megan thought, stilling a desire to fan herself. And he was so close, so dark, so large, and. . . .

"Listen . . ." Her voice sounded rather panicked to her own ears. "Justin, I—I—"

The waiter returned, cradling a bottle for their inspection, but Justin had little time for interruptions and nodded dismissively.

"I shouldn't be here," she finally said, pulling her eyes back to his. "I don't belong here."

She waited for a response, but instead he reached out to take her hand from where it rested on the table. Turning her palm upward, he placed a gentle kiss at its center. Her arm jerked and he lifted his gaze, smiling with lazy pleasure before lowering his head again to touch his lips to her wrist.

She tried to speak—in fact, her lips were slightly parted—but no words came. She watched him silently, as if mesmerized, as his kisses trailed higher, blazing a course along her shivering arm to the elbow.

"What were you saying, Megan?" he asked finally, lifting his face again but still holding her quivering limb.

"I—I said . . ." She paused for a moment, having no idea what she had said, and searching frantically for the phrase. "I shouldn't be here," she finished, ridiculously relieved her memory hadn't failed her completely.

His eyes were the most wonderful, frightening things, so warm and alive and able to light her life with a glance.

"You're right. You should not. You should be in my bed, love." He smiled a little at her shocked expression. "But I suppose we have to eat sometime."

"Justin," she gasped, "have you no morals?"

"Yes." He raised his brows at her. "But not where you're concerned."

She mouthed a soundless reply and he laughed low in his throat.

"Does that shock you?"

"But . . ." She found her breath. "Justin . . ."

"Remember our first night?"

The question shocked her even further and she stared, wide-eyed, wondering if he actually thought she might forget.

"Remember?" he asked again, his umber gaze

caressing her face. "I didn't realize it was your first time." He seemed suddenly serious now, and allowed his fingertips to graze the tender flesh of her arm as she shivered at the touch. "I want to ask your forgiveness for that foolish bet, Megan. I want to make it up to you now."

"There's no need for . . ."

"Yes, there is, love," he breathed. "It was a precious gift you gave me. And I hope to give you something in return."

She was melting, along with her inhibitions, along with her good sense, along with any hope of ever abolishing him from her mind.

"I hope to give you pleasure, love. Equal to the pleasure you've given me."

She was gone, far past the point of no return and found she could not even manage to try to pull her arm from his grasp. She should leave. She should pray. She should run from the room like a hunted hare. But she did none of these things. Instead she simply stared, her eyes wide and unfocused, trying to draw enough breath to maintain her equilibrium.

The server returned but Megan was far beyond an ability to order leaving Justin to do the honors.

"So . . ." She took a deep breath, watching the waiter depart and silently vowing to be a model of decorum. "You've always lived at Manor Royal?" she asked primly, well knowing the answer and praying he would play along with her chit-chat. "Have you never wished to live elsewhere to—"

"Megan," Justin interrupted smoothly, "are

you really so interested in this subject or are you simply trying to avoid my ever-so-obvious seduction?"

Raw excitement flashed through her body like crackling lightning. Decorum flung itself from the nearest window. "No, truly, I simply was wondering if—"

"If we can leave and find our mutual bed?" Justin's mouth lifted at one corner, teasing her with the suggestion of a smile as his free hand suddenly contacted her leg beneath the table.

Megan gasped aloud as flames spit outward from his hand, careening wildly from her thigh to the rest of her body. Time ceased to be a reality as he worked his magic on her, whispering naughty suggestions and now and then brushing a kiss against some shivering part of her anatomy.

"If you can't wait, love," he said finally, "we could forget our meal and leave this very minute." His lips were so near her ear she could feel his breath tickle her lobe and through the fabric of her gown she could feel each stroke of his fingers against her thigh.

"Justin, please," she pleaded, not knowing how to finish her request or react to such shocking stimulus, but he only laughed.

"I like it when you beg, Megan," he teased, the words feather soft as they caressed her ear yet again.

Whether her gasp was caused by the erotic movement of his recalcitrant hand or his implication that she begged for his favors, even she was uncertain. And neither could she know she leaned toward him as one does when bracing herself against a powerful wind.

"Megan, my love," Justin warned as he removed his hand from her tingling thigh to take the stem of his glass. "I think our meal is about to arrive. Perhaps it would be best if you didn't greet our waiter with that exact expression." He smiled into the stark passion of her face. "It might be a bit much for the uninitiated male to withstand."

Megan stared at him with a total lack of comprehension, but finally his words permeated her dazzled brain and she jerked herself upright, wondering if she were salivating like a starving dog. How had she sunk to such depths of depraved desire? All the man need do was touch her hand and she was lost. It was disgusting. She stared numbly at her meal, then, in the hope of ignoring Justin's presence, dug into her food with desperation.

Justin, however, remained unmoved, watching as she ate.

She persevered for a time, but her calm finally crumbled. "Justin, please," she begged, unable to bear his scrutiny any longer. "Eat."

His smile was slow and devilish. "You're right of course. I'm sure we'll need all our strength for the night ahead."

"Please, Justin . . ." She was honestly pleading for mercy, feeling she was unable to bear his suggestions any longer without her mind and body turning to ash beneath his heated gaze.

He chuckled, the sound low and lovely, and nearly as provocative as the feel of his hand had been. "All right, love, I'll wait until the meal's end. But after that ..." He leaned toward her, his eyes a deep shade of desire. "There'll be no holds barred."

Chapter 22

$\longleftarrow \textbf{OO} \longrightarrow$

Justin touched her cheek with gentle fingertips. "We're here, love," he whispered.

The heavy room key hung from a silken ribbon, forgotten in his opposite hand. Megan's breath rushed like a tornado through her parted lips. *No holds barred.* Her numbed mind already buzzed with his nearness. Her bedazzled body could take no more of his hot sensuality. She was certain of it, but the truly frightening thing was she felt this giddy responsiveness while fully clothed and standing safely in the hall of the inn. What would she find on the opposite side of the door? It was entirely possible, she thought, that his blatant masculinity would sear her mind from her body and leave her blundering about witless for the rest of her days.

Placing the key in the hole, he turned it, then pressed the door inward and paused to look down at her. "Are you ready, love?" he whispered.

She couldn't move, couldn't speak. How had she come to this pass when all she wanted was him?

Justin leaned down, kissing her lightly, then

sliding his arms behind her to lift her from the floor. The door closed softly, sealing out the world.

It was only a few paces to the bed where he seated himself. His thighs were tight and hard against Megan's buttocks. His chest was taut and mounded against her shoulder. Moonlight was scattered about the room, illuminating and shadowing and shedding its pearly light on the bed where they sat.

Megan's arm loosely hugged Justin's neck, bringing their faces only inches apart. There was a breathlessness between them, a wondrous, heart-pounding tension that drew them even nearer. And then he was kissing her again, his lips moving like satin against hers.

"Megan," he breathed. His hand moved to the buttons that ran down the gown's back and she shuddered as the garment fell away from her quivering flesh. "Megan, love." Drawing the satin from her shoulders, he blazed a trail of kisses down the length of her throat. "It seems such a miracle that you saved such loveliness for me."

The bodice dipped farther downward, and his gaze followed. The upper portions of her breasts were bare, with the rosy peaks still covered by the soft cotton of her chemise. His gaze roamed over the beauty of her torso and his fingers followed, feeling her quiver at his touch. With tender care, he reached out, smoothing his palm over the tip of one breast.

Air hissed between Megan's teeth. The feelings were too sharp, too intense. Her eyes found his. Her hand slipped from his shoulders to his neck, pulling him closer. Their lips met again. Justin eased her onto the feather tick, covering her body with his own, moving his lips upon hers with tantalizing slowness.

The world ceased to function for Megan. There was only Justin and this night. Nothing else mattered now.

He moved from her lips, letting his kisses wander downward over the sheer barrier of her chemise. She gasped when he reached the crest of her breast, but he remained there only a moment, smoothing the gown lower.

He kneeled on the floor. The gown dropped between his knees and then his hands were on the sheer fabric of her undergarments, tugging them downwards to finally join the dress. He kissed the graceful length of her legs. His hands skimmed along them, caressing, tickling, awakening every nerve to vibrating awareness.

He came to her finally, crawling over her sprawled form so that he straddled her small body with his. "Every time I see you, you seem more beautiful," he said.

Lowering his head, he tasted the nectar of her lips. Her arms crept around his back, hugging his strength to her but there was an irritating barrier. She lay naked while he was fully clothed. It hardly seemed right. Her hands pushed at his chest now and he drew away slightly.

"Is there something wrong, love?"

"Yes." Her voice was husky.

In his eyes she could see his worry and smiled wickedly at his concern.

"I can't go on," she murmured, feeling his

body tense with aching disappointment. "Not with this in the way." She tugged at his shirt, and understanding dawned on his face.

"You're teasing me," he accused hoarsely.

She chuckled, the sound so low and seductive that it sent a shiver up his spine and he drew his head back, watching her awakening sensuality unfurl like a rose in bloom.

She was so utterly desirable, so undeniably woman, all softness and fire. Her fingers grazed his buttons and he waited expectantly as his shirt was tugged free of his breeches and the buttons released. He watched her nostrils extend and felt the burn of his own desire as her hands touched his chest. She smoothed her fingertips across his torso and he held his breath, feeling her touch to the depths of his soul and closing his eyes languidly.

Megan drew her gaze from his face to watch her fingers find their way down the hard, bronze center of his chest. Never in her life had she seen anything like him. He was so finely sculpted, so wonderfully created, that just the sight of him took her breath. He rested on his hands, with his wondrous chest propped above her and his lower body pressed to her with an intimate warmth that made her breathing come in hard, primitive gulps.

She slipped her hands behind his back, feeling the great masses of muscle that extended from his shoulders to the taut circumference of his waist. He felt like a wildcat beneath her hands, untamed and sleek. Her hands slid along his sides, then followed the slant of his ribs to meet at a point just above his navel, where his hair grew dark and thick. She ran her fingers through it, then traced a line downward with her index fingers until they were met by the edge of his trousers.

Her hands stopped. Beneath the taut fabric of his pants a prominent bulge was evident. She hesitated a moment, but then she reached forth, brushing the swelling gently with her knuckles.

His inhalation was long and low. He pressed more firmly against her, his great body tense and she raised her gaze.

Justin's broad neck was arched, his chest rounded and hard above her, tempting and lovely and male. Her fingers ran over the bulge again. She watched him shudder, and feeling her own excitement mount with his, lifted her head to kiss the warm indentation between the hard masses of his pectorals.

Megan drew back and Justin tilted his head downward, meeting her eyes with his own. It took him a moment to find his voice and when he did it was husky and stilted.

"Aren't you going to finish what you started, love?"

She stared at him, mesmerized by the beauty of his masculinity. "What?"

"Weren't you disrobing me?" he asked, his eyes heavy with desire.

Megan bit her lip. He was indescribably attractive, desirable beyond reason but to uncover the remainder of his bold form was beyond her daring.

He watched her silently, then chuckled, the sound filling the room with its provocative tone. "I'd love to allow you to finish, Megan, but you've made me too impatient." Leaning down, he kissed her lips with a lusty passion, then stood abruptly to remove his clothing with hurried hands.

In a moment the length of his hot body was pressed up against her and she was gathered into the taut strength of his arms. Their kiss was long and possessive, shattering all thought of the outside world and leaving them open to the vibrant intensity of their lovemaking.

Her hands skimmed the sculpted muscles of his hard form, while he grazed languidly down her back, pulling her ever nearer until he gripped her rounded buttocks in his palms. Like silken magic Megan's slim legs slipped over his and suddenly she was atop him, nestled against the planes of his tense form as she straddled him.

His kissed flowed downward, igniting a fiery trail toward her breasts and she arched away from him. Her nostrils were flared, her body like dry kindling above the flame of his desire, and he drew away slightly, drinking her in with his eyes and his fingertips.

"Megan." He growled her name. She felt him tremble. "I need you, love," he whispered.

She arched nearer, then gasped as his mouth found the summit of one breast. Fire engulfed her. Her hands gripped his hair. She could feel the turgid heat of his shaft against her bottom and could wait no longer.

Her legs gripped him with astonishing strength. Her body bucked against his and suddenly he was inside, gliding into the utopia of her satin sheath.

"Megan." He moaned again, but her kiss stopped his words.

She could wait no longer, for she'd learned his lessons of pleasure too well to brook delay.

The earthy rhythm of their movements increased in speed and intensity. Flesh pressed against flesh, gliding, stimulating—heating them both to feverous pitch until Megan was riding him like a galloping stallion, unaware of her wild abandon.

The tempo increased. The room seemed to whirl until finally they were thrown over the crest of their pinnacle to fall into the feathery softness on the far side of desire.

Justin awoke slowly to find Megan's soft, smooth back pressed to his chest. Shifting his weight slightly, he studied her serene features.

Tangled locks of sun-streaked waves swirled about her peaceful face, then flowed downward to encircle her rounded shoulders and delicate throat. But there his view was halted by the rude interruption of the one sheet that had survived their night's play.

She looked so very different in the morning light, he mused silently. It was certainly not that she looked any less lovely, he thought, but simply that the former tigress had been replaced by a soft and sleepy lamb whose very presence screamed for gentle affection. How was it that such an unpredictable woman could arouse both the gentleman and the beast in him?

How as it that she had stormed into his life, stolen his pants, and eventually stolen his. . . .

Justin drew a deep breath, stopping his

thoughts. He didn't truly know this woman who shared his bed. Too much had passed between them to be forgotten. It was possible, after all, that little Megan was simply biding her time, awaiting the day when she could once again gain from his misfortune. She had promised him she knew nothing of Manchester or the stallion he had sold and reclaimed. But was it the truth? Or was she playing him for a fool?

Justin scowled at her. He had no answers, only a longing ache that no one but she could satisfy.

He touched her cheek and she sighed under his fingertips as she turned onto her back.

"Good morning." He stared into her emerald eyes, finding her soul in their depths. "Did you sleep well?"

She was silent and he realized in a moment that the hussy of the previous night had fled. In her place was a lovely, young woman with enormous eyes and a shy smile. She pulled the linen a bit higher under her little chin. "Yes," she managed in a small voice.

He couldn't help smiling at her quiet answer. If he let his imagination run riot he could almost believe there was the hint of suggestiveness in her tone. And run riot it did. Justin leaned forward, kissing her lightly. The touch of her lips against his only fed his imagination and it seemed he had little control over the direction of his hand. It slipped beneath the sheet she held like a shield between them and found the soft fullness of her breast.

Megan gasped against his kiss and he slid his hand about her back, pulling her nearer. She had no defense against him and felt herself melt into his embrace, falling under his masculine charm.

"House servants," a voice announced from the hall. "Come ta see ta yer room."

Megan jerked from Justin's arms, her cheeks burning with embarrassment, but Justin suffered no such emotion and kissed her neck with slow tenderness.

"The room can wait," he announced, drawing away from her slightly. "But we'd like a bath brought up as soon as possible."

"Yassah."

Footsteps were heard in the hall, allowing Justin to find Megan's lips again with his own, but she pushed desperately at his chest.

"Justin," she gasped frantically, embarrassed to the bone. "They'll be back in a minute."

"Let them come." His voice was husky, his eyes dark with mischievous desire.

"I——Justin," she repeated, wiggling wildly in an attempt to free herself from his embrace.

"Really, Megan," he said, his expression impenetrable. "I don't think your wriggling about is helping your situation at all."

Against her thigh, Megan could feel the hard evidence of his desire and wished she could control the blush that spread from her cheek bones to her curling toes.

"I love it when you blush." He was staring into her face, she knew, though she refused to meet his eyes. "Your entire body turns all pink, like a rose in bloom. I doubt I'll ever quit teasing you so long as you blush so prettily. Can you do it on command, or is it a sort of involuntary thing?"

She had no intention of answering, but he waited in silence until there was no way of avoiding the question. "I——I can't help it," she murmured, scowling.

"Ah." He nodded his understanding. "There are certain bodily functions beyond my control also."

Megan's face steamed. The man had no shame whatsoever. Had his sense of modesty been stunted at birth?

"Bath, sir."

Megan jumped again, unable to calm her nervousness.

"Just a moment." True to his nature, Justin was completely nonplussed by the arrival of their bath, and grinned into Megan's burning face. "You'd best cover yourself better, love. Even if our company is able to resist the sight of you, I can no longer guarantee my own self-control."

Megan jerked the bedsheet to her nose, but that flimsy blanket seemed inadequate. With one skittered glance at Justin's grinning face she scrambled, bare-bottomed to the end of the bed where she dredged up the blankets from beneath the tick.

His amused chuckle grated on her pride but the security of multiple blankets tucked snugly under her chin, made his humor well worth the irritation.

"Little Megan." He sat, naked as an egg upon the bed, living proof of his shocking lack of modesty. "You are, without a doubt, the most entertaining woman I have ever known."

Megan narrowed her eyes at him. She didn't know what he meant by 'entertaining' but she didn't like the sound of it. Being the object of his amusement was becoming painfully tiresome.

Justin watched her for a moment longer and then stepped to the floor to pull his breeches over his bare skin and turn to find her gaze glued tightly to the bedsheet once again.

The bathing tub arrived a moment later. It was a weighty, claw-footed porcelain and Megan eyed it with amazement. It was, she thought, the most glorious vat she had ever seen. Bucket after bucket of warm water was poured and tested. Finally a lacy dressing screen was set up before the elegant tub and Megan watched from the security of her cocoon as the last servants exited and Justin closed the door behind them.

"Well . . ." He turned from the door to raise his brows at her. "Are you ready for your bath?"

She eyed him narrowly. He was naked to the waist, long muscled and deadly masculine, and she'd greatly resented how the serving women had looked at him—like he was some sweetmeat, cooked to perfection.

"Come on, love," he urged. "Charleston awaits."

"No." She dearly longed to lounge in that tub, but her temper kept her immobile. How dare he flaunt his nudity before all those women and expect her to jump at his beck and call?

"What do you mean, 'no'?" he asked, scowling a little and placing his hard-knuckled fists on his hips. "You need a bath."

Megan glared at him, becoming angrier by the moment. "Then you'd best leave the room," she replied.

"Leave the . . ." Justin began in disbelief. "What are you cackling about now, woman?"

"I'm not bathing while you're here."

Justin stared in dumbstruck amazement. The woman had been as hot as a lynx beneath his hands only a few hours earlier and now she refused to bathe in front of him? "What's the reason for this new foolishness?" he asked impatiently.

"Foolishness!" she sputtered, almost forgetting to hold the blankets nose high. "You would call it foolish, I suppose, but I call it modesty. Of course you don't mind parading around like a buck in rut, but it so happens that *I* have higher morals."

He stared at her in wordless amazement, his mind trying to absorb her seemingly senseless ravings.

"You're jealous," Justin finally deduced, then gave with a slow, wicked grin.

"Jealous!" Megan gasped, shocked by his idiotic assessment. "Jealous of what?"

"Of me." He approached the bed slowly, grinning like an ill-mannered cat. "You're jealous of me."

"I am not," she spat over the blankets but Justin only laughed now, his naked chest heaving slightly in his amusement.

"You most certainly are." He chuckled, trying

to bring his humor under control. "But don't let it upset you. I think it's sweet."

She glared at him with all the heat she could muster. "You couldn't make me jealous if you bedded every woman in Carolina simultaneously. So don't flatter yourself."

"Flatter myself?" Suddenly Justin was upon the bed, braced on hands and knees as he stared at her eye to eye. "I don't flatter myself, love," he said huskily. "You flatter me, with your looks, your touch . . ." He paused, his hot gaze boring into her. "Your kiss."

His lips were warm and supple. She knew she should be angry. She was certain of it, and yet, it hardly seemed worth the trouble, not when he was so brazenly masculine, so nearly nude, so hard and lovely and . . .

"Come take a bath, love," he whispered, drawing away slightly.

How was it that he could mold her so easily? It seemed she no longer had a will of her own but was flung about, willy-nilly at the ends of her rampaging emotions.

"Come, love." He tugged gently at the blankets, but she had found the edges again and hung on for dear life.

"I—I can't."

"You can't?" His brows raised again as he tried to figure this new problem. "Can I ask why?"

"I——I'm naked."

Justin did his best to contain his mirth. Call him foolish but he thought that was the best way to bathe. "I know you're naked, love. But it's all right. I've seen you like that before. Remember?"

His voice sounded husky even to his own ears and he had to stop himself from pulling her into his arms and abandoning the entire idea of a bath.

"But, but," she stuttered nervously. "It's daylight."

Ah, so it was daylight. An astounding fact. "I know love, but don't worry, I won't tell anyone."

"But I can't just prance about in front of you in the daylight."

She was honest-to-God serious, Justin thought in amazement. She was embarrassed, ashamed of her own nudity. The idea was astounding to him. He knew women who would give their eye teeth to spend one hour inside a body like hers. She was, after all, at least as far as he knew, physically perfect.

"You haven't grown fat and ugly overnight, have you, love?" he questioned, not quite able to contain his humor. "You'd best stand up so I can check."

She didn't budge, didn't so much as raise her eyes.

"Really, Megan. This is ridiculous. You have to bathe and I've always found it most practical to bathe while disrobed." He raised one hand and the corner of his mouth. "Call me a cad."

"You'll have to leave the room." Her gaze finally found its way from the bedsheets.

"You must be joking," he said in disbelief.

"No." She shook her head with determination.

"But think on it, love. How would it look with me standing about in the hall? Suspicious, don't you think?" Who would believe I'm your lawfully wedded husband? He scowled at her as if actually considering her proposition. "I tell you what. How about if I turn my back?"

She was silent then. "You wouldn't look?" she asked uncertainly.

"Not until you're behind the screen and immersed in water," he promised.

She finally nodded her agreement and he stepped from the bed to turn his face into the wall.

"Now . . ." she said nervously. "You stay as you are." He heard her patter across the floor to the dressing table. "I have to put my hair up." He grinned, hearing her rummage about. "Don't turn," she reminded him. "Just a while longer." Her bare feet tapped across the floor and it was only a moment later that he heard the water welcome her entrance. Life could be a bundle of fun, Justin thought joyously.

"Are you safely hidden?" he called, doing his best to keep his voice from breaking with humor. Lord knows, he wouldn't want to be shocked by the sight of her awful nudity.

"Yes." Her voice sounded stronger from behind the barrier of the screen, as if she felt safe because of that flimsy piece of wood and cloth.

"Good." Justin smiled as his fingers whizzed over his trouser buttons, then nearly laughed as he pulled the garment from his legs. "You're fully immersed, I hope."

"Yes."

Was it his imagination or did her tone suggest

she didn't trust him completely? Oh well, no matter. Dropping his pants, he strode across the floor to step behind the screen.

"You!" Megan gasped. "You said you wouldn't look." Warm water splashed over the tub's edge as Megan slid down. Her fiery hair had been hastily pinned up so that a few filmy tendrils trilled to her shoulders while her arms did their inadequate best to cover her breasts and her legs shimmied over each other, trying to cover her woman's secrets.

He stood not three feet from the tub, absolutely naked and showing not an iota of decent modesty. "Now, that's not true, Megan," he chided. "I said I wouldn't look until you were completely immersed." He eyed her with the audacity of a wild animal. "And it looks to me like you're immersed. In fact, if you got any deeper I'd have to jump in and save you."

He grinned, raising his brows suggestively. "As a matter-of-fact, that's not a bad idea," he said, stepping nearer.

"What are you doing?" Megan asked, sliding even lower. He was an arrogant pain in the hindquarters and although she was tempted to slap that smug smile from his face, she was in a poor position to do so.

"I'm preparing to bathe," he answered casually. "Did you think I was simply modeling my wares for you? Slide over."

"You're joking!" Truly there was something wrong with the man. Where had he been when God handed out shame? Parading down the streets of gold, buck naked? "Don't you dare come in here."

His foot reached the water.

"Justin," she shrieked. "There's no room!"

"Certainly there is. We did this all the time as children."

Water splashed, Megan gasped, and Justin chuckled as he squeezed himself into the tub like a pickle beside its mate. "You know, love," he admitted wryly, "there's not quite as much room as I thought there would be. But then, such are the hardships of life."

Justin smiled, his face mere inches from the bounteous twin breasts, pressed together by Megan's well-meaning arms. "Well, isn't this cozy?"

She glared at him, not knowing if she should scream, kick, or merely incinerate into a smoking pile of humiliated ash. "Get out of my bath," she ordered.

"Now, Megan, it's not *your* bath. Honestly! You're so selfish with your goods." His gaze hadn't left the deep valley of her cleavage since his arrival. "While I, on the other hand, am so very willing to share."

Beneath the surface of the water Megan could feel the hard length of his shaft pressed intimately to her thigh.

"In fact, if there's anything in particular I could share with you at this very moment, I'm at your service." His face drew marginally nearer her breasts that remained uncovered by her arms.

"Justin," she gasped, honestly appalled by his lack of shame, "you—you—can't be in here."

"Why—why—not?" he asked, mimicking her

stutter as his dark, handsome face finally lifted
to look into hers.

"Be—because . . ." She tried to speak more
fluently. But Mother Mary, he was pressed to
her with the intimacy of a bloodhound in season. "It's a bathtub."

"So it is, love."

His statement ended abruptly, as if he awaited
a more expanded explanation.

"I have to bathe."

"Oh." Understanding seemed to dawn on
Justin's face and he squeezed his body upward
slightly, sliding his hard, heavenly form against
hers. "So that's the trouble. Well, it's no problem, really. I'll be happy to help you bathe.
Think of me as your servant. Where's the
soap?"

He lifted a hand from the water, doing nothing to prevent his arm from pressing gently
against the upper regions of her breasts. "Where
is it?" he repeated, scowling dramatically into
Megan's face as he rummaged about on the
short table that held the towels and soap. But
the bar of cleanser seemed to elude him until he
slipped his wet body over hers and peered over
the tub's rim to the table's top.

"Ah, there it is," he called triumphantly, lifting the cake of soap in his hand, then glancing
down into her reddened face. "I found it."

The entirety of his body was now pressed to
hers and although the tub was fair sized, it certainly was not large enough for him to stretch
out. He supported himself on his knees, with
one on either side of Megan's hips and the

shocking heat of his manhood sandwiched between them.

They stared at each other, Megan's eyes wide and skittish, Justin's warm and aroused.

"What would you like washed first?" His voice was as deep as his eyes and even if Megan could have thought of something to say, it was impossible for her mouth to form the words.

"It's a difficult decision, isn't it?" He grinned a little, canting his head. "I have the very same problem. But since space is a bit cramped, I guess I'll have to make do with the most accessible parts."

His gaze slid slowly from her face to her bunched breasts then upward again as he grinned his devilish smile. "Here goes," he drawled.

Easing back onto his knees, Justin made a show of ambitiously rubbing the soap to a froth. "Hold out your arm."

"Justin, really, I—"

"Oh, come now, Megan. One would think you didn't trust me. Give me your arm."

He took the limb from over her breasts. It was stiff in his hands as one rosy breast was uncovered. Megan saw his nostrils flare slightly as his eyes fell to the bare mound, but he said nothing, instead soaping each individual finger, then sliding the cake up her arm toward her shoulder, leaving a track of small, white bubbles. He dropped the soap to the water, then applied his attention to her fingers again, gently massaging each one between his large, dark hands.

Megan's lips parted slightly as her body relaxed. It was impossible to remain unmoved.

Her legs were bent to the side, while his large-muscled limbs pressed against them and his flat, rippled stomach stretched upwards into the glorious strength of his broad chest. His arms were heavy with muscle, his neck wide and dark. She felt the rhythm of her breathing increase.

Justin's hands moved towards her shoulder, smoothing along her arm. "I'm out of soap."

"What?" She'd been so involved with the lovely feel of his massage, it was difficult to focus on his words.

"I'll have to find the soap."

It took a moment for her to absorb his meaning, but suddenly his arms were on each side of her body as he fished for the missing cake.

"There. . . . Oops! Missed it." His chest was pressed to hers as his hands skimmed along the nether parts of her body. "Got it! Oops, missed again."

Megan felt the slippery missile skid beneath her legs and lodge against her bottom. Her eyes widened. Justin twisted slightly, eyeing her legs, then bent as if ready to dive beneath the surface.

His hand rose. There was a squeal and a splash as Megan lunged from the tub.

"Megan," he called, catching a glimpse of the towel as she snatched it from the table and dove to the opposite side of the screen.

"Well." He sighed, settling back against his feet and finding the soap with ease. "I suppose she's clean enough."

Chapter 23

Megan sat atop Rainstorm, dressed in her mauve gown and laughing. They'd been touring Charleston for several hours now. It was a lovely city, filled with beautiful sights and wonderful aromas, but it was Justin who thrilled her.

His wit was particularly sharp today, his smile always ready, and his eyes filled with a tender emotion that held her mesmerized.

"Are you hungry yet, love?" he questioned. "There's a nice inn not far from here. We could go there if you like."

"Whatever you wish," she said.

"Truly?" His brows rose suggestively. "Why couldn't you have had the same attitude this morning?"

She blushed readily and he laughed deep in his throat.

"Let's go. The inn's just down the street."

They hadn't ridden far when they heard the auctioneer's voice coming to them from down a tree-lined boulevard.

Megan frowned a question, but Justin was silent for a moment, then said, "Horse auction."

He smiled sheepishly. "I should have remembered it was today, but I fear I've been distracted with . . . ," he let his eyes skim her curvy form, "more pleasant things."

"I . . ." She couldn't breath when he looked at her like that. "I like looking at horses."

"I like looking at you," he said, leaning sideways to touch her hand.

Megan drew breath through her teeth, her eyes widening at the shocking sensation such a simple gesture created.

"And touching you," he added quietly, letting his fingertips run up the bare flesh of her lower arm.

Shivers proceeded his caress, careening up her forearm to scurry riotous messages to her buzzing brain. Her lips parted slightly but she said nothing and Justin chuckled.

"You'd best not look at me like that, Megan," he warned in a husky whisper as he leaned close, pressing his gelding up against her mare. "Or I'll forget completely about the auction and find some grassy spot in the dappled shade of an elm."

Her jaw dropped lower as she mentally visualized such activity. Could they do it outdoors? In the shade—in front of God and everyone? Her eyes widened and Justin laughed aloud.

"Come, love. We'll appease your curiousity in flesh," he murmured, turning his mount but she failed to follow, seeming stuck in her tracks. "Megan," he chided glancing over his shoulder. "I mean horseflesh, of course."

There were horses everywhere, some being shown to prospective owners, some being ridden, but the vast majority stood tied in rows to ropes that ran from tree to tree.

It was a large grassy area with a livery barn behind and black carriages all about.

Tying their own mounts to an available tree, Justin and Megan wandered about. The sun was warm, flies buzzed, and horses lazily swatted their course tails. People milled about, laughing and talking, some picnicking on the outskirts of the grassy scene, lending an almost fair-like atmosphere to the scene.

But Justin's attention was on Megan alone. Her eyes were alight with pleasure, her step quick and energetic as she strode from horse to horse.

The comments she made were not the giddy statements of a pampered southern belle but rather were intelligent observations from a woman who knew and understood the equine species.

A dark, long-limbed young stallion caught her eye and she wandered in that direction, surreptitiously watching as he was trotted out for another's inspection.

Justin followed her, admiring the gentle sway of her hips and catching up as she slid her hand along the hip of a sway-backed mare. She was absorbed in the study of the flashy stallion and he smiled to himself, loving the intensity in her pert face as she peeked over the chestnut toward the now returning colt.

"Nice horse," he said, leaning against a nearby tree to cross one leg before the other.

"Yes," she murmured, her gaze not lowering from the prancing gait of the two year old.

"Good eye. Nice bone."

"Beautiful," she agreed, mesmerized by the stallion's movement.

"Rich color."

"Ummm." She sighed dreamily.

"Little long in the back though."

"What?" She turned to him with a scowl. "Long?"

"The mare," he said, indicating the cock-hipped chestnut she was stroking. "She's a little—"

"The mare!" Megan scolded quietly. "How can you be looking at her with him ..." She nodded unobtrusively toward the arrogant stallion.

"What?" Justin feigned an expression of surprise. "You like that little runt?"

"Runt!" she chided. "He's wonderful. I've never seen more fluid action."

"Him?" Justin straightened, scowling slightly as if in disapproval. "Too narrow."

"Narrow!" Her voice was rising. "You don't know a thing about horses. He's—"

Justin laughed out loud, stepping close to slip his arms about her waist and whisper. "But I know a good deal about women." He kissed her ear lightly, causing her jaw to drop. "And I've got myself a woman who knows all about horses, so I can concentrate on other things."

Gooseflesh was spreading from her tingling ear, but Megan frowned. "You were teasing me," she accused shortly.

"Me? No."

She glared at him, trying to be angry. "You know very well he's a beauty."

"I know you're a beauty," he countered.

"He'd . . ." She was losing her line of thought. "He'd produce beautiful babies," she said breathlessly.

"So would you," he whispered, his hands slipping lower.

"Are . . ." She was breathing hard and leaned back slightly, trying to maintain some decorum. "Are you trying to seduce me . . . again?"

He chuckled. "I can't do it too often." His hands cupped her buttocks through the few layers of her garments.

"I . . . Justin!" she gasped. "This is hardly . . . proper."

"I can't help it," he murmured back. "I don't feel . . . proper . . . when I'm near you." He pressed one hand upward, following the course of her spine and causing her to arch slightly toward him.

"This isn't . . ." she began in a scandalized tone, but at that moment Justin pressed the hard evidence of his desire up against her thigh and she gasped. "It's not—" she tried again, but her thoughts ran riot. "Where's that dappled shade under the elm?" she whispered breathlessly.

Justin chuckled again, drawing away slightly. "I'd love to, Megan," he admitted. "But . . . I have things to do." He stepped back. "You look about. I'll catch up with you soon."

"But . . ." she sputtered. "But . . ."

"Sorry." He grinned. "Hold that thought. I'll be back."

He strode off, hard desire and all, and Megan scowled. The man was a tease!

Ten minutes passed quickly for if Justin

wasn't about to distract her Megan was more than happy to peruse horses. A young foal cavorted beside its mother and she stopped for a moment, smiling at its antics, but a movement caught her attention, a flash of red hair, and she turned quickly.

Michael? Had it been Michael? She searched the crowd, but he was gone. And then there he was again, a narrow back and auburn hair.

She hurried after him, squeezing through the crowd toward the livery.

It was slightly cooler in the shade of the building, but she was alone there. If it had indeed been Michael, he was gone now. Megan turned.

"Miss Welsh!"

Robert Tolbert stood not two feet from her, smiling drunkenly.

"Or is it Miss Megan today?"

Megan froze. What was he doing there?

"Don't look so surprised," Tolbert crooned. "We were bound to find each other again. It's fate."

He took a step toward her.

"Get out of my way."

"Oh no, Buttercup. I've been dreaming about you for weeks. I ain't going to give you up so easy this time."

"Let me pass," she insisted, stepping to the side, but suddenly Tolbert lunged, grabbing her and pressing her up against the wooden building.

She tried to shriek, but his hand covered her mouth, pressing the scream down her throat.

"Don't act so cold, Buttercup," Tolbert said. "I

know your kind. I've been remembering your kiss ever since that first time. And I know you liked it too."

Megan tried to relax. He was drunk. She would get away unscathed if she kept her head. She forced her shoulders to drop slightly.

"Thatta girl. You're remembering now, too, aren't you?"

She nodded, slowing her breathing.

"You must have seen me back here and come looking, huh? Finally lost Stearns!"

Megan nodded again, thinking hard.

"Then kiss me, girl," he demanded, and suddenly his hand was replaced by his mouth.

Megan remained motionless, readying herself, but suddenly Tolbert was ripped away and thrown to the ground where he crumpled like a crushed doll.

"Get back to your horse, Megan," Justin snarled, not looking at her.

"Justin," she breathed but he didn't turn.

"Go!" he raged.

Megan raised her hand to her mouth, truly afraid. "What are you going to do to him?"

Justin remained silent, his body as large and stiff as a tree, but he turned his head finally, the movement slow. "I didn't know you cared," he said coolly.

"He didn't hurt me," she breathed, reading the rage in his eyes.

Tolbert scrambled to his feet. "Touch me and my daddy'll have your hide," he sputtered, backing away.

A growl rose from Justin's throat and he took

a step toward him, but Megan caught his arm, terrified.

"No! Justin! Don't!"

He turned to her again. A muscle jumped in his cheek. His face was stonily cold. "Very well." He grasped her arm in a hard grip, turning her away. "If he means that much to you."

Chapter 24

Megan paced the length of her simple room. It had been three days since their return to Free Winds and in that time Justin had barely spoken a word to her.

He blamed her for Tolbert's attack. She knew it, although he'd not said it in words. Megan paced again, clenching her fists.

Wasn't it just like a man to blame the victim for the crime? Michael had been known to do the same. She scowled at the black square of window, thinking. But at least Michael would have voiced his accusations.

Not Justin, however. He'd hardly entered the house, not even complaining about her poor culinary attempts.

What little time he was abed was spent in the smaller room, leaving his bedchamber for her. He never spoke and the anger emanating from him seemed almost a tangible thing. Anger at her! And for what?

She'd had her fill! Megan gritted her teeth angrily. She couldn't bear any more of his silent accusations. Tonight was the night to get things out in the open and if he couldn't believe she was innocent she'd leave. He wouldn't stop her now. She was sure of it. The only problem was she didn't want to go.

Megan turned abruptly, pacing to the far side of the room where she pressed clammy fingertips to her forehead. She didn't want to leave. It was true. When it had happened, she didn't know but the thought of leaving left a cold, hard knot in the pit of her stomach. What would she do if she couldn't see him again—not see him smile, not hear his laughter?

The door slammed below her and Megan jerked into rigid immobility. He was home! Her eyes skittered to the door as she pressed her hands together again in nervous worry. Would he come up or would she have to seek him out?

In the end she found Justin in the kitchen, seated before a half-empty bottle of whiskey.

"Well . . ." His voice was slightly slurred, his eyes somewhat unfocused. "If it isn't my beautiful Megan."

She stiffened, scowling at his unusual condition. He was drunk and disheveled, with his shirt opened nearly to the waist, baring the tan of his sloping chest. "I need to talk to you, Justin."

"Truly?" He raised bloodshot eyes to hers. "What is it my dear lady wishes to discuss?"

Megan paused a moment, resisting the urge to wring her hands together and forming them into tight balls at her sides. "I want to speak to you about Charleston."

"Ah . . ." he murmured, taking a swig straight from the bottle. "Our time together in Charleston." He leered up at her, lifting the whiskey in a salute. "I remember it well." He paused again, pushing his weight against the back of the chair and canting his head at her. "And what would you like to say about it, Megan? That you've never felt ecstasy in all your life? That you dream every night of our time there together? Or perhaps you wish to explain your meeting with Tolbert." His face was dark and taut. "Now there's a likely subject. Our dear—and let us not forget—rich—Robert Tolbert, the sole heir to his father's fortune."

Megan scowled at him, her gut twisting.

"Couldn't you have found a more secluded place to meet with him, Megan? Couldn't you have at least waited until I was out of sight?"

"I had no intention of meeting with him," she whispered.

"No intention," Justin scoffed, lifting the bottle again. "How is it then that you so conveniently met him alone there?"

"I—"

"And isn't it a coincidence that it was mere days after I confessed I would gain none of my father's wealth?" he questioned caustically. "Mere days, Megan. One would think you could have waited a week, that you could have borne my company that long. But not you, huh? You're an opportunist to the last, aren't you?"

She was silent, staring at him, feeling as though her heart had been crushed.

"Aren't you?" he asked again, louder now.

"No." She shook her head. "I don't care about money."

"Don't lie to me, woman!" he roared suddenly, lunging to his feet and overturning his chair.

Megan gasped and backed away. He was large and dangerous. His eyes looked haunted and frightening.

"Do you know how it feels to be lied to again and again?" he asked, rounding the table to step toward her. "Do you know what it's like to wonder constantly if this will be the day she'll disappear with your money or your horses or . . ." He lifted his arms, at a loss for words. "And yet . . ." He paused, glaring at her with hot intensity. "She's so lovely, so soft, so filled with life and . . ." He shook his head, his voice dropping. "That you can't let her go."

Megan stared at him. Her throat ached with loneliness; her heart ached with blinding hopelessness. "I *need* to go, Justin," she whispered. There was no other way, no way he'd ever trust her.

"Go?" he asked, snorting as if she'd told a silly joke. "I'm not letting you go, Megan. You owe me."

"What do I owe you?"

"Money," he said coldly. "A good deal of money. And how will you pay it off, Megan? I can't trust you out of my sight. But . . ." He stepped closer and she backed away. "If I keep my hands on you, perhaps you could work off your debt on your back."

"Don't touch me!" she warned, fear tightening her throat.

"But you want to pay what you owe, don't you? After all, you'd hate to be indebted to me when you go to another." He approached again, his strides unsteady.

"I'm warning you, Justin. Don't come nearer."

"Or what?" He didn't heed her words but continued across the floor, backing her finally against the table that stood near the wall.

"Or . . ." Megan's eyes skimmed the room, searching desperately for a weapon as her hands braced behind her on the table's edge. Her fingers skimmed over the implements on the table as she prayed for a cleaver. But there was nothing more deadly than a castiron pan. She grasped the handle, lifting the heavy thing to brandish it before her. "Or . . . you'll regret it. I promise."

Justin merely stared for a moment, seeming stunned by her choice of weapons and then he chuckled, the sound coming from somewhere deep inside as he shook his head.

"Oh, Megan! It's true you're not easy to live with, but goddamn if you're not entertaining. Put down the pan."

"I'll die first." It sounded melodramatic even to her own ears, but her fear was fading, her temper rising. She held the pan over her shoulder, ready to remove his head.

"Put it down."

"N—" Megan began but suddenly the pan was wrenched from her hands and Justin towered over her, glowering into his face.

"Hear this, woman," he growled. "If I wanted to take you here and now, I could." His breath smelled like death, his eyes looked no better and his hands burned on her arms. "But it's not worth the trouble."

Justin dropped her arms suddenly and stepped back. Megan glared at him, hating him, then watched in utter astonishment as he crumbled to the floor.

Chapter 25

"**J**ustin?" Her mouth dropped open and she bent slightly, brushing her hair aside in an attempt to see his face. Was he playing a trick, paying her back for her own theatrical performances? "Justin?"

He was as silent as death and she approached slowly, finally touching his arm tentatively. It was hot beneath her hands. She scowled, then placed her palm to his forehead. It burned like fire.

"Justin," she called frantically. "Justin, what ails you?"

His eyelids lifted slowly, showing the tortured orbs behind. "Megan," he breathed. "I'm sorry." He was silent for a moment. "Seeing you with another . . ." He closed his eyes. "I can't hold you here. Against your will."

"You're ill," she said, not understanding his words but desperate to help him.

"It's just a fever. Not uncommon. Don't worry."

Don't worry? Don't worry? Mother Mary, the man was dying on the kitchen floor.

"I just need sleep. Couldn't sleep—without

you. Couldn't sleep—with you. Couldn't eat."
He snorted a derisive laugh. "I'm a fool." His
lids drooped, but Megan shook him frantically.

"Justin," she called. "You need to get to bed.
I'm taking you to bed."

Her statement failed to register in his burning
brain, a true measure of his illness, and she
grasped his arm, trying to pry him from the
floor. It was hopeless. He outweighed her by a
good one hundred pounds.

"Megan." His eyes opened again, like a
drunken man's. Only he was not. "I need to get
to bed."

"Yes." Hadn't she just said that? "I'll get you
upstairs. Don't worry." She tried again to coax
his arm over her shoulder while dragging at his
substantial weight. She tugged with all her
might and he assisted finally, slowly rising to
his feet.

It took a full ten minutes to get him up the
stairs. Megan leaned against the doorjamb of
the small room, gasping for breath as Justin's
weight dragged at her shoulder. "Just a little farther," she rasped.

They started again, limping with painful
slowness across the room until Justin collapsed
on the bed. Megan paused for breath, then bent
and with great effort was able to lift his legs and
drag them onto the feather tick. She staggered
back a step, staring at him. He seemed to be un-
conscious. She should cover him, she thought.
But since there was no hope of getting the blankets from beneath him, she hurried into his
room and returned just as quickly to cover him

with the blankets she had jerked from his bed. She leaned forward, scowling her worry.

"Justin?" she whispered. Was it possible he was feigning sickness? she wondered hopefully, but when her palm touched his burning forehead that hope vanished. "Justin, I'm going for a doctor. I'll be back soon."

He remained silent. Smoothing the blanket fretfully, she turned away but his hand lifted abruptly, grasping her arm in a weak grip.

"Don't leave me, Megan," he whispered painfully. His lids lifted for just an instant, his reddened eyes haunted. "Please."

She stared at him breathlessly. She should leave. She knew nothing of sickness or fevers. She needed help. She couldn't care for him alone.

"Please," he whispered again, his voice hoarse and she shook her head emphatically.

"No. I won't, Justin. I won't. You sleep now. I'll be here."

His eyes fell closed, as if the effort needed for speech had taxed him, but she thought she heard 'thank you' in a tone too soft to fully discern. A tremor shook him and she bit her lip, pulling the blankets closer to his chin.

"I'll get more quilts," she said, gently pulling her arm from his grasp and he did nothing to stop her.

Running from room to room, she collected all the blankets she could find before hurrying back to Justin. He lay curled up on his side, unwarmed by the fever that made his massive form tremble. Megan spread the multiple blankets over him.

His eyes wavered open, focusing poorly but his fingers caught her arm again, tugging at her. Megan scowled, not understanding his wishes at first. Finally she lowered herself beside him and he seemed content, drifting off into a too-deep sleep within seconds.

Megan lay awake in the darkness. Panic seared her brain, guilt gnawed at her conscience. What if he died? She had never shown him kindness. She'd never told him how she felt about him.

Perhaps he had malaria. She pushed the terrifying idea from her head, trying to forget the endless, mosquito-infested nights he had remained outside too long.

Maybe he had cholera. She knew little of either disease but had seen the devastating effects and knew the probability of death. Without thought, her arms found their way about his damp back and she hugged him to her, desperate at the thought of losing him.

She should go for a doctor now, while he slept, she thought, but her slightest movement disturbed him. Megan closed her eyes, trying to still her worry. He was strong, she reminded herself, but her heart continued to thud frantically against her restricted chest. He'd lived near the Carolina swamps all his life. Surely he would fight off this fever. And perhaps there was something she could give him. Quinine. They gave quinine for fever. But where would she find some?

She bit her lip and prayed numbly, remembering the things he had said about past illnesses. She should have delved into his past, but he

had always seemed so strong—almost inde-
structible. She'd never dreamed he was becoming sick. But she should have known. She
should have read the signs. It was her fault that
he had worked so late each night. After all, it
was her presence in his house that had made
him avoid the protection provided there.

It was her fault. She prayed more feverishly,
feeling him tremble against her.

The night seemed to last forever. The silence
was intolerable as doubts raged in Megan's
head. She couldn't find comfort, only fretful
sleep, interrupted by Justin's moans of pain and
the choking heat that held her.

Dawn came after a lifetime. Justin opened his
eyes groggily to the light of day. Megan lay in
his arms, watching him awaken, and praying.

"Megan." His voice sounded fairly lucid, but
surprised as if he had no recollection of the
night just past.

She scowled and raised a hand to his brow,
wondering if, perhaps, the night had been nothing more than a horrid dream. But the ravishing
heat remained, embedded in his skull like a
venomed arrow.

"Are you feeling better?" she asked softly.

He smiled, but the expression did nothing to
decrease the dreadful haggardness of his face.
"I'll survive this." His dark brow furrowed with
the effort of speech. "It's not as bad as it seems."

Not as bad. Holy Patrick, Megan thought
wearily. He looked as if he were about to die yet
had the unmitigated nerve to spout platitudes.

"I'll go for a doctor," she said quickly, but he

tightened his arms about her, preventing her escape.

"There's no need." He sounded exhausted and seemed to struggle to keep his eyes open. "I'm sorry to trouble you, Megan." His eyelids drooped but he snapped them open, a panicked expression crossing his face for a moment as he jerked back to wakefulness.

"Don't leave me," he rasped. His eyes burned hers. His fingers clawed desperately at her back but then he drew a heavy breath, forcing himself to relax again as he quieted his words. "Please."

Megan remained motionless, watching his face. Her chest felt compressed with pain. "No," she whispered. "I won't."

Hours passed in silence as worry burned at Megan's mind. He opened his eyes finally and she watched as his gaze settled on her.

"Water," was all he managed.

She nodded, then slid away, careful not to disturb the blankets, but he seemed beyond awareness already.

Outside, the breeze felt cool compared to the stifling heat of the bedroom, but she hurried to the well, not noticing the freshness of the air. No one was about, an affirmation that it was Sunday, the only day when Zeke didn't come.

She needed help. She needed someone, but she was alone. Lifting the bucket, Megan hurried back to the house. He wouldn't die. He wouldn't.

"God!" She felt the prayer like an ache in her soul. "Don't let him die, Lord." She drew a deep breath, praying for strength, then hurried up the stairs, with hands slightly steadied.

"Justin," she called softly, touching his brow again to feel the consuming heat. "I brought you water."

His eyes opened painfully and he struggled to sit, but the debilitating weakness brought him no farther than his pillow's edge. Megan bent, wincing at his obvious pain and pressing at his back to help him sit.

He drank deeply, gulping at the water with parched lips until she withdrew and refilled the cup. He drank again and finally tipped his head back to rest it against the walnut headboard. "Thank you." His eyes caught hers and in their depths she could see a gratitude much deeper than his thankfulness for water.

"Are you still cold?" She tried to hide her worry, but she was no actress, only a young woman, alone and afraid.

He nodded and she set the cup aside. "I'll heat some broth."

"No." He didn't lift a hand but stared at her silently, his face gaunt and haggard. "Please stay."

She nodded, searching the room for a chair, but he couldn't bear her distance.

"Here," he said weakly.

He didn't explain his words, but she understood and slipped into bed beside him, fully dressed except for her bare feet. He slid downward, and in a moment his breathing came deep and heavy again.

Megan shifted her weight slightly, careful not

to disturb him, but his eyes opened groggily, finding her face.

"I won't leave." Even she wasn't sure why she said it, but when his expression showed his relief, she felt a confusing gratitude. He didn't trust her, never would. She should have some pride—pride enough to leave. But she didn't. Instead she was willing to live in sin—so long as she lived with him. She closed her eyes and he relaxed again, but just when she thought he slept, he lifted one hand. She watched as his dark, tapered fingers lifted to the top button of her simple blouse.

She didn't draw away but examined his lean features. The fever had not only robbed him of strength but of flesh too. He looked gaunt and hungry, with slight valleys shadowing his cheeks. Her gaze fell to his fingers, noting the three buttons he had loosed. His eyes lifted to hers for a moment, his expression gentle and guileless before his mahogany eyes were hidden behind his lids again. He drew her closer. She felt the rasp of his neglected whiskers against the tender flesh of her upper breasts and pulled him tightly into her embrace.

It was some hours later that she awakened. The room felt hot and stifling yet Justin shivered beside her. She pulled the blankets higher and waited.

The day passed slowly, finally falling into darkness. The night seemed longer still.

Dawn came. Megan awoke from an uneasy nap to find Justin had pushed his blankets aside.

"Megan." His eyes opened to meet hers, his

tone breathless with surprise. "You've returned."

"I'm here," she said softly, brushing the damp hair from his forehead. "I haven't left. Do you want water?"

He nodded and she lifted the cup to his lips. "Not so fast, Justin. Are you hot?"

He nodded again.

"Maybe it'd be best if you took off some clothes."

"Good idea."

His answer was hoarse but had come surprisingly quickly and she eyed him cautiously, wondering if there had been an edge of suggestiveness in his tone. But looking at his lean, feverish face she banished the thought, feeling guilty for her suspicions.

Slipping his shirt buttons loose from their holes, Megan pulled the sleeves from his arms and eased the garment from behind his damp back. His eyes dropped closed again and she studied him for a moment.

Even in sickness he was a masculine masterpiece, so beautifully sculpted that she found herself indecently attracted to him. Every muscle was wonderfully carved into hollows and hills, every bone broad and strong. Her gaze slipped from his wide throat down his smooth chest to his flat, hard belly.

He was stunning, truly. . . . What was wrong with her? The man was sick, she reminded herself sternly. And she was even sicker to entertain such lascivious ideas when he was caught in such a terrible fever. Scowling darkly, Megan hurried from the room, but after rummaging about in his wardrobe, she returned to his bedside.

"Justin," she said softly, standing beside him with towels and a washcloth. "If you're not too tired I could bathe you somewhat. It might make you more comfortable."

His eyes opened in an instant with just the mist of a smile. "Please," he said, beginning to sit, but she pushed gently at his chest, feeling the heat that dwelled there.

"Just lie back," she ordered. "You don't suppose you're strong enough for a tub bath, do you? I brought some water to sponge you off."

Justin settled back, watching her with his warm, steady gaze as she dipped her cloth in the basin and squeezed out the excess water. She lifted the rag then, and beginning at his broad throat, smoothed it along his endless shoulders and heavy arms until she reached his hands.

Picking up his right hand, Megan washed each digit separately. He closed his eyes to her administrations, enjoying the cool massage against his flesh. She moved finally up his arm again, then across the broad expanse of his chest. It was smooth and hard, bulging with rigid muscle and beautifully sculpted with bone and sinew.

Megan took in each detail there, appreciating every masculine quality, until she realized his velvety gaze and fallen upon her again. Embarrassed by her obsession with the task, she bit her lip and settled uneasily against her bare feet.

"If you moved to the other room I could get

you from these damp linens and wash your back," she suggested after a moment.

Justin made no comment but studied her for a moment before easing his stockinged feet to the floor. Megan hurried to assist him and in a few seconds he lowered himself to his own soft tick, careful not to jar the headache that accompanied the terrible fever. He didn't lie down immediately, however, but sat on the edge of the bed to undo the buttons that bound the top of his well-tailored trousers.

Megan frowned, bit her lip, and frowned again. Removing his shirt had seemed a fairly harmless idea, but removing his pants. . . . It seemed rather. . . . But, well . . . surely she could stay and watch. But. . . . Turning with the shyness of a spring hare, she scurried from the room in search of the clothes and water left behind.

It was not much later that she returned. But the situation had not improved. For now Justin lay absolutely naked beneath the sheer white sheet. She could tell he was naked, for the sheet was low enough to reveal the paler skin, usually hidden by his britches.

Megan stopped in the doorway, immobilized by the sight of him. The man had no modesty whatsoever, she reminded herself, but it hardly seemed proper to criticize someone who was so obviously ill. With faltering steps, she ventured slowly into the room to place the basin near the bed.

Settling onto the mattress, Megan immersed the cloth to begin the job of bathing his back. It stretched out beneath her hands, dark, broad, and beautifully muscled. And while his chest and shoulders had been distracting, this new situation proved to be nearly painful. True, his most private parts were covered by the light-weight sheet, but even so, the nearly transparent linen did nothing to hide the smooth masculinity of his back that flowed so wonderfully into the curve of his hips.

Idly she wondered if, perhaps, he planned to seduce her, then discarded the idea quickly, chastising herself for such an uncharitable thought. The poor man was deathly ill, after all.

The bathing went on interminably for it was not an unpleasant task, with his warm flesh so firm and smooth beneath her hands. Perhaps, she thought, avoiding any regions lower than the slight indentation of his waist, it'd be good if she washed his legs too. But the warmth that already diffused to her face warned her against such a task.

Feeling Megan's movements slow, Justin rolled to his back and rested his gaze on her wide, emerald eyes. "Thank you." He smiled gently, but Megan failed to notice that movement of his body had displaced the protective sheet just enough to reveal the full effect her touch had produced in him.

Her gaze held awkwardly on the swollen proof of his desire, standing erect and ready above the white sheet. Mother Mary! Her gaze shot upward, her face beaming red.

Perhaps he was not so ill as she had thought. Or, perhaps nothing affected that particular part of him. "I—I . . ." she stammered. "I'll bring that broth."

Upon returning, Megan was relieved to find the naughty sheet was once again in place, hiding everything below the thickest matting of hair that furred his rigid and undulated abdomen. Setting the bowl of broth aside, she leaned across the bed to help him to a seated position.

He scooted himself upwards readily enough, but when his eyes did not rise to her face, she lowered her own gaze in search of an explanation. Her blouse! She gasped in dismay. Somehow in her concern for his care, she had forgotten the buttons he had opened the night before and now as she bent to help him, her breasts had fairly fallen into his face.

Megan stiffened, prepared for retreat, but his hands were suddenly on hers, holding her steady as if to view her for just a moment longer.

"Your broth is certainly cool by now," she said, fumbling for something to keep her heart from pounding from her chest. He didn't seem to hear her. His hand lifted and he ran gentle fingertips with feather lightness, down the crevice between her breasts.

She realized with frightening clarity that the heat in his eyes had little to do with the fever that plagued him.

"You should eat," she rattled on quickly. "Or you'll never regain your strength. I—I mean," she stuttered, realizing her statement sounded as if she worried over his future sexual performances, "you look hungry. I mean," she stumbled, "can you manage the soup yourself?"

Her face was bright with embarrassment now and she couldn't trust herself to sit so near the flame of his person. Justin, however, seemed to be completely unaware of her blundering and said softly, "I don't feel terribly strong."

His answer sounded beguiling, as if it came from a charming boy. Yet the dark body that leaned back against the pillows was that of a man, fully mature and more than able to create a bundle of trouble for any healthy woman.

Calming her trembling and reminding herself that he *was* a sick man, Megan seated herself again at Justin's side. His eyes never left her face while she fed him, and though he didn't talk, she felt as if she read his thoughts—not in any coherent way, but in a strange sort of understanding that made her feel unreasonably content.

She rose finally, setting the bowl aside and turning to the window. Somehow evening had come.

"Are there any chores that I should do before nightfall?" she asked softly.

Justin shook his head, loath to speak for the effort it took. "Zeke'll see to them." He paused. "You look tired. Come to bed."

The beguiling boy was back and though Megan tried, she found she couldn't resist him. He was too charming, too dependent, and she fell asleep quickly in his arms, her back braced against the warm firmness of his wide chest.

Midnight had come and gone yet dawn was hours away when Megan was wrenched from her sleep. She jerked herself upright, frantically searching the room for the noise that had awakened her, but no demons were there, only Justin's rigid body beside hers.

He sat erect, his massive chest heaving from the effect of his dreams. "Megan," he choked, his quick gaze searching her for injuries and his trembling arms enfolding her. "I thought ..." His eyes closed, his breathing harsh and quick against her neck. "It was only a nightmare, I guess," he whispered, and yet that realization would not allow him to release her, and he lay back finally, bringing her with him.

No more words were spoken. He gave no explanation, but pressed the full length of his taut body against hers, holding her as if the demons of his dreams might snatch her away. Still, sleep returned eventually, enfolding him once again in blessed oblivion.

Megan lay in the darkness, unable to find the comfort of slumber as she tried to understand herself and the man who slept beside her. During his illness she had viewed a side of him she'd not known existed, a facet she guessed few others had seen. It was softer, less independent. Weaker, she supposed. And yet, it was a weakness that appealed to her, a soft, new element that made him turn to her for help.

Dawn came after a turbulent eternity for Megan and she opened her eyes to find Justin staring at her.

"I think the worst is behind us." He reached up to caress a curl that lay over her shoulder. "Just the aches and pains left," he added, moving one muscular leg beneath the sheet in an effort to relieve a cramp.

Megan searched his eyes. She'd failed to realize how wonderful it would be to see him well, to see his smile and the warm cider wonder of his clear eyes.

"I . . ." Justin paused, lifting his arm and settling his head onto one broad wrist. "I want to apologize for last night. I must have scared you nearly from your wits."

Megan shifted her eyes downward, remembering the frightful shriek that had awakened her. "What did you dream?" she asked finally, lifting her gaze to his.

He didn't answer for a time but watched her face as if searching for something, then, shifting his weight, he turned his gaze to the ceiling.

"I dreamed about your brother." His voice was little more expressive than a monotone, the only evidence of his emotions revealed in the stiffness of his body, the tightening of his bunched muscles. "You left with him." He drew a deep breath, thinking he shouldn't tell her, shouldn't reveal the depth of the concern he had for her, the need he had for her presence. But she'd stayed with him through the fever—when she could have left. Perhaps she cared. Perhaps. "I searched for you," he said softly. "But when I found you—you were dead."

There was fear in his face. Pain and fear. It was camouflaged, but it was there. Suddenly she could see it as clearly as if it were chiseled in stone. She should say something, she thought—should tell him how she couldn't bear to leave him. But she didn't dare. He'd made no commitment to her. She was only his mistress, possibly one in a long line. Tomorrow he may tire of her and what then?

"Thank you for staying, Megan," he said

softly. The monotone was gone and in its place was a grateful warmth.

There was so little she could say, and yet, there remained so much that should be spoken, so much his illness had revealed to her. "I had no idea you were becoming ill," she said softly.

Justin retrieved another bright curl from her shoulder and grinned. "I think it was your cooking."

Megan dropped her eyes. It could very well have been, she thought, for she herself was losing flesh. "I'm sorry."

"Megan." He touched her chin, lifting her face. "I was only joking. It's my own fault. I've had this fever enough to know when to expect its assault. I should have rested. I shouldn't have been drinking. But the thought of you . . ." His words stopped and he drew another heavy breath. He loved her. There was no point in denying it. He loved her beyond all reason and he would do what was in his power to keep her. But if he couldn't?

Justin's muscles tightened and he forced himself to relax. If he couldn't hold her, he would love her while he could.

"I'm sorry for my behavior in the kitchen," he said quietly. "I seem to remember saying it wasn't worth the effort of taking you . . ." Justin shrugged one heavy shoulder, smoothing the curl against her elegant throat. "I lied."

His eyes were as full of promise as April, and when he leaned forward to kiss her, there seemed nothing she could do but melt in his warmth.

A heavy rap at the door below caused Megan

to jerk away, scrambling from the bed to straighten her gown. "Someone's here," she said breathlessly, hurriedly fastening her wayward buttons.

"Its seems so, love," Justin agreed slowly, settling his dark head against his lower arm again.

"I'll—I'll go see who it is."

The crinkles about his eyes proved his mirth. "That would seem very practical, Megan."

After a poor attempt to smooth her hair into place, she scurried down the stairs to open the door. Zeke stood holding a covered basket, his impish face alight with happiness.

"Had t' tell y' the good news," he declared with a crooked grin. "The missus birthed a right healthy baby."

"Oh, Zeke, I'm so glad."

"Yup. Me, too. But that ain't all of it." He shook his head as if shocked beyond belief. "It's a girl."

"A girl!" Megan was genuinely thrilled. "That's wonderful!"

"Well, thank y', Miss Megan. Oh, and the missus sent this here for y'," he added, lifting the basket. "How's Justin fairing?"

"You knew he was sick?"

"Well sure. I've been around a while, y' know. Long enough to know he don't like nobody hangin' round when he's feelin' poorly." He looked at her with that unique blue-eyed twinkle. " 'Ceptin' you of course, miss."

She blushed to the roots of her hair, accepting the basket and wishing she could bury her head in it. "Your wife shouldn't have gone through all the trouble," she said. "In fact she should still be in bed."

"My missus?" he asked with a proud laugh. "Not likely. She was up and about the next morning, and a worryin' bout Justin. But I see you been takin' good care of him." For a moment she thought he was going to burst into laughter, but he confined his mirth to a broad, knowing smile. "You tell him not to worry 'bout nothin'. Me and my boys are here and we'll see everything gets done up proper."

Back upstairs, Megan set the basket on the small commode beside the bed. Justin was lying on his side and watched her as she fiddled with the checkered napkin that covered the basket's contents.

"Zeke's wife had a baby girl," Megan said, not raising her eyes.

"Really?" He seemed genuinely pleased and chuckled aloud. "Lucky for them. They were fast running out of boys' names. And the baby and mother, they're doing well?"

"Apparently so. She sent this basket to help you mend."

"Ahh—" Justin drew a deep breath, inhaling the aromas coming from the basket. "Sara's pastries. She's a rare woman."

Megan stood beside the bed, silent and still, and Justin watched her quietly before reaching up with a gentle expression.

"Of course, not so rare as you, Megan."

She was acting like a fool. She knew it, and yet she couldn't help but shuffle her feet and stare at the floor. The last thing she needed was to be jealous of Zeke's wife when there was enough honest competition to go around.

"I can't bake pastries," she said, realizing that she sounded as immature as a child.

Justin laughed deep in his throat, tugging at her hand and causing the sheet to fall lower across the dark skin of his bare chest. "But there are other things you do so incredibly well, love. We can hire a cook, but I would not hire another to take your place in my bed."

"J—Justin! Really. You need to eat to get your strength back. Really."

He chuckled again but succumbed easily to her demands. "I suppose you're right, love. Bring on the basket." His hand touched hers, his eyes dark and suggestive. "Dessert can come later."

Chapter 26

"**D**o you miss your brother?"
Justin's voice was quiet and Megan found herself lost in the deep recesses of his eyes.

"A bit, perhaps," she said softly, fiddling with the checkered napkin that covered the remains of Sara's feast.

"Just a bit?"

His body was tense again, making her wonder at his thoughts.

"We've been together for some time," she said, shifting her eyes to the basket she held in her hands. "He was all I had before ..." She stopped, raising her gaze to his.

"Before what, Megan?" Justin asked, his expression taut.

She felt breathless and terrified. Before she'd fallen in love with him, she thought. But she couldn't tell him that, couldn't trust him with the knowledge of her feelings for him, for the pain of his rejection would be doubled if he knew.

"I ..." She caught her breath. "I'm worried about him. He's not a bad person. He never meant to harm anyone. He's simply high spir-ited. And it gets him in trouble sometimes."

Justin hid his scowl, not wanting to discourage her from talking, but justifying the scoundrel's crimes by calling him high-spirited seemed overly generous at best.

"And your lifestyle?" He watched her closely, trying to read her thoughts and knowing the course of his future depended on her response. "Do you miss that?"

Miss the horrible anxiety, the endless travel, the gnawing guilt? Megan let her eyes fall closed. "No. I've longed for a home," she an-swered softly, "for many years."

Quiet took the room, holding it for a breath-less moment.

"And is this home, Megan?" he asked finally, forcing the words out in a whisper.

She wanted it to be, she thought hopelessly. But what was her position here? How long would she be welcome? As long as she pleased him in bed? Until another woman captured his interest?

"Why am I here, Justin?" she murmured, needing to hear some confession of his caring.

Justin lay still. She was utterly lovely and looked so vulnerable that he longed to take her in his arms and promise her a lifetime of happi-ness. But what was she truly thinking? Perhaps she would be gone in the morning. And per-haps if he held her too tightly she would flee all the faster. "I'll never find another to warm my bed so well," he said, forcing a roguish grin.

Megan stiffened, doing her best to hide her

expression, and Justin watched, not certain what she felt. Was it pain? Had he hurt her?

"Being with you," he breathed, not able to stop the words, "makes me happy." He touched her cheek, feeling overwhelmed by her nearness. "Very happy."

Megan stared at him, feeling the pulse of excitement. Perhaps he would never love her. But perhaps there was a chance—if she made him happy.

"I . . ." She felt so utterly weak when he was near. "I have duties that need attending. I—should see to them."

"No, you shouldn't."

"You're feeling better," she said. "You don't need me here."

"Oh, but I do, Megan," Justin breathed, thinking he needed her far more than she knew and vowing to make her need him. Bending one leg beneath the linen sheet, he moaned piteously. "I'm in a great deal of pain, you know." He was not above using his illness to keep her near. He was not above using any means, he admitted.

Megan eyed him dubiously. He looked as hale as a horse and though she ached to touch him, to lose her thoughts in the overwhelming pleasure of his lovemaking, surely it was foolhardy to become more enmeshed in his irresistible allure.

"Truly. I get terrible head pains after these fevers. My mother used to rub my back to help me relax. It did wonders. Not that I would ask you to do the same, of course," he added, looking up at her like a small, innocent boy.

Megan watched him with thoughtful eyes. "Just rub your back?" she asked skeptically.

He nodded, maintaining a serious expression.

"All right," she agreed finally. "I hate to have you hurt."

"That's very good of you, Megan," he said. "Very good." Rolling onto his abdomen, he smiled into the pillow and waited.

Megan took a deep breath. His back stretched beneath her hands, dark, well-muscled, and strong. Mother Mary! She couldn't remember the last time the man had enough decency to wear clothes and his nudity was beginning to tell on her nerves.

She kneaded the heavy muscles of his shoulders and arms, concentrating on her task with conscientious ambition. It was amazing, she thought, how the job warmed her. After all, there wasn't a great deal of exertion involved, yet she felt positively overheated as her hands eased the tension from the large muscles just below his shoulder blades.

"You're very good at this," Justin said. "Have you done this sort of thing much in the past?"

"Certainly not," Megan said, glad he couldn't see the color that diffused her face.

"Oh, well, I was just wondering. I didn't mean to disturb you. It feels heavenly."

Time passed and though Megan had expected her skin to cool it seemed the heat was increasing. She sat propped upon her bare feet, with her knees touching the lovely flesh of his side and her wayward hair falling upon his back as her hands moved to and fro. Beneath the shameless sheet she could see the dramatic rise of his buttocks and did her best to avoid looking in that direction.

"Ohhh, Megan." He sighed, stretching like a cat beneath her hands. "This is so kind of you. The ache in my head is completely gone. Of course my chest feels terribly cramped." He rolled to his side, watching her with those sinful eyes. "Would you mind?"

"Mind what?" A woman couldn't trust a man who spent days on end without any cloth on.

"Would you mind rubbing my chest?" Without awaiting an answer he rolled to his back, placing his hardened hands beneath his head and staring at her with his hot eyes.

"I—I . . ."

"Just a little, Megan. My mother used to."

There was really no point in resisting him.

The heat from his chest seemed to sear her hands and burn upwards over her arms and into her face. He was so large, so beautiful and so ungodly immodest.

"Ohhh." He sighed again, closing his eyes as if there was ecstasy in her touch. "You can't imagine what this does for me."

Megan refused to look downward, but she was certain, after the previous day's bath, that she could very well imagine just the effect her administrations had on him.

"I'm sure I'll be able to return to my duties very soon, with the wonderful care you've given me," he continued, as he drew up one long leg. But the movement was interrupted by another groan of pain.

"What is it?" Megan asked, worried by his sound of agony.

"Oh. It's nothing to concern yourself with. Just my legs," he said dismissively. "They always stiffen up when I become ill." The words fell flat into the silence of the room.

She stared at him, wondering at his honesty, but his next prolonged groan of pain decided her.

"I could rub them for you, I suppose."

"Could you?" His smile beamed from his dark, handsome face. "How generous of you."

Megan glanced furtively downward, assured herself that his lower regions were decently covered, then set her hands on the sheet over the large muscles of his right thigh. She massaged gently, careful to not disturb the linen that shielded her from his nakedness, but no sighs of pleasure escaped him.

"I fear it's just not as effective this way," Justin said, scowling as if puzzled by the thought. "I think the direct warmth of your hands on my skin makes the massage doubly healing." He scowled again. "You don't mind if I lower the linen do you?"

Megan's jaw dropped open. Lower the linen? She grappled frantically with this shocking idea, but before she could formulate an objection he had pushed the sheet far past the point of no return.

"You can continue now," he said casually, smiling with gentle good grace.

"I—I—I ..." Her body was frozen, her eyes fixed on an unoffensive point just below his nose.

"This won't bother you, will it, Megan?" he asked thoughtfully.

Megan's mouth moved noiselessly but search as she might she couldn't think of a single, mature excuse that could extract her from such an embarrassing situation. Her hands trembled slightly as they moved downward and although she tried to make her gaze follow her hands, she couldn't force her eyes to leave his face. She prayed frantically as she groped along, but as her hands touched a hot, turgid appendage, he gasped and she jerked away as if burned.

"Really, Megan," he admonished gently. "Perhaps we should leave *that* massage until later."

He was laughing at her. Megan narrowed her eyes, burning with embarrassment. So he thought she couldn't bear the sight of his nakedness, did he? Well by all that was sacred, she'd show him. She set her jaw as if preparing for an arduous task and jerking her eyes from his face, moved her gaze slowly down his body.

The hard evidence of his desire stood erect and prominent. She swallowed hard, moved lower, and placed her hands on his thigh.

Her movements at first were stiff and unyielding, but gradually she began to relax somewhat. Her hands moved with a measured cadence, roaming downward, massaging each group of muscles before moving on to the next. Down, over the bent knee to the heavy calf, and then to the next leg and upwards she moved, finding the task not at all unpleasant. In fact, it filled her with a sort of warm, heady feeling that lifted her above her embarrassment.

With fingers warm and fluid now, her hands skimmed upward, ever more daringly, slowly moving past the upper thigh and over his lean

hip to his flat abdomen. Justin's low hiss of inhaled pleasure was barely noticed, for her own
warmth was now too consuming.

Megan's hands floated over his heated flesh
with feather-soft lightness, caressing each dip
and rise in the rippled expanse of his belly. Her
eyes no longer avoided the hard ridge of his
manhood that rose as evidence of his arousal.
Instead she watched it pulse, her fingertips
brushing it now and then, eliciting excited trem-
ors from Justin's massive body.

With her shyness completely abandoned now,
Megan moved her hands to his inner thighs, her
wrists just touching the lowest regions of his
most masculine parts.

Justin's large hands gripped the pillow as if
he was fighting for control. And as Megan lifted
her sultry eyes to find his, she discovered that
the velvet browns were now closed. His wide
neck arched backward, pushing his dark head
into the pillow beneath him.

Seeing his so-evident arousal only increased
Megan's own desire. She trembled lightly, then
leaned forward, touching her lips to the tight
ridges of muscles that lay across his flat abdomen. Kisses smoothed across his body with ex-
cruciating slowness, working upward to his flat,
smooth nipples. Letting her hair fall upon him,
she eyed his wonderful chest, then bent again to
touch her tongue to one small nub.

Justin bucked beneath her, his eyes flying
open, and she smiled at him with devilish glee.
Who would have suspected his nipples were as
sensitive as her own? It seemed a wondrous se-

cret and she ran her tongue about her lips once before touching it to the other peak.

"Megan!" The single word was little more than a growl, gasped from the volcanic center of his molten body.

"What?" she asked huskily, her lids at half-mast over her lazy eyes.

"Attila the Hun doesn't like to be teased," he gritted.

Megan raised a brow and brought one knee across his tight form to settle her light weight upon his abdomen.

"Tease you?" She moved her fingers to her own buttons, easing one, then the next from their holes until her blouse opened, revealing more and more of her rounded bosom.

Justin watched, his eyes dark, his lovely body taut and waiting until she dropped her blouse to the floor.

Her torso was covered by an eyelet fabric. The frilled garment was laced down the front, pressing her soft breasts upward, and she leaned onto his chest, touching her own burning flesh to his.

He felt like magic beneath her and she closed her eyes before lifting her head to touch her lips to his.

He kissed her with the intensity of a building storm. Then, with taut slowness, he moved downward over the ivory flesh of her throat and further to where the rapid beat of her heart could be felt through the trembling softness of her breasts.

He tasted the glory of her skin, loving her with his touch and kisses, until, no longer able to await the pleasure, he tugged at the lace. Her breasts came free, spilling from bondage.

She could feel his breath coming in a rush against her flesh and arched against him in prickling excitement. His fingers touched her, tracing a pattern of pleasure against her skin, and where his fingers went, his kisses followed, flowing over her torso like intoxicating fire, then spiraling toward the peak of her breast with breathtaking anticipation.

Megan waited, suspended in agony until his mouth found the rose-tinted tip. She gasped against the exhilaration, pushing her body toward him with new abandon.

The world halted its progress. Vaguely, she felt his hands on her skirt and then the thing came away, followed by her pantalettes.

They were naked together, trembling with anticipation, until they could wait no longer.

His thick rod thrust into her enveloping warmth and they groaned in unison, closing their eyes to the feeling. The rhythm was slow at first with her riding high, her hands on his chest, her head slightly back. But in a moment the intensity built, flooding them with raw, electrifying sensations until Justin rolled her to her side, driving with deep strokes.

Megan clung to him now, her breathing coming hard and fast against his chest. But they noticed only the glory of their pleasure as they were consumed by the inferno that raged between them. They were forged into one inseparable being until they slept finally, wrapped in each others arms.

It was sometime later that they awoke to smile into each other's eyes.

"Megan," Justin whispered, touching her face with gentle fingertips. "I . . ."

She waited breathlessly. His eyes spoke of things she could only hope for, but he stopped the words before speaking them.

"I need a bath," he said quietly.

What had he intended to say? Megan wondered, wishing she could see inside his soul.

"I'll heat some water." She did her best to hide her emotions as effectively as he hid his.

"No, Megan." He caught her hand. "I know of a place where we don't need to carry water."

She scowled at him, but he stepped to the floor, taking her with him.

"Put this on," he said, handing her the discarded chemise.

She hurried into the garment, but when she reached for her blouse, he stopped her.

"No, love. It's dark. No one will see." His eyes caressed her face, then turned to search for her skirt.

"But . . ." she objected, but he had found her skirt and turned now to kiss away her modesty.

Drawing away finally, he pulled his trousers over bare flesh as she donned her skirt. He wore no shirt and they found no shoes before he pulled her down the dark stairs after him.

Running like wayward children, they raced hand in hand to the barn and laughed, breathless and exhilarated, when they reached the barn.

They kissed again, but Justin drew away first. "I'll get Rum."

Megan nodded and turned to fetch her mare, but he caught her hand again. "No love. Ride with me."

She nodded numbly.

He placed a bridle over the stallion's head, then boosted Megan onto the animal's broad back and swung himself lithely up behind.

Outside the barn, the moon cast fleeting shadows about them, broken by the movement of the stallion's hooves as they rose from the ground in a steady cadence.

Justin's left hand held the reins with easy grace, allowing his other hand to roam with free abandon over Megan's lacy chemise.

Their journey was short, but his patience was shorter still, and he finally tugged at the lace again, allowing her breasts to come free of their bindings.

A fragrant breeze touched Megan's bared skin. She leaned her head back against Justin's shoulder, soaking in the sensation of his hands as they mingled with the refreshing air.

Time ceased, leaving only the night bird's songs and the swaying movements of their mount until Megan heard the unmistakable sound of the tide.

Accustomed to the ocean's fretful waves, the stallion stepped willingly into the soothing, gemstone liquid, wading outward until his master's hand stopped his motion. The water lapped about the riders' bare feet and they sat together, watching the play of moonlight on the gilded water, and letting the contentment of the moment reach their souls.

With the slightest nudge Justin urged the stallion forward again. The animal moved like a giant sea horse, carrying them farther out until his hooves no longer touched the sand and his huge body was taken with buoyancy. He lifted his chin, letting his head float on the waves and paddling with strong, sure strokes.

Water pressed about the riders' hips in flowing waves of midnight blues and greens. The stallion turned finally and when his pumping hooves touched the sand again, Justin turned Megan in his arms and kissed her as the world swayed about them to the eternal rhythm of the sea.

Megan sat sideways across the withers of the horse beneath her, steadied and caressed by Justin's tender hands. Slowly, he removed her chemise.

The moon was too bright, the world too hushed and beautiful for her to be offended by the sight of her own nudity. They seemed at one with the world, an inseparable part of the elements that surrounded them.

Justin's hands were warm and gentle against her flesh and she leaned against him, allowing him full access to her bared skin. But her skirt stopped his progress, causing him finally to slip from the stallion's back, bringing her along with him.

Cool water gripped them. Megan's skirt rose up around her, allowing Justin to reach her softness beneath. They played together, lapped by the waves and caressed by the moonlight, until, unable to resist her nearness any longer, Justin pulled her weightless body into his arms to take her gently to shore.

He spread her skirt upon the sand and in a moment eased her down atop it. The moonlight was blocked for an instant as Justin's large, masculine form hovered over her and then he was beside her, taking her again in his arms.

Megan smoothed her hands over his chest, marveling at the similarity between him and the glistening stallion that grazed not far away. The power was the same, rugged and formidable. The curving muscle seemed similar, with the long, smooth lines of each moving with the fluidity and grace of a wild beast's.

Fingertips frosted bared flesh with dark shadows as they roused and caressed, smoothed and excited, until once again they became one and rose to ecstasy on the waves of sensual pleasure.

They lay together far past midnight, peaceful in each other's arms, but Justin rose finally, drawing Megan with him. Dressing was no easy task, for the clothing was wet and binding, and they laughed at each other's difficulties and finally ran, wrinkled and sodden, to where the stallion waited at the bluff's edge.

The journey to Free Winds was filled with low chuckles of laughter and warm, deep caresses that held them tightly together until they reached home.

They turned the stallion into his stall. The moon seemed to follow them as they crossed the yard and entered the house. Stairs creaked as Justin carried Megan upstairs to his bed.

Her skin tasted of salt. Justin closed his eyes, luxuriating in the feel of her hands on his body. He couldn't bear to lose her. He couldn't pretend any longer. She'd captured his soul and he lay defenseless in her arms.

"Why were you with him, Megan?" His words crept out, unwanted but unstoppable.

She stiffened in his arms, closing her eyes. "Tolbert?" She said the name with dread, remembering his horrid presence, remembering Justin's anger.

"Yes."

Megan forced her eyes open. He must care for her. He must, for surely no man could make her feel as she did unless he cared—at least a bit. "I didn't know he was there, Justin. I swear it."

His eyes held hers in the dimness, questioning, probing.

"I swear it, Justin," she whispered, knowing she had no pride.

"Why were you there—behind the livery?" he asked stiffly.

Megan paused, feeling the air leave her lungs, feeling her chest compress. She could lie, but not to him. "I thought I saw Michael," she admitted.

His face showed no sign of his thoughts. "And so you went to him? You risked your life?"

Megan scowled at him. "Risked my life? I had no idea Tolbert was there. How was I to know?"

"Don't you see, Megan?" He frowned back, pulling away slightly. "Can't you see your brother is dangerous?"

"Michael?" She propped herself on her elbows. "He cared for me, Justin. When there was no one else, he was there to protect me."

"To use you for his own devious purposes!"

Justin said, his voice rising. "Because he could gain from your presence, from your pain."

"And what about you?" she shot back, humiliation and uncertainty sparking her anger. "How are you different? You've offered me no security. No promises. And haven't you used me for your own pleasure?"

"I thought I gave pleasure in return."

"Pleasure's a simple thing for men," Megan whispered. "They stand to lose nothing."

"And what have you lost?"

My heart, she thought. "My virtue!"

"Virtue!" Justin scoffed, his tone made harsh by his jealousy and anger. "You dare to say you were virtuous, after what you've done?"

Silence echoed through the room.

"Get out," she said finally.

"Must I remind you this is my property?" he snapped.

She drew herself away, rising on her knees. "Then I'll leave."

"No!" The single word was sharp. His hand grasped her arm, his grip hard. "I bought you with hard-earned money. You'll not go until I say."

"I'll go when I please," she replied.

"Would you rather go to your brother, then?"

She stared at him. Tears burned her eyes. "At least he cares about me."

"Cares about you!" Justin shook his head, his tone hushed. "Your naivetè is stunning." He loosened his grip with an effort. His hand dropped away. "You have no idea what love is, Megan. No idea."

The door closed softly behind him.

Megan turned her face into the pillow, letting the loneliness consume her and feeling the hot tears soak in the linen casing.

Chapter 27

Justin stared through the smoke of the gambling hall. He couldn't bear to lose Megan to another man, even when that man was her brother—or perhaps especially knowing it was Michael.

Justin narrowed his eyes, searching for a thatch of red hair. Megan thought she had seen Michael. Justin clenched his teeth and tried not to think of her—tried to concentrate on his task. Michael was a bastard to the bone, he reminded himself. He'd not leave Megan, not when she could make his lousy schemes work.

Very probably Michael was near. Near enough to find him and bribe him to leave. And if payment didn't work, threats would!

But first he had to find him. And it was all a matter of asking the right person. Someone was bound to know his whereabouts.

From a dim corner, Tolbert stood noiselessly, slipping from his chair to hurry from the inn.

Hastening down a poorly lit street, Tolbert stepped into Rae Ann's. The setting was similar to the hall he'd just left. Gamblers were seated around several tables. The smell of smoke was heavy, and sitting near the far wall was Michael O'Rourke.

It took Robert only moments to reach him. Only a moment to whisper the news in his ear.

Michael jolted up straighter in his chair, his freckled face going pale. "In Charleston?" he blurted, then hushed his tone, excusing himself from the game to find a quiet corner.

The hour was late. Michael faced Robert, running a nervous hand through his stiff curls. "Stearns is here?" he asked. There was a hint of panic in his tone. "Looking for me?"

Tolbert nodded. "I heard the word passed around. It's only a matter of time before he finds you."

"Well . . ." Michael clenched and unclenched his fists, trying to calm his jangling nerves. "Then we'll do it tonight," he declared suddenly. "While he's still in town."

"Tonight? Right now?" Tolbert asked.

"Yeah. Tonight. While she's alone. You know where to bring her?" Michael asked nervously.

"Of course I do," Tolbert snapped. "Of course I do." He took a deep breath.

"You think you can do the job?" Michael asked worriedly and Tolbert scowled.

"I'll do it all right. She'll be there." His eyes narrowed. "Even if I have to tie and gag her."

Michael scowled, watching Tolbert closely.

"If y' hurt her, you'll answer t' me," he warned.

Robert drew himself up, looking haughtily offended. "You don't trust anyone, do you *Michael*?" he asked.

"I told you t' only say that name t' her," Michael hissed and Robert laughed.

"She'll be there," Robert said, his tone stronger now as he nodded solemnly. "Just you make sure *you* are." He turned quickly, striding for the door, and Michael watched, eyes narrowed warily.

Megan sat bolt upright in bed, her frantic dreams shattered. The frenzied knocking sounded louder.

Pulling her thoughts together, she slipped from bed to find and don her crumpled blouse. The pounding increased.

She scrambled down the stairs in the dark. The hammering of her heart echoed the fist on the back door.

Where was Justin? She'd heard him leave the house and knew he'd not returned.

She felt panicked at the thought. Maybe he could no longer bear the sight of her. Or. . . . Her breath lodged in her throat. Perhaps he'd gone for the sheriff and it was the law that waited at the door.

Or perhaps Justin was hurt.

Terror seized her!

Without another thought she jerked the door open.

"Michael's been wounded," Robert blurted.

Megan stood speechless, stunned to silence.

"You must go to him!" Robert said. "He begged me to bring you."

"But . . ." Megan trembled. "How? Where?"

"There's no time for questions. He's hurt bad," Tolbert gasped. "Bad!"

"No!" It was the only word she could manage. Her thoughts scrambled as she remembered her childhood, Michael's impish, freckled face. But Justin's dark countenance appeared suddenly in her mind as well, his eyes fathomless. The two faces shifted and Megan gasped. "Justin! Where is he?"

Tolbert stiffened. "Don't you know?"

Megan felt the blood drain from her face. "He didn't . . ." Her voice failed. "He didn't . . . hurt Michael?" she whispered.

"Stearns?" Robert frowned, remembering his lines. "No. Michael was gambling. There was a . . . misunderstanding. Michael was shot. There was nothing I could do but get him out of there. But he doesn't have much time. We've got to hurry."

She hesitated only a moment. "I'll get my horse."

"No! Megan." Robert gripped her arm suddenly. "There's no time. I brought Michael's gelding. Ride him."

"Joker?" Megan questioned, turning her gaze to the chestnut. "You brought Joker?" Perhaps she had held some hope that Tolbert was lying, but the sight of Michael's prized mount assured her of the truth. Michael was indeed in trouble. Megan clenched her fists. He was her only brother. Blood kin!

* * *

From the shelter of the towering elms Michael watched Robert and Megan ride past. Everything appeared to have gone smoothly so far. Lending Joker to Tolbert had been a brilliant move. Megan was bound to believe the story now and apparently had because they were riding hell bent for the west.

All Michael need do now was deliver the ransom note to Stearns and wait for the cash. After the ruckus at the horse auction, Michael was certain Stearns was taken with his little sister.

But ... so was Robert Tolbert. Michael frowned, hurrying to his rented mount. He'd followed the man to make certain Tolbert played the scam straight and if he didn't want to lose them, he'd better hustle.

"I heard you're looking fer a short red-headed fella."

Justin raised his eyes, looking into a fleshy, reddened face.

"Yes." He'd been waiting with feigned patience, nursing a drink and letting the word of his search circulate. "Sit down. Can I buy you a drink?"

The stranger swiped his hands on his soiled britches and licked his lips. "Yep. That'd be 'preciated."

The barkeep arrived in a moment, but Justin noticed the man's eyes never strayed from Justin's liquor until his own arrived.

"Maybe ..." The stranger raised bloodshot

eyes to Justin's. "Maybe we could keep the bottle, huh?"

"Sure." Justin nodded to the barkeep who placed the whiskey on the table and left.

The man's hand shook as he raised the glass to his lips. His eyes closed for a moment as he savored the taste. "Thank y'."

"Did you have something to tell me, sir?" asked Justin, noting the sorry signs of alcoholism but prodded by his own nagging impatience.

"I think I know the fella you're lookin' fer. He's a freckled faced Irishman, short, quick smile. Kinda likable but not too trustable. That him?"

"Could be," Justin said. He couldn't have described the boy better himself.

"Well, I know of him, but I don't know where to find him. Not right now anyhow."

Justin sat in silence, waiting.

"But I know who might be able t' tell y'."

"Who's that?"

"That dandy Tolbert fella."

Justin stiffened. "Robert Tolbert?"

"Yeah. That's him. They chum up together sometimes. 'Specially when Tolbert's losin' at cards—which is most always."

A cold knot formed in the pit of Justin's stomach. "You've seen them together?"

"Yessir. A fair amount. But not tonight. Tonight Tolbert was here alone."

"Here?" Justin looked around, a warning bell clanging in his mind. "Now?"

"Nope. He left. Not long after you come in."

The man shrugged, licking his lips. "I'm here a good deal of the time and when I don't have nothin' t' drink—well, then I just watch folks."

"Thank you." Justin rose quickly, drawing several bills from his pocket and handing them to the man. "Thank you."

It was dark, but the road was good. Justin urged his mount into a faster lope, his heart pounding to the same rhythm. If Tolbert and Michael were friends, then perhaps it hadn't been a coincidence that Megan had seen them at the auction. Perhaps they were working swindles together. Perhaps they had meant to take Megan then. And perhaps . . . , Justin leaned low over the gelding's neck, perhaps they meant to take her now. Perhaps that was why Tolbert had left.

Dear Lord! He prayed in silent earnestness. If she was there, he'd tell her the truth. He'd tell her his world was empty without her. He'd take the risk. If only. . . .

His horse galloped into the yard. The moon had long since faded. The house was dark. Justin left the gelding with dragging reins and raced to the door. He reached out to grasp the handle, but his knuckles brushed a note tacked to the portal. He tore the thing free and burst into the house.

"Megan!"

Silence answered him. He yelled again, taking the stairs by threes.

Her bed was empty, as were the other rooms.

His chest ached. His breathing came fast and hard. He clenched his fists. The note crumpled in one hand and he looked at it dazedly before lighting a lamp to read it.

Justin, I left with Michael. I'm safe. Don't try to find me. By the time you read this we'll be far away.

Megan.

His world fell apart.

She was gone. Far away. Out of his life. He let the paper fall, lifting his hand to shield his eyes.

He should have stayed home. Should have been there when her brother had come. Should have fought to keep her.

But what good would it have done? he argued. He couldn't hold her against her will even if he wanted her that way. He couldn't keep her when she chose to be with her brother instead.

It was his fault! He'd driven her away—had accused her of a lack of virtue when in truth he'd been the one who was lacking, for he'd been more conniving and less forthright than she. There had been times when he could have sworn he could see her emotions in her eyes—could read her feelings. Times when he knew she cared, but he had not dared to believe it.

The emptiness closed in around him. He needed to get out. The place was stifling without her.

He extinguished the lamp and then he was

outside. Catching his gelding's reins, Justin led the horse toward the barn. A whinny sounded from the corral. The gelding answered back and Justin lifted his head.

Rainstorm was still there!

Justin froze in his tracks, his heart thumping. She'd left Rainstorm. But why?

He gripped the reins, his mind spinning. She wouldn't have left the mare. Not Megan. She loved the horse.

That meant. . . .

She'd been taken against her will! He knew it suddenly, without a doubt. His soul soared. She hadn't wanted to leave him. All he had to do was find her.

But where had Michael taken her? Or. . . .

Justin halted in his tracks, his mind spinning with possibilities. Had it been Michael who took her? If Megan was taken by force as he suspected, surely it wasn't she who wrote the note. And if Michael was the culprit, it was doubtful he'd claim the crime as his own.

So who?

Tolbert!

Of course! Tolbert wouldn't have known about Megan's attachment to Rainstorm. He could have written the note, not knowing he'd left a loose end. But where would he have gone? Would he take the girl to his father's plantation?

Definitely not. Unless. . . .

Justin pulled the girth tight on a fresh horse and swung aboard. Years ago Tolbert had used the old Burdock house for gambling. Might he not use it now to hide Megan? Justin kicked his horse into a gallop.

God help Tolbert if Justin's guess was right!

Chapter 28

Damn, damn, damn! Michael stomped around in a circle and clenched his teeth. It was nearly dawn. He'd been riding most of the night and Tolbert had just abducted his sister.

He swore again, ground his teeth, and watched the ramshackle house where his gelding stood beside Tolbert's mount. What the hell was going on? Why hadn't Robert followed his instructions? He'd been promised half the take, which was likely to be a goodly sum if Justin was as fond of little Megan as Michael suspected.

Stearns could afford to pay a bundle to buy her back. And Robert needed the money to pay for his gambling debts, so why was he here?

Damn again. The only answer that came to mind wasn't a soothing one. After all, Megan was a pretty thing and Tolbert had been craving her for a long time.

And here Michael was, stuck out in the middle of nowhere by a forgotten old, broken-down house with no way out of the mess he was in. What was he supposed to do?

Save her himself?

Oh damn! If she wasn't his sister. . . .

But she was.

He should have brought a gun. But he never carried a gun.

Then again, Megan did. Or she used to. Michael waited, hoping she'd kept her fighting edge sharp. Minutes passed. Michael ran a hand through his hair.

It was his fault of course. She wouldn't have come if she hadn't believed he was hurt, and he'd never forgive himself if *she* got hurt.

He'd have to rescue her.

The decision caused his stomach to turn nervously.

Michael took a step, but another thought stopped him.

Tolbert probably had a gun if he were planning something nasty. Megan was smart and could be mighty mean when she was cornered. Maybe she'd still figure a way out.

A muffled cry came from inside. Michael gritted his teeth. Lord help him! Taking a deep breath, he bolted for the house.

"Robert?" Michael kept his tone intentionally nonthreatening. No point in offending the man right off the bat. His wits had gotten him out of tighter spots. All right. Well, maybe it was Megan's wits that had gotten him out. And maybe he owed her one.

Taking the steps slowly, Michael headed for the light at the top of the stairs. The door was open. He stepped inside. Tolbert stood to the left and Megan was with him, her hands and legs tied, her mouth gagged. She was sprawled on her back on a tattered, straw-filled tick.

"Hey, Robert," Michael repeated. "I thought we was meeting in town. But you're right. This is better. Stearns'll never find her here. Right in his backyard, huh?"

Tolbert's expression showed his irritation as well as a streak of blood that ran from his cheek to his chin. Apparently Megan hadn't taken kindly to being hogtied. "How'd you find us?" Tolbert's tone was tense.

"I followed y'," Michael said casually. "I got t' thinkin' she can be mighty difficult if she gets it into her mind, so I thought you might need some help. But ..." He chuckled, stepping forward and taking in the details of the room. The single window was glassless, the chair broken. Only the bed was intact and that was grimy and bowed in the center. "I see y' tied up all the loose ends." He chuckled again, eyeing his sister's bound limbs. Megan's eyes drilled into him, snapping with rage.

"Yes, I got things well in hand," Tolbert replied grimly.

"Well then, I'll stay with her. You can deliver that note t' Stearns," Michael offered, keeping his tone casual."

Tolbert didn't move.

Michael swore in silence. His luck seemed to be running low. "You'd best get goin' before Stearns gets home. I'd hate t' be around if'n he's mad and this little ransom note ain't likely t' make him happy."

Tolbert smiled, but the expression was not soothing. "I already left him a note, Michael. I said she went with you."

"With me?" Michael's voice squeaked. The

thought of Justin Stearns raging after him was enough to make him consider becoming a monk and moving somewhere cold and preferably un-inhabited.

Tolbert smiled again, hearing the fear in Michael's voice. "He'll never trace her here, never consider I might be involved. No." He shook his head. "He'll be looking for you and you alone. So if I were you, I'd start running now and not look back." —

"Why . . ." Michael shuffled his feet and looked offended. "Why'd y' tell him I took her?"

"I was quite clever if I say so myself. I wrote the note and signed Megan's name, then tacked it on his front door. Said she was far away and that he shouldn't bother looking for her. But . . ." He shrugged. "Of course he will. She's such a pretty thing." Anger seethed in his eyes as he fingered the fresh wound she'd inflicted on his cheek. He glanced at her. She'd propped herself to a seated position, her eyes flaming. "And spirited. Who wouldn't search for her?"

Michael shook his head. "This is a bad idea, Tolbert. Real bad. Someone's likely t' get hurt."

"Yes." From an inner pocket a pistol appeared in Tolbert's hand. "You are—if you don't get out and get out now."

"Hey! Listen." Michael raised his hands. "I'm willin' t' give y' a bigger split. In fact you can have—"

"I want *her*," Tolbert interrupted "She should have been mine from the first."

"You want . . ." Michael backed away a step and grimaced. "You want *her*?" he asked in amazement. "But she damn near broke yer nose. Remember? And now your cheek. Hell, man, if she's with you an hour longer you'll be lucky t' have a face at all."

"We'll see," Tolbert said stiffly. "We'll just see."

"You don't know her temper," Michael said, shaking his head and trying to think. "She can even get meaner—meaner than a sow with younguns once she gets riled." He glanced toward his sister's smoldering eyes. "And she looks awful riled now." If he could just get her hands loose, Michael thought, Tolbert would be lucky to live out the day.

"I think she won't be so feisty after I apply a little discipline."

"Discipline!" Michael scowled, lowering his hands a smidgen, but Tolbert motioned with his gun.

"Get out while you still can, Michael," Tolbert advised. "Because I'll turn you over to the sheriff first chance I get."

"I could do the same to you," Michael reminded him quickly, but Tolbert laughed.

"They'd never believe you. Now get out." He shifted his eyes to Megan for a moment. "I've got something that needs attending."

"If you're going to shoot, Tolbert," a deep voice rumbled from the hall, "you'd better shoot me first."

Michael gasped aloud. Tolbert's face blanched white. Justin Stearns stepped into the doorway, filling the opening.

His eyes shifted momentarily to Megan, then back to Tolbert. His gaze was scalding, filled with an unspeakable rage. His fists clenched and a muscle jumped in his cheek. "Better shoot to kill, boy," he snarled, his tone low. "Because when I get my hands on you, you'll not see the dawn." He paused. "That's a promise, Tolbert!"

Robert shifted his weight, then his eyes. This wasn't how he'd planned things. "It was all her brother's idea. All his," he squeaked suddenly.

"You're standing between me and my woman," Justin said flatly, ignoring his words. "You can't bring me down with that peashooter. Not before I reach you. And then it'd be too late." His fists clenched, loosened, clenched.

Robert dropped his gaze to that threatening movement. "Listen." He stepped abruptly to the side, glancing once at the window. "None of this was my idea. I was trying to save her from her brother. I—"

"I'm going to kill you, Tolbert," Justin warned calmly, and took a step forward, but suddenly Robert dove, flinging himself through the nearby window.

There was a muffled shriek, a thud, and, "Ohhh, My leg! I broke my leg!"

But Justin failed to notice the screams from below. "You're next, O'Rourke."

Michael drew himself up, his eyes wide, his breathing rapid. "Go ahead then. Go ahead. Have at it." He motioned erratically. "I'll welcome the chance to beat the tar outta the man who mistreated my sister."

"Mistreated!" Justin growled, his fists clenched again, aching to pummel the lad. "You're the rat who mistreated her!"

"You know nothin' about it," Michael snarled

back, his own temper steaming. "I saved her
when there was no one else. When she was just
an ugly, little tadpole, not nearly good enough
fer the likes of you. High and mighty Justin
St—"

Justin's snarl was little warning. His shoulder
hit Michael midchest, knocking him against the
wall with the power of a charging bull.

"She was good enough," Justin raged, catching Michael's fist in his abdomen. "Too good for
your company."

"But I never let her ... be ... defiled,"
grunted Michael, clinging to Justin in an attempt to avoid his fists. "It took a lowdown
snake like you to—"

Justin's knuckles grazed Michael's cheek,
lacking the full impact as the lad ducked.

"I never defiled her," Justin retorted. "I—"

Michael was small, wiry, and as dirty a fighter
as could be found. His knee came up with a jolt,
jarring against the other's groin.

Justin's moan filled the house as he dropped
to his knees, loosening his grip. Michael scrambled away. But Justin's anger was boiling and he
shook off the paralysis to grapple for Michael's
leg. "Come back, you little rat. You'll pay for
what you put her through."

"No!" Michael had reached the remains of the
broken chair and smashed the thing across
Justin's back. "*You'll* pay for soiling her reputation."

Justin crumpled for a moment, still weakened
by his illness, but he came up with a grunt,
crawling along Michael's body as he dragged
himself upward. "You'll apologize to her today,"

he croaked, his fingers clasping the other's neck. "Or you die!"

"Stop it!"

Megan had wriggled free of her bindings and stood near the window, one hand on the sill. "Back away from each other, both of you," she gritted, "or I'll be gone and not come back. I swear I will. And neither of you will see me again."

"Megan!" both men gasped, but she stood stone-faced and serious.

"I'll do it! Back away!"

They did so. Justin limped. Michael's face was smeared with blood.

"I didn't mean t' get y' hurt, Meg," Michael whined. "I just couldn't leave y' in bondage t' the likes of him." He nodded jerkily toward Justin. "I had t' get you away."

"So you thought you'd ransom me?" Megan stormed.

"Well, I thought the money wouldn't do us no harm. We could head north. Start up that horse ranch of yours. Just like you wanted."

"Huh!" Justin scoffed. "You lying little weasel. You never planned to take her home. You just used her for—"

"And what about you? What about you?" raged Michael. "You sayin' you didn't use her? Huh? Deny it then. Say you didn't bed her. Say you didn't plan to—"

"I planned to make her my wife." Justin's tone had dropped and his gaze shifted now, settling on Megan's tense form. "I hoped to make her my wife. If she'd have me."

"Wife?" she whispered. "Wife?" And then suddenly she was in his arms.

"Marry me, love," Justin pleaded. "Say yes."

"Yes," she breathed and then he was kissing her.

Michael watched with a scowl. "I woulda took her home," he muttered irritably. "I woulda."

Chapter 29

"**M**rs. Stearns," Justin said, reaching up to help Megan from Rainstorm's back. "Welcome home."

Megan smiled, her heart so filled with love, she felt it would surely burst. Home. Free Winds was her home. And Justin was her husband. She slid down before him, reaching up slowly to touch his cheek with her fingertips. "Thank you, Mr. Stearns," she whispered. "And thank you for allowing Michael at the wedding. It was generous of you."

She felt like heaven in his arms. "I fear my reasons were far from unselfish," Justin confessed huskily. "He'd only promise to leave the area if he could see you properly wed." He shrugged. "Perhaps he's got some good to his soul, after all."

"He tried to save me from Tolbert," Megan reasoned.

"Of course he was the one to endanger you at the start," Justin reminded her.

"True." She sighed.

"I'm sorry, Megan," Justin said softly, drawing her eyes to his.

"For what?"

"For what you've had to endure. For all the hardships."

"But without that"—she smiled—"I'd never have made you pity me enough to marry me."

Justin scoffed. "It was hardly pity. Self-preservation maybe."

She frowned a question.

"I thought it was safer to keep you close at hand. No telling what kind of God-awful scheme you would have trounced me with next."

"I wouldn't have," she denied hotly, trying to pull away, but Justin had her in a firm grip and eased her body back against his.

"I love you, Megan Mary Stearns," he vowed gently.

"You do?"

He nodded. "Are you certain you didn't want an extended honeymoon? I know a nice inn with large bathing tubs and—"

"There's nowhere I'd rather be than here," she confessed, her face uplifted.

There seemed to be nothing he could say, for her small impish face was too beguiling, her eyes too mesmerizing, her small, luscious body bedecked in a mint green, satin gown that slipped beneath his fingers. He bent his neck, kissing the softness of her delicate throat. "Then you don't regret marrying me?" he murmured. "You could have had Robert Tolbert, you know. He's very wealthy."

If Justin's kisses hadn't felt so wonderful she would have pushed him away. "I could have killed Tolbert, you mean."

He chuckled against her neck. "Me, too, love. Me, too. But I fear we'll not get the chance. It seems his father has banished him from Carolina. We'll not be seeing him again."

"Then we can live our lives in peace," she said, luxuriating in the feel of his fingers on her waist, his kisses on her neck.

"Peace?" he questioned, drawing away to look into her emerald eyes, and remembering how they could flash with anger. "I have my doubts."

"Well!" She tried to sound affronted, but his hands had slipped lower and were now raising the hem of her elegant gown by slow increments. "I suppose I'll have to prove my docile nature to you then. But I'm not worried." Somehow he'd pulled her skirt up high enough to allow his hands to reach beneath it. Little shivers skittered up and down her legs. "I plan to make you very happy, Mr. Stearns."

"Truly?" He breathed the word hopefully against her throat.

"Yes," she murmured. "I'm going to be the most wonderful wife. I'll cook your meals and—"

"Cook my meals!" His hands dropped away as he drew his head back. "Cook my meals?"

"Why yes." She smiled sweetly. "All your meals." Primly she fluffed her skirt about her, settling it demurely over her hips again and turning away. "I'm going to cook and cook—"

"Please." Justin caught her hand, propelling her back towards him. "Please don't cook for me, Megan. Please. Let Missy cook."

"But Missy . . ." Megan shook her head. Now

that we've hired Missy and brought her home with us, she's moping, I think."

"Moping?"

"She misses Nat. She's in love with him, you know."

"She is?"

"Yes. You can't expect her to cook when she's lonely."

"I'll buy him!" Justin said with sudden hope. "If I buy him and set him free, will you promise not to cook?"

Megan tilted her face at him, trying not to laugh and pretending to think. "Ahhh. No! It's my duty. I'm going to cook until—"

A clatter of hooves sounded on the hard-packed lane and Justin drew his eyes from his little bride with an effort. Down the road pranced the dark two-year-old Megan had ogled at the auction.

"Then I suppose I might just as well return the colt," Justin said, motioning to the rider who led the haughty young stallion.

Megan gripped her husband's arm, pulling it down and hugging it to her body. "You bought him for me?"

"Yes," he said casually, still pretending to try to draw the rider's attention. "If I hadn't spent so much time haggling over him at the auction, you'd never have been molested by Tolbert so I see now the colt's caused trouble from the very beginning. Best to get rid of him before—"

"No!" She was nearly jumping up and down, pulling on his arm like an impatient child. "No, Justin. I love him. Don't send him back. I won't cook. I promise."

He laughed out loud. "I never gave you a wedding gift," he confessed, losing himself in her eyes. "I had to try to compete with Manchester's."

Megan laughed. Horace had returned Sure Gold himself, saying the golden stallion was a gift for the woman who could keep Justin too occupied for petty rivalries.

Justin's chuckle joined hers. He planned to be well occupied, devoting his life to loving Megan.

"What will you do with all your horses, my love?"

"Not to worry," Megan whispered, pushing her arms about his waist and looking up through her lashes. "I've got plans for each one of my studs."

Avon Romances—
the best in exceptional authors and unforgettable novels!

LORD OF MY HEART   Jo Beverley
76784-8/$4.50 US/$5.50 Can

BLUE MOON BAYOU   Katherine Compton
76412-1/$4.50 US/$5.50 Can

SILVER FLAME   Hannah Howell
76504-7/$4.50 US/$5.50 Can

TAMING KATE   Eugenia Riley
76475-X/$4.50 US/$5.50 Can

THE LION'S DAUGHTER   Loretta Chase
76647-7/$4.50 US/$5.50 Can

CAPTAIN OF MY HEART   Danelle Harmon
76676-0/$4.50 US/$5.50 Can

BELOVED INTRUDER   Joan Van Nuys
76476-8/$4.50 US/$5.50 Can

SURRENDER TO THE FURY   Cara Miles
76452-0/$4.50 US/$5.50 Can

Coming Soon

SCARLET KISSES   Patricia Camden
76825-9/$4.50 US/$5.50 Can

WILDSTAR   Nicole Jordan
76622-1/$4.50 US/$5.50 Can

Avon Romantic Treasures

*Unforgettable, enthralling love stories,
sparkling with passion and adventure
from Romance's bestselling authors*

ONLY IN YOUR ARMS *by Lisa Kleypas*
76150-5/$4.50 US/$5.50 Can

LADY LEGEND *by Deborah Camp*
76735-X/$4.50 US/$5.50 Can

RAINBOWS AND RAPTURE *by Rebecca Paisley*
76565-9/$4.50 US/$5.50 Can

AWAKEN MY FIRE *by Jennifer Horsman*
76701-5/$4.50 US/$5.50 Can

ONLY BY YOUR TOUCH *by Stella Cameron*
76606-X/$4.50 US/$5.50 Can

FIRE AT MIDNIGHT *by Barbara Dawson Smith*
76275-7/$4.50 US/$5.50 Can

ONLY WITH YOUR LOVE *by Lisa Kleypas*
76151-3/$4.50 US/$5.50 Can

MY WILD ROSE *by Deborah Camp*
76738-4/$4.50 US/$5.50 Can